ALAN MOORE

BOOK ONE
The Compleat Scripts

Illustrated by
Eddie Campbell

Edited by
Stephen R. Bissette

BORDERLANDS PRESS
Baltimore ☐ 1994

SPIDERBABY GRAFIX
Wilmington VT ☐ 1994

FROM HELL: *The Compleat Scripts*
Introduction copyright © 1994 by Alan Moore
Original scripts copyright © 1994 by Alan Moore
Interior illustrations copyright © 1994 by Eddie Campbell
Afterword copyright © 1994 by Stephen R. Bissette

All rights reserved.

A numbered, slipcased edition of this book, limited to 1000 copies and signed by Alan Moore, Eddie Campbell, and Stephen R. Bissette is available for $95.00. To order, call (800) 528-3310 or write to Borderlands Press at the address below.

No part of this publication may be reproduced or transmitted in any form or by any means, electronic or mechanical, including photo copy, recording, or any information storage and retrieval system, without explicit permission in writing from the Author or the Author's representative.

The chapters herein of the serialized graphic novel *From Hell* appeared originally in *Taboo 2-4* (SpiderBaby Grafix & Publications, 1989-1990). These chapters were subsequently collected as *From Hell vol. 1* and *vol. 2* (Madlove Publishing in association with Tundra Publishing Ltd./Kitchen Sink Press, 1991-1993).

Write for order information to: Kitchen Sink Press, Inc., 320 Riverside Drive, Northampton MA 01060.

ISBN #1-880-325-07-1

Cover illustration copyright © 1994 by Alan Moore
Afterword illustrations copy © 1994 by Stephen R. Bissette
Graphic Imaging by Roger F. Powell
Typesetting & Design by
Elizabeth E. Monteleone, Thomas F. Monteleone, & Shanny Luft

Printed in the United States of America

Borderlands Press P.O. Box 146 Brooklandville, MD 21022
SpiderBaby Grafix P.O. 335, Marlboro VT 05344

ACKNOWLEDGMENTS

Alan Moore would like to thank Debbie Delano, Phyllis Moore, Jamie Delano, Steve Moore, Hayden Paul, Mike Crowley, George Woodcock, Neil Gaiman, Judith Clute, Iain Sinclair, Bob Goodman, Steve Bissette, and Marlene O'Connor.

Eddie Campbell would like to thank Ed Hillyer, Des Roden, April Post, and John Barry for their invaluable assistance.

Steve Bissette would like to thank Marlene, Maia & Daniel; Diana Schutz for proof-reading; and Elizabeth Monteleone for retyping and typesetting these pages from the original materials.

This book is dedicated to *Polly Nichols, Annie Chapman, Liz Stride, Katie Eddowes,* and *Marie Jeannette Kelly.*

You and your demise: of these things alone are we certain.

Goodnight, ladies

Contents

INTRODUCTION   Alan Moore   9

PROLOGUE: The Old Men on the Shore   19

CHAPTER ONE: The Affections of Mr. S.   54

CHAPTER TWO: A State of Darkness   105

CHAPTER THREE: Blackmail or Mrs. Barrett   235

AFTERWORD   Stephen R. Bissette   329

APPENDIX   337

INTRODUCTION

In the last days of 1988, on the cusp of the dark centenary, I began work on *From Hell*. To be more accurate, a different person began the work, in a different world. The Soviet Union had yet to collapse, the Berlin Wall and Margaret Thatcher were as yet untoppled. I was living in a different house, in different circumstances: had not entered in amongst the streets of Whitechapel save in my speculations, had not read a fraction of the Ripper lore that I have since absorbed. I did not have the first idea what kind of mind, what kind of being might have made that fucking mess in Millet's Court on that apocalyptic evening in November, just a century before.

I still don't. No-one does, despite the vast range of "final solutions" to the contrary. The source informing Stephen Knight's *Jack The Ripper: The Final Solution* (which theory *From Hell* uses as a starting point) is Joseph Sickert, putative son of the more famous Walter. Since I started work upon *From Hell* this junior Sickert has again emerged into the light of print, this time with an expanded cast of villains that include not only William Gull but also Randolph Churchill. Other theorists have revived the notion that the crazed misogynistic poet J.K. Stephen (who died in Northampton, not a mile away from where I type these words) might be our man, while the most recent and most publicized "solution" hinges on a "Hitler's Diary"-esque discovery of certain papers in a house in Liverpool, less than a mile from where my daughters currently reside.

At least we had the sense, thank God, to label *From Hell* honestly as fiction, from the start. The hours of picking through my teetering piles of reference books in search of facts (or things that look like facts) have taught me this at least: In all our efforts to describe the past, to list the simple facts of history, we are involved in fiction. Even assuming all the data that we struggle to include within our various historical mosaics happens to be true, the moment we attempt to order it or to extract a meaning we are trafficking in fictions. History, as I was taught the subject in my youth, was based upon a viewpoint that could not see further than the cliffs of Dover; based upon the fiction of a British Empire as the perfect culmination of those centuries of cultural adventurism. Whether we discuss events surrounding the Gulf War, the progress of the economy or the Whitechapel murders, we are dealing, unavoidably, in fiction. Better that we recognize this. Better that we choose a fiction that holds a hope of truth within its meaning, rather than within the "fact" from which we have assembled it. That way lies madness. That way lies dogma and an end to thought.

Fiction is a more expansive process with the freedom to explore those areas that scientific inquiry is by its nature unequipped to deal with. Fiction can apply itself to sounding out the inner lives of its protagonists, to their subjective points of view and feelings, territories, which are necessarily forbidden to the scientist, to the historian. Fiction is at liberty to delve into the underlying myths that shape each culture and its peoples; shape their every word and deed. Myth, though it fuels the various wars of culture and religion going on around the globe as of this writing, is deemed inadmissible evidence in any formal mapping of events. Only in fiction, it would seem, can this important yet unquantifiable terrain of legend be included in our picture.

In my pursuit of this specific fiction I have often found myself in unfamiliar territory, in the literal sense as well as in the intellectual. In Princelet Street there is a residence, unoccupied save for a brace of tailors on the third floor. Seventeenth Century in origin and once the home of Hugenots who prospered in the East End prior to their suppression by the government, the house is not without its share of morbid history: in the early nineteen-hundreds it saw service as assembly rooms where various groups, political and social, would deliver well-attended flights of oratory. At one such meeting, someone shouted "fire." There was no fire in any real material sense, yet scores of the stampeding, trampling attendees still lost their lives in the imaginary blaze.

My visit, made under the auspices of Channel Four as part of the *Without Walls* presentation "The Cardinal and the Corpse," was peculiar and memorable. In company with poets Brian Catling, Aaron Williamson and Iain Sinclair (eminence gris behind the project in his role as co-director and, according to the schedule notes, "freak wrangler"), I crouched there in the attic room and clutched a first edition of *The Magus*, an Alchemical text penned by Francis Barrett in the Eighteenth Century. This was my final scene: typecast as an occult fanatic by the mordant Sinclair, raving and obsessed by the geometries of Whitechapel, I find myself alone, condemned to spend eternity in a bare attic overlooking Christchurch, Spitalfields. The Barrett book (which has its own abnormal history) is open at a page of illustrations that depicts the fallen angels, or the "Vessels of Iniquity & Wrath." It strikes me that the picture of

From Hell
Introduction

Christchurch, Spitalfields — Alan Moore casing the joint, early '89

Apollyon, a vessel of Iniquity, bears an unsettling resemblance to the photograph of me that's on the dust jacket of *Watchmen*. Out through the window looms the spire of Hawksmoor's awful church. I look up from the book and gaze in panic at the empty room in which I am to spend forever as a prisoner of my obsession. It's a wrap.

Downstairs, I watch while former soldier of the Kray twins Tony Lambrianou is interrogated on the finer points of gangster fashion by the maniacal book-finder and career-suicide Driffield. Later on, back in the attic, I stand listening to the mesmerizing croak of dying visionary John Latham, mad conceptual artist and exponent of a science dubbed "Spatterphysics" by the Sunday supplements. Latham, cancer-ridden, is explaining his idea of books as the receptacles of time to Brian Catling, whose profoundly deaf "familiar," Aaron Williamson, stands between the two and acts as their interpreter, sign language flashing from his fingertips. When books are closed, they represent a model of post-Stephen Hawking spacetime, the events within the book depicting past, present and future all contained within a simultaneous whole. When books are opened, two more modes of time come into play; time as it seems to pass for characters within the book and time as it appears to pass inside the reader's mind. Sat by the window in the Portland Stone-white light of Spitalfields, Latham is breathless and his words are painfully slow. The camera rolls. I think of Latham, Lambrianou, all the victims of the phantom fire: Hugenot communards that fell beneath the cudgels of the troops who barracked down in Hawksmoor's church: the vast procession of humanity, of individuals that left some faint impression of their passing in the ancient brickwork of this house, this attic room. In Hawking's space-time mode this is truly where we spend eternity, pressed there between the pages of John Latham's book.

I tiptoed torchless through the unlit, derelict vault of Hawksmoor's St. Luke's Old Street; spent a glorious evening getting drunk with brilliant noir crime-writer Derek Raymond, half Old Lag, half Old Etonian, there in the front room of the Kray twins' public house in Brick Lane; was followed home from my first visit to the site of these allegedly Masonic murders by a monstrous truck that clung to our back bumper for a thirty mile long stretch of motorway, the legend "Widowson, Ltd." stenciled on its bonnet. "Well. This is it," I thought. "The Brotherhood are going to take me out. I know too much. I'll end up as a sinister footnote in someone else's Ripper book, my fatal car-crash there right next to Stephen Knight's undiagnosed brain tumor and Dr. Thomas Stowe's untimely heart-attack."

Luckily, the truck turned off near Watford, leaving me to ponder the morass of paranoia that surround all ventures to the occult territory, the slippery descent to twitching lunacy that are, it seems, a hazard that comes with the terrain, though not the only one. At best, a book or any other work or artistry should alter, at least briefly, the perceptions of those who come into contact with it. This includes the author and the audience alike. With some books, this can be a glorious and light-filled experience, I'm sure. With others, the change in perception is of a more Stygian nature. You have to be careful, to watch yourself so you don't slip in the dark.

To give an example, while gathering data to aid in *From Hell*'s reconstruction of the final murder, I was in receipt of a generous offer made by Martin Fido, noted Ripperologist and true-crime writer. Referring to details unearthed in his then still-to-be-released Ripper Compendium and A–Z, he suggested I might like to see newly-published post mortem details that related to Jack's final victim, the hideously-mutilated Marie Jeannette Kelly, including some previously undisclosed facial wounds.

Now, I suppose that if you happen to be somebody who hasn't spent the last four years engrossed in coroner's reports and mortuary photographs, the obvious appeal of such enticing information might conceivably be lost on you. "Does it matter", you ask, "if the first cut was made in the face? He made hamburger out of the woman, for God's sake! Who wants to know the precise order he did it all in?"

I do. I know it's a sickness, but I do. You see, that first facial incision can be matched exactly with cuts in the bed-sheet, which means that when she saw the man with the knife crossing over the dark, twelve-foot square parlour-room to her bed, she pulled up the bed covers instinctively, just like a small child afraid that the monsters will get her, to cover her face. It's so poignant, the image: how can I resist it?

The surge of excitement I felt on receiving the offer of yet more details of the hideous things that were done to this woman was frankly as close as I've come to pure horror throughout this whole exercise. Not a revulsion at what had become of Marie Jeanette Kelly, of her purely physical disfiguring, but a nausea predicated on myself on all the Ripperati fumbling elbow deep in pools of ancient blood, hoping to find some previously undiscovered talisman amongst the viscous, clotted bedsands: half a railway ticket, or a broken comb: a grape-stem or a ginny kidney.

Luckily, however, this rare flash of self-awareness passed, and I returned to work. Another year to eighteen months and by the reckoning we should be done. I honestly have no idea what I'll be like by then.

These scripts you are about to read were written, as I've said, for someone else. Moreover, they were written in the main without regard for necessities of literary style, intended only for the eyes of my esteemed collaborator, the cosmetically-retouched Mr. Campbell. While I still have no idea why anyone would find a mass of long-winded and often repetitious stage-directions edifying, I have bowed to the exhortations of my knowledgeable colleague, Stephen R. Bissette, a man who finds the cataloguing of a cannibal motif in early "Mondo" movies edifying. My hopes for this collection are twofold, and humble:

First of all, I hope that you will find these scripts instructive.

Secondly, and in realisation of the hope expressed above, I hope that you are not a freestyle vivisectionist. Other than that, enjoy them in whatever way you're able.

Alan Moore
Northampton, October 1993.

au•top•sy (ô'top'se) n. 1. dissection and examination of a dead body to determine the cause of death.
2. an eyewitness observation. 3. any critical analysis.
[from Greek *autos*, self + *opsis*, sight: the act of seeing with one's own eyes]
—Collins English Dictionary

One measures a circle, beginning anywhere.
—Charles Fort, *LO!*

Everything must be considered with its context, words, or facts.
—Sir William Withey Gull, *Notes & Aphorisms*

Prologue: The Old Men on the Shore

PAGE 1

(PANEL) 1

Okay ... Let's get out there and win one for the Ripper! (Actually, that's Robert Bloch's joke, but I thought I'd stick it in anyway.)

This first page has nine evenly-sized panels, all taken from a fixed point of view. The year is 1923, and we are in Bournemouth, down on the beach quite close to the tide-line. The month is September; a leaden and overcast day with a blind white sky and grey tides sulkily coming in to the damp sand of a pale grey beach. The time is late afternoon or early evening, and if we could see the sun it would be going down. As it is, the sun sinks unseen and without spectacle behind the smothering, featureless duvet of cloud. Its only visible effect is that throughout this entire eight-page episode, the light gradually worsens through dusk to the beginning of darkness.

We are looking down the beach, looking along the edge of the tide from a ground-level viewpoint. To the right of the picture, stretching away towards the distance, we see the grey-black waves washing sluggishly in with their skirts of grubby white foam. To the left we have a smoky impression of the granite sea wall and the buildings of

"The Old Men On the Shore," is based upon a tentative suggestion put forward by the late Stephen Knight in his book Jack the Ripper: The Final Solution (Grafton Books, 1977).

From Hell
Prologue: The Old Men on the Shore

the Bournemouth sea front rising up stolidly behind it. This too stretches away into the distance, meeting with the line of the sea's edge at the vanishing point, with a ragged ribbon of grey sand and occasional tufts of black maram grass lying between the two. (I'm guessing here, Eddie, since I haven't yet tracked down any references for Bournemouth during that period. When we finally do locate references we'll just have to adapt these descriptions as best we can to fit the facts.)

The beach is deserted, and if there are any people strolling on the sea front they are much too far away to see as more than indistinct dots. In the very foreground of the shot here, right under our noses as it were, there lies the inert body of a decomposing seagull. It lies there with the remains of one wing sticking up scraggly: a few ribs already jutting through the soiled white down of its breast. Its chipped beak hangs open stiffly, stupidly. Its staring eye is a tiny white blob of mucus that has become cloudy and opaque, reflecting only blind white clouds. A number of sand-flies are hopping and picking over the corpse . . . little black dots with legs that you see hopping around near the water's edge and at first mistake for the beginnings of some optical disorder. Since we have this rotting bird right under our noses for nine panels, making it pretty large and right up close in the foreground, maybe we can actually show the idiosyncracies of insect feeding habits going on: An insignificant little ballet going on while the real action gradually encroaches from the background. All I mean by this is maybe we have one fly up on the head who remains almost motionless throughout the entire sequence. Another hops about all over the place, looking for the right dining ambience. A third turns up half way through and presumptuously starts to tuck in right next to the second, who takes umbrage and flies off . . . Just black dots moving around, to give the unpleasant impression of teeming bugs as naturalistically as possible, without overdoing it.

While this is going on in the foreground, we gradually become aware of two figures approaching along the beach from the background, following the line of the tide as they walk slowly towards us. Here, they are tiny little black dots, no bigger than the flies that we see feeding in the foreground. The title lettering, either in black on white or reversed, as appropriate, is superimposed somewhere in the centre of this first panel as if it were the opening title of a film. The lettering is that upon the heading of the note received by the Whitechapel police in the October of 1888: Stark, simple and scruffy: a couple of tiny spattered ink blots to the right of the "F" and just above the "r" in "From".

Okay, so that's the set up for this first page. Before we carry on though, I should just reiterate what I was saying over the phone about how I work: none of this rambling junk is sacred. If there's stuff that doesn't work visually or that you think would work better another way then just go ahead and do it. I only put all this laborious detail in so that you'll have an idea of the effect that I'm after. If you have a better way or a more practical way to achieve it then that's fine by me. For fuck's sake don't be intimidated by it, and please sling in all the ideas and suggestions that you want. I want you to have as much fun on this as I'm having, so just kick off your shoes, loosen your belt and relax. Just don't fall asleep.

LOGO: *From hell*

(PANEL) 2
Same shot exactly, except the flies have maybe moved around a bit and the waves are either crashing in or rattling back across the shingle ... whichever they weren't doing last panel, basically. The two black dots of the men approaching down the beach are larger here, though not by very much. The sub-logo and credits are superimposed across the middle of the panel again, this time probably in an elegant and antiquated Victorian-looking typeface.

CREDITS: *Being a melodrama in sixteen installments by Alan Moore & Eddie Campbell*

(PANEL) 3
Same shot, the tides and the flies having moved accordingly. The figures, again, are a little closer here, although still very small. Once more, the title lettering is superimposed over the panel's centre, probably in the same pseudo-Victorian typeface used last panel.

From Hell
Prologue: The Old Men on the Shore

TITLE: *Prologue: The Old Men on the Shore*

(PANEL) 4
    Same shot. We can now see that the figures are those of two men, both wearing long coats and muffled against the cold. One of them is quite slender and delicate looking, a man of around fifty years old. He wears a scarf, topcoat and gloves, but is bare-headed save for his full and neatly groomed head of grey hair, his greying moustache and beard. He is the more genteel-looking and slightly the better dressed of the two men, but from his attitude he seems to be attentive and fussing in regard to the older man who walks beside him, as if concerned that the old man should over-exert himself for something. I don't mean that that's his physical attitude to the old man in this specific panel . . . I just mean that's the overall impression he gives off when we see him with the older man: respectful and solicitous, albeit occasionally prone to impatience when goaded by the older man's cantankerousness. Here they just walk side by side, hands deep in their greatcoat pockets. The younger man is called Robert Lees. His associate is Frederick Abberline. Abberline is the older of the two men, and more noticeably from yeoman stock than the rather effete Lees. He is pushing seventy, although he still looks a fairly sturdy and solid figure, if slightly inclined to portliness in these, his later years. I don't have a photo reference of Fred Abberline yet, but I'm guessing that he's the fairly stocky figure described above, with a mousey moustache and muttonchop sidewhiskers. His hair, though receding, seems to have kept at least some of its colour. As we see him here he is wearing a derby hat and carrying a gentleman's walking cane. He moves more stiffly than Lees, and it is his difficulty in walking that accounts for the pair's snail-paced progress along the beach towards us here. When Abberline gets closer, I fancy that we might see his nose as being slightly red and bulbous, though not to excess. By all accounts he drank rather a lot, and walking round White Chapel in the fog swigging raw spirits wouldn't do anybody's nose a lot of good, would it? Anyway, we can't make out any of this detail yet since the pair are still too far away. The caption giving the place and date are somewhere up towards the top left of the panel. Since there won't be many captions at all throughout this entire book (just place-and-date captions, like here) the captions can either be lettered in the

Victorian typeface mentioned above or in a more normal and prosaic fashion . . . I leave it entirely up to you. Whatever you think looks best.

    CAP.: Bournemouth. September 1923.

(PANEL) 5

    The two figures continue to get closer. The flies continue to feed on the dead seagull and the waves continue to lurch against the shore. Abberline, who is probably the figure on the left of the pair as they walk towards us, appears to be saying something to his companion here: He sprouts a small word balloon, but there isn't any real lettering in it . . . just a bunch of tiny unreadable scratches that look like words and convey the impression of inaudible conversation.

    ABBERLINE (v. small):
    ....on the dead seagull and the waves continue

(PANEL) 6

    The figures continue to get closer, more and more detail becoming evident as they do so. Here, they both have word balloons. The balloons are still very small, and the words in them are lettered as tiny as possible while still remaining just-about-legible, to give the effect of a conversation gradually becoming audible as the speakers get closer to us.

    ABBERLINE (v. small):
    . . . bloody shambles, this last six years.

    LEES (v. small):
    A shambles inflicted from WITHOUT. Foreign interference hardly invalidates 'Capital's premise.

(PANEL) 7

    The figures come still closer. From their attitudes now we can see that they are debating. Lees looks the more agitated of the two, gesticulating as he attempts to make his point. Abberline continues to plod slowly and implacably forward, digging the end of his cane into the damp sand as he does so. He needs all his energy for walking and can spare none of it for extraneous hand movements. Their

From Hell
Prologue: The Old Men on the Shore

The dialogue between the two men is thus a fabrication: Lees always claimed his psychic abilities were perfectly genuine, and the confession I have attributed to him here is based upon my own intuitions and prejudices. Similarly, while Lees himself claimed to have received an ex gratia pension for his part in solving the Whitechapel murders, and while various authors----notably Stephen Knight----have suggested the; Abberline may have been paid to keep his mouth shut, there is no real evidence to support either suggestion. This doesn't mean the claims are necessarily untrue, but simply that they cannot be taken as hard an proven fact.

word balloons here are bigger than last time, although still not quite as big as the full sized normal lettering that we will see in our next panel.

ABBERLINE (small):
Oh DO come on, Mr. Lees! Really! They've had nothing but war, poverty . . .

LEES (small):
Despite which they have SURVIVED! Surely that confirms rather than contradicts what Mr. Marx has said:

LEES (small):
Socialism is INEVITABLE.

(PANEL) 8

They are very close to us now, filling the whole panel. Abberline is a few paces ahead of Lees, and thus the closest to us here, walking along swinging his stick and then digging it down into the sand, so that its point, when visible, has a clinging sheath of damp grey sand adhering to the last few inches of its tip, a few grains falling off here and there. As he walks towards us he doesn't look round at Lees. Rather he looks down at the dead gull in his path. A slight frown of distaste wrinkles his features as he stares at the decaying bird and the flies feasting upon it. Lees, slightly behind Abberline as the pair walk towards us, does not appear to have noticed the bird and is looking at the back of Abberline's turned back. Lees' expression is very earnest, his sad eyes more or less begging Abberline to see reason and accept his argument. Lees has eyes like a spaniel, and looks sorry for the world, particularly himself.

LEES:
Why, I myself am testament to its increasing influence. I am undoubtedly a product of the middle classes, yet none espouse socialism more volubly than I . . .

(PANEL) 9

In this last panel, Abberline has moved so close that we can no longer see his upper body at all . . . We see him from around about the knee down here. In another step he'll be out of the panel entirely. With the end of his walking cane he swats the dead gull to one side so that it flies limply up into the air, spinning beak over tail with a miniature thunderhead of black flies billowing up from it in search of less hazardous pastures. Lees, still trailing a couple of steps behind the older man, is still not looking at the gull. Instead, he directs his gaze towards the point off panel above where Abberline's head must be. He looks puzzled, in a troubled sort of way, as he gazes at the back of Abberline's off panel head. Abberline's balloon issues from off panel above in the F/G.

ABBERLINE (off):
My point precisely, Mr. Lees.

ABBERLINE (off):
My point precisely.

PAGE 2

(PANEL) 1

Seven panels on this page. Although the final decision regarding layout is obviously up to you, I see this page as having a wide panel spanning the top of the page and then two tiers of three smaller panels beneath that. See what you think, anyway, and do accordingly. In this first panel we are looking down the last few yards of the beach before the tide line, and out to sea. Running at intervals down the beach away from us and into the encroaching surf there

From Hell
Prologue: The Old Men on the Shore

Knight goes on to claim that upon the death of Fred Abberline in 1928, one Nelson Edwin Lees was appointed the old man's executor. The implication is that the two men may have kept in contact long after the events of 1888's terrible Autumn, from which I have gone on to hypothesize concerning the walks the may have enjoyed together, the topics their conversation may have spanned.

are a number of pitch-blackened groins jutting up from the grey sand like decayed wooden teeth. Abberline, plodding across the picture towards its centre, pauses near the groins and stands for a moment gazing out towards the distant steely horizon, leaning on his cane. A very faint sea breeze is starting to rise as the sky gradually darkens and night draws in. Entering from the left of panel, Lees trudges into the picture in the wake of his old friend, gazing queryingly at the old man's back here. Abberline doesn't look back at Lees as he replies, staring reflectively out to sea.

LEES:
What do you mean?

ABBERLINE:
I mean MOST socialists are middle class . . . your late friend Mr. Hardie, for one. Mr. Ramsay-Leader-of-His-Majesty's-bloomin'-opposition-MacDonald for another.

(PANEL) 2
Change angle so that Abberline is now gazing out of the panel towards us, a head and shoulders close up in the foreground. We see Lees standing some few yards behind Abberline, hands deep in his pockets as he stares at the back of the old man's neck. Abberline, gazing out in the foreground has a sort of insufferably smug grim and knowing smile upon his face . . . Not so much a smile really as a tightening of the corners of the mouth and a narrowing of the

eyes beneath their straggling and slightly overgrown brows. Abberline believes himself to be a canny old bugger who knows a thing or two. Most of the time, he's right, but this doesn't stop a brief look of resentment stealing across Lees' melancholy features as he looks on from the near background. Abberline still doesn't look round at Lees as he speaks. The wind is rising slightly here, and the sky gradually darkens behind the two men as dusk encroaches.

> ABBERLINE:
> Now, myself, I come from a working family: We vote Tory. Always have done.

> ABBERLINE:
> The working class don't WANT a revolution, Mr. Lees. They just want more money.

> ABBERLINE:
> This next election, you watch.

(PANEL) 3

Change angle so that Lees is now head and shoulders in the foreground, roughly in profile here. He isn't looking at Abberline, but is gazing down at the ground before him, glaring in a faintly sulky manner, like a reprimanded child. Looking beyond him we see that Abberline is lowering his arthritic and portly frame to sit upon one of the jutting groins. As he does so, he glances round over his shoulder at Lees, a smile upon his ruddy features. It's sort of patronizing and mocking smile of disbelief.

> LEES:
> You're wrong, Abberline. The Labour Party will win the election.

> ABBERLINE:
> " . . . and the band played believe me if you like."

> ABBERLINE:
> You seem very sure, Mr. Lees. Had one of your visions, 'ave yer?

(PANEL) 4

Reverse angle again so that Abberline is now seated on the groin in the F/G, turned slightly to face towards Lees in the near

From Hell
Prologue: The Old Men on the Shore

background. Abberline's can lies propped up against the groin on which he is sitting. As he looks at Lees he has at least one arm slightly raised with palm outwards as if to both deflect what Lees is saying and to calm the younger man down. Once again, there's something annoyingly patronizing about the gesture, as if calming a silly child that's getting heated up about something trivial and silly. In the near background Lees rounds upon Abberline and looks for a moment genuinely angry, stung by the old man's condescension.

LEES:
Yes.

LEES:
Yes, damn you, I HAVE! I saw a calendar dated 1924 ... Mr. MacDonald on the steps of Number 10. I saw it, I tell you.

ABBERLINE:
Alright, alright. Keep your shirt on.

(PANEL) 5
Now we see both men full figure, studiedly ignoring each other in the wake of this sudden flare up of political opinion. Abberline sits on the wooden groin, staring out to sea and away from Lees. He has taken out a hip flask of brandy and is seen here unscrewing it. Lees stands a couple of yards away, glaring in the opposite direction, his hands deep in his trouser pockets. The rising wind ruffles his hair. The September sky grows gradually darker.

No Dialogue

(PANEL) 6
Same shot. Abberline is now tilting back his head to take a swig from the flask, still seated so as to be facing slightly away from Lees. Lees, over more towards the right of the panel has now sat down and is staring out of frame right. The anger has evaporated from his face, leaving the usual sad and anxious look in his deep set eyes. If anything though, he looks even bleaker here than he did previously. He still doesn't look at Abberline but stares hopelessly out of the right of the panel. Swigging his brandy, Abberline is oblivious to what Lees is doing or thinking.

Alan Moore

No Dialogue

(PANEL) 7

Same shot, with Abberline just removing the flask from his mouth and wiping his lips with the back of one liver-spotted hand here. He still isn't looking at Lees. Lees sits motionless over on the right, gazing out of the right of panel, just staring into space. He looks haunted and bleak and miserable.

LEES:

I made it up.

PAGE 3

(PANEL) 1

Another seven panel page here. As I have it laid out in my head, this time the wide panel is at the bottom of the page, with six panels up above it. The first three panels are almost identical to the last three panels on page 2, showing the two men sitting on their separate groins, Abberline to the left and Lees to the right. Lees hasn't moved since last panel, continuing to sit and stare glumly off to the right of the panel. Abberline, however, has turned his head. He stares at the back of Lees' head with an incredulous frown creasing his features.

No Dialogue

(PANEL) 2

Same shot exactly. Nobody has moved. Abberline is still frowning at the back of Lees' neck and Lees is still gazing mournfully out of panel to the right. The only difference is that Abberline has his mouth slightly open here as he speaks.

ABBERLINE:

What?

(PANEL) 3

Same shot. Lees shifts slightly, as if to ease the cramp in his buttocks against the hard, uneven wood of the groin, but doesn't look round. Abberline continues to gaze at Lees' back in increasing mute bewilderment. Lees looks miserable.

From Hell
Prologue: The Old Men on the Shore

> LEES:
> What I said: I made it up.

> ABBERLINE:
> The vision of Mr. MacDonald.

(PANEL) 4

Change angle now so that we are in front of Lees, looking towards him as he sits gazing morosely and defeatedly towards us, his back still turned to Abberline who we see seated behind him, also looking towards us as he stares at the back of Lees' neck. His eyes have a look of bewilderment in them that grows slightly more troubled over the next few panels. It's as if Abberline didn't want to hear this: as if he really wanted to believe all along that Lees possessed the mysterious psychic powers that he claimed to. There's something rather sad and child-like about Abberline's old and bewildered face over this next few panels, like that of a kid being told that there's no Father Christmas. Lees looks miserable as he confesses, still staring bleakly into space.

> LEES:
> All of them. All the visions. I made them up.

> LEES:
> You have to remember I was very young and frail.
> The attention, that was the thing . . .

(PANEL) 5

Same shot, but whereas Lees was full figure as he sat facing us last panel, here we have closed in slightly so that he's more or less half figure to head and shoulders staring bleakly towards us in the F/G here, still not so much as glancing round at Abberline, too wrapped up in his own awful confession. Abberline, seated behind Lee, is also closer now, his face growing more ambiguously troubled by the moment.

> LEES:
> I was seven, the first time. The family cat had been missing for days, and I said I'd had the STRANGEST dream: On May 25th, our cat should be RETURNED to us.

LEES:
A complete lie, of course.

(PANEL) 6
Now we are in the act of closing in still further, over Lees' shoulder, so that his face is no longer visible here . . . maybe we just see a bit of his shoulder at the bottom of the panel and one ear entering the picture from the left, but not much else. His balloons issue into the picture from off. Over his shoulder we are now focussed on a half figure to head and shoulders shot of Fred Abberline, the ambiguously troubled look in his eyes clearly evident now as he sits and listens silently to Lees' extraordinary confession.

LEES (off):
But after the fuss they made of me . . . How? How could I admit I'd invented everything? I chose to keep up the pretense . . .

LEES (off):
. . . and the longer I did, the harder it became to extricate myself.

(PANEL) 7
Now the wide cinemascope panel that spans the bottom of the page, if you decide to follow my layouts. We are down at the water's very edge, with grey waves crashing and foaming and booming dully in the foreground. Looking up the beach and along it a way, we see Lees and Abberline, both seated upon the groins, very small and poignant little figures here, surrounded by the flat and featureless landscape of the beach, the stone sea front looming up in the distance behind them against the slowly deepening twilight. They look very isolated and lonely.

LEES:
Be a good fellow, Abberline.

LEES:
Don't tell anyone.

From Hell
Prologue: The Old Men on the Shore

PAGE 4

(PANEL) 1
Eight panels here. I suggest two panels on the top tier and three on each of the two lower tiers. In this first one we are behind Abberline and Lees, and looking out between them to sea. Both men are off panel to the left and right respectively. All we see of Lees is his slightly hunched-over back entering into the panel from the right as he sits leaning forward with his elbows resting on his knees, his head off panel right here. All we see of Abberline is one of his arms, entering from the left of panel to lay itself reassuringly on the back of Lees' shoulder. Looking between the two partly revealed men and out to sea we can see a few wheeling seagulls swooping over the iron ocean in the failing light.

ABBERLINE (off):
Mr. Lees . . .

ABBERLINE (off):
Mr. Lees, you're pulling my leg, surely. What about the SEIZURES, man? I've seen you myself, rigid as a sleeve-board; eyes like blessed millwheels . . .

(PANEL) 2
Perhaps a slightly larger panel here. We pull back so that we see both men full figure. With a sort of depressed and miserable dignity, Lees starts to stand up, lifting himself from the groin. Abberline just stares at him, puzzled.

LEES:
Oh, the SEIZURES . . .

LEES:
You liked the seizures, did you?

LEES:
Here. You watch this.

(PANEL) 3
Now a bank of three panels all from the same fixed point of

view. In the F/G, entering the panel from the left, we can see just a little of Abberline... Maybe one buttock visible sitting on the groin facing away from us, his can resting against the groin and his aged and liver spotted hand resting upon the knee of his trousers as he watches Lees, who is now standing in profile in the middle foreground, staring ahead of him into space and poised as if about to attempt some difficult performance; standing for a moment and marshalling his resources first. There is something quietly theatrical about it.

No Dialogue

(PANEL) 4

Same shot, with the shot of Abberline's knee unmoved in the F/G. In the middleground, Lees stiffens, suddenly and dramatically, as if he's having some sort of dreadful heart attack, his fingers tensing into hooked claws by his side, his head lolling suddenly back on his shoulders and a spastic tremor running through his body.

LEES:
Unh...

(PANEL) 5

Same shot. In the foreground perhaps Abberline shifts slightly, a little uncomfortably. Beyond him, in the middleground, Lees is in the process of collapsing, his limbs suddenly nerveless like a puppet with the strings cut. His legs turn to jelly and fold pathetically beneath him as he starts to collapse towards the sand. His eyes are wide and terrified and transfixed and gazing, his teeth gritted together with a little spittle escaping from the corners of his mouth as he starts to fall, still making inarticulate noises and grunts. It's all very convincing, and not a little unnerving. Behind Lees the grey sea stretches away impassively towards a darkening horizon.

LEES:
aa-huch!

LEES:
aahuch...

LEES:
Guhhuh...

From Hell
Prologue: The Old Men on the Shore

(PANEL) 6
Now three panels from a different angle. We have reversed the shot, and are not down at ground level with Lees lying prostrate in the foreground, his back arching and twisting as he thrashes and writhes in the damp sand. His wide and terrified eyes stare transfixed into space, and there is now slobber spraying from the corners of his mouth as he talks through gritted teeth, a veritable study of divine possession. Looking past him we see old Fred Abberline sitting on his wooden groin, looking wide eyed and utterly gobsmacked as he stares in disbelief and astonishment at the writhing psychic thrashing on the ground before him. This is really rather a grotesque little scene, with Lees talking to thin air of the awful visions that he is "seeing".

LEES:
Hhhuughhh . . .

LEES:
Hhhhuughhh . . . Duh . . . death. See death . . .

LEES:
Five . . . HHHUGHHHH . . . five years . . .

LEES:
Five years . . .

(PANEL) 7
Same shot. In the background, Abberline doesn't move. He just sits there staring utterly transfixed. In the foreground Lees slumps suddenly, as if into unconsciousness or a swoon after his psychic exertions. His body goes limp and his head rolls towards us, so as to face us. The eyes are closed and Lees seems to have blacked out.

No Dialogue

(PANEL) 8
Exactly the same shot. In the background, Abberline hasn't moved, still sitting staring at Lees' inert body. In the foreground Lees opens his mouth just slightly to speak, although he doesn't yet move or open his eyes. He looks very calm.

LEES:
There.

PAGE 5

(PANEL) 1

Seven panels here, with the final one being another wide one that spans the page, if that looks okay to you. I like these wide panels because they sort of emphasize the loneliness and isolation of these two men; they are isolated by the knowledge they share. In this first panel we seem to pull back a little from the short in the last three panels of Page 4, so that we see more or less the whole of Abberline's back as he sits facing away from us towards Lees, his cane. leaning against the groin on which he sits. Beyond him, in the immediate background, Lees is getting up from the sand and fastidiously brushing its clinging grayness from the folds of his well-tailored clothing. Abberline, if we can see any of his face from this angle as he stares dumbfounded at Lees, looks completely lost and bewildered. Lees, dusting himself down, looks sad and matter-of-fact, looking more at his sand-soiled clothes than at Abberline as he speaks.

LEES:
I'd sometimes pee in my trousers, as well. For emphasis.

LEES:
Only during childhood, naturally. I'd purged my repertoire of that device long before I was nineteen and first introduced to Her Majesty.

(PANEL) 2

Reverse angle. In the F/G, Lees stands dusting the clinging sand from his clothing. Sitting facing us in the near background, Abberline looks lost and bewildered, gesturing uncomprehendingly with his withered hands as he talks to Lees. There is a certain amount of pathos in the way he struggles to take in the implications of what Lees is saying. In the foreground, Lees doesn't look at Abberline as he continues to brush down his clothes with the same sad and guilt-haunted expression.

ABBERLINE:
But . . .

ABBERLINE:
What you SAID. EVERYTHING you said. It all HAPPENED.

From Hell
Prologue: The Old Men on the Shore

> ABBERLINE:
> It was all TRUE...

(PANEL) 3

Reverse angle again so that once more we have a little bit of Abberline entering the panel in the foreground. We can't see his head and shoulders here but we can see enough of him to realize that he is slowly rising to his feet, placing one hand on the groin to assist in raising himself up from it. In the background, Lees has finished dusting himself down and is standing with his hands in his coat pockets gazing mournfully and motionlessly out to sea, not looking round at Abberline as he speaks. The breeze is still rising, and his hair is even more ruffled now. It looks as if its getting quite chilly. As the sky and the sea both darken towards an indistinguishable and amorphous band of blackness we see a few last gulls swooping above the foaming grey caps of the waves.

> LEES:
> Oh yes.

> LEES:
> On May 25th we found the cat under a hedge, poisoned by weed preparation. It was small; stiff; nothing interesting about it whatsoever...

> LEES:
> I made it all up, and it all came true anyway.

(PANEL) 4

This last bank of three panels before we get to the wide angle shot at the bottom are all from the same angle. We have Lees head and shoulders facing us in the F/G as he stares out to sea. Behind him and full figure we see Abberline rising unsteadily to his feet beside the groin he's been seated upon. He is staring at Lees with an odd expression, as if seeing him in an entirely new light and not knowing quite what to say. As Lees looks out towards us in the foreground his eyes are still haunted and full of sorrow and tragedy, but one corner of his mouth lifts up slightly into a sad little half-smile.

> LEES:
> That's the funny part.

(PANEL) 5

Still with the same expression, Lees continues to stare out to sea in the F/G. Behind him, Abberline is stooping slightly to retrieve his walking cane from where it rests propped against the blackened groin. The wind looks quite stiff now. Abberline gazes at his stick as he reaches for it while Lees looks out to sea. Neither man looks at the other.

No Dialogue

(PANEL) 6

Same shot. In the F/G, Lees remains unmoved, still staring out over the darkening off-panel ocean with the same half smile upon his wan features. Behind him, Abberline stands up straight, bracing himself against the wind and supporting himself upon the cane, planted firmly in the sand at his feet. He looks at Lees with a neutral expression as he speaks, resuming the bluff tone of their normal relationship, as if trying to put a full stop after the odd and disquieting little exchange that has just occurred. We sense how much it has disturbed him from how little Abberline is looking disturbed: He is obviously trying to shut the incident out: almost pretending that it hasn't happened.

ABBERLINE:
It's turned quite cold, hasn't it?

Knight points out that Robert Lees, the alleged psychic who claimed to have "solved" the Whitechapel murders, had his family roots in Bournemouth. He also points out that Inspector Fred Abberline went to live in Bournemouth after his somewhat abrupt retirement from the police force in the wake of the Cleveland Street Scandal in 1889 (the scandal involved a police raid on a male brothel situated at No. 19 Cleveland Street; the raid unearthed several wealthy or high-placed clients, including Prince Eddy, the Duke of Clarence and Avondale, and becomes relevant later in the course of our narrative).

From Hell
Prologue: The Old Men on the Shore

> ABBERLINE:
> Shall we be heading back?

(PANEL) 7
    Final wide-angle shot spanning the bottom of the page. We just see a panoramic shot of the grey beach beneath the blackening sky. The two old men are plodding across it, heads tucked down against the rising wind. Dunno if it'll be evident here, but they're making their way towards the ramp or flight of stone steps that lead up from the beach onto the sea wall and the seafront beyond. Huge dark clouds move almost invisibly against the dark sky above them.

PAGE 6

(PANEL) 1
    A nine panel page, probably with three tiers of three. These first three panels are all from the same fixed vantage point: We are up just under the sea wall, which is behind us and thus invisible here. Entering from the left of panel and towards the middle ground we can see the lower reaches of the ramp or steps leading up onto the sea wall from the beach. In the very F/G, down low near our ground-level eyeline, we see an old fashioned empty bottle of INDIA PALE ALE. Draped casually across its brown glass contours and partially obscuring its quaint old label there are a pair of old fashioned women's bloomers. Looking beyond all this towards the background we see the small figures of Lees and Abberline walking slowly up the beach towards the ramp or steps (We'll know which it is when we find some reference.) They are chatting together as they come towards us, and as we see them here they are still some good few yards away from the bottom of the ramp/steps.

> LEES:
> Abberline . . . my performance back there. Please forgive me.

> LEES:
> It's just September; this time of year . . .

(PANEL) 2
Same shot. Lees and Abberline have just reached the bottom of the ramp/steps and are starting to mount them, still talking casually. Lees looks at Abberline somewhat anxiously, while Abberline gazes gruffly down at the ground before him as he mounts the steps/ramp. In the F/G, as yet unnoticed, the pair of bloomers still lay motionless, draped over the empty ale bottle.

ABBERLINE:
I know.

ABBERLINE:
It all comes back to you doesn't it? Bloody September. Gets you down . . .

ABBERLINE (separate balloon):
Mind you, I've always though that, even BEFORE what happened. There's something that's . . .

(PANEL) 3
Same shot. Halfway up the ramp, Abberline stops dead in mid step. Frozen and motionless he stares down towards a point just off panel to the left of the foreground, near the inert bloomers and beer bottle. Abberline's eyes widen and his face sets in a look of dawning outrage and anger. Behind him, Lees almost stumbles as he's brought to a halt by Abberline's sudden and unexpected cessation of movement.

ABBERLINE:
What the bloody hell do you call THIS?

(PANEL) 4
Dunno whether one of Abberline's hands should be visible entering the panel from one side of the foreground, as if we were behind him and looking down past him at the scene taking place up against the sea wall immediately before and below him: We see a young woman of about twenty-two with dirty blonde hair in a contemporary working class style. She lies on her back with her head and shoulders resting against the base of the sea wall, her knees bent and raised and her legs parted. Her skirt is rucked up around her waist. Lying on his side beside her with his own legs bent and tucked

From Hell
Prologue: The Old Men on the Shore

under the woman's we see a dark and surly looking young man with his trousers around his ankles. As he rolls back slightly from the woman his rapidly deflating penis slides wet and dangling from her vagina. The man looks momentarily startled and confused, frowning with incoherent belligerence at no one in particular while the woman stares levelly and coldly at both us and Abberline. She makes no movement to cover herself. Her expression is contemptuous.

The phrase "butcher's" here is a contraction of the Cockney rhyming slang expression "a butcher's hook," meaning a "look."

YOUNG WOMAN:
'Ad a good butcher's, 'ave yer?

(PANEL) 5
We are now looking up at Abberline and Lees, the young woman and man now off panel behind us somewhere. Abberline's fists clench and his face starts to redden as he becomes angrier. Behind him, a worried looking Lees places a restraining hand upon Abberline's shoulder. Abberline ignores it.

ABBERLINE:
Had..?

ABBERLINE:
I'll have you inside, that's what I'll have! The PAIR of yer!

LEES:
Fred, let's just leave it. You're retired...

(PANEL) 6
Pull back so we can see the young

man and woman in the foreground, looking past them at Abberline and Lees standing looking down halfway up the stairs/ramp leading from the beach to atop the sea wall. Abberline still looks furiously angry, shaking Lees' hand from his shoulder as he glares, enraged, down at the man and woman in the foreground. Both of these have risen and are standing now. The man, one hand still engaged in pulling up his trousers, points with rather unconvincing menace at Abberline, more a display for the woman's sake than anything else. The woman, stooping to pick up her knickers from atop the empty beer bottle glances back contemptuously over her shoulder at Abberline as she speaks to her boyfriend.

ABBERLINE:
I don't care! I'll not have prossies whoring on my front doorstep!

YOUNG MAN:
Oy, YOU! You WATCH it, all right?

WOMAN:
Oh, let's go somewhere else. He's just browned off because he's not had a bone on in years.

(PANEL) 7

A longish shot, showing all figures, but with all of them quite small. Abberline and Lees stand on the steps/ramp, over to the left of the panel and facing right. The young man and the young woman are walking off along the beach, heading towards the right of the panel and not glancing back at Abberline as he rants and rails after them. The woman, not turning round as she speaks, stuffs her knickers into her coat pocket as she walks off. Abberline looks absolutely furious as he roars after the departing twosome. Again, Lees attempts ineffectually to restrain the old retired policeman from his fury.

ABBERLINE:
You WHAT?

WOMAN:
You heard.

ABBERLINE:
You come back here and say that!

From Hell
Prologue: The Old Men on the Shore

Michael Caine played Abberline in David Wickes' two-part centenary TV movie Jack the Ripper *(BBC/Thames Lorimar TV, 1988)*

LEES:
Fred...

(PANEL) 8
Close up now of Abberline, head and shoulders, as he bellows after the off panel retreating pair of lovebirds. Abberline looks ugly. A vein stands out in his temple, another beneath his eye. His face is dark with blood and he raises one old and knotted fist as he roars. He looks murderous, and with this panel we realize (a) that Abberline isn't a very nice old man and (b) he doesn't like sex, women or prostitutes, which are all lumped together in his head. This isn't the likeable cheery Cockney of Michael Caine's television portrayal ... Or if it is, he's a lot older, more bitter and more fucked up. As he stands behind Abberline, Lees looks for a moment disgusted in his old companion's choice of phrase, as well as with his behaviour in general. He grimaces in appalled disgust as he prepares to turn and walk away from the situation, leaving Abberline to it. He glares at the red and bristling back of Abberline's neck here as he speaks.

ABBERLINE:
You COW!

ABBERLINE:
You cheeky little CUNT! You come back here, I'll 'ave your guts for GARTERS!

LEES:
Abberline, for God's SAKE man! Let's just DROP it.

(PANEL) 9
Same shot as last panel, with Abberline staring head and shoulders out of the panel at us in the foreground still, presumably still gazing after the off panel departed woman and man. His eyes are rheumy and narrowed slits of malice here, and one corner of his lips curls and distorts as he speaks through it, voice icy with contempt. Behind him we see Lees' back as he walks away from us up the steps/ramp to the top of the sea wall and the sea front beyond.

ABBERLINE (small):
Fucking tart.

PAGE 7

(PANEL) 1
We are now atop the sea wall, on the sea front. Lees stands in the foreground, waiting for Abberline to catch up, his back turned to the beach behind him. He glances around absently, staring into space with, again, a look of annoyance on his face. Behind him we see Abberline mounting the last few steps/feet of ramp towards the sea wall. His head is lowered and his face lost in the shadows his derby hat. He seems to have recovered his composure a little. Maybe he's even feeling a little ashamed of himself in a gruff and uncommunicative fashion. In the foreground, Lees doesn't look round as Abberline approaches from behind. Lees still looks a bit miffed and sulky.

No Dialogue

(PANEL) 2
Same shot. Lees has remained standing still, probably somewhere towards the middle ground. Abberline has walked past him without looking round at Lees, but as he passes him he speaks a word or two in passing, not looking at Lees as he does so but continuing to hobble towards us in the foreground, eyes still hidden by his hat brim and its shadows. Lees is slightly further away from us as Abberline walks past him now, and is looking towards the ex-inspector's back with a sort of quiet and querying frown, as if trying to figure out what Abberline is all about.

From Hell
Prologue: The Old Men on the Shore

>   ABBERLINE:
> September. You're quite right.

>   ABBERLINE:
> That time of year.

(PANEL) 3

(Before I forget, this is a six panel page . . . up to you how you lay it out.) This third panel shows a full figure profile of Abberline and Lees as they walk across the traffic-less roadway dividing the sea front promenade itself from the other side of the street, where some posh-looking Victorian terraced houses stand in a row, looking squarely out to sea. As they cross the empty road in the near darkness we can maybe see that down along the promenade the gas lamps are coming on. The wind is quite sharp now, with Abberline having to hold his hat on as he walks, a few paces in front of Lees here. Lees quickens his pace to catch up with the older man as he follows him, addressing his remarks to Abberline's back. Abberline doesn't look round as he replies.

>   LEES:
> Do you think about it a lot?

>   ABBERLINE:
> About the thing itself? No. Can't say I do.

>   ABBERLINE:
> I just think about how I was treated, that's all. All those years on the force . . .

(PANEL) 4

Now Abberline and Lees have reached the other side of the street and are walking down it towards us, with Abberline half figure head and shoulders in the F/G and Lees full figure, just mounting the curb a few paces behind Abberline. In the F/G, Abberline's face is cold and grim and bitter as he stares into space. Behind him, Lees addresses his comments to Abberline's back with a slightly pained and disbelieving look.

>   ABBERLINE:
> It's being lied to, that's what gets my back up.

>   ABBERLINE:
> It's the DISRESPECT.

LEES:
And that's ALL?

(PANEL) 5
Reverse angles so that we are behind Lees as he follows Abberline along the street. The houses all have high front steps leading up to the front doors with a wrought iron railing beside them. Abberline is just approaching the bottom of one of these railings here, placing his hand on it to steady himself, still facing away from us as he speaks. In the F/G, Lees faces away from us, hands spread imploringly as he speaks to Abberline's turned back, trying to get some kind of human response out of him.

LEES:
Don't you ever feel GUILTY?

LEES:
We could have SAID something; we could have DONE something. WHY, Fred?

LEES:
Why did we just let them BURY it?

(PANEL) 6
Changes angles again. In the foreground, Abberline is just starting to slowly and laboriously mount the steps towards his front door, coming towards us roughly half figure here as we look down past him from the top of the steps towards Lees, who stands on the pavement at the base of the steps looking up at Abberline's turned back. His face looks sad and defeated. Abberline has down cast eyes, as if admitting his physical cowardice only with difficulty.

ABBERLINE:
Because we didn't want our throats cut.

ABBERLINE:
Because we didn't want our lights hung over our shoulders.

ABBERLINE:
Give us a hand up these steps, would yer?

From Hell
Prologue: The Old Men on the Shore

The term "lights" mentioned on the previous page is an English colloquialism meaning "lungs" or in more general terms here "innards."

PAGE 8

(PANEL) 1
There are seven panels on this last page, probably with the wide-screen one at the bottom of the page this time. In this first small panel we see a side-on shot of Lees and Abberline as they slowly mount the short flight of steps to Abberline's front door. Abberline is slightly in the lead with Lees a step behind him, holding his arm and semi-supporting him, looking as usual a little worried for the old man's physical safety. As he mounts the steps of his elegant sea-front house, Abberline is fishing inside his coat and waistcoat for his front door key.

LEES:
I think about it constantly.

LEES:
The sweet-shop girl, the widow Queen, the little barge-boy and the barrister...

(PANEL) 2
We are now at the top of the steps looking down, with Abberline just mounting the last step as he retrieves a key from his inside pocket. His eyes are lowered slightly, not looking at us. Though his tone is matter-of-fact and casual there is a certain gravity in his face, a certain bluff guilt that is only expressed by the stone-like quality that steals over Abberline's face as he mentions Druitt. Behind him, Lees looks on, his pained-looking eyes gazing penetratingly at Abberline, as if trying to

read the older man's soul from the back of his neck.

> ABBERLINE:
> Ah, yes. Mr. Druitt.

> ABBERLINE:
> I've been meaning to visit him since I retired . . . although I don't suppose he's much bothered.

> ABBERLINE:
> Seems silly not to, though; him just up the road . . .

(PANEL) 3

Reverse angle so that we're slightly behind Lees, with him looking away from us in the F/G at a slight angle so that we can see his face in profile as he stands at the top of the steps talking to Abberline's back, a look of sad and sympathetic understanding in his eyes. Abberline stands with his back to us, busy unlocking his front door. He doesn't move as Lees speaks. He just stands with his back to us, listening in motionless silence.

> LEES:
> You want to visit DRUITT, but you say you don't feel GUILTY?

> LEES:
> It's the money, isn't it? You could shrug off anything but that.

> LEES:
> We both did well out of doing nothing, Abberline.

Abberline's somewhat cryptic reference to a Mr. Druitt being situated "just up the road" is accurate even though it may be initially puzzling to anyone with more than a surface knowledge of the Whitechapel murders. Rest assured that all will be explained.

From Hell
Prologue: The Old Men on the Shore

(PANEL) 4

Change angle again so that Abberline is now facing us head and shoulders in the F/G, with Lees a dark and sombre figure standing listening behind him. In the street below them, on the seafront, the sickly glow of the gas lamps serves only to reinforce the darkness. Abberline's face, as he gazes out of the panel at us, is naked. It seems to sag, and the eyes look almost as sad as those of his younger companion. Bleakly, he faces the unpleasant truth about himself. He has neither the heart nor the conviction to defend himself against what Lees is saying. He simply accepts it, having no other choice.

ABBERLINE:
Yes.

ABBERLINE:
Yes, you're right. Nice pension, plus perks. Nice expensive residence on the sea-front at Bournemouth . . .

ABBERLINE:
Didn't do bad out of it, did I?

(PANEL) 5

Side-on shot now as a sad-faced Abberline starts to open the door of his house, turning the heavy brass knob while staring at it as if its extravagance makes him sick somewhere inside. Lees, sensing that he has gone too far, places one hand gently on the old man's shoulder as he stands behind him, his face pained as he tries to apologize. Abberline doesn't look round as he replies. He just shakes his head and stares at the fucking posh door-knob.

LEES:
Abberline, I'm sorry. I didn't mean to open old wounds . . .

ABBERLINE:
No, no, it doesn't matter. You're quite right: Those awful days, and Fred Abberline got a fancy new address out of 'em.

ABBERLINE:
A bent copper, by God.

(PANEL) 6

We are now just inside Abberline's large and quaintly furnished hallway, with the old man hobbling towards us. Behind him, Lees hovers uncomfortably in the doorway, looking as if he wishes he could just go home. Abberline, in the F/G, doesn't look round as he speaks, brooking no argument. Perhaps he waves one ancient hand dismissively. Outside the distant waves boom; the gas lamps hiss and glow softly.

LEE:
Um . . . look, perhaps I should be heading home myself . . .

ABBERLINE:
No, no, I insist. You've walked me all that way, you'll come in for a nightcap, surely?

ABBERLINE:
After all, Mr. Lees, this is the very place . . .

(PANEL) 7

This final wide screen panel shows the stately facade of the terraced house that Abberline resides in. We stand in the street looking up at it. The door is open with a pale light within the hallway against which we can just see the hunched shape of Abberline as he hobbles off up the hallway, not looking back to see if Lees is following. Lees stands poised in the doorway, perhaps with one hand on the brass knob as if ready to step inside the house and pull the door shut behind him. Before he does so he has a last look out into the cold, brine-scented darkness of the Bournemouth sea-front, his dark eyes full of trouble. His shadow falls down the steps towards us, the fine-looking house rising up impressively to fill the background with its dated and sombre lines, the pale light filtering through the thick net curtains that veil its windows.

ABBERLINE:
This is the house that Jack built.

(Sickert's red handkerchief) was an important factor in the process of creating his picture, a lifeline to guide the train of thought, as necessary as the napkin which Mozart used to fold into points which met each other when he too was composing.
—Marjorie Lilly Sickert, *The Painter and His Circle*

She says he knew who Jack the Ripper was.
—Violet Overton Fuller, referring to artist Florence Pash, friend and confidante of Walter Sickert, as quoted in *Sickert & The Ripper Crimes* by Jean Overton Fuller

later, there is a room a bed
the dissection of time
meat decor, exorcism in blood
the carving of forbidden words
on clean flesh pages
—Iain Sinclair
from "Painting With A Knife"
The Birth Rug (Albion Village Press, 1973)

Chapter I: The Affections of Young Mr. S.

PAGE 1

(PANEL 1)
    There are seven panels on this first page, probably with a big wide one at the top of the page here, spanning its full width. The date, as we shall see, is July, 1884, and the place is Cleveland Street, London, one of the more fashionable and upmarket areas of that period, as far as the metropolis went. We are inside a confectioneres-cum-tobaconist situated at No. 22 Cleveland Street, and in this first panel we are looking at a long shelf that neatly fills the space allowed by this first wide, horizontal panel, stretching from one side of the page to the other. Upon the shelf there are old-fashioned sweet jars containing old-fashioned sweets: aniseed balls, winter mixtures, mint imperials, sugared almonds, acid drops, bon-bons and so forth... along with some evidence to show that the shop is also a tobacconists's... perhaps a box of

The bulk of the narrative in this episode is drawn from the sequence of events given in Stephe Knight's Jack The Ripper: The Final Solution, *in which he recounts the tragic story of Walter Sickert, the incognito Prince Eddy, and his doomed marriage to Annie Crook, the sweetshop girl. Knight's theory has been roundly attacked and derided in recent times, and indeed there are grounds for supposing that much of* Final Solution *may have been intended as an ingenious hoax. This will form much of the basis for a proposed appendix to appear after the completion of* From Hell, *titled "Dance of the Gull Catchers," in which we will attempt to document the interplay of the various "Ripperologists" who have tried to solve the mystery since its inception.*

From Hell
Chapter One: The Affections of Young Mr. S.

cigars, or partitioned tray of different tobaccos. Maybe we can see a hint of the tops of the jars on the shelf below this one here, but only if there's room. Over on the right of the wide panel, we see the arms of a twenty-five year old shopgirl named Annie Crook, a sturdily built and tidily dressed young woman, as she reaches up from off panel below to take a few more pieces of barley sugar out from a jar on the top shelf. One of her hands manages to hold the jar's lid and also to tilt the open jar over towards her. Her other hand dips in to retrieve a couple of single pieces of deep orange barley sugar. We cannot see any more of her than her arms, entering the picture from below. The rest of the panel is just tobacco and different sorts of sweets: I want this to be a panel that you can almost smell, if you know what I mean. The title lettering is superimposed over the left of the panel somewhere, down towards the bottom.

Title:

Chapter I: The Affections of Young Mr. S.

(PANEL) 2
Now we are behind the counter of the shop, with the shopgirl, looking out over it. On the shop's counter there is an old fashioned weighing scale or balance, into one of the pans of which we see Annie Crook dropping the couple of pieces of barley sugar that she's just taken from the jar, as if to make up the weight. We can still see no more of her than her hands and cuffs, entering from the left of the foreground here. Looking out across the counter and into the shadowy remainder of the shop we see two young men standing waiting for the woman to finish delivering the sweets that they are purchasing. One of these, dressed in a mustard colour check suit of somewhat questionable taste and loudness, is young Walter Sickert, aged 24 years old. The other young man is much more somberly and elegantly dressed in a gentleman's black coat, and although he will be introduced to us as Sickert's younger brother Albert, he is in fact the young Duke of Clarence, Prince Albert Victor Christian Edward . . . or Prince Eddy for short. At the time of this first scene, in 1884, he is only twenty years old. He's quite good looking, but there's something rather bovine about his expression. He isn't terribly bright, knows it, and feels wretchedly self-conscious about it. He's naive to the point of being infantile, and having led a relatively

Alan Moore

loveless existence is inclined to fall passionately in love with anyone he meets. Coupled with this, his infantile needs for gratification manifest themselves in his sex life to make him fairly promiscuous . . . although that's somewhat too knowing a term to convey the childishness, almost innocence, of his emotional and sexual experience. He has had syphilis since the age of sixteen, although this will not manifest its worse effects until later in Eddy's life. As he stands with Sickert here he holds a top hat nervously and awkwardly beneath his arm, and is staring almost slack jawed at the off panel woman behind the counter, far too gauche to conceal his wide-eyed interest, or even to be aware that he is showing it. Sickert, on the other hand, is comparatively easy and relaxed, a confident young Bohemian about town. He has a smart derby hat tucked jauntily under his arm, or is holding it in one hand. His gaze is directed at the last pieces of barley sugar being dropped into the scale, rather than at the young woman doing the dropping, as is the case with

From Hell
Chapter One: The Affections of Young Mr. S.

his companion. He smiles faintly, relaxedly, utterly at ease. The shop has a large front window, and the bright sunshine falls in from outside in shafts, a solid edged rhomboid of white gold light against the musty umber darkness of the sweetshop, with its jars and trays and selections of briar pipes. Fallen from the off panel woman's fingers, the last piece of barley sugar hangs suspended magically in mid air, caught frozen between hand and weighing scale. The caption can be at the top or bottom. Up to you.

CAP.: London, July 1884.

(PANEL) 3
Now a side on shot, looking down the length of the counter towards the shop's front window, so that we can see all the three participants clearly. Annie stands, fully visible for the first time, behind the counter, over to the left of panel here. She's pouring the barley sugar from the pan of the scales into a little triangular bag made of white paper. The barley sugar lumps are somewhat melted and stuck together, on account of the ferocious and sweltering July heat. Annie is a large and sturdily built woman with broad features . . . She isn't fat, you understand. Just big . . . only a little shorter than Prince Eddy. She isn't immediately pretty or beautiful, but her character and warmth are evident, and do much to compensate for this by lending her own unique air of animation and charm. She smiles quietly as she pours the barley sugar into the white paper bag, eyes twinkling with friendly amusement as she speaks directly to Sickert. Prince Eddy, in the background, holds his top hat wretchedly in both hands and stares at the woman behind the counter with a moonstruck expression that borders upon the imbecilic. Sickert grins at Annie as he speaks to her. She's modelled for him in the past and the two are quite friendly and relaxed around each other. Annie comes from Scotland originally, by the way.

ANNIE:
There. Two pennorth on the nail. I'd not want to jew you now, would I?

ANNIE :
I'm sorry they're all of a lump. It's this weather.

SICKERT:
Nonsense, Annie. They look mouth-watering.

(PANEL) 4

Same shot exactly. All of the sweets are now in the bag and Annie is placing the bag (with a twist at the top corners) onto the counter. Sickert is in the act of taking a couple of copper pennies from his coat pocket. Both Annie and Sickert sort of pause in mid movement and turn their heads to look slightly away from us towards Eddy, who stands semi-facing us in the immediate background here, in more or less the same position as last panel. He looks dreadfully embarrassed, and, as is usual at such times, starts to evidence a faint stammer, a mere echo of his father's far more serious speech difficulty. He gazes at Annie with childish, awestruck adoration. You can see how people might be touched by the naked sincerity of a young man of Eddy's years and station. Sickert and Annie look surprised.

EDDY:
A-as do you . . . i-if I may say so.

EDDY:
That is, ah . . .

(PANEL) 5

Reverse angle now, so that Eddy faces slightly away from us, head and shoulders in the foreground as he gazes towards Sickert and Annie in the centre of the immediate background, standing to either side of the shop's counter. Eddy looks wretchedly agitated and anxious and worried in the wake of his outburst, fearful that Annie has taken offense. Annie, standing behind the counter, turns and gazes at Eddy while she speaks to Sickert. Her eyes are wide with surprise and she has a faint smile that is slightly mocking, but kindly. Sickert, laying his two pennies down on the counter top, turns also to look at Eddy, grinning broadly with amusement at the young chap's obvious discomfort. With his other hand he is picking up the small white bag of barley sugar.

ANNIE:
Why, Mr. S. You do entertain the most IMPERTINENT companions.

From Hell
Chapter One: The Affections of Young Mr. S.

Putting aside doubts about Knight for the moment, the following facts would seem to be generally agreed upon by most reliable sources: Annie Crook definitely existed, and definitely worked in the sweetshop at No. 6 Cleveland Street;

A male brothel definitely existed at No. 19 Cleveland Street, just across the road from the sweetshop. There would seem to have been at least some connection between the sweetshop and the clients of the brothel in that various people working at the sweetshop were questioned in the wake of the Cleveland Street, Scandal of 1889. Since Prince Eddy, supposedly identified in police documents of the time as "P.A.V." (Prince Albert Victor), was said to be a client of the brothel, it would seem possible that he and Annie Crook may at least have met on occasion.

EDDY:
I . . . please, I apologize. I only meant . . .

(PANEL) 6
Now back to an angle similar to that employed in panels three and four, with the counter running away from us, Annie on one side and the two gentlemen on the other. Towards the foreground, Annie is placing the money in the drawer of an old fashioned Victorian till. In the near background, against the light of the shop window, Sickert has taken a step across so that he's behind Eddy with his hands clasped fatherly upon each of Eddy's shoulders from behind as he steers the reluctant and lovestruck young man towards the counter, in order to properly introduce him to Annie. Sickert looks at the frightened and uncomfortable-looking Eddy with amusement dancing in her eyes. She thinks he's cute. Eddy shuffles forward under Sickert's gentle pressure from behind, his top hat in his hands.

SICKERT:
Oh, come on, old chap. She's just having you on.

SICKERT:
Annie, this . . . this is my younger brother, Albert.

SICKERT:
Uh, Albert, this is Miss Annie Crook.

Alan Moore

(PANEL) 7

Similar shot now. In the foreground, Annie smiles and reaches one hand across the counter top towards Eddy, as if to shake hands. Eddy stares down stupidly at the hand as if not sure what to do with it, his own hand rising only hesitantly to meet it. In the near background, Sickert has taken a step away and is in the act of setting his derby atop his head in preparation to going outside. Perhaps he's checking his reflection in a glass fronted cabinet or something while he does so . . . In any event, he is no longer looking towards us, or towards Eddy and Annie. Annie almost looks as if she's going to laugh at the awkwardness of the handsome young Eddy as he gawps at her offered hand.

> ANNIE:
> Oh, a YOUNG Mr. S., eh? I didn't KNOW there was a young Mr. S.

> ANNIE:
> Well . . .

> ANNIE:
> Pleased to make your acquaintance, I'm sure.

PAGE 2

(PANEL) 1

A nine panel page here. In this first panel we are more or less looking through Annie's eyes, so that all we see of her is her outstretched hand, entering into the picture from off panel below. We are looking at Eddy as he takes her hand and bends over to plant a gentle kiss upon its back, his eyes upturned to gaze at us and at Annie. There is a sadness and vulnerability in his widely spaced eyes that is touching. In the background, Sickert finishes adjusting his derby and glances over at the pair with a non-committal expression, unless you want to leave him out all together and just concentrate on Eddy kissing Annie's hand.

> EDDY:
> The . . .

> EDDY:
> The honour is all mine, dear Lady. I . . .

From Hell
Chapter One: The Affections of Young Mr. S.

>EDDY:
>I hope we may become better acquainted.

(PANEL) 2

Back to a shot looking down the counter from the end with Annie on one side and Eddy on the other. He is still holding her hand, although the hands are lowered now and his is about to release it, having straightened up after stooping to kiss it. He stares directly into Annie's eyes. She stares back into his eyes and she is no longer mocking or amused. Her eyes have a wondering and almost startled look as she stares into Eddy's eyes. Seemingly oblivious to what is going on in the empty space between their eyes, Sickert calls out cheerily from the near background, gesturing with this thumb towards the front door of the shop that we can see in the right of the background behind him. It has a glass panel set into its top half, though not a terribly big one.

>SICKERT:
>Albert, I hate to be a bore, but Netley's waiting outside.

>SICKERT:
>We really must dash, Annie. No doubt we'll call again shortly.

>SICKERT:
>Come along, youngster.

(PANEL) 3

Same shot. Annie stands motionless behind the counter, looking towards the door of the shop. The two men have just gone outside. Eddy, closing the door behind him, looks back into the shop through the glass pane set into the top half of the door, his lovestruck gaze serious and meaningful. Annie, unconsciously, touches one hand to her breast as she gazes after him. The little bell that's rigged to the shop door tinkles in the otherwise dead silence following the gentlemen's departure.

>F.X. (small):
>tilting

Alan Moore

(PANEL) 4

We are now outside the shop. (For the basic look of the place, see the enclosed reference photograph. I figure that the sign above the window reads "Morgan's Tobacconist & Quality Confectioner." The shop has never been named, to my knowledge, but the proprietress was a Mrs. Morgan, so the sign outside seems feasible.) The shop was at Number 22 Cleveland Street, only a little way down from one of the street's ends. Closer to the end was Number 6 Cleveland Street, where Annie the shopgirl lived in a basement flat. Walter Sickert's studio was directly over the road from the flat, and the shop and the flat were close enough together for one to see both of them from the window of Sickert's studio. I figure the houses were smaller and the streets were shorter then . . . Everything was more cramped and eccentric looking. I figure that the coach that is waiting for Sickert and Eddy outside is not actually outside the shop so much as a little way down the street, towards the corner, facing in the opposite direction from the corner towards the other end of the street. In this panel here, we have the blinkered head of one of the coach horses as it stands steaming in the sunshine at the mercy of the numerous flies evident during that particularly hot summer. We are looking past the head of the horse at a slight angle, so that we're looking up the street somewhat towards the front

References to the general character of the weather in 1888 are also as accurate as possible. Accounts from the time in question refer to 1888 as an unusually lightless year, although a number of peculiar atmospheric effects such as green or blood-red skies are reported, supposed at the time to be a result of the aftermath of Krakatoa's explosion in 1885.

From Hell
Chapter One: The Affections of Young Mr. S.

of the sweetshop. We see Sickert strolling along the pavement towards us, smiling indulgently as Eddy hurries to catch up with him, setting his top hat on his head as he does so, he is grinning foolishly and excitedly, babbling like a schoolboy as he hurries to catch up with Sickert, who is walking towards the coach that is waiting off panel to the left of the F/G, behind the horse whose head we can see. As a general note about the streets, even though Cleveland Street was in one of the most fashionable areas of town, running parallel to the Tottenham Court Road, it would still have looked fairly crumbly and dirty. Nothing near as bad as what we'll later see in Whitechapel, of course, but as a general rule of thumb, everything was dirtier then: the streets, the buildings, the people and in particular the skies. There were tons of factories in London belching out black smoke day and night, accounting for the "London Particular" fogs and at least part of the ill health suffered by the average inhabitant. I'm not sure what we want exactly here, as regards the visual treatment of London here. It doesn't want to be quite so stylishly sinister as the London David Lynch portrayed in *The Elephant Man*, nor yet so heart-tuggingly sordid and melodramatic as Dore's engravings of the period, but we definitely want to give the world a feel that is subtly different to the world of today. Maybe this is something more to with psychological ambience than visual treatment, but if you try to consciously think your way into the London of 1888 while you're drawing this stuff I think it'll help. Everything would have been more permanent then, wouldn't it, and less susceptible to change. The Eighties were around the turning point of the empire, and I figure things were already starting to look old, their textures abraded by the rigors of the urban environment at its most squalid. I figure everything was starting to look a bit melancholy and sad, like beer cans and decorations do when the party's winding down, whereas they'd just looked somehow festive a moment before. Albert's dead and Victoria has taken the whole empire into her obsessive mourning with her. Somehow it shows in the defeated lanes, in the litter, in the dirty light.

Anyway . . . Here the horse chomps its bit and tosses its head to clear the flies in the foreground while Sickert strides towards us along the street from the background with the moonstruck young prince at his heels like a great stupid over-eager dog.

EDDY:
I say, Sickert! Isn't she the most enchanting creature? Have you known her long?

SICKERT:
Eddy, you've been too long in captivity and you're mooning after the first shop-girl you meet.

SICKERT:
What would your mother say?

(PANEL) 5
Change angle. We are now behind Sickert and Eddy as they prepare to board the coach. The coach doors and windows fill much of the background here as it stands beside the curb, with the horses off panel somewhere on the left. In the top left corner we can see the lower half of the coach man as he sits atop the coach, holding the reins in his hand. He wears a long and dirty light coat that hangs down over the box seat here. Eddy is opening the coach door and preparing to climb into its interior. (The outside of the coach is black, by the way, but there is no royal crest on the side.) As he does so he pauses and looks with almost comical earnest at Sickert, who laughs and turns his head to speak up to the off panel coach driver, whose name is John Netley.

EDDY:
She rather RESEMBLES mother, doesn't she?

SICKERT:
Oh, Eddy! What ARE we to do with you?

SICKERT:
Netley? Take us to Claridges. I intend to render this young pup incapably drunk before he gets us ALL into trouble.

(PANEL) 6
Change angle so that we're up in front of the coachman, and he sits facing us head and shoulders to the left of the panel here. Looking down beyond him we can see Sickert looking up at Netley and laughing good naturedly as he himself prepares to climb into the coach after Prince Eddy. Netley doesn't look round at Sickert as

From Hell
Chapter One: The Affections of Young Mr. S.

he speaks to him, but continues to survey the off panel road ahead of him with wary and watchful eyes that always seem to be looking for the main chance in a crafty and calculated way. Netley is twenty-four years old, and 5'5" tall. He has a fair complexion, dark hair, a small dark moustache . . . hardly more than a dirty growth on his upper lip really, of no great substance. It makes him look a bit unwashed and smelly, which of course he is. He has a full, wide face with a wide mouth and quite thick lips. He's a womanizer and a bit of a jack-the-lad, and there is something cruel and stupid about the grin that he customarily wears spread across his wide mouth. His shoulders are broad, and he has a build a bit like a pit bull. Atop his dirty, dark hair he wears a black leather peaked cap. We don't see Netley again for a couple more episodes, but I want to fix his face in readers' minds since he plays quite a large part later. Bear in mind when giving him a face that this is the man who wrote the "From Hell" letter: He's a cocky and egotistical little sod who's ruthlessly ambitious and wants to get to the top by the shortest route possible.

NETLEY:
As, insobriety's no proof against trouble, Mr. Sickert. I once got a cousin o' mine in FEARFUL trouble, an' she were as tiddly as I were!

SICKERT:
Ha ha ha.

SICKERT:
Carry on, Netley.

(PANEL) 7

We are now standing in the road on the other side of the coach from the pavement side that Sickert just entered by. Netley is now visible sitting up to the top right corner atop his box . . . or rather, his lower half is visible. Perhaps we can see the whip in his hand as he gathers up the reins. Looking through the carriage window we can see Prince Eddy leaning forward earnestly to talk to Sickert, who sits opposite him. Sickert laughs and shakes his head in disbelief at his young charge's infatuation. Behind the coach we see the facade of the houses down towards the corner of Cleveland Street (The corner itself is just off panel left in the background here, if that helps you get your bearings.). The horses are off panel right. Netley's face is not visible here, being off panel above, but his balloons issue into the panel from off pic, up at the top somewhere.

    NETLEY (off):
GYAP! GYAP, ya bugger! YAA!

    EDDY:
No, but seriously, Sickert . . . she DOES look like my mother, doesn't she?

(PANEL) 8

Same shot. The coach is now pulling away out of the right of the panel, so that only half of it is visible now. Perhaps we just catch a blurred glimpse of Eddy through the rear side window as the coach pulls away over the cobbles, still talking earnestly to his chum. As the coach moves away we can of course see more of the houses behind it, which were previously obscured by it. Netley's balloons trail back into the panel from off-pic right, while Eddy's issue from the coach.

    NETLEY (off):
YAA! YAAA!

    EDDY (in coach):
She has mother's eyes.

(PANEL) 9

Same shot. The coach has gone and we can now see the houses that were behind it, down on the corner of Cleveland street, standing fully re-

John Netley, the coachman, is more elusive and, aside from the various sources Knight alludes to in The Final Solution, there seems no concrete proof that he even existed. He appears in this story because he fits, and the actions and motivations attributed to him here are those supplied in Knight's book.

From Hell
Chapter One: The Affections of Young Mr. S.

vealed. If you can manage it, given the logistics of the shot, we can see the corner of Cleveland Street, at least to the point where the street sign is visible bolted up on the wall, even if we can't see the actual corner itself. The sign has the words "Cleveland Street" in stark black lettering. If it's possible, we can also see the front door of Number 6, three doors down from the corner, with steps leading down from street level to its basement. If you can't get both these things in comfortably then just make sure that we see the "Cleveland Street" street sign as the coach pulls away and forget about the shot of Number 6 and its basement. The street sign is the main thing, striking and somehow ominous as it hangs there on the wall, giving the name of the place where all that followed was to have its origins.

No Dialogue

PAGE 3

(PANEL) 1
It is now a month later, during the same year. We are inside the basement of Number 6 Cleveland Street, in the bedroom. It is late afternoon, and only a few last shafts of sunlight penetrate the chink between the railings at street level outside and the top of the basement window. There are just little random blobs of shapeless sunlight on the walls and floor here and there, but for the most part the room is slightly dimly lit. We can't see any of the room in this first panel however, since we open with a tight close up of the couple on the bed. To the left hand side of the bed, Annie lies on her left side, facing inward. We cannot see her head and shoulders here ... no more of her than her torso really. Lying on his back on the other side of the bed with his head turned to face inwards, is Eddy. Annie leans up on one elbow so as to let her breasts trail close to Eddy's face. One hand enters the picture from the left to hold the left breast so that Eddy can get it into his mouth. Eddy sucks at the nipple, which is wet with saliva. His eyes are closed. One of his own hands enters the picture and rests gently over Annie's as she cups her breast for him to suck at. Annie is naked, while Eddy wears only a gentleman's white singlet with nothing on his lower half.

No Dialogue

(PANEL) 2

Now we are looking down on the bed from roughly above it, so that we can see both Eddy and Annie more or less full figure as they sprawl beneath us. Leaning up still, Annie pulls back slightly, withdrawing her breast from Eddy's mouth, although both his and her hand are still touching it. She smiles as she looks down at him. He gazes up at her across her breast as he speaks. His penis is lolling and half erect. He looks lovestruck.

ANNIE:
Do you like my bubbies, Albert? See . . . they're standing up for you.

EDDY:
They're very beautiful.

EDDY:
YOU'RE very beautiful.

(PANEL) 3

Now we are down towards the foot of the bed, looking along the length of Eddy's body as Annie sits up in bed beside him. She gazes softly down at his hardening cock. Eddy directs his soft doe eyed gaze at her as he reaches out to lightly touch her elbow, taking hold of it lightly in his hand. Both of them have quiet expressions here, and there is something a little sad in Eddy's despite his burgeoning tumescence.

ANNIE:
Ah, go on. It's you's the beauty, if you weren't always mopin'. Lookin' after's what you need.

EDDY:
No. That's the TROUBLE. My FAMILY look after EVERYTHING, plan my whole LIFE for me . . .

EDDY:
Put your hand on my pego.

(PANEL) 4

A different angle now, as if we were on the far side of the bed, looking across its lower half at Annie as she kneels up on the bed. All we can see of Eddy is his lower half. His speech balloon enters

From Hell
Chapter One: The Affections of Young Mr. S.

the panel from off-pic to the right here. Leaning up on one of her hands, Annie takes hold of Eddy's cock in the other and begins to masturbate him. She stares down at the hand working on Eddy's penis with a kind of distant and detached look . . . Apparently absorbed in what she is doing and yet with her mind somewhere else. The basement's front window is behind her somewhere to the right of panel here, with the bed running parallel to the wall and window. It doesn't need to be visible here, but that's where what little dappling of sunlight there is is issuing from.

ANNIE:
Like this, now?

EDDY (off):
Oh yes. Yes. Frig me, will you?

ANNIE:
Mm. Your brother doesn't seem much bothered by your family.

(PANEL) 5
Now we pan up the bed so that we can only see Eddy's top half and perhaps a little of Annie's back as she kneels up halfway down the bed, her face off panel here as she continues to jerk Eddy off, also off panel in this instance. Eddy turns his face towards us, eyes closed and mouth open in a gasp of pleasure. Eddy is lying so that looking beyond him we can see the basement window here. It looks out onto brickwork with a little ribbon of railings and sky visible at the top.

EDDY:
You . . . you don't understand. It isn't the same for him. He isn't . . .

EDDY:
Oh.

EDDY:
Oh, Annie . . .

(PANEL) 6
Now we're at the foot of the bed again. Turning her back towards us and thus facing Eddy as he lies there on his back, Annie

swings one leg over Eddy to kneel straddling his hips. Lowering herself, she reaches down between her legs to take hold of the head of his penis, guiding it up between the lips of her vagina. She looks down away from us in a businesslike way at what she is doing, while Eddy gazes in soft awe at her face.

ANNIE:
Oh, dear. I think your Mr. Perkins has got himself all restless. I think he wants to go somewhere.

ANNIE:
Hold still . . . and never you mind about your rotten family.

(PANEL) 7
We look at the bed side on now. Annie lowers herself down onto Eddy's cock, still reaching behind her with one hand to guide it into her. Eddy starts to gasp straight away, coming almost as soon as he's inside her. As he closes his eyes and gasps breathlessly through gritted teeth, Annie's expression remains calm.

ANNIE:
We'll do as we please, and they'll not prevent it.

EDDY:
Oh Annie. Annie, my love, I'm going to spend . . .

(PANEL) 8
We close in, past the couple, upon the basement window. It looks out onto red brick, moss growing in the chinks between the bricks and a slight deposit of soot and grime adhering to the brickwork everywhere. There is something cruel and sad and surreal and ominous about a window that looks out onto solid brick. It looks as if the only way out is blocked, but more cruelly than if it were blocked by a wall. Windows are a symbol of freedom and escape, and to have one blocked by dirty brickwork has a certain poignancy about it. As we study the dull and uninteresting brickwork beyond the glass, the cries of the lovers issue into the panel from off picture.

EDDY (off):
Uh . . . uh . . . oouh . . . uh . . .

From Hell
Chapter One: The Affections of Young Mr. S.

> ANNIE (off):
> Oh Albert.

> ANNIE (off):
> Oh, my lovely boy.

(PANEL) 9
In this final panel we simply reproduce part of a contemporary street plan of London during that time, showing Cleveland Street and its tributaries from above, all clearly labelled. The words "Cleveland Street", as with the last panel on page two, are the most prominent here.

> No Dialogue

PAGE 4

(PANEL) 1
We now jump to the January of the following year, 1885, and also to the upstairs studio of Mr. Walter Sickert, on the opposite side of Cleveland Street from Annie's basement flat and the sweetshop eight doors down the street from it. Both of these are at least partially visible from Sickert's window, and indeed, it is Sickert's studio window that we are looking out through here. Up in the foreground we can see Sickert's hands entering the panel. He is busily sharpening a pencil or crayon with a sharp-looking knife in preparation to doing some sketching. Pencil shavings unpeel lazily and drop to the floor like the turds of wooden birds. Despite the fact that he is indoors, Sickert is dressed up very warm. There was no central heating, and I imagine in the coldest weather he's probably had to work in a coat and scarf in his studio. Out through the window here snow is falling upon Cleveland Street. Looking through it we can see the tobacconist/confectioners down in the street below growing gradually more Dickensian and picturesque as the snow gets deeper.

> No Dialogue

(PANEL) 2
We now pull back so that we can see Sickert maybe three quarter figure as he stands by his easel, which has its back to us, with the

Alan Moore

Mary Kelly

window behind him. Framed thus against the falling snow he stands looking towards us with his sharpened pencil or crayon in one hand and the knife in his other. He is just absent mindedly placing the knife down on the window sill here, having finished with it. Since we have pulled back some way across the studio now, we can now see in the foreground the knee of the young woman sitting posing for Sickert, her hands resting demurely upon her knee or lap, folded together quietly and passively. The woman's name is Marie (or "Mary" ----she changed her name in 1886) Kelly, and although we

From Hell
Chapter One: The Affections of Young Mr. S.

A black and white reproduction of William Richard Sickert's painting "Blackmail (or Mrs. Barrett)" (1908) appears with the original publication of From Hell, Chapter Three in Taboo 4 (SpiderBaby Grafix & Publications, 1990) on page 149. We regret being unable to reproduce the painting herein.

can't see her face or much else of her here, she is a young woman of Irish parentage, aged about twenty here, and she is probably the most conventionally pretty of all our female characters. As far as reference for her face goes, I'm trying to dig up photographs, but for the moment you'll have to rely upon the face in the Sickert painting "Blackmail, or, Mrs. Barrett," allegedly based upon Kelly and reputedly bearing a more than passing resemblance to her. Her voice issues from off panel here. As far as Sickert's studio goes, I'm not sure what the decor would be like. At first I'd thought of something picturesquely cluttered with the odd peacock feather here and there, but that seems more the style of a pre-Raphaelite like Holman Hunt (who lived just up the road from Sickert, also in Cleveland Street). As I understand Sickert, he was relentlessly and passionately modern, and despised the use of classical themes and technique in modern art. Maybe his studio would be pretty austere and functional, with sketches and paintings all over the place, pinned to the walls or scattered and piled on the floor in drifts. Assuming you can't find any reference to the contrary, then just do what feels right to you. He smiles faintly here as he glances up at the off panel Marie, muffled against the cold in his studio. His breath actually fogs slightly upon the air, escaping his smiling lips in a little silk wisp of vapour.

Alan Moore

MARIE (off):
And there was I thinkin' you'd be wantin' me with not a stitch on.

MARIE (off):
You'll have me doubtin' me attractions, Mr. Sickert.

SICKERT:
Never, Mary. Perhaps when it's WARMER . . .

(PANEL) 3

Full back still further so that Marie is now head and shoulders in the F/G, in profile as she sits there posing for Sickert. She wears a broad hat atop her dark hair (see "Blackmail, or, Mrs. Barrett") and around her pretty throat she wears a noticeable and identifiable red scarf tied in a gay and casual knot. I dunno how you'll manage to make the red scarf identifiable in a black and white comic . . . maybe a pattern of black spots on it or something. As she poses thus, seated in profile, she has a pleased smile on her small lips, satisfied by the compliment that Sickert is paying her. She knows that she's pretty and she likes it, but while she's a bit immature and prone to put on airs, she's not an unlikable girl. She's had a pretty rough and poverty stricken time during her life thus far, and was a widow at nineteen. As she smiles contentedly at Sickert's words we look beyond her to see the artist himself, standing by his easel and starting to sketch. He looks down at the picture rather than up at Marie as he speaks, and she doesn't look at him as she carefully holds her pose.

SICKERT:
Besides, I wanted you how I first SAW you, on the convent steps.

SICKERT:
The way the light caught you, in that red scarf . . .
you looked saintly, Mary. Religious.

(PANEL) 4

Change angles so that we are now looking at the scene through Sickert's eyes, with his easel now turned towards us in the F/G, a piece of drawing paper tacked to it. We see Sickert's hand entering from off panel in the F/G, loosely sketching the shape of Marie Kelly's head. What Sickert is doing here is a preliminary sketch that

From Hell
Chapter One: The Affections of Young Mr. S.

will eventually become the painting, "Blackmail, or, Mrs. Barrett", so make the rough sketch here look like a conceivable rough sketch for that painting. His speech balloon issues from off panel here. Looking beyond what he is drawing we see Marie as she sits there, posing for him. She laughs, face crinkling delightfully and peculiarly Irish wrinkles forming on the bridge of the slightly upturned nose. Somewhere on the wall behind her, pinned up, is a calendar, although we needn't be able to see it clearly here, so long as we establish its presence.

MARIE:
SAINTLY! Will you listen to HIM, now! He takes me into his house, feeds me, finds me a job . . .

SICKERT (off):
Oh yes. The confectioners. How's it going?

(PANEL) 5

This shot is almost the same as that in panel two on this page, with only Marie's knee and resting hands visible in the F/G here, with her balloon issuing from off panel left. Looking beyond her we see Sickert, now sketching furiously, with a frown of concentration as he stares fixedly at his drawing while he replies to Marie.

MARIE (off):
Oh, it's very nice . . . and so's Annie. Lovely couple, her and your brother.

MARIE (off):
Doesn't look much like you, for saying, does he?

SICKERT:
No. He, uh, favours his mother more. Do you see much of them?

(PANEL) 6

Now, from the front, we have a head and shoulders close up of Marie as she turns to stare at Sickert, smiling knowingly and a little saucily. Sickert's balloon enters into the panel from off. On the wall behind Marie we can now clearly see the calendar, open at January 1885.

Alan Moore

> **EDDY:**
> Not your brother, no . . . but there's been more to see of Annie lately, if you take my meanin'.

> **SICKERT:**
> I'm not sure I do. I've not seen her recently. I'm courting myself, you know.

(PANEL) 7

Full back from Marie so that in the F/G we see the drawing that Sickert is doing and his hand as he works upon it. Looking beyond this we see Marie sitting there posing. She laughs at Sickert's words, a little scornfully. In the foreground, the point of Sickert's pencil suddenly breaks against the surface of the figure he is drawing. The face on the paper now is almost exactly a pencil sketch for "Blackmail, or, Mrs. Barrett." The picture is set up so that we see the pencil point snapping after we've heard Marie's words.

> **MARIE:**
> Ooh, and is it "Courtin'" your brother's been doing, then?

> **MARIE:**
> The girl's six month's pregnant if she's a day.

(PANEL) 8

We are now looking at Sickert half figure as he stands there facing us by his easel with the window behind him, grey snow falling dreamily by. He stands just staring at us and the off-panel Marie in stunned disbelief, the broken pencil still clutched uselessly in his trailing, dangling hand. The news of Annie's pregnancy has obviously come as something of a shock to him. On the window sill behind Sickert, the knife is still resting where he put it. Marie's balloon enters the panel from off pic in the F/G.

> **MARIE (off):**
> Whatever was that? Is that your pencil broken now? You shouldn't be after pressin' so hard, Mr. Sickert.

> **MARIE (off):**
> Now you'll have to sharpen it again.

From Hell
Chapter One: The Affections of Young Mr. S.

(PANEL) 9
For this final panel we close in upon the window, so that we can no longer see either Sickert or Marie. We just see the window, the snow falling outside and the little sweetshop across the street. Lying on the windowsill is a very sharp knife.

No Dialogue

PAGE 5

(PANEL) 1
Another nine panel page. It's now the 18th of April, 1885, and in this first panel we see Walter Sickert, hurriedly dressed in an unbuttoned topcoat, rushing hurriedly through the streets towards the austere front steps leading up to the equally grim front door of Marylebone Workhouse. Maybe as we see him here he's just starting to run up the steps two at a time to the front door of the workhouse, the words "Marylebone Workhouse" carved in the stone above its door. It is night time, and the gas lamps are alight. Sickert looks very pale and anxious as he races through the crepuscular London streets.

No Dialogue

(PANEL) 2
We are now inside the chilly looking lobby of the workhouse, just inside the front doors. Sickert stands, breathless, just inside the front doors and facing towards us as he enquires after

Annie's baby, Alice Margaret, was born at the workhouse in Marylebone on 18 April 1885. No father's name or father's occupation is given on Alice's birth certificate, although Knight's critics have pointed out that when Alice grew up and married, her marriage certificate listed her father's name as "William Crook. I have attempted to explain this discrepancy in Chapter Three *of* From Hell, *and thus will save a fuller explanation until the relevant footnotes for* Chapter Three.

Alan Moore

Annie's whereabouts. In the F/G, behind a wooden desk that faces the door, we have an elderly and formidable looking woman dressed in the austere uniform of the workhouse staff. There is an inkpot on the desk, and with an old fashioned pen the elderly woman is filling in the particulars of the birth upon an appropriately headed sheet of paper. This is not the birth certificate, which will be filled in later, but just something headed "details of birth" that will be used to supply the workhouse's own records later. We needn't be able to read it here, so long as we can see that the woman is writing on it as she sits in the cold and shadowy hall of the workhouse, lit only by gas mantles or oil lamps. The place is very big and dark and sombre, and the woman doesn't look up as she speaks to Sickert, who stands panting by the door and staring at her hopefully.

SICKERT:
Hello. I'm . . . huhh . . . huhh . . .

SICKERT:
I'm here to . . . huhh . . . see Annie Elizabeth Crook . . .

SICKERT:
Huhhh. Huhhh.

WOMAN:
Are you the baby's father?

(PANEL) 3

Reverse angle so that Sickert now stands facing slightly away from us in the foreground towards the woman, who sits facing us behind her desk. She still doesn't look up at Sickert, but continues to fill in the details of the birth, peering at what she is writing perhaps through little half-glasses. Sickert, from what we can see of his expression in the foreground looks breathless, nervous and somewhat guilty.

SICKERT:
No, I . . . I'm afraid I don't even know the father.

SICKERT:
I'm a friend of Annie's. My name's Sickert.

WOMAN:
Hummph.

From Hell
Chapter One: The Affections of Young Mr. S.

(PANEL) 4

Now we are right down on the desk top, so that in the F/G we can see only the woman's hand, her pen and the sheet of paper. The paper, headed "Details of Birth", contains as much of the following information as you can realistically fit on . . . District: Marylebone. County: Middlesex. Where born: Marylebone Workhouse. Date: 18th April, 1885. Name: Alice Margaret. Sex: Girl. Father's name: _____. Mother's name and Occupation: Annie Elizabeth Crook, Confectionery assistant from Cleveland Street. Occupation of father: _____. Mother's address: 6, Cleveland Street, Fitzroy Square.

Don't worry if you can't show all of that . . . The only important bits are the two significant blanks after "Father's name" and "Father's occupation." As we see the old woman's hand here she makes two strokes, one after each of the aforementioned categories, to signify that the information is unavailable. Looking beyond her hand as she does this we see Sickert, still hovering nervously, gazing towards her and awaiting directions. He look flustered. The old woman's voice issues from off panel, since we can't see her face here.

WOMAN (off):
Do you know the least used boxes on a birth certificate, Mr. Sickert?

SICKERT:
What? I'm sorry . . . I don't . . .

WOMAN (off):
Never mind. She's along at the end.

(PANEL) 5

Cut now to Annie's bed. We see this panel through her eyes, so that all we see of her is a little of her arms and a little of the heavily wrapped baby that she is sitting up in bed holding in them as she feeds it. Looking beyond the bed we see the nervous and apprehensive figure of Sickert as he tiptoes closer to the bed. His face looks incredibly anxious as he speaks hesitantly to us. Behind him we have a ghostly suggestion of other bunks stretching away into the distance, other women sitting or lying on some of them. Looking at Sickert, it's difficult not to notice how his manner is slowly changing as the situation slips out of his control. From the cocky young buck around town of the opening pages he is slowly transformed into a worried man who is trying not to admit to himself that the situation has become too big to manage and is heading inexorably for disaster. He has a certain doom-haunted look which will progress and worsen as the story continues to unfold.

SICKERT:
Annie?

(PANEL) 6

Reverse angle so that in the foreground we can see a little of Sickert, maybe one hand reaching into the panel from above and dragging a stool or a wooden chair across so that he can sit by the bed. Looking beyond what little of Sickert and the chair we can see, we see Annie as she sits up in bed, breast feeding her baby. She looks happy and relaxed, smiling softly with an ominously misplaced confidence in the safety of herself, her baby and their bright future together. She looks up at Sickert and smiles as little Alice Margaret continues to suckle.

ANNIE:
Walter. It's so good of you to come.

ANNIE (separate balloon):
Is Albert here?

SICKERT (off):
No. Uh, no, he couldn't make it. He had business with . . .

(PANEL) 7

Now we have a side on shot, looking from the opposite side of the bed to the side upon which Sickert has drawn up a chair and sat down. Nearest to us, its head towards the right of the panel, we have the bed in which Annie sits up in profile and suckles the child. Beyond the bed sits Sickert, lowering himself into the chair here and looking wretchedly guilty as he tries to reassure Annie. Annie looks resigned, but even this disappoint-

From Hell
Chapter One: The Affections of Young Mr. S.

ment cannot seriously dent her new found optimism and confidence. She looks down at the baby with a sad little smile, not looking at the uneasy Sickert while she speaks to him; speaking to the baby.

ANNIE:
Don't tell me. With your family, was it?

SICKERT:
Annie, listen. Albert's not . . .

ANNIE:
Och, it doesn't matter. I don't give a fart for your family. Little Alice here'll not go short of company on their account.

(PANEL) 8

Close in now, so that Annie and her feeding child are right up in the foreground, Annie still smiling down indulgently at the suckling infant. Beyond the bed, Sickert looks at Annie and tries to rally her spirits by attempting to be brisk and cheerfully efficient as he tells her his plans to help her. Gazing at the baby, Annie doesn't seem to be over-impressed. She has plans of her own.

SICKERT:
Certainly not! I'll pay little Mary Kelly to help with the baby. She could share your basement with you.

ANNIE:
Well, that'd be nice, but Albert'll have more time with me and Alice himself . . .

(PANEL) 9

Complete the close in so that the baby's face is right up close. It has briefly let the nipple fall from its mouth, although breast and baby's lips are still connected with delicate chains of milky saliva. Looking beyond this we see Sickert, who is staring at the baby. A look of doomed realization is stealing over his face, and he stares at the baby as if it represents doom itself. Sickert is starting to admit to himself that he's trapped on a train to hell with nothing to do but cover his eyes and wait for the crash. Since Annie's face isn't visible here then her balloon issues from off panel.

ANNIE (off):
After we're married, like.

PAGE 6

(PANEL) 1

A nine panel page again here. We are now inside the small church of St. Saviours, and its a month or so after the birth of the baby. In this first panel we have a long shot of the small congregation gathered with the vicar before the altar. The church is more or less empty apart from the wedding group, and is dark save for what sunlight falls through the high tall single window behind the vicar. The wedding party consists of Eddy, Annie, and Sickert and Marie Kelly at witnesses. With the exception of the vicar, other than these four there is nobody else in the church.

VICAR:
Dearly beloved...

(PANEL) 2

Now a vicar's eye shot, so that all we see of the vicar are his hands and the open prayer book he is reading from, up in the foreground. Looking beyond him we see the wedding part, with Annie and Eddy closest to us and Marie and Sickert standing slightly behind them and to either side, the left and right respectively. Marie Kelly is smiling happily. Annie, the bride, has a serene and contented smile. Eddy, the groom, looks very calm: He isn't really bright enough to see the danger in what he is doing, or to understand the potential consequences as being real in any way. The only member of the wedding party who looks agitated is Sickert, standing slightly behind and to the right (our right, that is) of Eddy. He is leaning slightly in Eddy's direction and whispering to the young prince as surreptitiously as possible through the corner of his mouth. His word balloon is a dotted-edge whisper balloon. None of the people present appear to hear Sickert... and if Prince Eddy does he doesn't look round or react in any way. The vicar drones on from off panel here.

VICAR (off):
We are gathered together here, at St. Saviour's, in the sight of God and in the face of this congregation to

From Hell
Chapter One: The Affections of Young Mr. S.

    join together this man and this woman in holy matrimony . . .

                SICKERT (whisper):
Eddy!

(PANEL) 3

Now a shot from a different angle, maybe arranged to get a profile of the happy looking Marie Kelly (wearing her red scarf) into the foreground, looking past her so that over to the right of the panel we can just see the back of Annie, and then a little of Eddy standing next to her. Further still, and a little back towards the centre of the picture, stands Sickert, still leaning forward ever so slightly as he hisses to Eddy. Again, despite the agitation upon his face, neither the vicar nor any of the wedding party appear to hear him. From off panel, the vicar continues to drone.

                VICAR (off):
. . . which is an honourable estate, instituted by God in the time of man's innocency, signifying unto us the mystic union that is betwixt Christ and his church . .

                SICKERT (whisper):
You KNOW you can't go through with this . . .

(PANEL) 4

Swing back round to the front of the party here. Eddy stands facing us, to the left of the panel, maybe half figure to three quarter figure here. Presumably Annie is a couple of feet to his right, somewhere invisible to us off the left of the panel here. To the right of the panel more and slightly behind Eddy we see Sickert. As Eddy speaks his face remains perfectly placid and calm, with only the smallest twitch of the corner of his mouth. He doesn't look round at Sickert, or even blink. His face has the same vacuous calm that we see on the reference photo that should be included in this package. Sickert looks sick with anxiety and exasperation, staring wildly and imploringly at Eddy's impassive back.

                VICAR (off):
. . . into which holy estate these two persons come now to be joined.

EDDY (whisper):
Annie arranged it, and I can't disappoint her. No-one need ever know . . .

SICKERT (whisper):
For God's sake, this is insane!

(PANEL) 5
We close in from the last shot so that now Eddy is right up close head and shoulders in the foreground, still with the same impassive expression and only the corner of his mouth ever so slightly contorted as he whispers, never taking his eyes off of the vicar, who continues to drone on from off panel here. Behind Eddy's shoulder we see Sickert. He stares at Eddy as if shocked by what Eddy is saying, stunned to a sort of mute helplessness, unable to think of a useful appeal against Eddy's judgement and probably knowing its already too late anyway. It's been too late since he introduced Annie and Eddy over the barley sugar back on Cleveland Street.

VICAR (off):
Therefore, if any man can show any just cause . . .

EDDY (whisper):
You're going to be married yourself soon, Sickert.

EDDY (whisper):
Be a good fellow and don't spoil things for us.

(PANEL) 6
We continue to close in until we can just see Sickert, standing facing us as the vicar continues with the service from off panel. Sickert stares out of the panel at us and looks trapped in horrifying circumstances completely beyond his control. His eyes are those of a drowning man.

VICAR (off):
. . . why they may not lawfully be joined together, let him now speak, or else hereafter forever hold his peace.

(PANEL) 7
Exactly the same shot, showing Sickert standing facing us. He

From Hell
Chapter One: The Affections of Young Mr. S.

lowers his eyes slightly in defeat and stares bleakly towards the ground. He doesn't say a word.

No Dialogue

(PANEL) 8

Pull back to a virtual repeat of panel two now, showing the vicar's hands on the prayer book in the foreground and the wedding party standing arrayed facing us in the middleground. Annie and Marie are still smiling. Eddy remains calm and impassive. Sickert is now standing with his head hanging, staring dejectedly at the floor. He looks wretched and defeated.

VICAR (off):
Wilt thou, Albert Sickert, have this woman to thy wedded wife? Wilt though love her, comfort her, honour, and keep her in sickness and in health, forsaking all others, so long as ye both shall live?

(PANEL) 9

We now cut to an exterior shot of the church, huddled on the corner of Osnaburgh St., just a stone's throw from Cleveland Street. Outside the dark church we see people going about their business through the late spring streets, all blissfully unaware of the ill-augured event going on inside the church scant feet away from them. Eddy's balloon issues from inside the church.

EDDY (from inside church):
I will.

PAGE 7

(PANEL) 1

An eight panel page here, in which we jump suddenly to the summer of 1886, to find ourselves aboard a ferry bound for Calais upon a beautiful summer's day. In this first panel we have a long shot of the ferry, moving through the swell at some featureless mid point in the English Channel. Following behind the boat, tiny specks here, we see a large cloud of wheeling and shrieking gulls. Other than a few high altitude ribbons of cirrus cloud, the gulls are the only cloud in the sky. This panel can perhaps be the largest on the page, to give a sense of open space to the seascape and a sense of isolation to the ferry. Annie's balloon issues from the ferry's decks, although it's up to you whether we are close enough to see the tiny black dots of people moving around on the decks or not. Behind the boat, the gulls wheel and scream.

ANNIE (from boat):
Mary? Don't you go too near the rail with her, now . . .

(PANEL) 2

We are now close in upon the ferry, so that the rail runs across the foreground of the picture here with the deck beyond it. Standing just on the other side of the rail and leaning leisurely against it is Walter Sickert, his eyes scanning the horizon as he gazes towards some off-panel point, looking relaxed despite himself on such a glorious day, with the salt breeze ruffling his hair. A step or two behind him we see Mary Kelly, smiling as she walks towards the rail with baby Alice snuggled contentedly in her arms. Alice is a little over a year old here, and looks around animatedly, having one chubby arm which she's worked free of her blanket. Mary doesn't look round as she replies to Annie, who stands some distance behind her, looking towards Mary's back and laughing good naturedly as she mocks the younger girl's pretensions and her schoolgirlish delight in visiting France. Annie wears a hat to protect her from the sun as she stands in mid deck, near some fixed deck-benches arranged for the passengers' convenience, which she will shortly sit down upon. Mary Kelly is bare-headed, but she wears the distinctive red neck scarf about her throat that we saw her in earlier. In fact, I should have mentioned during the church scene that she was wearing it then as well. Sorry about that. In this panel, as Mary walks towards the rail holding the infant, all three travellers look relaxed and happy.

MARIE:
Ah, away with ye. She's wantin' to see France.

ANNIE:
SHE'S wanting to? It's YOU'S been calling yourself "Marie Jeannette" since Mr. Sickert took us LAST time.

From Hell
Chapter One: The Affections of Young Mr. S.

The incidental historical information here derives from standard historical sources: Sickert did found his New English Art Club in 1886, the same year London suffered a wave of Fenian bombing. Possibly as a result of public outrage over the bombings, Mr. Gladstone's electeral gambit failed and there was no home rule for Ireland. The struggle for independence became more bitter as a consequence of this, and the "Special Irish Branch" that Sickert mentions on the facing page were transformed into today's less specific "Special Branch."

(PANEL) 3
Pan across slightly now and move in so that Sickert is more central and in the F/G. We needn't really see Mary Kelly here, unless you want a bit of her visible over to the left of the panel. We are mainly looking at Sickert, and, beyond him, towards Annie, still standing over by the bench and looking towards the back of Sicker's head, smiling affectionately.

SICKERT:
We can ALL use a change from England. Establishing my New English Art Club's been such hard work . . .

ANNIE:
Well, it's awfully good of you, finding time to take us places while Albert's away on business.

(PANEL) 4
Reverse angle so that Annie is in the F/G now, maybe lowering herself to sit upon the bench. Looking past her we see Sickert, still leaning on the rail but turning round to speak directly to Annie. His face has an expression that's the facial equivalent of a pessimistic shrug. He obviously doesn't place much faith in Gladstone's home rule initiative. Mary Kelly turns form the rail to look at Sickert and Annie, a slight frown wrinkling her nose. Annie, in the F/G, just looks sniffy and disinterested as she speaks, looking at nobody in particular. Beyond the rail, the slate grey ocean pitches and tilts gently.

ANNIE:
For me, I'll be glad to hear no more of this IRISH blather for a while.

SICKERT:
That's UNLIKELY, Annie. Gladstone's gambling this whole election on the home rule issue.

(PANEL) 5

Reverse angles so that we're again on the other side of the rail looking in onto the deck. In the foreground we see Mary Kelly to the left, leaning against the rail with the baby in her arms, her head turned slightly in profile so as to look at Sickert as she speaks to him. Her face looks slightly angry and indignant. Sickert, over to the right, looks at Marie with the same pessimistic and unhelpful shrug upon his features. He's a knowledgeable armchair political theorist, while Mary grew up in Ireland before her father had to leave. She feels the issue on an emotional level and responds accordingly, while Sickert can only offer a sort of useless and patronizing liberal sympathy. If we can see Annie in the background she is just gazing out into the distance off panel somewhere, having seemingly lost interest in the conversation.

MARIE:
Only 'cause he needs Parnell's backing. He took long enough makin' up his mind.

SICKERT:
Even so, he may lose. Feelings are high over these Fenian bombings. That's why they set up the Special Irish Branch . . .

(PANEL) 6

Reverse angles. Annie sits in the foreground on the bench, still gazing at some point off panel and enjoying the view, taking no interest in the conversation going on over at the rail. She has one hand raised to hold her hat on in the stiff breeze. Over by the rail, Sickert looks at Marie and blinks in surprise as she suddenly looks quite heated and venomous and bitter. Beyond the rail, a few gulls turn and circle above the listing grey waves.

From Hell
Chapter One: The Affections of Young Mr. S.

> MARIE:
> No "Special Branch" 'll staunch the blood if Gladstone loses and there's no home rule.

> MARIE:
> You don't know what it's like over there. Me dad had to take us children and leave, the unemployment was so bad.

(PANEL) 7

Now Marie and the baby are in the foreground, and we are looking past her down the length of the rail that she is leaning against towards where Sickert is also leaning against it. Marie looks away from Sickert, lowering her eyes to look down as she cuddles the baby in her arms. Her mouth has a sulky and resentful pout as she speaks. Looking beyond her we see Sickert, leaning against the rail. He is staring at the baby in Marie's arms with a look of unreadable disquiet. He looks very worried about something, suddenly out of clear sky.

> MARIE:
> D'you know what we call Her Majesty over there?

> MARIE:
> "The Famine Queen".

> MARIE:
> To Hell with HER, and her CHILDREN, an' her CHILDREN'S children.

(PANEL) 8

In this last panel we are up in the sky above the ferry, looking down upon the small, smokey, sooty metal lozenge of the ferry as it makes its way across the steely waters of the English Channel. Marie's balloon issues form the deck, even though she herself is too far beneath us to detect at this height. Wheeling through the foreground and skirling in the wake of the ferry we see lots of gulls with made and staring eyes, beaks open in raucous pandemonium. They flap above the tiny ferry far below like an omen.

> MARIE (from ferry):
> To Hell with all of 'em.

Alan Moore

PAGE 8

(PANEL) 1

These last four pages are devoted to a single scene, this taking place in the early winter months of 1888, in and around the location of Cleveland Street. The time, according to Sickert's own later account of what happened, is late afternoon. The page we have here is a seven panel one, with maybe two panels on each of the top and bottom tiers with three panels in the middle. The first and last panels on the page should perhaps be the largest here. This first one just shows an establishing shot of the late afternoon London skyline around Cleveland Street. The balloon issuing from the off-panel Walter Sickert enters the panel from off pic below. Before us, the windows and rooftops of London roll away into the smoldering distance. It's a fine day, but there is no sun, and a brisk, cold wind drags the heavy fleece of white cloud relentlessly across the sky.

SICKERT (off, below):
MARIE?

SICKERT (off, below):
Marie, WAIT!

(PANEL) 2

We pan down now to find ourselves in Maple Street, one of the streets running off of Cleveland Street at right angles. We are down towards the Cleveland Street end, looking along the length of the street in the other direction. Marie Kelly is walking towards us, carrying the two year old Alice Margaret in her arms. While not a big child, Alice Margaret has grown some since the last time we saw her, and Marie is only carrying her for quickness here. Normally, the child would walk. Marie is dressed up warm against the cold, and she is wearing the red scarf wrapped around her throat. Hurrying along the street towards her from behind comes Sickert, hastening his pace to catch her up. She turns her head to look round at him and smiles in greeting. Sickert, rubbing his hands together against the cold and exhaling a cloud of

From Hell
Chapter One: The Affections of Young Mr. S.

Other verifiable fragments of information include the fact that Mary Kelly was living with a Mr. Joe Barnett of New Street in early 1888. It is also true that Walter Sickertt in later years, kept a red scarf to which he seemed to attach tremendous significance. He would wear it habitually while he painted, and he seemed to associate it with the notion of murder (see Sickert, The Painter and His Circle by Marjorie Lilly, published by Elek in 1971).

steamy breath into the cold air, smiles back at her while looking discomfited by the severity of the weather. The breeze looks quite cold and strong.

MARIE:
Oh, it's you now, Mr. Sickert.

MARIE:
Where is it you're off to? Back to your studio out of this cold, I'll be bound.

SICKERT:
Yes. 1888's looking like a devil of a year, isn't it?

(PANEL) 3

Same angle, but closer now upon Marie as she walks along a pace or two in front of Sickert. She smiles down at the infant she is holding as she walks, not looking round at Sickert. In Marie's arms, little Alice Margaret has become interested in her nanny's red scarf and is pulling with her chubby little arms, loosening the knot and pulling the scarf away from Marie, who smiles indulgently and does not resist. A pace behind Marie and the child, Sickert laughs good naturedly and points to what the child is doing.

MARIE:
You're not wrong. I'm just heading for Cleveland Street myself. Been takin' little Alice Margaret for an outin'.

SICKERT:
Ha ha! Look, she's after your red scarf ..

Alan Moore

(PANEL) 4

We are now behind Sickert and Marie as they continue to walk down Maple Street away from us towards Cleveland Street, which we can see Maple Street intersecting in the near background. It's cold and dusky, and there are only a few people about, mostly hurrying home, holding their bonnets and hats on in the rising wind. Marie is facing away from us here, tending to the child in her arms as it pulls the scarf clear of her throat triumphantly. Sickert looks inquiringly at Marie, his face turned in profile to us here as they approach Cleveland Street.

MARIE:
Sure, she's welcome. There's little enough warmth in it.

SICKERT:
Where are you living now, Marie? I'd heard you'd taken up with a Mr. Barrett . . .

(PANEL) 5

Reverse angles so that we are now in Cleveland Street, on the corner where it connects with Maple Street. Up on the wall in the F/G we can see a sign on the corner that reads "Cleveland Street." Looking beyond this and along Maple Street we can see Marie and Sickert still walking towards us and the corner, chatting casually while in Marie's arms, Alice Margaret is waving the red scarf frantically.

MARIE:
BARNETT. Joe Barnett. It's a sort of married arrangement. We're living in New Street.

SICKERT:
And he doesn't mind you coming here to help Annie with the child?

(PANEL) 6

Same shot, only now Marie and Sickert have reached the corner and have entered Cleveland Street standing right in the foreground facing us here. Marie looks dismissive, turning her nose up and sniffing contemptuously. The baby is still playing with Marie's detached scarf. Sickert, having entered Cleveland Street is gazing at something going on off panel down towards one end of the street.

From Hell
Chapter One: The Affections of Young Mr. S.

He frowns slightly, as if puzzled by something.

MARIE:
East End men are bone idle, Mr. Sickert. They can hardly afford to be choosy over how their wives earn a crust, now.

SICKERT:
I suppose not. Well, here we are: Good old ...

SICKERT:
Wait a minute ...

(PANEL) 7
A largish panel, as seen through Sickert's eyes, with neither him nor Marie visible here. We are looking with him down towards the end of Cleveland Street farthest away from the studio, basement and sweet shop, all behind us here. We are looking towards where Cleveland Street connects with Howland Street, where there are a large and scruffily dressed crowd of ruffians loitering upon the corner, some of them glancing meanly in our direction. While they are dressed as ruffians, however, there is something sinister in the way they stand around, and in their general bearing. They are in fact plain clothes police officers who have been given the task of staging a diversion. Here they loaf upon the corner of Howland Street as if anticipating something. Sickert's balloon issues from off pic in the foreground.

SICKERT (off):
What's that going on up at the end there? That crowd of ruffians ...

PAGE 9

(PANEL) 1
A nine panel page here. In this first panel we have a half to three quarter figure shot of Marie and Sickert still standing on the corner of Maple Street, gazing in bewilderment and some consternation at the off panel ruffians down at the far end of the street. Running across the foreground we see a young Victorian street boy of the lower classes, maybe about sixteen years old. He is running past and turning his head towards us and looking back over his shoulder as he calls to some

comrade who is off panel behind him. He seems to be running in the same direction as Marie and Sickert are looking, down towards the end of the street with the men. Perhaps only Marie is still surveying the far end of the street here and frowning suspiciously while Sickert is just directing his gaze at the urchin running past in the F/G. Sickert suddenly looks a bit quiet and pale, as if suddenly afflicted by a dreadful apprehension in the pit of his stomach.

MARIE:
Sure, an' they're the cleanest-looking ruffians I'VE ever seen.

SICKERT:
Something's wrong . . .

STREET BOY:
'ERE! Come ON! Some cove's startin' a BARNEY!

(PANEL) 2

Now we are behind Marie and Sickert as they stand looking away from us towards the end of the street where the men are. There seems to be a fight starting amongst the small black smudgy figures of the ruffians. More figures, quite small, hurry along the street to watch the fight. Marie looks at the people running to watch the fight in disgust, her head turned mostly away from us. Sickert also faces away from us towards the end of the street where the altercation is going on. We can't see much of his face, but he looks pretty uneasy and disoriented.

Eddie Campbell's own rigorous research efforts corrected an error in this sequence as scripted. The actual location of Maple Street in proximity to the Cleveland Street sweetshop required that Eddie rework the action. In the final version, Marie and Sickert make their way past Maple Street and through the organized streetfight to witness the events at the sweetshop at the other side of the staged riot.

—SRB

From Hell
Chapter One: The Affections of Young Mr. S.

> MARIE:
> Look now, they're after fightin'.

> MARIE:
> Tch . . . and just look at all THESE nosey beggars runnin' towatch 'em at it!

> SICKERT:
> Marie, something's wrong. We'd better go and get Albert from my . . .

(PANEL) 3
    Same shot, with Marie still facing away from us watching the fight down at the end of the street. Sickert, however, has turned to look towards us, directing his gaze towards the off-panel far end of the street where the studio and sweetshop and basement flat are situated. As he does so his eyes widen with a look of sick alarm. Unnoticed, little Alice Margaret loses her grip upon the red scarf, and it floats forlornly towards the pavement here while the infant girl watches it fall in dismay.

> SICKERT (small):
> . . . studio . . .

(PANEL) 4
    Now three panels through Sickert's eyes, with neither him nor Marie visible. We are looking up towards the end of the street with the studio on the left and the basement flat (and farther down the sweetshop) over on the right. As we see it here, this end of Cleveland Street is completely deserted. Everyone has rushed to watch the fight at the other end of the street, and there's nobody watching this end of Cleveland Street at all, except for the off panel Sickert.

> No Dialogue

(PANEL) 5
    Same shot exactly . . . except that a dark police coach pulled by black horses is just rounding the corner towards us, about to park in front of the basement flat where Netley's coach was parked earlier. It's arrival in the cold and windswept empty street looks very ominous.

> No Dialogue

(PANEL) 6

Exactly the same shot. Things get more ominous still as a second coach also comes round the corner after the first one, looking as if it's going to draw up across the street from the first coach. The first coach is coming to rest outside the basement, while the second coach is heading towards the front of Sickert's studio, on the other side of the street. This second coach is black and elegant, pulled by black horses. It is the royal carriage, and it looks very sinister in this context.

No Dialogue

(PANEL) 7

Change angle so that we are now in front of Sickert and Marie as they stand on the corner of Maple Street looking towards the end of Cleveland Street where the coaches have just arrived, off panel here. Sickert, slightly closer to us, looks sick with fear, his face sheet white. Marie, behind him, looks confused, with just the beginnings of an uncomprehending fear starting to show in her pretty face. In her arms, little Alice Margaret struggles, staring down at the floor off panel below where she has dropped the red scarf, and reaching out with one stiff and pudgy arm as if straining to pick it up, even though it's way out of her reach.

SICKERT (small):
Oh my God . . .

MARIE:
Mr. Sickert? Whatever's going ON?

MARIE:
That rear carriage . . . that's the royal livery!

(PANEL) 8

Now we change angles so that we are down at pavement level at the feet of Sickert and Marie. We see their feet pointing away from us, framing the foreground. On the pavement in the F/G lies Marie's fallen red neck scarf. Looking beyond this and up the street we see at least the police coach parked outside the basement of No. 6 A fat man and a police woman have alighted from the coach and are heading down the steps towards the basement, with the fat man already going down the steps here and the plain clothes policewoman

From Hell
Chapter One: The Affections of Young Mr. S.

just climbing down from the coach. Marie and Sickert's balloons issue from off panel above.

> MARIE (off, above):
> They're going into the studio . . . and Annie's basement!

> MARIE (off, above):
> Oh, Mr. Sickert, whatever do they want?

> SICKERT (off, above):
> Marie, take the child. Get the child away from here.

(PANEL) 9

Change angle so that now we are facing Marie and Sickert from quite close up, with Sickert's staring and terrified face gazing at us head and shoulders in the F/G. As he raises his voice to shout at Marie, behind him, he doesn't look round. He can't take his eyes off of the dreadful events unfolding at the end of the street. Marie, behind him, is now starting to look very frightened and confused. The baby is starting to struggle and whimper in her arms, as if sensing that something is wrong.

> MARIE:
> But what are they . . . ?

> SICKERT:
> For God's SAKE, woman! Just take the child and RUN!

PAGE 10

(PANEL) 1

There are seven panels on this penultimate page, with a wide panoramic one for panel seven, spanning the bottom of the page. This first small panel is exactly the same in set up as the last panel on page 9, except Sickert has his mouth shut now. He is just standing motionless and helpless, staring out of the panel at us with a doomed look of horror in his eyes at the inevitability of it all. Behind, Marie has turned and is running as fast as she can back down Maple Street away from us, holding the wailing two year old girl in her arms as she runs.

> No Dialogue

Alan Moore

(PANEL) 2

We are now behind Sickert at about waist level, looking past him towards the studio end of the street so that we see one of his arms hanging down inertly into the panel to the left of foreground as he stands looking on helplessly. Up at the end of the street, we see that the fat man and the woman are leading a dazed looking Annie out of her basement flat and into the street. If we can see it, two men in brown tweed suits are also leading Prince Eddy, equally dazed, out of the door of the studio opposite. These will all just be small figures at the end of the street here.

No Dialogue

(PANEL) 3

We are now up at the studio end of the street, amidst what's going on. In the foreground, on the right, we can see a little of Annie's side and back as the firm hands of the plainclothes policewoman guide her out into the street. Her head and shoulders are off panel above, however, so we cannot see her face. Instead, we look past them for the focus of our panel to where Eddy is being led out of the studio between the two brown-tweed-clad detectives. He hasn't noticed Annie in the foreground, and is directing his questions at one of the two men who escort him by the arm. Eddy looks bewildered and very frightened. The two detectives are stone faced as they steer him towards the coach outside the studio, being polite to him but not responding directly to his questions.

EDDY:
Wh-what's the meaning of this? I, I demand . . .

DETECTIVE IN BROWN TWEED:
This way, please, your highness.

(PANEL) 4

Now we reverse the shot so that we have a little of the back and side of Eddy in the foreground as he's steered by the two detectives. Looking up past him we see Annie in the grip of the tough looking police woman while the fat man opens the door of the police coach,

From Hell
Chapter One: The Affections of Young Mr. S.

ready to bundle her in. Annie is staring at the off panel point where Eddy's head must be. She looks stunned, as if she's just been poleaxed. Her face sags, the muscles giving up the ghost, and her eyes look dazed, like those of someone you'd find wandering up the embankment after a train crash.

ANNIE (small):
Your ... highness ... ?

(PANEL) 5

Now a half figure to head and shoulder reaction shot of Eddy as he looks into her eyes, held as he is between the two brown tweed policemen. He seems to sag in their grip as he looks into Annie's off panel eyes, his lower lip trembling as if trying to form words where there are none to say. The guilt and misery in his eyes are unbearable to look at. He is starting to cry, the tears welling up to blur his vision.

No Dialogue

(PANEL) 6

Now a reaction shot of Annie. The fat man and the woman are bundling her into the dark interior of the police coach. As she is shoved away into the darkness she stares back at us through the door of the coach, her eyes wide and her face still frozen with shellshock. Bye bye, Annie.

No Dialogue

(PANEL) 7

Widescreen final panel. We see Eddy and his two accompanying detectives maybe half figure over towards the left here with a lot of white space over towards the right. The coach is presumably somewhere over towards the left, and it is towards this that the two detectives are attempting grimly to bundle Eddy. Eddy, though too weak to break free of their grasp, flings himself in the opposite direction towards the off panel Annie over on the right, his arms outstretched with hopeless and painful longing towards her. His face is an awful, naked picture of childish loss and shock and horror, and he lets out a great sick bellow like the lowing of a wounded animal.

EDDY:
ANNEEEEEEEEE!

Alan Moore

EDDY:
OOOHUUUHOOOOUHH . . .

FIRST TWEED DETECTIVE:
Get 'im in the coach . . .

PAGE 11

(PANEL) 1

A seven panel page, again with the widest panel at the bottom. These first three panels are all from the same angle, being similar to that used in panel two of page ten, with Sickert's arm hanging down into the left of the F/G throughout the three panel sequence, with a view of the studio end of Cleveland Street remaining static beyond that. In this first panel, the two captives are within their respective coaches, and the coaches are starting up. We see what are presumably Eddy's arms reaching out of the window of the royal coach, reaching uselessly towards the other coach as it pulls away from the opposite side of the street. Eddy and the detective's balloons both issue from within the coach.

EDDY (from coach):
ANNNEEEEEEE . . .

DETECTIVE (from coach):
Your highness, please . . .

(PANEL) 2

Same shot. The coaches are leaving Cleveland Street by the way they entered it. As they reach the corner, they both start to turn in opposite directions, heading away from each other. Sickert's hand remains immobile in the F/G as he watches this.

No Dialogue

(PANEL) 3

Same shot. Both the coaches have gone. The street is empty save for Sickert's hand hanging down limply in the foreground as he stands gazing at the vacant street.

No Dialogue

From Hell
Chapter One: The Affections of Young Mr. S.

(PANEL) 4
Change angle. We are now at ground level, a couple of paces behind Sickert, pulling back and down from our last panel so that we see Sickert standing full figure, looking up at him from the rear as he stands facing away from us towards the studio end of the street. In the foreground, lying on the floor, is the fallen red scarf that little Alice Margaret dropped earlier. Sickert glances round over his shoulder and catches sight of the scarf, looking down at it over his shoulder here, his eyes still pained and shocked from what he's just seen.

No Dialogue

(PANEL) 5
Still at ground level, but looking in the other direction now, towards the end of the street where we saw the ruffians staging their "fight" earlier. In the foreground we see Sickert's hand as he reaches down to pick up the fallen red scarf. Looking beyond this we see, down at the end of the street, that the fight has broken up as suddenly and mysteriously as it started. People are starting to drift away in ones and twos as if the fight has never happened.

No Dialogue

(PANEL) 6
Now a three quarter to full figure shot of Sickert as he stands there alone in the bleak and almost deserted street. He holds the red scarf he has retrieved in both hands, staring down at it as if trying to glean some meaning from it that will explain what has just happened. He trembles slightly as the shock starts to set in.

No Dialogue

(PANEL) 7
Same angle, but we pull back and away from Sickert to the end of the street that he is facing, so that he is now just a small figure standing in the centre of the street clutching at the red scarf, stupidly, looking like he's just survived a bombing, albeit only just. Around him the grey and windswept street is horribly empty and bleak and chilly looking. Down at our end, to one side of the panel, we see the street sign bolted up on the brickwork to one side of the street, still

legibly reading "Cleveland Street" in big black letters as it stretches away from us. This is a wide panel, to emphasize Sickert's dreadful isolation.

                      No Dialogue

Do you think the sun gets dazzled by its own light?
    —James Hinton
    The Life and Letters of James Hinton (1878)

As we watch Hinton in this struggle we seem sometimes to be conscious of a prophet who is caught up from the Earth in a whirlwind he cannot control, and borne away in a chariot we cannot follow.
    —Mrs. Havelock Ellis
    James Hinton: A Sketch (1918)

Oh me! I am happy and sorry; and just now I cannot see a bit whether that gladness I think is coming on the Earth is coming or not.
    —James Hinton
    The Life and Letters of James Hinton

Were such a thought adopted, we should have to imagine some stupendous whole, wherein all that has ever come into being or will come coexists, which, passing slowly on, leaves in this flickering consciousness of ours, limited to a narrow space and a single moment, a tumultuous record of changes and vicissitudes that are but to us.
    —C. Howard Hinton
    What Is The Fourth Dimension?

I must be a person not making things evil.
    —James Hinton
    The Life and Letters of James Hinton

(Hinton) was one of the pioneers of humanity through the obscure and dark ways of the senses to the region of truth.
    —William Withey Gull
    Introduction to *The Life and Letters of James Hinton*

Chapter II: A State of Darkness

PAGE 1

(PANEL) 1
We kick off this third installment of "Ripping Yarns" with a couple of pages of nice, restful, undemanding blackness. On this first page, there are nine completely black panels, and in this first one we have the white, reversed lettering of the chapter and title heading. nothing else is visible. We are completely in the dark. Titles (reversed):

Chapter II: A State of Darkness

(PANEL) 2
Another solid black panel, this time with a caption box hanging there in the darkness of the panel's upper reaches.
CAP: The Limehouse Cut. July, 1827

(PANEL) 3
Again, solid blackness. In the centre of the panel floats a word balloon without a tail. It just hangs there, unattributed, in the darkness.

TAILLESS BALLOON:
What is the fourth dimension?

(PANEL) 4
Blackness. This time, towards centre panel there hang two unattributed balloons. They could perhaps be linked

The Limehouse Cut is a canal with one end in Limehouse, not far from Hawksmoor's ominous church, St. Anne's. The other end is in Essex, a short overland coach jaunt from Thorpe-Le-Soken, where the Gull family and their barge company had residence.

All geographical references throughout From Hell are drawn from commonplace maps and street plans, such as the A-Z Guide to London, except in specific noted instances where historical maps, such as the Godfrey Edition Series of old ordnance survey maps, have been consulted.

From Hell
Chapter II: A State of Darkness

in some way . . . maybe touching slightly, one above the other. . .but as before they do not have tails issuing from them. They just float there.

    TAILLESS BALLOON:
Less than a thimble-full of Iodine divides the intellectual from the imbecile. . .

    TAILLESS BALLOON:
. . . of which phenomenon I shall henceforth attempt a demonstration.

(PANEL) 5

More Blackness. This time there are three Tailless balloons. As before, since they are all being said by the same person they could perhaps be linked in some way, possibly overlapping slightly as above. (When I say "The same person", incidentally, I mean the same person as the other balloons in that panel . . . The balloons in different panels here are all the echoes of different voices.)

    TAILLESS BALLOON:
Oh NO! William, it's too BIG.

    TAILLESS BALLOON:
Take it OUT!

(PANEL) 6

Solid blackness, with only one Tailless Balloon suspended therein.

    TAILLESS BALLOON:
Do you feel anything?

(PANEL) 7

Solid blackness, again with just one Tailless Balloon.

    TAILLESS BALLOON:
What is the fourth dimension?

(PANEL) 8

Solid blackness. Two linked balloons, both without tails.

    TAILLESS BALLOON:
Can history then be said to have an architecture, Hinton?

TAILLESS BALLOON:
The notion is most glorious, and most horrible.

(PANEL) 9
Blackness.

TAILLESS BALLOON:
What is the fourth dimension?

PAGE 2

(PANEL) 1
This page too is mostly black, but as of the third panel we see a point of light in the distance which gradually grows closer over the next two pages. We are in a long canal tunnel, moving towards the daylight at the far end, and even though we can't see either of the two people who are talking on this page, I want you to know where they are so that their respective speech balloons can issue from the right point int he darkness. (these are different voices to the ghostly echoes and premonition on the previous page. These are real—time voices, belonging to Bargee and Wharfinger John Gull and his ten year old son William, who are guiding their barge down the long dark tunnel here.) If this panel where not totally black, we would be able to see the head and shoulders of John Gull pressed against the side of his barge's forward cabin as he uses his off-panel feet to walk the barge along the tunnel, bracing them against the tunnel's walls. If we could see him, he would be in profile, a man of between fifty and sixty who looks strong and weathered but with grey hair that has already receded to leave the top of his head completely bald, with hair only around the back, apart from the gray-white whiskers running muttonchops fashion down beside his ears. Other than these, he is clean shaven. He works wearing breeches, a white shirt with its sleeves rolled up and a waistcoat. Perhaps a neckscarf, although since this the summer of 1827 the weather probably wouldn't warrant it. He sweats and grunts as he walks the barge along the tunnel, and although he doesn't know it yet, he has the beginnings of cholera, and will be dead within the year. Atop the cabin roof and a little further away from us than his father, sits young William Withey Gull, aged ten years old. While

From Hell
Chapter II: A State of Darkness

William Withey Gull was born in Colchester on 31 December 1816. His family moved to Thorpe-Le Soken in the early 1820s. Details of Gull's early life, including his initial interest in the sea, his oft-noted resemblance to Napoleon, and his father's death from cholera are drawn from William Withey Gull, A Biographical Sketch *by Gull's son-in-law Theodore Dyke Ackland (Adlard & Son, 1896). This book is available at the British Library, and in this instance the necessary locating and photocopying was performed by Neil Gaiman, to whom many thanks.*

not a tall boy he is stocky and solid, and already has something fo the bearing of a pocket Napolean sitting atop the cabin looking out over the prow as if commanding his fleet at Waterloo. His hair is cut short with brutal severity at the sides, with a patch of longer brownish locks atop his weighty cannonball head. He sits with his broad little back turned towards both us and his laboring father, his stout legs dangling over the front of the cabin as he watches for the light at the tunnels other end. He is dressed in knee-length trousers, a shirt and bare feet. Despite all the preceding descriptions, however, the tunnel's interior is completely black, so we can see nothing here but darkness as solid as that on page one. John Gull's balloons issue from a point towards the lower left of the panel. This location remains unchanged throughout these next two pages, as does that of his son, whose subsequent balloons will issue from somewhere around the upper right of the panel.

JOHN GULL:
William?

JOHN GULL:
Did you speak, lad? I thought I heard your voice . . .

JOHN GULL:
Ump.

(PANEL) 2
Again, this panel is completely black. William's balloon issues from the

darkness towards the upper right of the panel. I should perhaps reiterate that unlike the balloons on page one, these balloons do have tails. We just can't see the people speaking as yet.

> WILLIAM:
> No. I just made a little sound. I was listening to the echoes in the tunnel.

> WILLIAM:
> Is your biliousness worse, father?

(PANEL) 3

This panel is almost completely black, but there is now a distant point of light visible. Over the remainder of these two pages this will grow into a small semicircle of brilliance and then finally into the mouth of the tunnel as the barge moves through it and out into daylight. Here, however, it is just a distant pinprick of light. John Gull's balloons issue from somewhere towards the lower left, as before.

> JOHN GULL:
> It's hurp . . .

> JOHN GULL:
> It's no worse, no better, It'll clear up. It's working on these waters does it.

> JOHN GULL:
> Uwp

(PANEL) 4

This little semi circle of distant light is gradually growing bigger by increments. The voices of gull and his son issue from their respective placed in the blackness.

> WILLIAM:
> I should like to work water, when I'm grown. God willing, I should like to go see.

> JOHN GULL:
> Bless . . . Gup

(PANEL) 5

The distant semi circle of light gets a little larger, a little closer.

From Hell
Chapter II: A State of Darkness

John Gull's phlegm-flecked wheezings issue from the darkness down to the lower left.

JOHN GULL:
Bless you, you look too much like old Boney, as came to grief by sea, year afore you were born.

JOHN GULL:
You ... ung ... you want to leave the ocean alone.

(PANEL) 6

The semi circle of light gets bigger. William's voice issues from the darkness to the upper right.

WILLIAM:
Mother says that when she were with child after Waterloo, the pictures of Napoleon everywhere impressed fearfully on her mind, and that's why I look like him.

WILLIAM:
Is that so, father?

(PANEL) 7

The semi circle of light is now growin noticeably much larger.

JOHN GULL:
Well, it is a medical fact that such things may occur. How it accords with scripture, I know not.

JOHN GULL:
Is there light ahead yet, lad?

(PANEL) 8

The tunnel mouth widens in the far background, growing closer and bigger. Issuing from the darkness towards the upper right, William's two balloons are interjected between by John Gull's retching, rising from the lower left.

WILLIAM:
A little.

JOHN GULL:
Ump

WILLIAM:
Well, if I may not work the ocean, I should like to work with something of a KIND to it. Something that flows like the ocean . . .

(PANEL) 9

In the background the white light of the tunnel mouth moves closer, getting bigger as it comes. It has widened so much now that we have a silhouetted glimpse of the side of young William's head from the back as he sits facing away from us . . . just one ear and the stubble above it, perhaps a suggestion of the side of his neck.

WILLIAM:
Something salt, and old.

PAGE 3

(PANEL) 1

A seven panel page here, with the last panel perhaps being a wide one that spans the bottom of the page. Over these first six panels the tunnel mouth in the background gets bigger and wider, and we see more of the silhouetted head and shoulders of young William, sitting atop the cabin facing away from us over the prow. Perhaps we also get a suggestion of John Gull, dimly becoming lit by the approaching light as it filters into the tunnel, perhaps so that his face and shoulders gradually emerge from cross hatchings of decreasing density against the black, over these six panels. He should still remain pretty obscure, since the focus of our attention is upon the gradual and eery illumination of little William, even though we do not catch a glimpse of his face.

JOHN GULL:
Think less on tomorrow's work, boy, and more upon today's.

JOHN GULL:
The Lord has his own plans for each of us, and 'tis vanity to speculate.

(PANEL) 2

The tunnel's end widens. Silhouetted against it we can see the side of William's head and one of his shoulders as he sits facing

From Hell
Chapter II: A State of Darkness

The Biblical Quotation that begins with "What doth the Lord require of thee . . . ." later became William Gull's favorite text, and now decorates his tombstone in the churchyard at Thorpe-Le-Soken, where he is reputed to rest (source: WWG, A Biographical Sketch).

away from us. Unless we can see the dim shape of his father also starting to emerge, head and shoulders profile down to the lower left, then John Gull's balloon issues from the darkness.

JOHN GULL:
The scriptures . . . ung . . .

JOHN GULL:
The scriptures say "What doth the Lord require of thee, but to do justly, and *hurp* to love mercy, and to walk humbly with thy God."

(PANEL) 3

The tunnel mouth continues to widen. It looks like a lovely sunny day beyond the canal tunnel, with sunlight rippling dazzlingly upon the water. As the semi circle of light that is the tunnel mouth continues to widen as it approaches, we can now see nearly three quarters of the back of William's head as he sits there in silhouette facing away from us.

WILLIAM:
Yes, father.

WILLIAM:
You are right.

(PANEL) 4

The tunnel mouth widens still further. We can now see the whole of the back of William's head in silhouette against its light, with his shoulder also visible. He sits perfectly still and doesn't move so much as a muscle. He isn't a fidgety child. Perhaps, as the light improves, we can also see a little of John Gull becoming cloudily visible down to the left of the foreground as he walks his barge laboriously along the inner wall of the canal tunnel.

JOHN GULL:
Uwp

(PANEL) 5

The semi circle of light in the background is now very large. In another panel it will almost fill the entire of the background. We can see almost all of William down to halfway down his back, albeit only from the rear and in silhouette. John Gull is similarly becoming more visible, perhaps emerging from a cross-hatched gray, depending on what looks right to you. We can at least get a sense of the shape of his profiles reclining head and also of his baldness.

WILLIAM:
Father?

WILLIAM:
Is it vanity to hope the Lord may choose for me
a task most difficult?

JOHN GULL:
No . . . that would seem a worthy Christian attribute,
so long as it were not for Glory's sake.

(PANEL) 6

Sitting atop the forward cabin, young William is about to pass under the rim of the tunnel and into bright daylight. Still silhouetted, his seated body is now visible down to the waist, or thereabouts, as he sits facing away from us. Through the gray cross hatching we can now distinguish John Gull's face, right down to the mole that marks the cheekbone nearest to us, quite a large and brown item that will help us to identify Gull Senior when we see him stretched out upon his funeral bier in our next page's sequence.

WILLIAM:
Oh no.

WILLIAM:
Though I should have a task most difficult; most

necessary and severe, I should not care in none save
I did hear of my achievement.

WILLIAM:
Only the Lord and I shall know ...

(PANEL) 7
Now, if it suits you, a big wide panoramic panel as the barge noses out of the tunnel and into daylight. In the foreground we can perhaps see enough of John Gull to understand that he is walking with his feet braced against the tunnel's walls, which are still just visible framing the picture to either side here with their dull red brick, already old and eroded and draped with filthy black weed and tar deposits. He squints as he walks his boat into the daylight. Further away from us slightly, young William sits atop the cabin, facing away, He does not move. Beyond him, the river's surface explodes into concentric conjuror's rings of silver light and mallards with heads like the mouthpieces of coloured oboes rise up complaining from the razor-sharp black reeds that fringe the river to either side as it stretches away from us through the flat fields towards the smudged urban skyline of London, barely even visible in the distance here. The ripples of light quiver and flash directly beyond the seated William, so that his solid little dark shape almost becomes lost in the dazzle. It looks like a glorious day. There's hardly a cloud in the sky.

WILLIAM:
... and that shall be sufficient.

PAGE 4

(PANEL) 1
A nine panel page here, with all the panels shot from exactly the same angle. We are in the front parlour of the Gull family household at Thorpe-Le-Soken, in Essex. The family is in mourning and thus long black drapes hang at the window which we see square on in the background. The curtains are drawn back here, making a rectangle of diffused white light filtering from the daylight beyond through the net curtains hanging over the lower half of the windows. In the extreme F/G we see the head and shoulders of

Alan Moore

John Gull, who is dead. He lies upon his back with his eyes closed, facing towards the ceiling off panel above. We see the mole upon his nearest cheek, perhaps with a hair growing stoutly from it. He is dressed more formally then when we last saw him, in his best Sunday topcoat and tie. His hair is neatly groomed, his face made pale and somehow oddly effeminate by the morticians art. We are looking at this scene through the eyes of young William Gull, aged ten, even though we cannot see any of him in this first panel. As he stands off panel to one side of the body and looking across it, we see beyond the corpse the figure of a doctor who is just turning away from the body and walking back across the room towards Mrs. Gull, who stands nearer to the window. Dressed in black mourning clothes, Mrs. Gull is a sturdy and handsome woman of medium height and with dark hair, her manner stern and formidable. Younger than her late husband, she is perhaps in her late forties, and has born six children of whom William is the youngest. Her bosom is like the prow of some stately ocean-going vessel, and despite her no-nonsense demeanor, she is not an unattractive woman for her age. As the Doctor walks solemnly back across the room towards Mrs. Gull as she waits by window looking expressionlessly towards him, he is rather self consciously cleaning his spectacles upon a small piece of muslim, as if to emphasise that he has finished examining the corpse and is cleaning his spectacles prior to putting them away, ready for the next thing he might be called upon to look at.

DOCTOR:
Cholera. Just as the London Doctors stated.

DOCTOR:
Your barges did well to bring the body back to Thorpe-Le-Soken so speedily, Mrs Gull.

(PANEL) 2
Having reached Mrs Gull where she stands by the window, the Doctor pauses and stands talking to her, both half turned away from us, gazing idly out of the window as they speak to each other. Putting away his folded spectacles within an inner jacket pocket the Doctor casts a glance of sympathetic warning at Mrs. Gull, who largely seems to ignore him, gazing out over her gardens beyond the window. In the foreground, entering the picture at the very bottom, we see one

From Hell
Chapter II: A State of Darkness

of William's hands. It very tentatively enters the panel and starts to reach surreptitiously towards the dead face of his father. Neither his mother nor the Doctor have noticed this as they stand chatting in the background. Being only ten, William's hand is small but quite meaty, in keeping with his general proportions.

MRS. GULL:
As Stockport folk may prefer their locomotives, but we'll stick to our barges.

DOCTOR:
A widow running a barge-firm should not dismiss the Public Railway's competition, Mrs. Gull . . .

(PANEL) 3

Now Mrs. Gull turns around to face us, looking directly out of the panel at us here. She gives a small smile, fond of her off-panel son as she gazes at him. The Doctor too stands half turned to look in the direction that Mrs. Gull is addressing, so that he too is looking at us here, In the foreground, William has whipped his enquiring hand back out of sight as his mother turned around. His balloon issues from off panel, but nothing else is visible of him here. In the foreground, John Gull lies facing the ceiling, eyes closed in endless sleep.

MRS. GULL:
Barge people are not WEAK folk, Doctor. We'll hold our own, and see off Mr. Stephenson's contraption.

MRS. GULL:
Won't we, William?

WILLIAM (off):
Yes, mother.

(PANEL) 4

The two adults now turn away from William again, their backs completely towards us as the gaze out of the window away from us. The Doctor has his hands clasped behind his back in a stance somehow characteristic of his profession. Neither of them are looking towards William. From the foreground, his chubby hand enters the panel again, reaching slowly and carefully towards his dead father's cheek.

> DOCTOR:
> I'm sure you'll manage your husband's business splendidly.

> DOCTOR:
> Have you considered moving? Thorpe Estate is pleasant; owned by Guy's Hospital . . .

> DOCTOR:
> . . . but perhaps you're attached to Thorpe-Le-Soken?

(PANEL) 5

Still facing away from us and thus not looking at either us or William, the two adults continue to talk. Mrs. Gull gazes out of the window as she speaks, with the Doctor looking towards her in polite attentiveness as he listens. Neither of them are looking at William. In the foreground, his fingers reach out and take hold of the eyelid of the corpse, peeling it back from the glazed eyeball so that the eye is open, and staring with what looks like alarm at the ceiling.

> MRS. GULL:
> Not especially, We only moved here seven year back, from Colchester.

> MRS. GULL:
> Even so, we'll not be moving again till I'm certain that the company is steady without John. He . . .

(PANEL) 6

Mrs. Gull turns round suddenly, wheeling around to stare at William. She seems to glare at him. The Doctor half turns to follow her gaze, also looking at us and the off panel William whose eyes we are looking through. William has again whipped his hand back out of the panel here, but he has left the eye of his dead father open, staring at the ceiling with a look of frozen apprehension. Since the eye is on the side of the corpse that Mrs. Gull and the Doctor cannot see as they stand on the other side from William they remain unaware of what the boy has done.

> MRS. GULL:
> William? Did you laugh?

From Hell
Chapter II: A State of Darkness

This incident (Gull opening and closing his dead father's eye) is an invention, although the dialogue between the doctor and Mrs. Gull is based on standard historical reference: at the time of John Gull's death, the Stockport-to-Darlington railway had only just been established, being the first commercial use of Stephenson's steam locomotive. This innovation would, of course, eventually replace the barge as the foremost means of commercial transportation.

Details of the Gull family history presented here are once again drawn from WWG, A Biographical Sketch.

MRS. GULL:
I thought I heard you laugh, boy.

WILLIAM:
No, mother. I just made a little sound.

(PANEL) 7

Placing a comforting and placatory hand upon Mrs. Gull's shoulder the Doctor turns back towards the window and in doing so turns Mrs. Gull too so that she is no longer looking at the boy. William's hand is still off panel in the foreground not daring to reach into the picture until his mother and the Doctor have turned completely away from him. His mother is looking at the Doctor here.

DOCTOR:
The poor child was doubtless attempting to stifle a sob.

DOCTOR:
Tell me, have the children taken their father's death badly to heart?

(PANEL) 8

The adults are now both facing fully away from us again as Mrs. Gull speaks and the Doctor listens. From the foreground, William's hand reaches into the picture from off panel and swiftly pulls the waxy eyelid down over his father's staring orb, closing the eye once more.

MRS. GULL:
Bargee's lives are cold, flat things, Doctor. We're not reared to make great displays of sentiment.

MRS. GULL:
We've private sorrows, private mirth, and strangers think us cold fish . . .

(PANEL) 9
Same shot. In the background, Mrs Gull and the Doctor are staring away from us out of the window into the wan sunlight outside. In the foreground, William has withdrawn his hand. His father's face is back how it was in panel one, the eyes closed so that none would suspect that his eternal sleep had been ever so briefly disturbed.

MRS. GULL:
Cold fish with no feelings at all.

PAGE 5

(PANEL) 1
Now we have the first of two nine panel pages that make up a sequence filling in the formative years of William Gull and explaining his means of introduction to Guy's hospital. The way I want to do these two pages is by means of rhythmic intercutting between two different scenes. I know this will probably feel a little foreign to you as a technique, but I think it'll work and in this instance I think the use of the technique is justified: I need to relate, by means of dialogue, the mechanical facts of William's life at this time. We need to establish that Mrs. Gull did move to Thorpe Estate, as suggested by the unnamed Doctor in the last scene, and that she did this when William was sixteen. We need to establish that once there she met a Rector Harrison of Beaumont Parish Rectory, who agreed to privately teach young William every day at the rectory, as opposed to the humble village school that he fancied the handsome widow Gull. His importance lies in the fact that he was the nephew of Benjamin Harrison, treasurer of Guy's hospital, thus forging the important link between Gull and Guy's. Okay . . . now all the above information is necessary, but it's probably a bit dull (I typed "Gull" there and had to go over it.) Now, the other information we have to get over, not necessarily verbally, is young William's fascination and delight in examining the flora and fauna available in the ground of Beaumont Rectory. This absorption in the intricacies and beau-

From Hell
Chapter II: A State of Darkness

ties of nature is one of the things that is the key to Gull's entire life and philosophy. The things that we show William doing in this sequence are, admittedly, invention. It's known that he took a wild delight in the flora and fauna available at the rectory, and it is also known that in later life he became an ardent vivisectionist. He also believed that there was no greater or more lucid expression of the mysteries of God's workings than in the flawless architecture of the organic body. Given the above, I don't think it's stretching things to suggest that if the adult William, ensconced in the responsibilities of age and position, could cheerfully cut up living animals, he might in the heady throes of adolescence have taken it upon himself to dissect a deceased rat or two. To me, it seems a reasonably mild and cautious assumption. Anyway, given that we have these two necessary strands of information to impart (one detailed, verbal and dull; the other simple, silent and gorily fascinating) I figure it's legitimate for us to intertwine them. What I'm trying to explain here is that I don't think the use of this technique violates the avowed simplicity of our story structure. Both strands are clearly explained in the very first panel, and both happen at the same time, albeit in different parts of the same rectory. Because one of the strands of narrative is wholly silent, and because the scenes with William are also all seen from his point of view, then I think the whole thing will add up to a fairly simple and coherent reading experience. (See how nervous I get when I'm working with a respected comic book theorist like yourself? All that writhing and wriggling just to assure you I'm not getting flashy)

Anyway, in this first panel we are slightly behind Mrs. Gull as she stands on the front doorsteps of the rectory of the parish of Beaumont. It is a sunny day, and she is dressed soberly, although in slightly more summery attire than usual. The heavy oak front door of the rectory is open, and we see Rector Harrison standing in the doorway, smiling as he ushers Mrs. Gull within, perhaps taking her hand lightly and courteously as he does so. She returns his smile. (I have no photo reference of either Rector Harrison or his Uncle Benjamin, who we meet in a couple of pages time. They aren't major characters, and only appear this once, so draw them how you like. I see the Rector as a bespectacled cleric in his early forties; a celibate man who does a lot of writhing in the dead of night and who clearly is in the early stages of an abiding love and lust for Mrs. Elizabeth Gull, widow of this parish.) As we see the rector in this panel he has taken Mrs. Gull's hand lightly in one of his own, while with his other hand he gestures towards the interior of the rectory, beyond the open door. Mrs. Gull smiles politely as she steps forward in obedience of his entreatment to enter.

RECTOR HARRISON:
My dear Mrs. Gull.

RECTOR HARRISON:
Welcome to Beaumont Rectory. I take it young William is already off exploring the grounds?

MRS. GULL:
You can be sure he is, Rector Harrison. Never knew a child so keen on nature.

(PANEL) 2

Now we cut to a panel seen through the eyes of young sixteen year old William Gull, so that all we can see of him are his thickening ruddy forearms and his broad, long-fingered hands. He is on his knees inspecting an area of the undergrowth somewhere in the grounds of Beaumont Rectory while his mother chats with Rector Harrison indoors. It's a hot summer day, slightly after noon, and as William kneels there in the grass that pricks his knees he glories in the thick and sickly green scent of the vegetation; the smell of insect sex and his own sixteen year old sweat. The sun burns red upon the back of his thick neck, but all we can see here are his hands, which are just in the act of plucking a particularly luscious and rare looking English woodland flower (I'll leave it up to you what type..if you have any favorites or if there's some species with a name that seems resonant to matters at hand then please stick it in.) Immediately beyond the flower is an hedgerow, with thorn-studded bramble stems looping stiffly down into the picture from off and forming part of the close-up of greenery immediately beyond the delicate flower that young William's hands are seen picking here.

No Dialogue

(PANEL) 3

Back to Mrs. Gull and the randy Rector. We are now inside the rectory, in one of its spacious and book-lined withdrawing

From Hell
Chapter II: A State of Darkness

rooms, light falling in through the tall and narrow stately windows off to one side. The rector still has not relinquished his light grip upon Mrs. Gull's hand, and is leading her across the room towards one of two elegant armchairs that are arranged with a low table set between them. Upon this low table rests a silver tea service comprising sugar bowl, milk jug, tea pot, two tea cups with spoons and saucers and a pitcher of just-boiled water with a lid to keep in the heat. As he leads Mrs. Gull with one hand his other hand is already reaching for one of the armchairs, pulling it up for her a she steps towards it. She listens to the rector's words with a look of polite interest, while the rector affects what he hopes is an authoritative air. Facially, he isn't a tremendously attractive man. Perhaps he has a weak chin, or a smile that cannot help but look ingratiating and creepy. A respected minor character actor playing a creepy vicar in an early film presentation would seem about the mark to aim for Rector Harrison, although not overdone to the point of farce.

> RECTOR HARRISON:
> At sixteen, William is hardly a child. Still, I'm glad he's taken your move to Thorpe Estate so well.

> RECTOR HARRISON:
> At very least it would appear our flora and fauna are of interest to the boy.

(PANEL) 4

Now another shot through William's eyes, still on his knees inspecting the same patch of undergrowth. With the plucked flower now held in one hand, he is using both hands to gingerly separate the looping strands of briar, as if to peer into the darkness immediately beyond them. Perhaps he has a white linen handkerchief wrapped around the briar stem he grasps most fiercely, to protect his hand from foliage to see what other treasures may be unearthed.

> No Dialogue

(PANEL) 5

Back in the rectory drawing room. In the background, we see Mrs. Gull seated daintily upon one of the armchairs. More towards the foreground we see Rector Harrison as he comes towards us, reaching out to draw up his own chair, his back turned briefly to Mrs. Gull as she speaks to him. Nevertheless, even though he faces us his eyes swivel sideways, as if vainly attempting to see over his shoulder to where Mrs. Gull sits behind him. The effect upon his face is somehow crafty and watchful, but since he is facing away from her, Mrs. Gull does not see this and continues to chat lightly and pleasantly.

> MRS. GULL:
> Aa. I just wish he'd put his interest into proper learning. He talks of nothing but going to sea.
>
> RECTOR HARRISON:
> What BETTER basis for an education than the appreciation of Nature in all her terrible glory?

(PANEL) 6

We are back on our knees, looking through William's eyes. His hands have drawn back the brambles like a pair of painful and prickly curtains to reveal the dark and leafy enclosure behind them, opening it to the light of the early afternoon sun. In the little hollow amongst the weeds and briars there lies a dead rat, perhaps dead less than a day, its grey body already stiff and hard to the touch, like a hard stuffed toy rather than a flesh and blood animal. As William's hands draw back the briars to reveal the dead rat, the flower drops from his hand, forgotten in the thrill of the moment and the superior

WWG, A Biographical Sketch *also documents Mrs. Gull's move to Thorpe Estate in 1832, and the development of her 16-year-old son's interest in flora and fauna. The same source would seem to imply that Rector Harnson's offer to tutor William personally may have been based upon his attraction to the strikingly handsome Mrs. Gull, which we have attempted to represent in this scene.*

From Hell
Chapter II: A State of Darkness

charms of this new discovery.

No Dialogue

(PANEL) 7

In the foreground now, Mrs. Gull sits in profile to us, so that we see the stately battleship line of her bosom swelling out in a shapeless but formidable hump against the bodice of her high necked dress. Her head should perhaps be off panel above here, so that all we see is the curve of her bust and her hands folded demurely upon her lap. Looking beyond this we see the rector as he lowers himself down into the armchair just across the low tea-table from Mrs. Gull. He is staring fixedly at Mrs. Gull's bosom as he speaks. He looks a little flushed and uncomfortable, quite overcome by this vision from which he cannot wrench his tormented eyes. Mrs. Gull's physical presence obviously quite unsettles the poor man, though she is by no means a raving beauty by most standards.

RECTOR HARRISON:
Why, the very foundation of science and medicine lies in a preoccupation with natural forms . . .

RECTOR HARRISON:
Their workings; their shapes . . .

RECTOR HARRISON:
The very marvel in them, that moves men's hearts.

(PANEL) 8

Back on our knees in the foliage, looking through William's eyes. His hands are both raised reverently before him and cupped in them is the stiff corpse of the dead rat. (It's just struck me that you might prefer a bird instead of a rat, in which place please make the substitution. Any small animal will do, so adapt this as you see fit.) The rat just rests there in William's powerful young hands, an object of awe and reverence where seconds before it had been only the merest carrion.

No Dialogue

(PANEL) 9

Back inside the rectory, in the centre of this panel we have the tea table. From the left enter the knees of Mrs. Gull, her hands folded primly upon them. From the right enter the knees and at least one hand belonging to Rector Harrison. He is carefully pouring hot water from the jug into the tea pot, with steam billowing up into the panel. Both his and Mrs. Gull's balloons issue from off panel to their respective sides. Looking beyond the tea table to the background we perhaps see one of the room's windows, the trees and grass and flowers swaying in the summer breeze outside. (Whoops. Just noticed that only Mrs. Gull is speaking here, so scratch that bit above about the rector's dialogue issuing from off. He hasn't got any. All we see of him are his hands and his knees as he sits pouring hot water into the tea pot. Mrs. Gull's hands perhaps gesture as she speaks from off panel. See what looks best to you.)

MRS. GULL (off):
Such talk, Rector Harrison. It makes me quite giddy.

MRS. GULL (off):
Besides, our William's tutoring at village school is all a widow's income can afford him, providing little opportunity for such fine notions to bear fruit.

PAGE 6

(PANEL) 1
Another nine panels, following the same pattern as on page five. We open here with a shot through William's eyes as he kneels. In the immediate background, the dead animal has been placed carefully so as to lie upon its back at the centre of William's outspread handkerchief. In the foreground, we see William's hands. He is carefully opening up an old-fashioned looking pen knife. It looks like it has a good edge to it.

No Dialogue

(PANEL) 2
Back in the rectory, we have the seated figure of Rector Harrison in the foreground, roughly head and shoulders to half figure. He is more or less in profile to us here. He's finished pouring tea, but the steam has fogged his wire rimmed spectacles, and he has removed them here to wipe them clean with his handkerchief. As he speaks to Mrs. Gull he does not meet her gaze but rather looks down at the

glasses as he wipes them free from fog and condensation with small circular movements of his linen-enshrouded fingers. Across the table from him and thus facing us from the immediate background we see Mrs. Gull. Her mouth opens slightly and her eyes widen in surprise as the rector makes his offer. She hadn't expected this, but then she doesn't realize the extent of the rector's crush upon her.

RECTOR HARRISON:
A shameful waste of one so bright. How would it be if I should tutor him myself each day, here at the Rectory?

RECTOR HARRISON:
Then we shall see what disciplines he turns his hand to best.

(PANEL) 3
Back in the undergrowth looking through William's eyes. Steadying the stiff dead rodent in one hand, positioned belly up, William pushed the knife blade into the centre of its lower belly and draws it up through the tough and resistant tissue, exposing a wet and sticky darkness within. Already dead, the vaguely-disappointed-looking minimalist features of the rat register no extra distress at this further outrage of its corporeal form. The knife slices upward, parting fur, parting skin and muscle.

No Dialogue

(PANEL) 4
Back in the rectory we have a floor level shot, down by Mrs. Gull's feet, which we see in the foreground here. Though she sits with her legs carefully and prudently crossed beneath her voluminous skirts, the hem of it has inadvertently ridden up to reveal perhaps three quarters of an inch of flesh in the vicinity of Mrs. Gull's ankle, just above the top of her black lace up boots. As we look beyond this we see the seated Rector Harrison, full figure in the background and looking towards us. He is just resettling the glasses (now wiped clean) upon the bridge of his nose, and as his world swims back into focus it seems that his gaze is fixed upon the limited erotic vistas of Mrs. Gull's ankle (a slightly thick one at that, it must be admitted.) The rector, in danger of becoming an erector,

crosses his own legs concealingly and shifts a little against the hardness of his chair. Somewhere within the room, a clock ticks as dust motes tumble in the sunbeams. The lace of Mrs. Gull's underskirt rustles inaudibly against the cheap silk of her stockings. The rector sweats.

>MRS. GULL (off):
>Oh, I could not impose upon you so. Surely you'd soon grow tired with both of us?
>
>RECTOR HARRISON:
>With one so charming?
>
>RECTOR HARRISON:
>Dear Mrs. Gull, I should as soon grow tired with life itself.

(PANEL) 5

Back in the undergrowth, the opening incision has been made and the sticky knife set down to one side. The rat lies on its back, legs skywards, there at the centre of the blood-specked handkerchief. A slightly cynical-looking sideways smile has been opened in the flesh of its stomach, and here we see William's blood-blackened and sticky fingers pulling back the lips of the smile to thrust inside after the tiny, exposed organs. The smell of blood and shit and rats' innards mixes with that of grass and sweat and sunshine in William's excited nostrils. The moment is timeless and glassy, glazed by the bumblebee-quiet of the summers afternoon.

>No Dialogue

(PANEL) 6

Virtually a replay of panel two upon this page in terms of camera angle now as we cut back to the rectory. In the foreground, Rector Harrison is reaching out with one hand to lift the silver teapot. With his other hand he gestures to Mrs. Gull, palm outward in denial of her dazed protestations. Eyes closed piously and mouth a prim little bud if you want to see the rector's face . . . otherwise his face could be off panel and just his hands visible here. Up to you. Across the table, Mrs. Gull looks flustered and astonished. One hand raised unconsciously to lightly touch the linen slopes of her upper breast.

From Hell
Chapter II: A State of Darkness

    Her eyes are wide and surprised as she gazes at the rector.

MRS. GULL:
    Wh-Why Rector Harrison, I . . .

RECTOR HARRISON:
    Hush. It is settled. Let us hear no more of it.

RECTOR HARRISON:
    My uncle Benjamin is treasurer at Guy's Hospital. Who knows? In time your son may find his true vocation there . . .

(PANEL) 7

    We are looking through William's eyes at his hands, which are raised before his face. In the upper hand, between finger and thumb, he holds the cardiac and digestive systems of the dead rat, removed from its open chest. The delicate little rubber tubes and the kidney-bean-pip miniature organs glisten wetly in the sunshine, a small and sticky bunch of grapes from which the stale black wine still drips. William's other hand is directly beneath the hand holding up the organs for inspection. The drippings from the eviscerated innards fall down to splash in a tiny pool formed at the centre of William's broad, upturned palm. Everything is still. William holds his breath.

No Dialogue

(PANEL) 8

    Back in the rectory, we are looking now through the eyes of William's mother, Mrs. Gull. Perhaps all we can see of her are her hands crossed demurely and almost protectively upon the slippery fabric of her knee. Looking across the table, we see the rector. With one hand holding the lifted and steaming tea pot and the other steadying one of the bone china cups ready to pour, he looks up brightly through his spectacles at us, leaning forward across the table perhaps a little more than one would really want him to in his attitude of eager entreatment. He smiles, his desire to impress himself romantically upon Mrs. Gull absurdly obvious behind his attempt at a restrained rectorial facade.

RECTOR HARRISON:
    . . . may find a calling deep enough to make him quite

forget the ocean's lure.

>   RECTOR HARRISON:
> Now, how do you prefer your tea, dear Mrs. Gull . . .

>   RECTOR HARRISON:
> Or might I know you as "Elizabeth?"

(PANEL) 9

Final shot through William's eyes. We close in upon the image in panel seven, so that all we see here is the lower of William's two hands, the palm upturned to catch the blood and the dead juices that drip into the picture from off panel above. The pool in the centre of William's hand has started to brim over, thin black rivulets running down across the blade-edge of William's hand to trickle round, defying gravity, and gather at his knuckles, whence they drip in small beads towards the off panel spears of grass below. All the time, fresh droplets continue to splash into William's palm from above. It's all very holy and mysterious, a personal grail revealed.

> No Dialogue

PAGE 7

(PANEL) 1

Now another nine panel page, this time jumping ahead almost ten years to when William Gull was twenty six years old and in the prestigious position of teaching materia medica at Guy's Hospital. On this page, we detail a conversation between William and Benjamin Harrison, the elderly and despotic uncle of Rector Harrison, and the treasurer of Guy's Hospital. Again, I have no photo reference, but I imagine him as a stern and whiskery victorian patriarch of perhaps sixty five years. His bearing is very commanding and imposing, but as he speaks to Gull in this sequence we get the sense that despite his gruffness he very much likes the younger man, and has indeed taken an active hand in William Gull's meteoric advancement. The nine panel here are again seen through William's eyes, so that only his hands and arms are revealed. They are now the muscular and densely-haired forearms and hands of a twenty six year old of considerable physical strength, and they have smart white cuffs rolled

From Hell
Chapter II: A State of Darkness

back here to allow Doctor Gull to work. The work in question is the sewing up of a surgical incision in the side of a patient who we see stretched out unconscious across the middleground of the picture here, an open incision in the side nearest to us, and a considerable amount of blood. Both participants in the conversation seem to utterly ignore the presence of the patient as they speak, but it remains mutely in the middleground throughout, with Benjamin Harrison standing immediately beyond it in this first panel, facing us. His thumbs are hooked into his lapels and he shoots us a questioning glance from beneath his slightly lowered white eyebrows here as he faces us across the motionless form of the patient under surgery. We are in a dark operating theatre at Guy's Hospital, with maybe a liberal use of black backgrounds if you like and only the patient illuminated by the overhead light shining down upon him or her. (I leave the gender of the patient up to you.) As Benjamin Harrison looks queryingly at us across the operating table, we see William Gull hold up one of his hands towards the older man, palm outward as if to banish Harrison's worries about spoiling Gull's concentration. The fingers and knuckles are bright and wet with blood. William's balloon issues from off panel in the foreground.

BENJAMIN HARRISON:
So, Master Gull, let us RECAP ... if it will not disturb your ministrations?

GULL (off):
Not at all, Mr. Harrison. Please continue.

(PANEL) 2
Same shot. In the foreground, we see William's hands. In one of them he holds a surgical needle, while in the other he holds the end of a strand of catgut thread. With his bloody fingers, he is deftly attempting to thread the strand of catgut through the needle's eye. In the immediate background, just across the white and illuminated body of the patient under surgery, Benjamin Harrison turns so that he is now in profile facing towards the right of the panel, thumbs still hooked into his lapels in an autocratic fashion. Being about to start pacing as he discourses, he is no longer looking at Gull as he speaks.

BENJAMIN HARRISON:
Very well.

Alan Moore

From Hell
Chapter II: A State of Darkness

> BENJAMIN HARRISON:
> Five years ago, aged twenty-one, you were employed at Guy's counting house upon the recommendation of my nephew, the Rector.

(PANEL) 3

Same shot. In the foreground, William Gull's bloody fingers have succeeded in passing the end of the thread through the needles eye and he is now drawing the whole length of the thread through the needle's eye with a flourish. Beyond the motionless body of the patient, Benjamin Harrison has walked almost completely off panel so that only the back of his body and head are visible here as he paces slowly and distractedly off the right of the picture, caught up in his lecture.

> BENJAMIN HARRISON:
> You received fifty pounds, and rooms upon hospital premises. I told you that if you helped yourself, I should be able to help you.

(PANEL) 4

In the background, Harrison is completely off panel now, his balloon entering into the picture from off panel right. In the foreground we see Gull's hands busy themselves with the patient. One hand holds the flap of the wound steady while the other digs the point of the needle through the thick layer of tissue, the tendons standing out with exertion upon the thick wrists, the blood gleaming upon the laboring fingers.

> BENJAMIN HARRISON (off):
> You won every prize available; graduating with honours in surgery and comparative anatomy; finally appointed to teach Materia Medica here at Guy's.

> BENJAMIN HARRISON (off):
> Your progress is remarkable.

(PANEL) 5

In the immediate background, beyond the operating table, Benjamin Harrison has turned ponderously on his heel and is now heading back into the picture face first, his thumbs still hooked meaningfully behind his wide lapels. He frowns in consideration as he listens in silence to what Gull is saying as he paces. Apart from the speech balloons issuing into the panel from off-pic in the foreground, all we see of Gull is the hands and the arms, cuffs rolled back and bloody to the wrist. Having penetrated both sides of the flap, Gull now pulls the needle through, dragging the catgut thread behind it.

>WILLIAM GULL (off):
>I owe it all to a rhyme learned at my mother's knee:

>WILLIAM GULL (off):
>"If I were a tailor, I'd make it my pride. The best of all tailors to be ... "

(PANEL) 6

In the near background across the table, old Benjamin Harrison has returned more or less to his original position, facing us square on across the table. His crusty old face creases into a slight smile of appreciation as he regards Gull. In the foreground we see Gull starting to push the needle point through the flesh again, working steadily while he talks to the older man.

>GULL (off):
>" ... and if I were a tinker, no tinker beside. Should mend an old kettle like me."

>BENJAMIN HARRISON:
>Well said! Exactly the attitude that brings me here with a PROPOSITION for you ...

(PANEL) 7

Same shot. In the foreground, Gull draws the needle through the sides of the wound in the opposite direction, trailing the thread behind it. Across the table, Harrison's face becomes serious and grave, and he leans forwards as if imparting a great honour and confidence upon the younger man, looking him in the eye as he does so.

>BENJAMIN HARRISON:
>I have nominated you as an elected Freemason.

From Hell
Chapter II: A State of Darkness

Details of Gull's meteoric medical career are accurate, and drawn from A Biographical Sketch. Gull's entry into Freemasonry is more problematic. The only source would seem to be The Final Solution *in which Knight dates Gull's involvement with the craft from 1842, when the 26-year-old was employed at Guy's Hospital. The Masons themselves have since denied that Gull was ever a member of their order, and have generally derided the claims made in Knight's books, including* The Brotherhood *(Grafton Books, 1989), wherein Knight suggests that higher-level Freemasons pay homage to a bizarre triple-deity known as Jah-Bul-On. In at least this last denial, the Masons it seems may be telling less than the full truth: Martin Short's* Inside The Brotherhood *(Grafton Books, 1989) seems to confirm that, despite Masonic denials, Jah-Bul-On is an authentic masonic deity. How much, then, can their denial of Gull's Masonic status be trusted? The problem we face here is that neither Knight nor the assembled ranks of*

BENJAMIN HARRISON:
It would further your career, and though the Brotherhood's standards are exacting, I am certain you should not disappoint me.

(PANEL) 8
Setting down the needle and thread, leaving it to dangle from the patient's partially-sewn wound, Gull's right hand reaches out excitedly to shake that of Benjamin Harrison, who reaches across the operating table so that they shake hands across the body of the unconscious patient. Sir Benjamin smiles proudly as he shakes hands with the younger man, staring him levelly in the eye as he does so.

WILLIAM: GULL (off):
The brotherhood...?

WILLIAM: GULL (off):
I'll not disappoint you, sir. You have my hand upon it.

BENJAMIN HARRISON:
Very good. Our Lodge meets Friday week. Once initiated, we'll teach you our etiquettes, our ceremonies...

(PANEL) 9
Same shot. Both men have withdrawn their hands, and have both belatedly realised that William Gull's hand is covered in the patient's blood. In the foreground, William gazes down uneasily at the offending upturned palm, streaked with scarlet. Across the table, Sir Benjamin stares down at his own upturned palm, now similarly streaked with blood. His face has an expression of controlled distaste and

disappointment.

BENJAMIN HARRISON:
... our handshake ...

PAGE 8

(PANEL) 1

Okay ... The next two pages show Wild Bill Gull's initiation into the traditions and mysteries of the free and accepted masons. In this first panel on a nine panel page we see him from the front for the first time, albeit only up to just below the nose. We can see his distinctive mouth and chin, and then his neck, shoulders, chest and belly. He is wearing only a shirt and trousers in so far as we can see here. Though only twenty six years old he already has the heavy-set physique that will characterise him in later years, with his chin and jowls inclined towards that distinctive owlish chubbiness even at this early age. Entering into the panel from off pic we see the sleeves, cuffs and hands of the freemason acting the role of tyler and preparing the initiate in the drafty ante-chamber appended to the main freemason lodge rooms. (This is all taking place in a freemasons hall somewhere in London. No specific details. As we see the Tyler's hands, they are wrenching open the front of William Gull's shirt to reveal the hairy stomach, already developing a slight bay window effect, and the slightly

Freemasonry are necessarily telling the truth, at which point an obscuring Victorian fog starts to engulf the facts of our narrative. Given that the tortuous story of the Whitechapel murders is filled with liars, tricksters, and unreliable witnesses, it is a fog we shall encounter often.

The suggestion that Benjamin Harrison provided Gull's entrance to the world of Freemasonry is entirely ny own invention, based upon little more than Gull's professed lifelong gratitude toward Harrison, Harrison's comment to Gull (reported in A Biographical Sketch) that "I can help you if you will help yourself," and the fact that he happened to be in the right place at the right time according to Knight's construction of events. In all other respects, Harrison's inclusion during this scene is simply a convenience of fiction.

From Hell
Chapter II: A State of Darkness

fleshy and pointed breasts, also ringed with hair about the nipples. Gull's mouth, the only facial feature we can see here, is set into a grim and serious line.

No Dialogue

(PANEL) 2

Now we are down at ground level, looking at Gull's feet as they stand upon the chill flagstone floor of the ante-room. His right trouser leg is as normal, but upon that foot he has no shoe, and is wearing only his sock. On the left foot he wears both shoe and sock, but here the left trouser leg is rolled up to reveal the knee. Again, we see the Tyler's hands entering as he kneels off panel, his hands adjusting Gull's rolled-up trouser leg here.

No Dialogue

(PANEL) 3

Now we have a head and shoulders profile shot of Gull, but only of the back of his head. His face is off panel to the right, so that we can only see as far forward as his ear. Again, the Tyler's hands are gently entering the panel from off and carefully placing a rope noose over Gull's head and around his neck, so that the knot hangs down the back between Gull's shoulder blades. Gull remains unflinchingly still during this ritual.

No Dialogue

(PANEL) 4

Now we are looking through Gull's eyes. The Tyler, a nondescript victorian gentleman of around fifty stands half figure towards the foreground. Over his ordinary victorian clothes he wears an apron embellished with whatever masonic symbols look cheerful to you . . . eye in pyramid, dividers and set squares, crescent moon ringed by seven five-pointed stars, two hands clasped in a masonic handshake, a trowel, an hourglass with wings . . . you can pretty well take you pick really. As I understand it most masonic lodges had aprons decorated with different mixtures of these various symbols and others, so as long as it looks suitably arcane and nutty then you should be okay. Behind the Tyler as he looks towards us we get a suggestion of the stone ante chamber that we are in, looking towards some impressive looking double wooden doors with gleaming brass trimmings over in the background. The Tyler wears a neutral expression as he leans forward, reaching towards us so that his arms are foreshortened here as they loom towards our face, a drooping blindfold held between them, which the Tyler is about to fasten across our eyes.

No Dialogue

(PANEL) 5
An all black panel as the blindfold goes on.

No Dialogue

(PANEL) 6
Now a half figure shot of the Tyler in his apron, roughly in profile. William Gull's right hand (of which the shirtsleeve is rolled up to reveal the elbow) enters into the panel from out of picture to one side, and is being lightly grasped by the Tyler, who has led Gull up to the wooden doors glimpsed in panel four. The Tyler faces the door, expressionless as he raises his knuckles to knock upon the door.

No Dialogue

(PANEL) 7
Now we are behind William Gull, so that we only see the back of his head, and only one side of it at that, over towards the left of the picture, facing away from us head and shoulders or thereabouts. We can see the blindfold knotted about his eyes, and we can see the hemp noose hanging grimly down his back. If we see his right hand it is being held by the Tyler, who stands off panel to the right here. Looking past these two we see that the inner lodge door has opened. Another man stands within, also dressed in a masonic apron. This man is the inner guard, and in his right hand he holds a ceremonial knife, holding it up as he opens the door so that the hand and the blade rest horizontally across his upper chest, on a level with his heart. His face is stern as he speaks, really laying on the ritual and dramatics.

INNER GUARD:
Whom have you there?

From Hell
Chapter II: A State of Darkness

(PANEL) 8
Now we reverse angles. In the foreground, we perhaps glimpse a little of the inner guard as he stands facing away from us at an angle . . . maybe we can just see the raised hand with the knife in it somehow. Looking beyond him we see the Tyler facing us as he stands on the threshold of the inner temple. His left hand still holds Gull's right, although Gull is off panel right here, with only his hand and arm visible, the shirtsleeve rolled back to the elbow as he faces us. The Tyler speaks, his face deadpan, his voice resonating in whispers against the marbled silence of the chambers.

Tyler:
Dr. William Gull, a poor candidate in a state of darkness . . .

Tyler:
. . . who comes of his own free will and accord, properly prepared, humbly soliciting to be admitted to the mysteries and privileges of Freemasonry.

(PANEL) 9
A profile half figure shot now, showing the blindfolded Gull and the inner guard. Gull stands to the left of the picture, with only his front half entering the panel here. If any of his face is visible, only the lower half of it is, the rest of his profile being invisible, off beyond the upper panel border. Gull faces towards the right of the panel, where the inner guard stands facing towards the left. He places the point of his ceremonial knife against Gull's left breast, pricking the flesh. The line of Gull's mouth does not flinch from its firm and resolved line.

INNER GUARD:
Do you feel anything?

PAGE 9

(PANEL) 1
A solid black panel, as seen through William Gull's eyes behind his blindfold. The dialogue balloon belonging to the inner guard does not have a tail. It just hangs there, against the solid blackness, an unattributed echo. This panel is an exact repeat of panel 6 upon page 1.

Alan Moore

TAILLESS BALLOON:
Do you feel anything?

(PANEL) 2
Now we have a tight frontal close up of Gull's face, filling the entire panel from border to border. The upper half of the panel is thus filled with Gull's blindfold, and only his nose and his mouth are visible. The blindfolded face stares out at us, unseeing. The lips move, framing Gull's response.

WILLIAM GULL:
Yes.

(PANEL) 3
Now a half figure shot from the back as the inner guard, satisfied with the response, leads Gull deeper into the inner chamber. Most of Gull is off panel to the left here as he walks blindly and slowly away from us, and we can see little more of him than his right arm, his hand gently guided by the inner guard who also walks away from us, more towards the right of the panel. In his right hand, the guard holds the ceremonial knife aloft in a ritualistic gesture. Looking beyond the pair as they walk away from us we see three men in aprons standing facing us full across the floor of the sizeable masonic hall. The man in the centre is the worshipful master of the lodge. Flanking him to either side are a pair of deacons, each holding a short and stout wooden wand with ceremonial fittings of brass at either end. (Don't mind if you can't get all this ceremonial detail in. I just include it as reference if you need it, and for your further edification.) The Worshipful Master speaks solemnly as Gull is led forward into the lodge.

WORSHIPFUL MASTER:
Dr. Gull. . .

WORSHIPFUL MASTER:
In all cases of difficulty and danger, in who do you put your trust?

(PANEL) 4
Now a virtual repeat of panel two. Once more, Gull's blindfolded face fills the entire frame. Only his lips have moved, to

139

From Hell
Chapter II: A State of Darkness

The ritual shown here is an accurate, if abbreviated, depiction of the Masonic initiation ceremony as described in Knight's The Brotherhood (see footnote to From Hell Chapter Three) and elsewhere. Other sourcebooks consulted on Freemasonry include The Spirit of Freemasonry by Foster Bailey (Lucius Press, 1957), A Treasury of Masonic Thought by Carl Glick (Robert Hale Ltd., 1961); Yeat's Golden Dawn by George Mills Harper (The Aquarian Press, 1974), and The Mythology of Secret Societies by J.M. Roberts (Secker & Warburg, 1972).

GULL:
In God.

(PANEL) 5
Now we have a floor level shot. Gull kneels in profile over to the right of the panel, facing left. He kneels with his bare left knee touching the floor and his right knee raised. His right foot is oddly twisted so as to be at right angles to his bare knee. (It looks funny, but its just about possible. If it looks too funny and comical then leave it out, and have the foot normally positioned.) We can, in addition to this, see Gulls arms and hands, and also the hands of the worshipful master entering from the left of the panel as Gull kneels before him. The Worshipful Master is placing an ancient looking volume of sacred law into Gull's right hand and a large and beautifully crafted set of dividers into Gull's left hand. (Gull's left shirt sleeve is rolled incidentally, unlike his right.) The Worshipful Master's balloons issue from off panel left here.

WORSHIPFUL MASTER (off):
Then kneel upon your left knee, your right foot formed into a square.

WORSHIPFUL MASTER (off):
Take in your right hand the volume of Sacred Law, and in your left these compasses, one point presented to your naked breast.

(PANEL) 6

Now we have a close up of Gull's right hand as he kneels. It rests reverently upon the volume of Sacred Law. His balloons issue from off panel. (The cover of the Sacred Law could be adorned with some striking masonic symbol or other, to lend it weight and significance.)

> GULL (off):
> I, William Withey Gull, in the presence of the Great Architect of The Universe, do solemnly swear to always hold, conceal and never reveal the mysteries of Free and Accepted Masons . . .

(PANEL) 7

Now a close up of Gull's left hand, holding the compasses, and his left breast, against which the sharp and gleaming compass point rests. Again, his balloons issue from off panel.

> GULL (off):
> . . .under no less a penalty than that my throat be cut across, my tongue torn out by the root, and that I be buried in sand a cable's length from the shore. . .

(PANEL) 8

Now a panel almost identical to the panels two and four, just showing a close up of his blindfolded face filling the entire panel. Only the shape of his emotionless lips is different here.

> GULL:
> . . . where the tide regularly ebbs and flows . . .

> GULL:
> . . . twice in twenty four hours

(PANEL) 9

Now we have a sudden cut to the beach in Bournemouth, 1923. The panel we show here is an exact xerox repeat of panel four, page one in our prologue episode, only without the caption. All we see is the beach with the tide surging greyly in, the two tiny figures plodding towards us from the distance and the decayed seagull in the foreground, its beak yawning open in death and the sand flies hopping about upon it. The waves crash in the sound of someone dumping thousands of crates full of milk bottles. The dead gull on

From Hell
Chapter II: A State of Darkness

the tide line stares stupidly into the blind white sky.

No Dialogue

PAGE 10

(PANEL) 1

There are seven panels on this page, maybe with the seventh one as the largest, perhaps spanning the whole bottom of the page. We have jumped a few years , and it is now 1847. Gull is thirty, a most successful young doctor. As we see him here he is going about his practice within the gloomy and echoing interior of Guy's Hospital. In this first panel we are looking through Gull's eyes as one of his arms reaches out from the foreground to shake the hand of a man who has approached him from the background. This man is the young Hinton, slightly younger than Gull here. The only reference I have of him is the badly sketched copy of a contemporary picture which I enclose. It's a pretty decent likeness despite the faults, so I hope it gives you something to work with. Hinton is a nervous and excitable ball of jumpy, twitchy energy, filled with great spiritual anguish at the miseries he sees about him in society, always writhing about his inability to do anything about it. He is disarmingly passionate, and there is also something quite comical and likeable about his babbled monologues upon wild philosophical notions. Mrs. Havelock Ellis in 'James Hinton- A Sketch'(1916) described him as follows: "As we watch Hinton in his struggle, we seem sometimes to be conscious of a prophet who is caught up from the Earth in a whirlwind he cannot control, and born away in a chariot we cannot follow." As we see Hinton here he is brimming with genuine congratulation for Gull's recent achievements, and is somewhat self consciously extending his hand for Gull to shake. Beyond Hinton as he as he stands there nervously shifting his weight from one foot to another, discomforted by the presence of the much-admired William Gull, we see the long hospital corridor, perhaps with nurses of the period walking back and forth in the distance. The echoes are filled with piss and disinfectant.

HINTON:
Dr. Gull? I am James Hinton. My congratulations

upon the gold medal your M.D. received. A supreme honour . . . especially for one of barely thirty years!

(PANEL) 2

Still looking through Gull's eyes here. He has released Hinton's hand and has instead pulled his watch and chain from his pocket, which he holds up to the foreground of the panel as he inspects it from off. The time can be whatever you want. Perhaps the view down the corridor in the background has changed somewhat, as if Gull had continued to walk briskly on after his handshake with Hinton, or he had turned a corner from the main corridor or something. Hinton is more to one side of the panel here, and more in profile to us, as if he is falling hopefully into step alongside Gull as the senior Doctor goes about his rounds. Gull's balloon issues from off in the F/G, and other than this all we can see of him is the hand holding the watch. Despite what he is saying, there IS something rather brusque and dismissive about Dr. Gull's manner here, a trait that apparently made his many enemies during the course of his considerable life. Away down the corridor, the nurses parade silently through the gloom.

GULL (off):
Why thank you, Dr. Hinton.

GULL (off):
You'll forgive my haste, but I must attend the deranged women kept here for me at Guy's. Do not think me brusque . . .

HINTON:
Not at all. May I walk with you?

(PANEL) 3

We are now approaching to top of a flight of steps that leads down to some unguessable subterranean depth below. Hinton walks along slightly ahead and to one side of us, looking back at us over his shoulder as he speaks to us. His eyes are haunted and deeply sad and passionate as he speaks about the unfortunate women that are the dominating obsession of his curious life. The stairs, if we can see any of them, are very dark and only just dimly lit by the few gas-lamps fitted to the wall at lengthy intervals as it

From Hell
Chapter II: A State of Darkness

runs down the stairs. Everything is very shadowy. Gull is invisible here.

> GULL (off, F/G):
> Certainly. accompany my inspection if you wish.

> HINTON:
> That would be most agreeable. I confess that unfortunate women hold a particular interest for me.

> HINTON:
> Their miserable condition haunts me. Shall it NEVER be alleviated?

(PANEL) 4

They are now on their way down the narrow staircase, as seen through Gull's eyes if that's possible as he goes down the stairs with Hinton in front of him. If all this 'eye of the camera' stuff gets tricky or tiresome then please handle the shot some other way. The only important thing is that the creepy atmosphere be preserved and that we do not show Gull's face. If we are looking through his eyes here then we can see that he has raised one hand to gently placate the hurt look upon the face of Hinton, who turns round to gaze woundedly at Gull, convinced that Gull is laughing at him (in which he is correct) and that Gull doesn't like him (in which he is incorrect ... Gull is warming to this zealous and eccentric young Doctor a great deal. They will become lifelong friends.) The gaslight and shadows play over them as they descend the stairs.

> GULL (off):
> Hahaha! My dear Hinton, are all your outbursts so passionate?

> GULL (off):
> No, no, come, do not look aggrieved. Such passion's admirable in a fellow.

> GULL (off):
> ... though concerning the objects of your pity, I fear there's little hope.

(PANEL) 5

Now perhaps we see Hinton descending the dark and winding

stair, turning back and raising his hands expressively as he speaks to Gull, his eyes genuinely pained and tormented by the idea that there may be no redemption for the unfortunate women he cares so much about. His shadow is on a wall behind him, a slightly distorted shape of flat black upon the damp and uneven bricks. So is Gull's shadow, which partly falls across Hinton as Gull casts it off panel right. We see his profile in the shadow. The jowls and chin, the suggestion of a short fringe atop his high forehead, his slightly owl-like posture, that of a predator at repose. The two men wind deeper into the bowels of Guy's Hospital as they talk, where there is no natural light. There is something suggestively hellish and Dantean about the whole scenario.

> HINTON:
> There MUST be . . . even for such unfortunates. Is not all base matter gradual ascending; refining itself into pure spirit?

> GULL (off):
> Assuredly . . . but some wretches have a downward momentum in their lives almost impossible to reverse.

(PANEL) 6

Now, in the near B/G, Hinton glances back towards us as he pauses by a large wooden door with a small barred window set into it at eye-level. (They have reached the bottom of the steps by now.) Hinton pauses at the locked door and glances back at Gull with a look of deep interest, albeit slightly anxious interest. Looking through Gull's eyes, in the foreground we see his raised hand, in which he holds a bunch of keys, one key uppermost upon the ring and gripped between thumb and forefinger as he produces it from some off-panel pocket, about to unlock the door that bars our way in the immediate background, Hinton waiting nervously to one side of it.

> GULL (off):
> Consider it: Water will of necessity flow downhill, thwarting all our best efforts that it should do otherwise.

> GULL (off):
> In order that water might rise despite itself, it must first be transmuted into steam . . .

From Hell
Chapter II: A State of Darkness

(PANEL) 7

Big wide panel, as seen through Gull's eyes. To one side of the panel we see his hand and forearm entering the picture, holding open the heavy wooden door as it swings inward, the bunch of keys now dangling from the key that is fitted into the door's lock. Looking beyond the hand and the open door we see the dimly lit room, which is large and dark and full of madwomen. They sprawl upon straw or untidy bunks, an ugly and largely unwashed collection of creatures with missing teeth and staring eyes and stringy hair. Some just sit in catatonic depression or stand with their foreheads resting wearily against the cooling stone of the walls. An old woman lets a long elastic strand of drool escape over her incontinent gums as she clutches between her legs with one wizened hand. Some of the women's eyes are bright, but most are dull and listless and uncaring. As the door swings open, we see the panorama of their wretched tableau through the curtain-like pall of shadow and gloom within the spacious, high ceilinged chamber.

GULL (off):
... It must be touched by the purifying spirit of fire.

GULL (off):
This way.

PAGE 11

(PANEL) 1

A nine panel page here. In this first one, we are within the gloomy chamber, the shambling and all but indistinguishable figures shifting upon their bunks in the background. We need not to be looking through Gull's eyes here... perhaps we see his hands and arms entering from one side of the panel as he reaches out to hang up his coat upon a convenient peg jutting from the rough wall. Somewhere lower, beyond this peg, we can perhaps see a crude stone sink with an antique looking tap above it, a brass one streaked black and green with verdigris. To the other side of the midground Hinton gazes away from us at the incarcerated unfortunates visible through the murk, looking as anguished as he does so. In the foreground,

Gull coyly hangs up his top coat before getting down to work in his waistcoat and shirt sleeves. His forearms are thick with muscle, those of a very strong man in the prime of his life.

> HINTON:
> Dear God. Are they all quite mad?

> GULL (off):
> Oh yes.

> GULL (off):
> . . . But tell me of yourself, Hinton. Are you a married man?

(PANEL) 2

Change angle as Gull sets about his examination of a new inmate, with Hinton looking on. We see Gull's hand reaching into the panel from off-picture to one side, cupping the chin of one of the more decrepit female inmates as she slouches nervelessly upon her cot, tilting her face up towards him so that he can examine her for facial indications of disease. The woman's eyes are heavy lidded and glazed, and she may even possibly be blind or partly sighted. Her hair is lank and stringy, and she is maybe fifty five years old. Her eyes do not seem to focus as Gull gazes into them from of panel. Hovering nearby in the semi-darkness of the near background, Hinton looks on somewhat apprehensively as he hesitantly replies. All of the inmates, incidentally, are dressed in long rough smocks of something that looks like sacking.

> HINTON:
> I, uh, no. That is, I hope to be, when my Margaret gives assent.

> GULL (off):
> Bravo. A noble institution, matrimony.

> GULL (off):
> Now, let's see what ails you, my beauty . . .

(PANEL) 3

Now a shot through Gull's eyes. Kneeling by the foot of the cot he takes the hem of the woman's sackcloth garment in one hand and throws it up over her slack belly. With his other hand he

From Hell
Chapter II: A State of Darkness

briskly and efficiently pushes the woman's knees apart, to expose the tuft of dirty gray hair between her thighs. We are more or less looking up the length of the woman's body here, and she props herself up on one elbow to gaze stupidly down at us as we kneel between her knees. Her eyes are not focused, and perhaps do not even see us at all. She's a miserable and doomed-looking specimen of humanity. Hinton needn't be visible here. Gull's balloon issues from far off.

> GULL (off):
> I myself am shortly to wed Colonel Lacy of Carlisle's daughter, Susan.

> GULL (off):
> Women are such elevated and agreeable creatures, are they not?

> MADWOMAN:
> My husban', 'e wenn out fer co-al . . .

(PANEL) 4

Same shot, still through Gull's eyes as he kneels there at the foot of the hospital cot, still keeping the woman's knees apart with one firm but gentle hand. He pushes two fingers of his other hand up into the patient's vagina, feeling the inner walls just inside the entrance. The woman continues to gaze stupidly down at him, her face slack and dead as she mumbles her non-sequiturs, memories of a life she perhaps once led before she became the thing we see lying here. Hinton is perhaps visible at least partially to one side here, looking on in mild alarm and unease. He is a Doctor, admittedly, but the plight of these women is an obsession too close to his heart to retain a wholly unflappable professional calm about this whole episode. He feels these women's degradation in a very real sense, and it tortures him.

> HINTON:
> Uh, yes. Most agreeable.

> HULL (off):
> Just as I thought: A syphilitic sarcocele . . . too late for iodide of potassium, it seems.

> MADWOMAN:
> Is 'e back yet?

(PANEL) 5

In the foreground we see the woman as she struggles up into a sitting position on the side of her cot, some animation returning to her lackluster body. Her face, however, still looks slack and dim. She perhaps frowns, slightly, trying to puzzle something out through the befuddling fog of her condition. She is maybe half figure in the F/G as she sits up on the edge of her bed. Beyond her, we see at least the lower portion of Gull and Hinton. Having walked away from the woman, Gull is now washing his hands at the stone sink mentioned earlier. A faintly grubby piece of towel hangs somewhere near to it. Hinton stands lightly to one side, maybe with his head off the top of the panel as Gull's is here, presumably looking on at either Gull or the patient as she struggles up to a sitting position. Probably,. he is looking at Gull. We can see neither of the two doctors above the neckline here, as they stand in the B/G.

GULL (off):
The disease appears to have traversed the spinal column, infecting reason's throne itself . . .

MADWOMAN:
Is my Jack back yet with the co-al? Warrit 'im just now, 'avin 'is 'andfull o' sprats?

(PANEL) 6

Now we are a pace or two behind Gull and Hinton as Gull stands drying

Gull's friendship with the volatile and eccentric James Hinton is noted in The Dictionary of National Biography *under its entry for* Gull, *and is confirmed by references in* A Biographical Sketch *as well as references in* The Life and Letters of James Hinton (1878) *and* James Hinton: A Sketch by Mrs. Havelock Ellis (1918). *The latter two volumes, which also detail Hinton's obsession with the prostitutes of Whitechapel, are also available at the British Library. In this instance, the copies were procured by the welcome assistance of Steve Moore, to whom thanks are in order.*

The assertion that Gull had charge of an asylum housing 20 insane women at Guy's Hospital originates with Knight but would seem to be supported by references in A Biographical Sketch *to his appointment in 1843 as medical superintendent of the lunatic ward at Guy's.*

The remark about water possessing the ability to rise only once it has been touched by the purifying spirit of fire paraphrases a comment by Gull found in the "Notes & Apho-

From Hell
Chapter II: A State of Darkness

risms" section of his biographical sketch, which is entirely composed of documents removed from Gull's study at the time of his alleged death in 1890.

Gull's ability to detect a syphilitic sarcocele, seemingly at a glance, is noted in A Biographical Sketch.

his hands upon the towel. We can see his back as he stands there in the shadows, but his face is, as ever, turned directly away from us. Hinton gazes at Gull as he speaks, with a poetic sadness in his troubled-looking eyes. We are seeing the two of them through the madwoman's eyes here. She has risen from her cot and is stumbling towards them, reaching up one scrawny, black-nailed hand and forearm into the picture as she reaches out for the back of Dr. Gull's shoulder as he stands turned face away from her. Hinton is looking at Gull rather than at the woman, and as yet appears to be as unaware of her presence as Gull. The woman's balloon enters the picture from off panel in the foreground.

HINTON:
How dismal. Just as a serpent climbs the bough in Eden, so does the disease progress.

GULL:
Haha! My word, what an imagination. We must stroll together sometimes.

MADWOMAN (off):
Jack?

(PANEL) 7

Now we are looking through Dr. Gull's eyes as the madwoman suddenly launches round to the front of him and reaches out to grab at his coat as she faces him. (His waistcoat, that is. Not the one that's still hanging up.) Her face, streaked with grime, has become suddenly animated, and her eyes are staring wildly at us, although no-one could say what she believes she is seeing. Gull's hands enter the panel from off, gently pushing the woman away and calming her patronizingly as one would a child. He is in a hurry to leave. Perhaps Hinton looks on from the B/G, shocked, but the main emphasis here is upon the madwoman's wild and staring eyes as she voices her monious question.

> MADWOMAN:
> Is that you, our Jack?

> GULL (off):
> There, there, my good woman.

> GULL (off):
> All is well.

(PANEL) 8
We are now somewhere towards the middle of the gloomy hell for women, looking towards the heavy wooden door with the single barred window set into it at eye-level. It is being held open by Gull here. He is just stepping through the door away from us and pulling his coat on as he goes. The gaslight in the corridor beyond the door, although weak, has a sickly brilliance when contrasted with the gloom of the asylum chamber, and Gull is silhouetted against it here, making him a faceless dark shape as he prepares to leave. Hinton hesitates briefly before following behind Gull, one side of his face lit by the weak light filtering from the door as he turns to look back towards us and the centre of the room, where the woman sits slumped and dejected, holding up one feeble and impotent hand towards the departing doctors.

> GULL:
> Come, Hinton, let us now depart. Time is but short, and I have other tasks.

> MADWOMAN:
> Jack?

(PANEL) 9
Same shot, but the two men have departed and closed the door behind them, shutting us into the darkness and gloom with the madwomen. This is very Alex Toth panel, almost pitch black apart

From Hell
Chapter II: A State of Darkness

Alex Toth is one of America's prominent comic-book stylists. Toth's assured and often stark use of black-and-white is evoked here. Toth worked in comics from the early 1950s through the 1980s before working almost exclusively in animation; prominent works include Zorro, Hot Wheels, stories for Creepy and Eeerie, and Bravo for Adventure.

—SRB

from the little barred rectangle of light towars one side of the background that is the closed door with its little window. The madwoman's balloon issues from the point in the darkness where we saw her sitting last panel.

    MADWOMAN (from dark):
  Jack, is it you?

PAGE 12

(PANEL) 1

A nine panel page again here, but since every panel save for the first one is entirely black then it shouldn't be too demanding. We are with William Gull and his new bride Susan upon their wedding night. I don't have details of the honeymoon, so in this first panel we are in a fairly generic honeymoon suite at some hotel, inn or other such place. We are looking through the eyes of William Gull as he sits on the side of the bed, undressing. We see his hands entering the panel from the F/G, and in one of them he holds his shoe, which he has just taken off as he sits there cross legged on the edge of the bed, one ankle resting on the opposite knee. From within the shoe or boot he is emptying a small shower of rice grains, his balloons issuing rom off panel here. Looking past his hands, legs and the shoe we see Susan Gull standing by a dressing table on the far side of the room, full figure. She is a sturdy and fairly good looking woman in her late twenties who will ripen into a Margaret Dumont figure, physically speaking, during her late middle age. Here she stands glancing nervously across the room towards us, about to undress and put on her night gown, ready for bed. (Perhaps the long night gown hangs over the back of a chair near the dressing table. See what you think.) There is a softly-glowing lamp upon the dressing table or somewhere near by, and it is towards this that the new Mrs. Gull's hand moves hesitantly as she addresses her faltering query towards us and her new husband, who sits on the bed in the foreground, emptying rice from his shoe with apparent casualness and indifference, perhaps using his Doctor's bedside manner to take the edge from his bride's nervousness.

SUSAN GULL:
William?

SUSAN GULL:
H-husband . . . ? Might I put out the lamp before I prepare to retire? I . . . I confess I am somewhat shy.

WILLIAM GULL:
Whatever suits you best, dear Mrs. Gull. Confound this rice! Is nowhere free of it?

(PANEL) 2
Now we have in all black panel. Susan has extinguished the lamp, plunging the room into a state of darkness. The balloons belonging to Susan and William Gull issue from their respective positions in the darkness.

SUSAN GULL:
There.

SUSAN GULL:
"Mrs Gull". How strange. I am not used to it, I fear.

SUSAN GULL:
The wedding was successful, don't you think? Papa looked splendid in his uniform. . .

WILLIAM GULL:
Indeed he did.

(PANEL) 3
Again, solid darkness, with the balloons still issuing from the same places within it.

From Hell
Chapter II: A State of Darkness

>SUSAN GULL:
>...and all your young friends from the Hospital! I-is Mr. Hinton always so excitable? I feared that he would burst! He...

>WILLIAM GULL:
>Susan...

>WILLIAM GULL:
>Are your preparations yet completed?

(PANEL) 4

Same again. Darkness, with William and Susan's balloons issuing from the same places.

>SUSAN GULL:
>I...

>SUSAN GULL:
>Yes. Yes, they are.

>WILLIAM GULL:
>Then come to bed

(PANEL) 5

Again, an all black panel, this time without any balloons.

>No Dialogue

(PANEL) 6

It is still dark, but the word balloons have resumed. They now issue from points much closer together in the darkness towards the foreground.

>SUSAN GULL:
>Oh.

>SUSAN GULL:
>Oh William, I shall faint! Um. Umm...

>WILLIAM GULL:
>Dear Susan. Dear Mrs. Gull. Just move your leg a little ...

>WILLIAM GULL:
>There. There, that is it...

(PANEL) 7
Now we have an exact repeat of panel five upon page one. The tailless but interconnect balloons just hang there in the darkness. It is uncertain at this point whether we are in the darkness of Gull's marital boudoir, or that of a canal tunnel some twenty years before.

    TAILLESS BALLOON:
Oh NO! William, it's too BIG.

    TAILLESS BALLOON:
William, stop it, you're hurting me. Take it out!

    TAILLESS BALLOON:
Take it OUT!

(PANEL) 8
We are still in complete blackness, but the balloons have tails once more. They are issuing from either side of the foreground, as if the couple are still in the same bed but have moved apart, their coitus broken.

    SUSAN GULL:
Oh.

    SUSAN GULL:
Oh William, I'm SORRY. I'm sorry, but it hurt so much, and I think there is BLOOD . . .

    SUSAN GULL:
Have I upset you, husband? You seemed to groan . . .

(PANEL) 9
Solid blackness. If Susan Gull's balloons issued from the left last panel, then

Gull married Susan, Colonel Lacy of Carlisle's daughter, in 1848, according to his biography. Details of their wedding night as presented here are obviously fiction.

From Hell
Chapter II: A State of Darkness

William's balloons issue from somewhere towards the bottom right in this panel.

WILLIAM GULL:
No.

WILLIAM GULL:
I just made a little sound.

PAGE 13

(PANEL) 1

There are four panels on this page. As I see it, we have three tall panels in a single tier to kick off with, taking up the top two-thirds or three quarters of the page. Beneath that we have a wide horizontal panel for the final one, stretched across the bottom of the page beneath the three vertical ones above it. The reason for this more spacious panel layout is to accentuate the scale and size of the architecture that we spend the next three pages discussing. In this first panel, it is six o'clock in the morning and we are in the abysmal setting of Dorset Street, Spitalfields. I've enclosed a photograph, but I'm afraid I don't know which way we are looking along Dorset Street in the photo. In this first panel we are looking along it towards the end where the front of Christchurch Spitalfields loom us, almost opposite the end of the street if a little to the left. On the photo there are vague shapes visible through the smog at the end of the street that could be the front of the church, but I'm not sure, so just soak up the detail of the street and fake it from there. As we see Dorset Street here it is horribly dark and deserted. The early morning light has a quality like smudged charcoal, obscuring the few solitary figures that move within it. This is our first shot of Whitechapel..reputedly the most evil and run down street in that neighborhood..so we ought to try and capture some of the dreadful lightless ambience and squalour of the place. Admittedly, here it is dark and there are none of the sordid denizens of the area littering the front steps, but the narrow row of buildings still gives off a palpable feel of lightless human misery, with the ambiguous stains on its cobbles and walls, and the dark Caligariesque rectangles of its shop-signs jutting out into the swirling, dirty fog. As we look down the street here, we are behind the shadowy figures of Gull and Hinton, dressed in cloaks or greatcoats with top hats and out for a morning stroll, as was their custom between the hours of six and eight. We can barely make them out here..just two masses of shadow moving away from us down a narrow and shadowy street towards the dark and forbidding church that looms up at the street's far end, visible in the background here. Over the next three panels I want too attempt Winsor McCay's trick for establishing scale where his camera-eye would 'follow' at a regular distance behind his characters as they approached some huge and distant monument, so that they remain the same size while the monument gets steadily more massive in the background beyond them. As Gull walks along away from us here, he is absently picking grapes from a stem he carries and eating them. We almost certainly can't see this here, since he's facing away in terrible light, but I thought I'd mention it just so you'd know. The two dark figures chat to each other as they glide along the deserted and claustrophobic shadow-paths of the "most evil street in London". If there's any room in the F/G, perhaps we could have just-visible streetsign bolted to a wall reading "Dorset Street". If not, then leave out. Gull and James Hinton are both in their late forties, early fifties here, some twenty years having elapsed since Gull's wedding night on the previous page. The year is 1868.

Winsor McCay was the creator of Dreams of a Rarebit Fiend *and* Little Nemo, *and was renowned for his extraordinary skill drawing imaginatively detailed city landscapes and unusual perspectives.*

From Hell
Chapter II: A State of Darkness

>HINTON:
>Dorset Street ... the most evil in London, I'm told.

>HINTON:
>I apologise. Our walks of twenty years so often lead to Whitechapel, where the plight of unfortunates first racked my heart.

>GULL:
>At six in the morning, its evil is evidently sleeping, Hinton, and we are quite safe.

>GULL:
>Do have a grape.

(PANEL) 2

Same shot, with the figures the same size as we follow the same distance behind them, following them Dorset Street towards Commercial Street and the Spire of Christchurch that dominates it. In the background the church is growing slowly and ominously larger. (Shots of the church's front are included, so you'll know what the place looks like. Big and old and hellishly creepy.) Hinton and Gull are now at the end of Dorset Street, about to cross the Tramway of Commercial Street, again more or less deserted, towards the 18th century church facing them from just across the way. It's perhaps a little lighter here, but not much, and as the two men walk away from us we don't get any hint of Gull's face or appearance from the front, through Hinton can turn his head in profile from time to time if you wish, glancing at Gull.

>GULL:
>No?

>GULL:
>You should. Grapes, or raisins-with-water enliven the blood, postponing fatigue

>GULL:
>As for Whitechapel, do not apologise. I enjoy visiting churches; attempting to fathom the minds of their architects.

>GULL:
>Few churches conceal secrets like Christchurch,

Spitalfields .. or like the mind of its maker, Nicholas Hawksmoor.

(PANEL) 3

Same shot, but now the shadowy mass of Christchurch fills the entire background of the panel as Gull and Hinton cross the Commercial Street Tramway towards it, leaving Dorset Street behind them. We are still the same distance behind their two dark figures as we were before, so that they have remained a consistent size while Christchurch grows bigger beyond them. Here, they approach its wide and sweeping steps that lead up to the doric columns framing the high and massive portico.

HINTON:
I've always found it UNNERVING ...

GULL:
Intentionally so! Hawksmoor designed several London churches to be of "Solemn & Awefull Appearance" following the Pagan traditions of the ancient Dionysiac architects.

GULL:
He'd possibly also read Thomas Hobbes, the only thinker preceding your friend Coleridge to suggest that certain symbols might subtly affect men's minds.

(PANEL) 4

Now the wide panel. We are still behind the two men, but here they are mounting the steps of Christchurch

No evidence exists to prove that Gull and Hinton ever walked together through Whitechapel, although in Gull's introduction to The Life and Letters of James Hinton *he confirms that they did indeed often take early morning walks together through the relatively deserted streets of London. Gull was during this time employed at Guy's Hospital only a moderate walk from the East End across London Bridge, and Hinton's obsession with Whitechapel and its prostitutes is well documented in Mrs. Havelock Ellis'* James Hinton: A Sketch. *It thus seems at least conceivable that they may have chosen Whitechapel as the route for one of their early morning strolls, as Knight suggests in* The Final Solution.

Gull's statement that he enjoys visiting churches and attempting to fathom the minds of the men who made them is based upon assertions to this effect in A Biographical Sketch.

From Hell
Chapter II: A State of Darkness

towards the Portico-Shadows framed between the Doric Columns. The width of the rising steps fill our panel here, with the bottoms of the columns visible towards the top of the panel, spanning the page. As Gull and Hinton ascend the steps, Gull gestures expansively with his grape-free hands towards the dark and vaulted roof of the Portico, high off panel above them. Hinton maybe tilts his head back to look in the direction towards which Gull is gesturing. Gull's face remains hidden throughout as we follow the two men up the steps of Christchurch.

HINTON:
Hawksmoor follows PAGAN traditions? I am astonished!

Nicholas Hawksmoor after bust by Sir Henry Cheere.

GULL:
His cunning rhetoric concealed it, but the evidence surround us . .

GULL:
This massive Doric Portico, meant to instill a sense of "Terrour & Magnificence", would to the ancients signify such awesome deities as Hercules; Minerva; Mars . .

GULL:
Gods of strength. Gods of wisdom and war.

GULL:
Come . . let us venture within.

PAGE 14

(PANEL) 1
Another four panel page, but with a different layout. Here, the two upper thirds of the page are taken up by one enormous panel, showing a gloomy interior view of Christchurch Spitalfields, as in the reference photograph provided, only darker. The shot of the church's interior can be more or less exactly like the photo, only with added shadows. The two figures of Gull and HInton are very small, somewhere deep into the church towards the background down towards the shadowy lower right of the panel, so that we do not notice them until we have followed the echoing trail of their speech balloons across the lofty heights of the church ceiling and down through the darkness, giving us the effect of the men's conversation flinging around

The information on Nicholas Hawksmoor and his creation----Christchurch, Spitalfields----is drawn from numerous sources. In straightforward architectural terms, the authoritative text must surely be Hawksmoor by Kerry Downes, published by Thames & Hudson as part of their art and architecture series. However, all contemporary theorizing as to the meaning of Hawksmoor's architecture can be traced back to the pioneering and visionary work of London poet, author, bookdealer, and Necronaut Iain Sinclair, who first noticed the odd characteristics of Hawksmoor's churches while employed in tending their grounds for the Council. His epic poem Lud Heat (1975) set out his intuitions on the subject and provided the inspiration for Peter Ackroyd's prize-winning novel Hawksmoor (Hamish Hamilton Ltd., 1985), and for the musings on Hawksmoor in this work.
From Hell's specific association of Hawskmoor and the Dionysiac Architects is based upon Hawksmoor's well-docu-

From Hell
Chapter II: A State of Darkness

mented obsession with the work of Vitruvius (see Kerry Downes and elsewhere). Vitruvius is identified as a member of the Dionysiac Architects by Manly P. Hall in his The Secret Teachings of All Ages (Philosophical Research Society, 1928---- kindly supplied by Steve Bissette and Marlene O'Connor), from which almost all of the information relating to the Dionysiac Architects in these pages is drawn, along with occasional reference to The Dionysian Artiffcers by Hippolyto Joseph Da Costa and Manly P. Hall (Philosophical Research Society, 1964) and The Ten Books of Architecture by Vitruvius (Dover Books, 1960).

the rafters of the church. The long stream of dialogue balloons winds in a reversed 'S' shape from the top left corner of the panel down towards the lower right corner, snaking right, then left, then right as it progresses. All the early balloons in the sequence have no tails, to suggest the disconnected echo effect. Only the last couple of balloons, where specifically indicated, are linked by tails to the tiny figures of Gull and Hinton down in the lower right background. The whole purpose of the picture here is to impart a weighty sense of architectural solemnity to the matters under discussion, emphasised by the vastness and deliberately frightening contours of the dark church that we are in, eavesdropping upon the conversation between the sanguine and erudite Dr. Gull and his excitable companion Hinton, in whom middle age has not dulled the propensity to let his imagination ramble.

TAILLESS BALLOON:
It's dark.

TAILLESS BALLOON:
Hawksmoor cut stone to hold shadows... a Gothic trait, though Hawksmoor's influences were somewhat.. older.

TAILLESS BALLOON:
The Dionysiac architects?

TAILLESS BALLOON:
Unmistakably. A secret fraternity of Dionysus cultists originating in 1,000 B.C., they worked on Solomon's temple, eventually becoming

the Middle Ages' Travelling Masonic Guilds.

TAILLESS BALLOON:
Their ingenious constructions merely symbolised their greater work: The Temple of Civilization; chiselling human history into an edifice worthy of God, its Great Architect.

TAILLESS BALLOON:
Borrowing proportions from God's Temple, the human body, they sought to become one with the processes of Nature, and thus IMMORTAL.

TAILLESS BALLOON:
Perfectly attuned, their monuments supposedly rang with the voices of the ages; the echoes of futurity . . .

TAILLESS BALLOON:
Their acoustic secrets included passageways where you couldn't hear your own screams; chambers that re-echoed your merest sigh . . .

HINTON:
Like St. Paul's whispering gallery?

GULL:
Hawksmoor assisted Wren with St. Paul's. Who knows which features were his?

GULL:
Such MINDS, Hinton, shaping infinity itself!

(PANEL) 2
Now, in the remaining three panels on this page we are looking through Gull's eyes at Hinton as they stroll along through the abysmally dark church. We are looking at Hinton here, with perhaps Gull's hands in the foreground just plucking a grape from the stem. Hinton looks at us thoughtfully as he speaks, gazing through the sooty darkness. We can still see him reasonably clearly here, but as he walks along, back towards the front of the church , he is approaching a denser patch of darkness that the one which he is walking through in this panel: perhaps the slab of shadow cast by a buttress or something.

From Hell
Chapter II: A State of Darkness

> HINTON:
> You know, Gull, this puts me in mind of some theories that my son Howard proposed to me.

> HINTON:
> They suggest Time is a human ILLUSION...

(PANEL) 3

Same shot, but Hinton, continuing to stroll as he speaks, is now walking face first into the slab of shadow mentioned last panel, so that he is rapidly vanishing from our sight. He is all but gone here, a dark mass slipping into darker shadows. We needn't see Gull's hand in the F/G unless you want to, holding up the grape about to pop it into his off panel mouth. Gull's balloon issues from off pic in the F/G.

> HINTON
> ... that all times CO-EXIST in the stupendous whole of eternity. He hopes to publish a pamphlet one day ...

> GULL
> Indeed? And how shall this pamphlet be entitled?

(PANEL) 4

A solid black panel now, repeating exactly the third panel on page one of this episode. A single tailless balloon hangs there in the otherwise empty blackness.

> TAILLESS BALLOON:
> "What is the fourth dimension?"

PAGE 15

(PANEL) 1

Now we have nine panels, still continuing with the same scene. This first one, from the same Gull's eye view, shows Hinton as he starts to gradually emerge from the slab of shadow he has just walked through, his face and forward parts swimming into murky visibility here out of the blackness. In the foreground, Gull maybe picks another grape from his dwindling stem, that is if you want to show his hands. Otherwise his balloon just enters the panel from off-pic in the foreground during this sequence, allowing us to concentrate upon Hinton as he strolls, showing his nervous little movements and mannerisms.

    HINTON:
Fourth-dimensional patterns within Eternity's monolith would, he suggests, seem merely random events to third-dimensional percipients...

(PANEL) 2

Same viewpoint as we continue to walk along. Hinton is more strongly illuminated here again as he walks through a relatively light patch, but there is another slab of shadow waiting for him just up ahead. He maybe gestures obscurely towards Gull as he explains his theories.

    HINTON:
... events rising towards inevitable convergence, like an archway's lines.

    HINTON:
Let us say something peculiar occurs in 1788...

(PANEL) 3

Now a panel very much like panel three on our previous page, with Hinton just about to vanish face first into the darkness again. This time, he gestures expansively with one hand as he does so, describing his imaginary curvature of

Hinton's paraphrasing of his son Howard's theories on time and space are based freely upon C. Howard Hinton's pamphlet What Is The Fourth Dimension?, *first published in 1884. For further information on C. Howard Hinton's extraordinary life and theories,* The Fourth Dimension and How to Get There *by pop mathematician and Science Fiction author Rudy Rucker (Penguin) is also highly recommended.*

From Hell
Chapter II: A State of Darkness

events rising up through history. He is about to be swallowed up by thedarkness.

> HINTON:
> A century later, related events take place. Then again, 50 years later . . . then 25 years . . . then 12 1/2 . . .

> HINTON:
> An invisible curve, rising through the centuries.

(PANEL) 4

Now a solid black panel that exactly repeats panel eight upon this episodes first page, with the two linked or overlapping balloons hanging their tailless and unattributed in the otherwise solid blackness of the panel.

> TAILLESS BALLOON:
> Can history then be said to have an architecture, Hinton?

> TAILLESS BALLOON:
> The notion is most glorious, and most horrible.

(PANEL) 5

Now we are behind the two dark figures as they walk towards the semi—lighted opening that represents the open front door of the church, leading out onto Spitalfields, the way they came in. I should have mentioned earlier that both men would have removed their hats upon entering the church, and would hold them in one hand throughout their stay indoors, so please adjust your thinking upon the foregoing panels accordingly. They have them in their hands here as they walk, silhouetted, towards the open front door of the church, both facing away from us.

> GULL:
> Yet consider this church: Built upon "Ho-Spital Fields" where plague victims were buried . . . Plague that entered London barely a mile away.

(PANEL) 6

Now we are out the Portico, walking towards the steps that lead down to the street. Hinton is in the foreground, facing slightly away from us as he walks after Gull. We see Gull in the near background, just starting to descend the Church's front steps back towards the street, settling his hat upon his graying hair as he does so. We do not see his face.

> GULL:
> In the 1760's, troops bloodily suppressing Weaver's Riots were barricade here in Christchurch.

> GULL:
> Nearby, in 1811, the Ratcliffe Highway murders engendered our Police Force, now imitated throughout Europe.

(PANEL) 7

For these last three panels, I figure we show a shot of the two men vanishing away from us along the south side of Christchurch (see reference photo), having returned down to streetlevel and continuing with their walk. Up to you how you do this . . the reference photo of Christchurch's south face is very long and horizontal, so maybe you could use it a continuous background stretching across all three panels, with Gull and Hinton walking across it in profile (shot so as to conceal Gull's face) until in panel nine we can only see their backs jutting into the panel from off pic right as they prepare to walk off-pic. Alternately, you could just use the reference photo as a guide and angle the shot differently, so that we are looking up along the south side of Christchurch rather than square on at it. In case, the two men would get smaller and smaller as they walked away from us until they almost vanish in the shadows in panel nine. See which way you fancy, and do accordingly. Here in this panel the two men are fairly prominent as they start to walk away from the front of the church, heading along the south wall towards the far end. If you go for the profile idea, it's shot so as to exclude Gull's face, but without it looking contrived, if that's possible. If not, then the two men just walk away from us towards the background, chatting as they go, Gull still plucking grapes from his stem and devouring them at intervals.

> GULL:
> Perhaps Hawksmoor gouged more deeply an existing channel of suffering, violence and authority?

From Hell
Chapter II: A State of Darkness

The reference to the spitalfields Weaver's riots and the barracking of troops at Christchurch is drawn from Leo Baxendale's excellent historical treatise The Encroachment, *publshed by his own Grim Reaper Press (1988).*

The siting of Westminister Abbey upon the remains of an ancient temple dedicated to Apollo is derived from page 169 of A Survey of London *by John Stowe (1598), in which he states, "In this place (saith Solcardus) long before, was a temple of Apollo, which being overthrown, King Lucius built therein a church of Christ."*

GULL:
Such PURPOSE! I am fifty, my OWN purpose unrevealed, despite meaningless laurels.

(PANEL) 8

The two men either get further away from us into the early-morning darkness of Spitalfields, or, if you use the continuous background idea, they continue to stroll across the picture from left to right.

GULL:
But not Hawksmoor: His final labours raised two towers, like jackal's ears, upon a monument at England's Governmental heart . . .

GULL:
.. an Abbey built upon the ancient temple-site of Anubis.

HINTON:
Really? Which Abbey is that?

(PANEL) 9

Final panel in this scene. The two men either vanish into the shadowy distance as they walk away from us down the south side of the church, or walk off panel right with just their backs visible to us here if you go for the continuous background approach. In either eventually, the panel has a air of finality and conclusion about it.

GULL:
Westminster.

PAGE 16

(PANEL) 1

It is now 1870-71, and we have a five panel page here, followed by a seven panel page on page seventeen, the two pages comprising a complete sequence filling in some of the esoterica of Gull's masonic background and also detailing the fateful moment in his life when the Masons asked him to take care of the Prince of Wales. I propose we do this by intercutting between brightly lit panels showing Gull in 1870-71 being interviewed by leading Mason Sir Charles Warren at Freemason Hall in Wild Street, and dark-background panels showing key points in Gull's various initiations, which have happened in the past and are seen in flashback here. The differentiation between brightly lit panels and very dark panels should help the reader keep the two time-strands separate, along with the clues provided by the narrative. This first panel is a full-width one spanning the whole top of the page and showing the huge scale of the Freemason Hall interior. If you can get a copy of *Murder By Degree* to watch, then the Freemason Hall in that is pretty accurate as reference. If you can't, then I hope the following description will suffice (and apologies for not giving it to you earlier, during Gull's initiation on pages 8 & 9): The lodge hall is like a temple, or perhaps like a cross between a temple and a

Bob Clark's Murder By Death *(1979) was a fictionalized account of the Ripper murders featuring Sherlock Holmes, as played by Christopher Plummer. I will discuss the film in Book Two's Afterword.*
—SRB

From Hell
Chapter II: A State of Darkness

These pages attempt, after suggestions made by Stephen Knight in Jack the Ripper: The Final Solution, *to explain why William Gull, ostensibly a talented doctor of no great social importance, should be appointed to treat the Queen's son, Albert, Prince of Wales, as happened in 1871. Gull's sudden appointment over the head of Sir William Jenner, hitherto the Queen's favorite physician, has never been explained, and thus the suggestion of Masonic influence proposed by Knight is extremely tempting in this context.*

Details of Masonic ritual recounted in these pages are inexact and drawn from numerous sources. Since the rituals depicted here are apparently kept secret even from lower-ranking Masons themselves, problems with accurate reportage will be appreciated. Gull's initiation ordeal as a Master Mason is based freely on the research of Robert Anton Wilson as utilized in his Illuminatus! trilogy *(Sphere Books, 1977) and in his various articles for* Gnosis *magazine. Wilson may also be given credit for identifying the Ma-*

court of law. It's very large, with impressively crafted and elegant stone work, and there are wooden benches set around it's walls, perhaps with wooden speakers podiums rising from them here and there. The floor is a checkerboard of black and white squares (this is probably the most important visual detail) and set into the stone work about the walls or engraved upon plaques we see various Masonic symbols, most notably the set square and compass motif, along with the seven stars ringing a crescent moon, or anything else that takes your fancy. In this first panel, facing us to the right of the wide foreground we have a grim-faced Sir Charles Warren (see reference photos), who although we only see him in head and shoulders or thereabouts here, is dressed in his masonic apron. As we look beyond him across the wide checkered floor of the brightly lit hall we see the form of William Gull, kneeling upon one knee with his head bowed and one hand upon his heart in ritual obeisance. He does not wear his apron, but is dressed instead in his ordinary frock coat and general doctor's attire. The light in the hall is all overhead, so Gull's face is turned into blot of shadow as he bows, staring floorward, with the lower surfaces of his kneeling body similarly darkened and a tar-black pool of shadow beneath him on the chess-board floor. Behind him, the doorways and arches and benches of the Masonic Lodge Hall look on silently. In the foreground, Sir Charles

Warren doesn't look round at Gull as he replies to him, remaining starting out of the panel at us, his eyes serious, his mouth set.

GULL:
You summoned me, Grand Sojourner.

WARREN:
I summoned you as Grand Sojourner, but speak to you as Sir Charles Warren, and as such may you address me.

WARREN:
Your rise in Masonry parallels your ascent in medicine, Dr. Gull. It seems not long ago you reached the third degree, manfully suffering the ordeal required to become Master Mason . . .

(PANEL) 2
Now we have a tier of three dark-background panels, all seen from the same angle, which is through the eyes of William Gull (remember this is a flashback). We are laying on our back, looking up at three figures: one holds a ruler, one holds a set square, one holds dividers. They stand about us, as if round a coffin, looking down at us with only solid blackness behind them. They themselves are shadowy , but we can that they are three men, each wearing bizarre and expressionless eye masks that come down from the forehead to just above the top lip. This is a shadowy and creepy ritualistic scene. The guy who stands to the left we shall

sonic verbal distress signal, "Will no one help the Widow's son?"

From Hell
Chapter II: A State of Darkness

call Jubela. The one in the middle, standing facing us from the floor of the 'coffin', we shall call Jubelo. The one on the right is Jubelum. These are three Masons acting out the role of the 'Juwes', just as Gull lies there re-enacting the role of the murdered Master Mason Hiram Abiff, also known (I believe) as Hiram, King of Tyre. The voice of the worshipful master, who isn't visible here, issues from off panel in the upper darkness, probably entering the panel from the left here.

    WORSHIPFUL MASTER (off):
Speak, thou JUWES, of thy interrogations:

    WORSHIPFUL MASTER (off):
Thou, Jubelo. Did he tell you the word?

    JUBELO:
I beat him and tortured him, but he would not reveal the word.

(PANEL) 4

Same shot, only this time, the other two having fallen silent, it is Jubelum's turn to speak. The Worshipful Master's voice still issues from off panel left here.

    WORSHIPFUL MASTER (off):
And thou, Jubelum. Did he tell you the word?

    JUBELUM:
I cut out his organs of generation, and he was mute. He did not reveal the word.

(PANEL) 5

Now, spanning the bottom of the page, we have wide horizontal panel showing the brightly gaslit immensity of the interior of the Freemason's Hall at the corner of Wild Street. Here, we have a longshot of the two figures, Gull and Sir Charles, as seen from right across the other side of the echoing and Cavernous Hall, across the gleaming chessboard floor. They are too far away to make out facial features, and Gull is standing with his back to us anyway.

    GULL:
Yes. Portraying Solomon's architect Hiram Abiff, I enacted his martyrdom and resurrection.

GULL:
I remember the symbolic execution of the three treacherous Juwes...

WARREN:
Ah yes... the entrails hung over the shoulder; the stomach burned to ashes and scattered... I recall my own initiation.

WARREN:
Yours happened twenty years ago, in 1850. Later, reaching thirteenth degree, you were exalted to the Royal Arch, learning its innermost secret...

PAGE 17

(PANEL) 1
Now we have a seven panel page, starting off with three black-background panels showing a flashback to one of Gull's previous initiations into mysteries. Again, we see this through Gull's eyes, and he himself is not visible. We are looking towards an elderly Freemason who we have not seen before, the Worshipful Master of Gull's current lodge, the Royal Alpha, and nobody of any great significance to our plot, so you can make up what he looks like. He stands there in a pitchblack room, wearing his apron over his everyday clothes, and he is gazing at us as he indicates three alcoves that are set into the wall at the far end of the black room, each one a perfect little miniature altar, and each illuminated by a solitary black candle so that they are the only illuminated objects in the room, apart from the light that plays over the Worshipful Masters face as he speaks solemnly and ritually in our direction, addressing the off panel William Gull. In this first panel, as the Worshipful Master stands at a slight angle to us with his head turned towards us, beyond him we can see the left-most alcove in its entirety, and a little of the middle alcove to its left (our right) just to establish there are a row of three devotional altars set into the wall here and not just one. We can only see the contents of the first alcove clearly here, lit by candle. (Or the alcoves be unlit and the Worshipful Master could be carrying a torch or candle, if you prefer that.) In the first alcove is a chunky looking tablet of black onyx. Set into it are the three hebrew

From Hell
Chapter II: A State of Darkness

letters J.H.V., signifying Jahweh. The gold glints white from the smooth black surface of the tablets in the shifting, tilting candlelight. The Worshipful Master's face is very grave.

> **WORSHIPFUL MASTER:**
> Exalted one of Enoch's Royal Arch, know ye now the true and hidden name of the Great Architect of the Universe.

> **WORSHIPFUL MASTER:**
> He is trinity, and in part he is JAHWEH, worshipped by the Hebrews.

(PANEL) 2

Same set up, but now the Worshipful Master has taken a step along left to right as he wanders down the line of alcoves, introducing us to the triple-faceted deity. We have also moved, closing in. Whereas the Worshipful Master was three-quarter to full figure last panel, here he is only half figure as he gestures to the alcove in the middle. Set within this there is a bust of Osiris, also made from onyx. It shows the god with his hands crossed upon his breast, one holding a crook and the other one a flail. Osiris, his black onyx skin gleaming, looks very stern.

> **WORSHIPFUL MASTER:**
> In part he is Osiris, Known to ancient Egypt...

> **WORSHIPFUL MASTER:**
> ... and also is he BAAL, the horned god of the Canaanites.

> **WORSHIPFUL MASTER:**
> In sum, know ye this; his awefull name...

(PANEL) 3

Now we have closed in further upon the Worshipful Master as he steps up to indicate the last illuminated alcove set into the wall of the black room. We are so close to him now that the top of his head is off panel, and we cannot see his eyes... only his stern mouth as he speaks the secret name of god, and perhaps a little of his arms and hands as he indicates the alcove, which is the focus of our attention here: the third alcove contains as onyx bust of a black goat, its horns long and curling, its eyes slanted and mad and gleaming, and the suggestion of a malefic smile hidden in the straggly shadows of its beard. The eyes are infinitely wise and all knowing. With eyes of black stone, BAAL the goat-god of the templars stares from the panel at

> Worshipful Master:
> ... which is JAH-BUL-ON.

(PANEL) 4

Now another wide and page-spanning horizontal panel to bring us back to present and brightly lit Freemasons Hall, deserted save for Warren and Gull. In this panel Gull stands facing slightly away from us towards the right of the foreground. We are behind him at about waist level, so that his head and shoulders are off the top of the panel border here and thus invisible. We can however see his hands as he raises them in hopeless apology and supplication towards Sir Charles Warren, standing over towards the left of the panel in the near background, seen full figure here. Sir Charles stands at a slight angle to us, with his head turned to look at Gull even though he stands side on to him, hands clasped behind his back maybe with s sort of Duke of Edinburgh Gait or posture. As Warren stares levelly at Gull, the empty and vast Freemason Hall rings with the echo of their conversation.

> WARREN:
> You've since advanced two degrees, becoming Knight of the Sword. We are impressed ... hence your presence here tonight, rather than at your Royal Alpha Lodge meeting at the Mitre Tavern.

> WARREN:
> Our situation's this: A fellow mason, Albert, Prince of Wales, is ill. We would prefer that you, a brother mason, treat him.

> GULL:
> But sir ... I cannot!

> GULL:
> Surely Sir William Jenner, the queen's favourite physician, shall attend the Prince?

(PANEL) 5

Now the first of three panels on the last tier, but still within the

From Hell
Chapter II: A State of Darkness

present and the brightly lit Freemason's Hall. We are looking through Gull's eyes and thus we cannot see any of him here. Instead, we are starting at Sir Charles Warren as he stands squarely facing us, looking us gravely in the eye as he speaks. His hands are by his side, and he is just starting to turn his palms upwards and outwards as he speaks here.

WARREN:
Jenner isn't on the square. He's not one of us.

WARREN:
"Will no-one help the widow's son", Dr. Gull?

(PANEL) 6
Same shot. We are still looking at Warren and he is still staring gravely at us without the slightest change of expression. Palms upwards, he slowly brings his forearms up until they are at right angles to his body, the palms turned upwards, the arms bent at the elbow. The gesture is so formal that we know it means something. Warren simply stares at us as he waits for us to understand and respond to his hidden Masonic command, demanding help and assistance. He doesn't speak.

No Dialogue

(PANEL) 7
Now we have a close up Gull's hand and Warren's hand as the two men shake hands. The handshake is the one shown on the front cover of Stephen Knight's book *The Brotherhood* a copy of which should be enclosed. Gull's voice issues from off panel here. Beyond the handshake we can see Freemason Hall, perhaps with some suitable symbol carved prominently and ominously into the stonework, visible beyond the sealing of a Masonic pledge that is going on in the foreground with the handshake.

GULL (off):
I . . . I understand your meaning, Sir Charles.

GULL (off):
I'll do my best.

PAGE 18

(PANEL) 1

Now we have a four panel page, the first of two in a sequence detailing an encounter between Dr. William Gull and her imperial majesty, Victoria Regina. The main point to get over in these two pages, aside from the obvious plot points like Gull's appointment as physician in extraordinary and so on, is the sheer brooding monumental presence of Victoria. She wasn't just a funny little old woman who said 'we are not amused' and refused to pass legislation against lesbians because she simple didn't believe that such creatures existed. She was a holy terror of a queen, a monarch who'd presided over the building of Britain's great empiric adventure, a presence at the heart of one of the world's greatest power-blocks. Her family and servants were all shit-scared of her, and for her part she seems to have had little time for any of them, holding even her family in obvious contempt much of her time. At the same time, she was the queen who'd gone into a truly monumental sulk upon the death of her husband Albert, a sullenness hewn in marble and enduring for decades while the empire began to atrophy and rot all around her. She is a presence that has somehow transcended mortal limits and entered history within her own lifetime, a woman emotionally and politically dead long before her elaborate

Gull was made a baronet in 1872, in acknowlegment of his role in saving the life of the Prince of Wales. The character and temperament of Victoria here is entirely my own interpretation, and has indeed been the subject of debate between myself and the otherwise genial and agreeable Mr. Campbell of Taringa, Australia.

Queen Victoria

From Hell
Chapter II: A State of Darkness

funeral. It is this quality in Victoria, stone-like, historic and monumental that I want to convey here, and the way that I to do it is by using a tense and repetitive sequence of static panels. You'll see what I mean as we go along, hopefully. This first page has one big panel at the top that takes up two thirds or three quarters of the whole page area. Beneath this there are three panels that gradually close in upon a detail of the opening image. The first and biggest picture is a shot of Queen Victoria sitting in a huge and shadowy stone chamber, all alone, somewhere within Buckingham Palace or thereabouts. The room is unbearably dark, but with suggestions of huge pillars and arches rising about the walls of the chamber in the background, indistinct and shadowy masses against the miasmic dark of the chamber. Perhaps huge drapes and tapestries, equally dark, hang in a dustbound silence from some parts of the chamber, perhaps concealing windows and blocking out the light. The chamber is almost bare, and in the centre of it upon a raised stone seat cushioned with sumptuous fabrics and plush bolsters sits her imperial majesty, showing us the distinctive profile that launched a thousand postage stamps. The only source of light in the room, a comparatively weak one, seems to be issuing from off panel left, behind Victoria as she sits facing to the right. Her face is therefore completely obliterated by a mask-like blot of shadow, with only the back of her head and a little of the side of her side of her face illuminated here. She sits perfectly still in the shadows, as if carved out of the shadows herself. She already looks like one of the statues that will be erected after her death, so unearthly is her motionlessness. She doesn't look round as she speaks, and her speech balloon is a small thing, hanging in the echoing vastness of her chamber of bled into the shadows of the chamber, heightening her visual ambiguity.

VICTORIA:
Dr. Gull.

(PANEL) 2
Now the first of the three small panels that conclude this page. I should point out that we are looking through the eyes of William Gull here, Although we do not see so much as one of his hands here, or throughout the rest of the sequence. The only thing announcing his

presence is the occasional speech balloon issuing from off panel in foreground. All of our attention is rivetted upon Victoria. In this panel we seem to have closed in slightly from the massive opening shot, as if Gull were approaching the queen over these next three panels as she speaks to him. She does not move even slightly as she speaks, and it strikes me that perhaps the best way to do these two pages would be xerox machine. I think that will capture the unreal and unliving sensation endangered by the Queen's chilling stillness. Here, we have closed in so that only about three quarters of Victoria is now visible. She still sits in profile, her face a blot of shadow.

                    VICTORIA
We are indebted to you.

                    VICTORIA
It is thanks to your interventions that the life of our son has been spared.

(PANEL) 3

The same picture, but we continue to close in, until we can now maybe only see half of her Imperial Majesty, from the waist up. She still hasn't moved so much as a hair, and her face is still lost in impenetrable shadow as she speaks, so that only her distinctive profile remains.

                    VICTORIA
We are informed that you spent many hours by his bedside, lifting him bodily upon your shoulders while his bedding was changed, conversing with him in his delirium.

(PANEL) 4

Same picture, but we have now closed in to a head and shoulders shot. If you so decide to use a photocopy and the enlargement here produced a grainy effect, then I shouldn't worry about it. I figure it will only add to the inhumanity of Victoria's presence, but as ever the final decision is in your hands. Just do what looks best to you, and if you don't like the xerox idea then just ignore it. Victoria still does not move as she speaks, and her face is still hidden in shadow.

From Hell
Chapter II: A State of Darkness

> VICTORIA:
> You saved his life, Dr. Gull.
>
> VICTORIA:
> We should be interested to learn if you thought it worth the saving.

PAGE 19

(PANEL) 1

Now a nine panel page. All of the panels are almost identical, carrying on the use of static Xerox™ images, if that's what you decide to do. This panel is an exact copy of the last panel upon page 18, with the shadowy queen in head and shoulders profile, her face invisible as she listens to Dr. Gull make his startled and hesitant diagnosis upon the Prince of Wales right to be alive. His balloons issue from off panel here, in the foreground.

> GULL (off):
> Your Majesty. . ?
>
> GULL (off):
> I, uh, that is, as Heir to the throne, His Majesty is, uh . . .
>
> GULL (off):
> That is to say, ALL life is worth preserving, Your Majesty.

(PANEL) 2

Now, for the first and only time during this entire sequence, Victoria turns her head just slightly so that she is looking directly at us and the off panel Gull. The left hand side of her face (our right) is obliterated by shadow here, but upon the other half we can clearly see her recognizable Saxecoburg features and her expression of regal scorn. It is not an especially endearing face. In the assumption of absolute power implicit in its every line, Victoria's face is indeed a little frightening as we catch our brief half-glimpse of it here, illuminated in a stray of light from off the panel.

> VICTORIA:
> If you mean "No", Dr. Gull, you have our leave to say "No".

> VICTORIA:
> Our son is a wastrel and a halfwit. We shudder to think of the throne in his hands ...

(PANEL) 3

Victoria turns her face away from Gull and back towards the shadows. This panel is thus an exact copy of panel one upon this page, a xerox if you like. Her face is again invisible as she speaks.

> VICTORIA:
> ... but he is none the less of our flesh, and our obligation is most severe. .

> VICTORIA:
> ... both to yourself, and to that loyal brotherhood which you represent.

(PANEL) 4

Victoria doesn't move a muscle. Gull's balloon issues from off panel in the darkness of the foreground.

> GULL (off):
> I ...

> GULL (off):
> I am honoured, Your Majesty.

(PANEL) 5

Same shot. Victoria doesn't move as she speaks, her face still concealed by its blot of shadow.

> VICTORIA:
> Honoured you shall be, Dr. Gull.

> VICTORIA:
> In recognition of your services, we appoint you Royal Physician in Extraordinary.

> VICTORIA:
> You will in addition be created a Baronet. Does this suit you?

(PANEL) 6

Same shot, Victoria doesn't move. Gull's balloons issue from off panel in the F/G.

From Hell
Chapter II: A State of Darkness

> GULL (off):
> Your Majesty, I . . .
>
> GULL (off):
> I did only my job. Such generosity is undeserved.

(PANEL) 7

We are still in close up, and Victoria still faces towards the right of panel with her face in shadow, but she drops her head slightly here, her chin lowering to her chest with an air of great melancholy, in so much as its possible to express melancholy in a near-silhouetted outline. Her face is still in shadow, and other than this simple movement of the head, nothing else in the panel has changed.

> VICTORIA:
> We think not.
>
> VICTORIA:
> These times . . . they are such a worry to us, and it has been too long since we had men about us who were strong and dependable.
>
> VICTORIA:
> Since dear, dear Albert . . .

(PANEL) 8

We have now started to back away, so that we are now looking at the profile of the seated Queen with about half to three quarters of her full body visible. Her chin is still sunk dejectedly upon her bosom. Gull's balloon issues from off in the F/G as he backs away from Victoria. Her face is still in deep shadow as she speaks to him.

> VICTORIA:
> Go.
>
> VICTORIA:
> Go now, Dr. Gull. We would be alone.
>
> GULL (off):
> Your Majesty

(PANEL) 9

Now a full shot. Gull has departed. The queen sits alone and motionless, in full figure profile, at the centre of her dark and lonely widows' chamber. Beyond her chamber walls, the once bright Empire grows faded and moribund, as if infected by the widow queen's morbidity. Slowly, perhaps even literally, England goes to hell one step at a time.

No Dialogue

PAGE 20

(PANEL) 1

A nine panel page here. It is now the end of 1875, late November, and we are in the warm and well lit interior of William Gull's residence at 74 Brook Street, Mayfair. It is morning, and perhaps it is a cold and bright November day with sunlight streaming in through tall windows somewhere off-panel here. We have a fairly fixed viewpoint throughout this page, and it is all seen through the eyes of William Gull, now Sir William Gull, as he sits at the desk in his spacious and soberly decorated study. We see some of the desk top right up in the lower foreground as we sit behind it looking through William's eyes. Upon the desk there rests a split paper bag containing a succulent bunch of dark grapes. All we can see of William are his hands, which have been getting steadily older-looking throughout this entire lengthy episode and are now those of a man approaching his fifty-ninth birthday, although they are still the hands of a very, very strong man. Here, they are engaged in nothing more strenuous than opening the morning post. In his left hand, Gull holds a wedge of opened envelopes and their partially removed contents, the uppermost of which here is a printed card that is too small to read properly but has the general demeanor of a wedding announcement or invitation. Beneath that there is an obscured letter, and behind those some envelopes, cut open, addressed to Sir William Gull, 74 Brook Street, Mayfair, London. You probably can't read these either, as seen here, but I thought I'd just tell you what's on them in case you need to know. In his right hand, Gull holds a wooden paper-knife of elaborate design . . . or any sort of paper knife that takes your fancy, really. He is just placing the knife down

From Hell
Chapter II: A State of Darkness

Gull's daughter Caroline eventually married Theodore Dyke Acland, son of Gull's old friend Henry Acland. Indeed, it was Theodore Dyke Acland who compiled **William Withey Gull, A Biographical Sketch**, *the memoir from which much of the material in this chapter is drawn.*

The announcement of a marriage between Florence Campbell of Buscott Park and Mr. Charles Bravo seems appropriate given the reputed friendship between Gull and Florence's father, as mentioned in Suddenly At the Priory *by John Williams (William Heinemann Ltd., 1957).*
James Hinton died in 1875, and the central quotation in the letter here is taken from a letter to his son C. Howard Hinton as quoted in The Life and Letters of James Hinton. *That Hinton's thinking may have at least partially influenced Gull is suggested by Knight in* The Final Solution. *In* White Chapell, Scarlet Tracings, *Iain Sinclair's own exploration of the territory suggested by* The Final Solution, *this suggestion is echoed more*

upon his desk and towards the background we see Susan Gull. She has aged and filled out appropriately since we last saw her, and stands here smiling at her husband across his desk top. She seems a nice enough woman, at least in her dealings with her husband. She can probably be dead snotty with the servants, though. Behind her on the wall hangs a framed print of Hogarth's 'The Reward of Cruelty' (again, we maybe can't see what it is from this distance, but I'm just telling you for future reference.) I was originally going to have Mrs. Gull dusting throughout the early part of this sequence, but it seems doubtful that a lady of her station would do her own dusting. Maybe she's just entered her husband's study and is absently arranging a few things upon his shelf-tops or just good naturedly tidying up here and there while she talks to her husband. See what you think. Otherwise, just have her standing there as she addresses William, without any extra business to give her something to do with her hands. Whatever looks most natural to you, basically. The only other details, semivisible somewhere towards the background, are a small selection of framed portraits, small ones in frames, probably including shots of Gull's friends and family. We needn't get more than a suggestion of them at this distance, just standing in their little frames upon a surface over in the background somewhere, unnoticed here. Lady Gull is laughing lightly as she speaks to the off panel Sir William, only his hands visible here as he puts down the letter-opener and prepares to read the post clasped in his other hand. (Afterthought: Maybe Lady Gull's just entering the study here?)

> *poetically and forcefully:* "[Hinton] left the harpoon on the table. He forced other men to take it up."

LADY GULL:
Young Caroline's blushing. I fancy her letter was from Henry Acland's son Theodore.

LADY GULL:
What of your own correspondence, husband?

WILLIAM:
Let me see . . . something from Mr. Campbell of Buscot Park . . .

(PANEL) 2
Same shot. Towards the background, Lady Gull turns away and fusses with some ornaments of something, so that she's in profile to us here. Though fussing with the contents of her husband's study in an absent minded way she is still listening attentively to what he is saying, even though she isn't looking at him. She wears a small and pleasant smile, enjoying hearing him read out the post while she tidies. In the F/G, Sir William's hands are still visible. He has put down the letter opener and it lies on the desk near the split bag of grapes. Using his right hand he is pushing the wedding announcement up and away to reveal

From Hell
Chapter II: A State of Darkness

the letter beneath, which is in a fine copper plate hand writing even if it's too small for us to actually read here.

WILLIAM (off):
His daughter Florence marries one Charles Bravo in December.

WILLIAM (off):
Ahh. One from Hinton's son, Howard: "Dear Sir William, I write with considerable regret to inform you . . .

(PANEL) 3
Same shot. Gull suddenly goes silent and stops reading aloud. Standing in profile concerned with her tidying somewhere beyond the desk, Mrs. Gull notices the pause and turns her head to look round at us and her husband, shooting him a faintly querying glance. She is as yet unconcerned, but just curious as to why he should suddenly stop reading in mid sentence.

No Dialogue

(PANEL) 4
Same shot. Mrs. Gull, in the background, now turns back full face towards her husband, a look of distress suddenly coming over her face. She raises her hands towards her mouth in surprise, her wide eyes pained, the brows sloping up in the centre. In the foreground we see William Gull's hands as he recovers himself and continues to read from Howard Hinton's Letter.

WILLIAM (off):
". . . to inform you that my father, James Hinton, passed away this Friday last after a further decline.

LADY GULL:
Oh, William, NO!

LADY GULL:
Oh, poor James.

(PANEL) 5
Same shot. In the foreground, Sir William continues reading from the letter. In the near background Lady Gull turns away,

walking slowly towards the dresser or whatever in the far left corner of the room, over in the left background. This is where the small framed portraits are standing. As she paces slowly across the room, Lady Gull is listening to her husband, perhaps with both hands up, the fingers covering her lips as she walks. She is dry-eyed, though deeply saddened, and the posture conveys a sort of thoughtful attentiveness as she crosses the room. See what looks most natural to you, anyway, and do that.

WILLIAM (off):
"Though delirious towards the end, he remained lucid until then.

WILLIAM (off):
"Recently, he wrote: "There is a wrong, an intense wrong, in our society running all through our life . . .

(PANEL) 6

In the foreground, William keeps reading from Howard Hinton's letter. In the background Lady Gull has reached the dresser or whatever it is and is gently reaching out to pick up one of the framed little portraits that stand upon it, gazing down at the portrait sorrowfully.

SIR WILLIAM (off):
". . . and it will be made righter some day. I dashed myself against it but it is no one man's strength can move it.

SIR WILLIAM (off):
"It was too much for my brain . . .

(PANEL) 7

In the foreground, William finishes reading the letter, perhaps lowering it slightly here. In the near background, Lady Gull has turned and is walking back towards us, carrying the little framed cameo portrait. The picture is turned towards her bosom here, so we cannot see who it is. Lady Gull looks sad as she walks slowly back towards us and her husband's desk in the foreground.

WILLIAM (off):
". . . but it is by the failure of some that others succeed, and through my very foolishness shall come better success to others . . ."

From Hell
Chapter II: A State of Darkness

> WILLIAM (off):
> "... perhaps more than any cleverness or wisdom of mine could have wrought."

(PANEL) 8

William sets the letter down, on top of the other papers he's been holding upon the desk top. His broad hand rests heavily and gravely upon the papers, weighing them down the framed picture for her husband to see. It is a cameo portrait of Hinton, set into an oval, although we needn't be able to see it clearly here.

> SIR WILLIAM (off):
> Poor Hinton.

> SIR William (off):
> You were the dearest of companions; the kindest, most thoughtful men. Would that your visions might be realised. Would that I myself had the strength ...

> SIR WILLIAM (off):
> I'll do my best, old fellow ...

(PANEL) 9

Sir William picks up the little portrait of Hinton in one hand and gazes at it while in the near background Lady Gull takes a handkerchief and dabs at her eyes. The grapes gleam upon the desk top. Over in the background, maybe invisible to us here, Hogarth's doctor's cut open a body with a noose about its neck, preparing to pare the flesh from the leg and hauling the entrails out over the corpse's shoulder.

> SIR WILLIAM (off):
> I'll do my best.

PAGE 21

(PANEL) 1

Now we have a page that takes place in the early months of 1876 and details Sir William's brief involvement the infamous 'Murder At The Priory' case, which entailed the sudden death by poison of a Mr. Charles Bravo, mentioned last page. This is a nine panel page, and in this first panel we are looking through Sir William's eyes as he hangs up his hat and coat upon a hatstand in the hallway. I've just realized Bravo was kept upstairs so maybe he could have already done this and be upstairs, heading along a landing towards the room of the priory. (I've enclosed what reference of the priory I have, but I'm afraid the rest you'll have to make up as you go along. I've also enclosed pictures of the the main participants in this sordid little drama, so you should be alright for reference.) As we see Sir William's hands entering the panel from the foreground to hang up his hat and coat we see the figure of the Bravo's housekeeper, Mrs. Jane Cox, hovering solicitously nearby. Along down the far end of the spacious and elegant priory hallway we see a closed door, although it needn't be too noticeable here. Mrs. Cox, a remarkably plain and somewhat creepy woman stands there with her hands clasped together before her, as servants are wont to do. She looks at Sir William with a puzzled little smile. Her eyes, behind her spectacles, are quite sharp and cunning. It's of no importance to this scene, but if it helps you visualize the characters, then it seems quite likely that Florence Bravo, Nee Campbell, conspired with Jane Cox to poison Mr. Charles Bravo. Neither were ever convicted, and all in all the

This scene is a condensation of the vital sequence in Suddenly At the Priory *by John Williams that recounts how Sir William Gull was called in shortly prior to the death of Mr. Charles Bravo, who many believe had been poisoned by his wife Florence or his housekeeper Mrs. Cox, or both. Gull was the only doctor to plead favorably for Florence Bravo at her trial, and, because of his public standing and fame, this testimony contributed greatly to her subsequent acquittal. Various commentators on the crime have suggested that Masonic influence may have played a part in Gull's decision to aid Florence, but since the sole source for these speculations seems to be Knight's* The Final Solution *there is no reliable confirmation.*

From Hell
Chapter II: A State of Darkness

Latest theories on the murder at the priory suggest, incidentally, that Florence Bravo may have accidentally poisoned her husband by secretly administering grains of arsenic to him in the hope of making him just slightly too ill to feel like making love to her. This covertly-administered oral contraceptive, a progenitor of "the male pill," was apparently resorted to by numerous wives during this period, when childbirth often involved a risk more fatal than that posed by arsenic. In Mrs. Bravo's case, the suggestion is that she misjudged the dosage because both she and Mrs. Cox were drunk on sherry at the time.

Gull's procedure regarding the vomit, and the chillingly callous remark to Bravo that he was "heart dead already" are as recounted in Suddenly At the Priory.

case remains quite a puzzling one. Here, Mrs. Cox smiles at Sir William in the gas-mantle illuminated hallway with its leaning shadows, watching as he hangs up his coat with the gas-light dancing in the lenses of her spectacles.

MRS. COX:
You're kind, attending Mr. Bravo at the priory, Sir William.

MRS. COX:
'Tis puzzling: Sending me with the message, Mr. Campbell said "Ask if no-one will help the widow's son". . . although Mr. Bravo's father still lives.

(PANEL) 2
With Mrs. Cox walking a little in front of him, turning her head slightly to glance solicitously back at him over her shoulder, Gull makes his way down the hall towards the closed door at the end, which gets bigger in the background accordingly. As she speaks to him in hushed tones, Mrs. Cox shoots Sir William a somewhat knowing look, part of her face perhaps occluded by the hallway's shadows here. The door of the sickroom approaches.

GULL (off):
I see. What exactly is wrong?

MRS. COX:
I fear Mr. Bravo's taken poison. Mr. Campbell thought spiteful folk might blame his daughter Florence; Mrs. Bravo.

MRS. COX:
He trusts you'll investigate sympathetically, Sir.

(PANEL) 3
We have now reached the sick room door, and Mrs. Cox has paused, turning slightly towards us she speaks. with one hand she reaches out and starts to open the sick room door, smiling sweetly at us she does so. Something about her manner and indeed this entire conversation is altogether wrong, although it's difficult to say exactly what. Jane Cox smiles, the gaslight glinting on her glasses.

GULL (off):
I think I understand you, Mrs. Cox.

MRS. COX:
Very good, sir.

MRS. COX:
Mr. Bravo's through here.

(PANEL) 4
Still looking through Gull's eyes we are now gazing into the sickroom. A window is open to one side of the room, quite near us, maybe with the curtain's blowing. In the centre of the panel stands the bed, with its foot towards us, and lying sick within it, propped up on a bolster, we see the horribly ill figure of Mr. Charles Bravo, who looks towards us with heavy lidded and feverish eyes. Sitting by the bedside is Mrs. Florence Bravo, who is holding a glass of Sherry in one hand and has the remains of a bottle standing down by her feet. She is pissed out of her mind, and, looking up along with her husband at Sir William's entrance, she gestures with one wavering hand towards the open window. The room is shadowy, gaslit and dark . . . unless you prefer candles or oil lamps or something. It's the middle of the night.

GULL (off):
Mr. Bravo . . . and Mrs. Bravo, presumably. Has any vomit been passed?

FLORENCE BRAVO:
Florence Bravo, S'William. S'great privilish.

From Hell
Chapter II: A State of Darkness

> FLORENCE BRAVO:
> Charles spewed owther window, onner leads outside...

(PANEL) 5

Now, as we continue to look through Gull's eyes he has crossed to the window and stands looking out of it, his hands resting palms down upon the sill as he gazes out and down into the dark garden below. On the leads outside the window some feet down there is a puddle of vomit, stinking in the clean air.

> GULL (off):
> I see.

> GULL (off):
> Have footmen scrape it up, using pure silver spoons which won't affect the vomit's constitution.

> GULL (off):
> Now, Mr. Bravo... what have you taken?

(PANEL) 6

Now Gull has turned from the window and is looking back towards the bed, where the stricken Charles Bravo lays dying. He looks to Sir William with his dark and sunken eyes, and his voice is a pitiful croak. He has the look of a man very afraid that he is going to die... not without good cause, I might add. By the bedside, Florence Bravo tilts back the glass of sherry to her lips, draining it. If there's room in the background, creepy Mrs Cox hovers solicitously, looking on with her shrewd little eyes. If there's not room to fit her in comfortably then leave her out. As he looks towards Sir William, Charles Bravo lifts one of his trembling arms as if reaching out imploringly towards his saviour.

> CHARLES BRAVO
> Luh-Laudanum. Before God, only Laudanum... yet I'm in such pain.

> CHARLES BRAVO
> Sir William, tell me there is hope... that I shall not die...

(PANEL) 7

We are no longer quite looking through Gull's eyes, but have dropped down to the eye level of Charles Bravo as he sits there propped up in bed. We are quite close to him, and from the left of the panel we see Gull's hand reaching down into the picture from off, expertly checking the pulse of the hand that Charles Bravo was holding up last panel. Beyond the hands in the foreground we see Bravo's face as he gazes up towards an off-panel point above somewhere, presumably looking up at the off panel face of Sir William. Bravo's face is a picture of horror and despair, his eyes widening with the pupils dilating to pinpricks, his mouth contorting around an express of mortal anguish. Gull's balloon issues into the panel from the upper right here, as opposed to entering via the bottom F/G as they have been while we've been looking through his eyes.

GULL (off, right):
Hmm.

GULL (off, right):
Looking at your condition, it wouldn't be right to give you hope. There's very little life left in you.

GULL (off, right):
In fact, you're heart-dead already.

(PANEL) 8

As Gull back from the bed and we resume looking through his eyes, Mrs. Cox steps into the F/G, smiling sweetly as she reaches out to take Sir William's arm, preparing to lead him from the sick room. Looking beyond her we see the sick bed. Turning his head to one side and throwing his hand over his eyes in an extremely over-the-top attitude of tragedy, Charles Bravo lets out an anguished, sobbing moan. By the bed side, Florence unconcernedly pours herself another drink.

CHARLES BRAVO:
Oh NOOOOOOOO! Dear God, noooooo ...

MRS. COX:
You can do no more Sir William. I'll show you out.

MRS. COX:
Thank you again for calling.

From Hell
Chapter II: A State of Darkness

(PANEL) 9
We are now outside the sickroom, back in the shadowy and gaslit hallway as Mrs. Cox shows us out, walking abreast with us here and turning her head to smile with polite gratitude at us. From the sick room behind us as we walk (probably off panel right here as we turn our head to looks at Mrs. Cox, walking beside us) the balloon of Charles Bravo issues, a frantic scream, a wail for pity that ends in racking sobs. If you want, you can make Bravo's balloon shapes a little more feeble or sick-looking and wobbly or something. See what you think.

GULL (off):
Not at all. I'm always gladly at hand to relieve human suffering.

CHARLES BRAVO (off):
Have Mercy! Oh god, spare me! Ahuhuhuhuhuh...

PAGE 22

(PANEL) 1
Now another cheering scene from the everyday medical life of Sir William Gull, to give us some insight into his character and his dealings with ordinary folk. Here, it is again night time, and we are in an autopsy room somewhere at a hospital in London. It is the October of 1887, and William Gull is almost seventy years old. We are looking through his eyes so that we can only see his hands as he reaches out and draws back the sheet, uncovering the body of the unidentified male pauper lying dead upon the mortuary slab. Across the slab from us sits the dead man's sister, an impoverished-looking woman dressed in black who looks as different as possible from the women in our last scene on page 21, so as to avoid confusion. Neither does the corpse look like Charles Bravo, for similar reasons. The woman looks bitter and accusing, her mourner's handkerchief balled up in her hand as she speaks to us over the corpse of her brother. Other than a light shining from somewhere off in the foreground that illuminates the area around the mortuary slab, the rest of the autopsy room is dark. In the left background, way beyond the woman seated facing us beyond the slab, we see an opened door that

admits a rectangle of light from the illuminated hospital corridor outside. The woman has been crying, and appears to be somewhat resentful of Sir William being allowed an examination in the first place.

> WOMAN:
> Now you mind, Sir William, you're only to examine my dead brother. . not take nothin' out!

> WOMAN:
> I've 'eard about you cuttin' up poor live animals. S'why the family insisted I be here, keepin' an eye.

(PANEL) 2
Same shot. The body on the slab now uncovered, we see Gull's hands as he takes a scalpel in one of them and places the point upon the corpse's breast, preparing to make an incision. The woman on the other side of the slab sits and looks down at this somewhat dubiously. Gull's balloons issue from off panel in the foreground.

> GULL (off):
> Madame, your brother died of an interesting heart complaint.

> GULL (off):
> Your family's refusal to let me remove the organ for study, along with your presence here tonight, is most tiresome.

(PANEL) 3
Pushing the point of the scalpel in,

The incident depicted here is drawn from A Biographical Sketch, with the dialogue concerning vivisection derived from Gull's widely publicized pronouncements on the subject. Gull's exit line is genuine, though the reference to Dr. Treves is an insertion for story purposes. The heart in question is, apparently, still preserved at Guy's Hospital.

From Hell
Chapter II: A State of Darkness

Gull draws it down. A pool of dark and stale blood wells thickly around the incision, obscuring it. Gull cuts with certainty, sure of what he is doing. Beyond the slab, sitting looking on, the dead man's sister doesn't look so sure. She looks down at the welling blood and her lips starts to curl despite herself in squeamish revulsion.

GULL (off):
As for your unenlightened thoughts upon vivisection, there is no doubt that physiological experiments have benefited both animals and mankind.

WOMAN:
Bakin' dogs alive, I 'eard!

WOMAN
Ooh dear . . .

(PANEL) 4
Now Sir William's hand, the one holding the scalpel, works deep within the incision, inside the corpse's chest cavity. His other hand is also inside the wound, fumbling and tugging at something. The woman, clenching the handkerchief in both fists, raises the knuckles to her mouth and starts to turn her head away, only looking sideways at what Sir William is doing as if this diminishes its horror in some way.

GULL (off):
Baking dogs? Be assured, the good we may obtain outweighs the immorality of any such process.

GULL (off):
Now. . let me just see if I can . . . unngh . . .

(PANEL) 5
Same shot. Gull's hands emerge from the man's chest, holding his dripping heart triumphantly. The woman's eyes widen as she gazes in mute shock at this grim trophy retrieved so unexpectedly from her brother's chest. She looks utterly stunned.

GULL (off):
There.

(PANEL) 6
Same shot. The woman sits frozen in the background, staring

straight at us across the hacked-open corpse of her brother. In the foreground, looking through Gull's eyes, we see hand as he very gravely holds up the glistening heart for the woman's inspection. She just sits there, staring at her brother's heart and paralysed by the dreadful unreality of the situation.

> GULL (off):
> Now, madame, I am going to place this object in my coat pocket and leave the room.

> GULL (off):
> I trust to your honor not to betray me.

(PANEL) 7

Our viewpoint hasn't changed since last panel, but we are no longer looking through Gull's eyes. It's as if we haven't moved, but he has. We see a little of him over to the left, just entering the panel from off as he walks round the bottom of the bed, wrapping the heart in a bloodied handkerchief as he does so, his head and shoulders well off panel here. The woman doesn't look st Sir William, but sits absolutely immobile with shock staring down at the bloody hole in her brother's chest.

> GULL (off, left):
> You will excuse my haste, but I have an appointment with my colleagues Dr. Treves.

> GULL (off, left):
> Good night to you, Madame.

(PANEL) 8

Same shot, only now Gull is a small figure in the background with his back turned towards us as he walks out of the room through the open doors in the background, silhouetted against the light outside the door and not looking back as he leaves. In the foreground, the woman sits staring at the hole in her brother's chest as we face her from the same position across the operating table. She doesn't look round at Gull as he leaves behind her, but continues to stare like a hypnotized rabbit at her brother's body.

No Dialogue

From Hell
Chapter II: A State of Darkness

(PANEL) 9
Same shot. In the foreground the woman continues to stare at the body with the bloody and gaping wound in its chest. In the background, Gull has closed the door behind him as he left, making the room somewhat darker. The woman sits there in the shadowy gloom, staring at the heartless body and looking terrified out of her mind.

No Dialogue

PAGE 23

(PANEL) 1
We cut now to the London hospital for a meeting with Dr. Treves and his more infamous charge, Mr. John Merrick. I don't have a photo of Treves or any good shots as yet of the London Hospital. Maybe Steve [Bisette] and Marlene [O'Connor] have a book, or if not I suppose that we could assume that David Lynch was as accurate in his portrayal of Treves as he was in his portrait of Merrick and Victorian London, and make Treves a dapper little dark haired chap with a small beard and moustache. This is a seven panel page, with a big wide single panel taking up the middle tier and three panels both above and below it. In this first one, we are looking through Gull's eyes as he stands within the brightly lit corridors of the London Hospital. We see his hand entering the picture from the F/G, shaking the beaming Dr. Treves warmly by the hand. Beyond them,

Alan's reference to David Lynch in his panel description here is, of course, a reference to Lynch's film about John Merrick's life, The Elephant Man *(1980). Dr. Treves was played by Anthony Hopkins.*

—SRB

hospital business goes on. Maybe a closed ward door is visible somewhere in the B/G, so that we can move over to it in our next panel.

> TREVES:
> Welcome to Whitechapel, Sir William. The London Hospital is honoured.

> GULL (off):
> Nonsense, Treves! You're now Royal Physician in extraordinary and I Physician in Ordinary, yet we meet so SELDOM.

(PANEL) 2

Still looking through Gull's eyes at Treves, who has now led Gull over the closed ward door, which he is just starting to push open for Gull here, ushering him through the door with an ingratiating smile. I may be doing the guy a tremendous injustice, but I don't see Treves as a very sincere man. Let us be blunt: He did little for Merrick that was not motivated by his desire for a reputation. If Merrick had been physically normal, Treves wouldn't have troubled himself however terrible Merrick's condition might have been. Anyway, here he smiles as he starts to push the door open for the off panel Gull.

> GULL (off):
> Besides, I must meet your discovery before leaving for my holiday in Scotland.

> TREVES:
> Ah yes. Mr Merrick's through here; expecting you. I'll leave you to make your own introductions . . .

(PANEL) 3

Now we are looking through Gull's eyes as he leaves Treves off panel behind him and ventures into the room beyond the door. It is much more shadowy and dimly lit that the corridors outside, and we shall perhaps have to turn a corner a little way in front of us before we can clearly see the bulk of the shadowy looking room. Here we see Gull's hands, or perhaps just one of them as he calls out into the odd-smelling and seemingly deserted gloom of the ward.

From Hell
Chapter II: A State of Darkness

Gull's meeting with John Merrick is fictional, although plausible. It is a matter of public record that Sir William Gull and Doctor Frederick Treves, the discoverer of the Elephant Man, were respectively Royal Physicians in Ordinary and Extraordinary during this period, and thus almost certainly knew each other. Since many London doctors flooded to view Merrick during this period, it doesn't seem unlikely that Gull may have used his connection with Treves to secure such an audience.

The information relating to Merrick, including his presence at The London Hospital in Whitechapel during these crucial months and the description of Merrick as being "like some Indian idol," are taken from Treves' own account of Merrick's life in his book *The Elephant Man and Other Reminiscences*, the relevant portions of which are reprinted in *Very Special People* by Frederick Drimmer (Amjon Publishers Inc., 1973).

GULL (off):
Hmmm. Mr. Merrick? Are you within?

GULL (off):
It is, Sir William Gull, come to visit you.

GULL (off):
Mr. Merrick?

(PANEL) 4
Now a big wide panel filling the whole central tier. John Merrick stands, dressed seemingly for dinner, in the centre of the shadowy and otherwise deserted room. He stands with his huge head cocked to one side, gazing at us from the single eye that can see clearly without the obstruction of the over hanging brow. I'm sending you the one photograph I have, plus a copy of Treves description of Merrick, which might help. As he stands there in the daintily furnished and tidy ward room, Merrick looks unspeakably bizarre and vulnerable and sad. He also, it must be said, is incredibly fucking ugly.

MERRICK
Fir Whiyum.

MERRICK
I yub moft dheepy honurrt.

(PANEL) 5
Now, in these final three panels we start to close in slowly upon Merrick's grotesque form as Sir William walks towards him. Here, Merrick faces us roughly three quarter to half figure, looking straight at us, his face capable

of only the most wooden expressions, and the only real look of humanity being in his single visible eye.

GULL (off):
By the Divine Creator.

GULL (off):
Mr. Merrick, you are the most dreadfully deformed human being I have ever encountered.

GULL (off):
It is a great privilege to make your acquaintance.

(PANEL) 6

Closing in still further, we now have maybe a half figure to head and shoulders shot of Merrick, still looking at us. He laughs. The only way we can tell this is that his huge head wobbles massively, thick as a man's waist.

MERRICK:
Huhuh.

MERRICK:
Yu nho, wen bhey fhea me, moft peeble fcreem of loff, or fubtibes bhey pwetebb I luk purfecky orbimary.

MERRICK:
Your hobbesty ib moft wefweffing.

(PANEL) 7

The elephant man's huge head now fills the entire frame, the single visible eye gazing out at us hauntingly. We see Gull's hands or at least one of them, entering the panel in the foreground and casually indicating Merrick's huge head as he speaks.

GULL (off):
As is your articulacy, Sir . . .

GULL (off):
. . . though indeed, I see you have some difficulty in speaking. Might I examine you more closely?

From Hell
Chapter II: A State of Darkness

PAGE 24

(PANEL) 1

A nine panel page here, continuing the scene with Merrick. In this first panel we are still looking through Gull's eyes at his hands as he gently tips Merrick's head back to examine more closely the thick pink stub of horn that juts out, deforming Merrick's upper lips. Merrick seems quite happy to let Gull examine him. He is used to this treatment, and has known none kinder or more respectful.

MERRICK:
Pleve, be by geffp.

GULL (off):
Thank you.

GULL (off):
Hmmm. I see there is a thick pink stump of bone, protruding from your upper jaw. It almost turns your lips inside out . . .

(PANEL) 2

No longer looking through Gull's eyes, we are looking at Merrick side on as he lowers himself down to sit in a chair, tired of standing. Gull stands behind the chair, his head and shoulders invisible off the upper panel border. As Merrick sinks wearily into his chair, Gull is reaching into his coat and starting to pull out a tape measure, which maybe isn't visible yet here. Perhaps we just see him reaching into his coat without knowing what he's reaching for.

MERRICK:
Yeff . . . wem I wof im buh fide-foh, bug poafpug-arpiff dwoo ip ab a fingle tufk.

MERRICK:
Bhey caw be bug "Eweffub Mab". Ip wof moft cwuel.

(PANEL) 3

Looking thorough Gull's eyes again as he stands slightly there behind the seated Merrick, whose great head is turned so we can see at least a sliver of his awful face as he sits facing mostly away from us in the near background, the shadows of the ward rising up all around him. In the F/G we see Gull's hands, looped between them we see a stretch of tape measure.

> GULL (off):
> Indeed. Yet perhaps those cruel poster-artists paid you a compliment without their realizing.

> GULL (off):
> Tell me, Mr. Merrick, have you heard of Ganesa?

(PANEL) 4
No longer looking through Gull's eyes we swing to the front of Merrick for a half figure to head and shoulders shot of him as he sits facing us, looking grave. Standing behind his chair is Gull, head and shoulders off the upper panel border, invisible to us here. Gull has looped the tape measure around Merrick's giant head and is starting to try and measure it. His balloons come from off panel above as he speaks. Merrick's one eye looks thoughtful, as if trying to recollect the name 'Ganesa'.

> MERRICK:
> Gameefa? Mho . . . buh mabe iff Umfabiwiuh.

> GULL (off):
> Ganesa is the Indian God of Wisdom: An elephant-headed deity with a single tusk.

> GULL (off):
> Just think . . . in India, you would be WORSHIPPED.

The identification of Merrick with Ganesa is a notion suggested in Iain Sinclair's White Chapell, Scarlet Tracings, *and is resorted to by a current author as an earlier attempt to identify Merrick with the demon Leviathan (sometimes depicted with the head of an elephant) proved abortive. Additional material gleaned from Donald A. Mackenzie's* Indian Myth and Legend *(The Gresham Publishing Co., 1913) would seem to support Sinclair's speculation by identifying Ganesa as the deity to be consulted at the commencement of an important venture, an attribute that assumes ominous significance in light of later events in our narrative.*

From Hell
Chapter II: A State of Darkness

(PANEL) 5
Closer up now upon Merrick, so that his face fills the panel again. He tilts it up slightly, as if looking up at an off panel Sir William, and his single visible eye is trained upon something beyond the panel border. Around his brow we see the tightly looped tape measure, with Gull's thumb just marking off a cranial size of some thirty four inches. Merrick's eye gazes upwards with a sort of sad interest that is quite poignant.

MERRICK:
Worfipped?

GULL (off):
Oh yes. Offerings are made to Ganesa at the commencement of any great journey or important venture.

(PANEL) 6
As with Panel Five, we are not looking through Gull's eyes here. Maybe we see a little of his front entering the panel from the left, his hands busily refolding or rolling up the tape measure, ready to pop it back in his pocket. Merrick sits in front of him gazing up at the largely off panel Sir William with rapt attention. Both men's large shadows are thrown upon the wall behind them, grotesquely, from some off panel, gasfueled light source. Merrick looks particularly strange in this light.

GULL (off, left):
Why, I've heard Dr. Treves himself liken you to "Some Indian Idol".

GULL (off, left):
Rest assured, Mr. Merrick, you are a creation of God, and all his makings are wondrous. . none more than yourself.

(PANEL) 7
Merrick seated, perhaps seen from a slightly different angle here so that we can see the door leading out of his ward over in the background somewhere. See what suits you best. Looking up at Gull's off panel face, Merrick extends one deformed flipper for Gull to shake, which Gull does warmly, his balloons issuing from off

panel. Merrick seems bemused to have met someone who treats him so perfectly ordinarily.

> GULL (off):
> Now, you must excuse me, but I have winter holidays to undertake.

> GULL (off):
> I hope I may visit you again, sir.

> MERRICK:
> Yeff. YEFF pleeze bu. I fudd like that.

> MERRICK:
> Gub evemim to yhu, Fir Whiyum.

(PANEL) 8
Same shot. Over in the back ground we catch a glimpse of Gull's back as he leaves. In foreground, Merrick sits staring reflectively into space, there within his shadowy little room. He doesn't look round at Gull as he leaves, less through bad manners than through his extreme difficulty in moving his enormous head.

> No Dialogue

(PANEL) 9
Same panel as our last one, Only in this one the door in the background is closed and Gull has departed, no longer visible here. In the foreground, Merrick cocks his head poignantly to one side and gazes up wistfully into the dark spaces of his chamber.

> MERRICK:
> Worfipped . . .

PAGE 25

(PANEL) 1
Now it is less than a week later, and we are up in October Hill of Scotland, near Gull's Scottish holiday home. We are looking through Gull's eyes here, as he is out walking with his daughter Caroline, now a young woman in her early to mid twenties. They

From Hell
Chapter II: A State of Darkness

are both bundled up against the cold, and Caroline is turned to look towards her father as she walks, smiling excitedly. They are walking up a relatively steep slope, and all around them there is a dense white mist blowing across the soaking grass at their feet. We can see Gull's hands here as we look through his eyes. One holds a bag of grapes, while with the other he gestures to his daughter to run on ahead of him up the hill. I've no reference on Caroline Gull, I'm afraid. Make her up.

CAROLINE:
... and you really met the Elephant Man, Papa?

GULL (off):
Yes, yes. Now run ahead to the house and tell your mother I'll arrive once I've negotiated this blasted hill.

GULL (off):
And tread carefully in this mist!

(PANEL) 2

We are still looking through Gull's eyes, and can maybe still see the hand holding the open bag of grapes, up in the foreground. He is trudging slowly and laboriously up the slope in the thick and rolling mist. Up ahead of him we can just see the rear of his daughter as she runs away ahead of him, vanishing within a few paces into the rolling eerie fog that has collected in the troughs between the hills. Gull's labored breathing enters the panel from off pic in the foreground as he ascends the hill.

GULL (off):
Huhhf ...

GULL (off):
Huhhf ...

(PANEL) 3

We continue to look through Gull's eyes as he continues up the slope, through mist that rolls slowly, like milk in tea. There is a figure standing in the fog up the slope ahead of Gull, standing as if waiting for the old man to catch up. Gull calls out in exasperation to it through the fog.

> GULL (off):
> Huhhf. .

> GULL (off):
> Who's there? Confound this Scottish fog . . .

> GULL (off):
> Caroline? Is that you?

(PANEL) 4

Sir William has climbed a few laboring paces, and we are nearer to the figure now. The mist billows back briefly, revealing the small intense man who stands there in the fog, staring coldly at Sir William. He wears the garb of the early Eighteenth Century, carrying a set of dividers in one hand and a set square in the other. Or maybe, since we've got the square and dividers coming up again in a minute, the man could be carrying a theodolite here instead. See what you think. The man has his hair worn long, in ringlets, according to the fashion of his day rather than the later roman-style haircut added by his sculptor, but otherwise the man's face is every bit as cruel and cold as that off his black plaster bust, now standing in All Souls College, Oxford. We can still see Gull's hand holding up the grapes in the F/G, but we are looking past them at the strange man who stands in the mist gazing unblinkingly at us. His name is, or was, Nicholas Hawksmoor. He remains silent.

> GULL (off):
> H . . . ?

> GULL (off):
> Hawksmoor? Nicholas Hawksmoor? Old Nick himself!

> GULL (off):
> You knew your purpose, Hawksmoor. H-have you come to tell me mine?

(PANEL) 5

Gull stumbles onward, up the slope and into the mist, reaching out one hand towards Hawksmoor. The grim faced and silent architect seems to recede, however, the mist billowing up to cover

From Hell
Chapter II: A State of Darkness

him and his gray shape melting away as if it had never been. Other grey shapes seem to billow up ambiguously in the mist, too vague to see if there is anything there or not. Sir William clutches his grapes defensively to his bosom as he stumbles on up the hill.

GULL (off):
Hawksmoor? Don't go, fellow!

GULL (off):
This hill is so steep, and I am of a sudden so confoundedly hot . . .

GULL (off):
See. I am sweating.

(PANEL) 6

We continue to look through Gull's eyes stumbles up the hill through fog. The mist draws back now to reveal another figure . . . That of an old man in a pair of breeches and a waistcoat, his shirt sleeves rolled up. One of the old man's eyelids is lowered, in a strangely lifeless and mirthless wink. Through the other eye, old John Gull glares reproachfully at his son. A vaguer grey figure is visible beyond him.

GULL (off):
F-Father?

GULL (off):
Are you here too? Father, I am almost seventy, and the Lord has found me no special task . . .

GULL (off):
Wh-who is that ahead of you, up the slope . . . ?

(PANEL) 7

Leaving John Gull behind somewhere, William Gull stumbles up the slope, towards its crest. Ahead of him now stands the sad and sympathetically pitying figure of James Hinton. He looks at Gull with infinite sympathy and sadness, and as he does so he is holding out one of his hands as if indicating something to Gull, something just out of sight over the crest of the hill. Like the other ghosts, Hinton says nothing.

Alan Moore

GULL (off):
Hinton! Dear chap, how splendid to meet with you again! I am so happy, my heart is pounding fit to burst.

GULL (off):
What are you indicating fellow? Something over the hill? Something you wish me to observe?

(PANEL) 8

We are no longer looking through Gull's eyes. Instead we have a ground level shot from the side as he trudges up the last couple of feet of the hill, towards its brow where the grass suddenly flattens out. Here we see Gull's lower body as he trudges weakly up the remainder of the slope, the mist clinging about his feet. There is no sign of Hinton, John Gull or Hawksmoor. There's just an old man staggering around in the blinding mist, suffering a stroke. He puffs as he stumbles up the hill, his head and shoulders and indeed most of his upper body off panel here. We can still see his hand clutching the grapes to his chest.

GULL (off, above):
Very well . . .

GULL (off, above):
Huhhf . . .

GULL (off, above):
Very well . . . let us . . .

(PANEL) 9

Same shot as last panel, only now Gull's feet have reached the top of the hill and take their first couple of steps along the flat grass at the top before stopping dead, staring at something off panel right, his balloon issuing off panel where his unseen head and shoulders are.

GULL (off, above):
. . . see . . .

PAGE 26

(PANEL) 1

Only one panel on this page, filling the whole area. We are up

From Hell
Chapter II: A State of Darkness

Alan Moore worked with artist Garry Leach on a two-part Warpsmith story, "Cold War, Cold Warrior," which was originally published in Warrior #9-10 (1983). This story was later reprinted by Eclipse Comics in the collected Axel Pressbutton. Another Warpsmith story that was written around the same time, "Ghostdance," was also completed by Garry Leach and published in A1 Book One (1989).
—SRB

way behind Gull somewhere, so that he is absurdly little figure standing facing away from us right at the bottom of the picture, probably too tiny to notice on first glance at the page. He stands at the mouth of a path leading towards the picturesque holiday home that the Gull family maintain up here in the hills of Scotland. The house too, though bigger than Gull, is very tiny here compared to the picture as a whole. The house is surrounded by a beautifully wild Scottish scenery with a huge expanse of sky like a giant's runny grey water-colour, in which pearl-coloured masses moves against fields of dark slate and even black. Gull stands frozen stock still at the neck of the path leading to his little holiday home, gazing fixedly up into the huge grey expanse behind the house is God. God, in this instance, is a triple entity around hundred feet tall. The three beings that make up God sit with their backs touching towards the centre, one in profile facing left, and seated upon some throne we cannot see, one similarly seated in profile facing right and one in the centre sitting on its haunches and facing us. I don't know if you remember the arrangement of the three giant black warpsmith in those old 'Warpsmith' stories that Garry Leach and I did, But I see these three giant entities as being seated in a similar triptych. They might be fused at the back for all we know. The one on the left is Jahweh, a humanoid figure that can either be William Blake's naked beard ancient of days of some more cloaked and hooded gnostic representation, with maybe a cloth over its profiled face with the Hebrew letters J. H. V. in gold upon the brow. In either eventually, the giant figure of Jahweh holds a set square in one hand and a compass or dividers in the other. Its face, if we can see it, is terrifying stern and angry. The one on the right is Osiris, for which see the reference photos. . . a mummy-god, with only the face and hands free of bandages, a great helmet set upon his head. His hands are crossed across his breast, and in one he carries a crook while in the other he holds a flail. The skin on Osiris is a solid and unreflective jet black as he stares out with a remote and inhuman expression across the bleak grey hills of Scotland. The God in the centre is BAAL, and it is the most frightening. Very simply, it is a giant black goat, and its slanted and all-knowing eyes are staring right at the little tiny figure in the pathway far beneath it, where William Gull feels the warm urine spreading down his trouser legs as he gazes back into the unblinking eyes of the goat that is the centermost component of the entity known as Jahbulon.

No Dialogue

PAGE 27

(PANEL) 1

Now a nine panel page. This first panel is a virtual repeat of the last panel upon page 25, in that we show Gull's lower body as he stands rooted to the spot and stock still upon the wet grass, some tendrils of mist still rolling heavily like cigarette smoke about his rooted feet. He wavers, trembling slightly, and the bag of grapes tumbles from his nerveless fingers towards the wet grass. Stabbing pains shoot along Gulls arms and legs and he hears a huge gong crash once, somewhere far away inside his head, deafeningly loud and reverberant.

GULL (off, above):
Juh . . .

(PANEL) 2
Same shot, but here Gull sinks slowly down upon one knee,

doing so without revealing his head and shoulders, which are still off the upper panel border. Maybe last panel was up to Gull's waist, so that he can still kneel here without revealing his head. As he kneels, the pose echoes exactly his posture when kneeling during his initiation to Freemasonry: He falls upon one knee as if in obeisance, and he clutches one hand to his heart, just as he presented the compass points to his breast back at the initiation. He is sweating profusely, if this is visible, and the fallen grapes lay scattered upon the grass at his feet. His balloon comes from off panel above.

GULL (off, above):
...juh...

GULL (off, above):
...jah...bul...on...

(PANEL) 3

Now we are in the kitchen or some equally suitable room of the Gull holiday home, with a big window looking on to the misty grounds before the house. Over by the window, looking at the tiny misty figure kneeling out at the bottom of the bath, we see Gull's daughter Caroline. She is looking very apprehensive and alarmed all of a sudden as she stares out of the window, maybe far enough away from us to be roughly half to three quarter figure here. In the F/G, looking both towards her daughter and the window we see Lady Gull, who is suitably aged since her earlier appearances. I figure Lady Gull is roughly head and shoulders here, facing slightly away from us with enough of her face visible for us to see the sudden pang of alarm that passes across it as she realises that her husband is having some sort of attack. Out in the grounds, indistinct in the mist, William Gull kneels looking upwards and struggling for breath, the sweat dripping from his brow. He need only be a tiny dot here, if indeed we can see him at all. Just the look on his daughter's face will probably be enough.

CAROLINE:
M-mother?

CAROLINE:
Mother, is something wrong with papa? He's kneeling down, before the house.

LADY GULL:
Oh dear God, it's his heart. Quickly, Caroline! Fetch your husband!

(PANEL) 4

We are now back out on the wet grass with William Gull. He kneels sweating and trembling in the F/G, still with his head and shoulders off panel, and we have a nearly ground-level shot here looking past him to where we see the house. Off down the path in the background, running frantically from the house towards us and her stricken husband we see Lady Susan Gull, her skirts gathered up as she runs, quickly as she can considering her years. Some way behind her, also running from the house but with considerably more vigour we see Caroline Gull and a young doctor of about thirty named Theodore Dyke-Acland, the husband of Caroline Gull. Lady Gull cries out, a look of dreadful apprehension upon her face as she runs towards us across the slippery grass, still adorned with torn tatters of mist. I don't know how much we can see of the house in the B/G here, but if we can see it we can no longer see anything standing behind it. . . Just rising hills and cigarette-ash-coloured clouds rolling off towards some Hibernian infinity.

LADY GULL:
WILLIAM!

LADY GULL:
William, husband, are you ALL RIGHT?

(PANEL) 5

Now we are looking through Gull's eyes as he kneels there. Lady Gull stoops down towards us with a look of tremendous worry and concern, perhaps reaching out one foreshortened arm to clasp our off panel shoulder as we kneel before her. Running up from the background we see Theodore Dyke-Acland and a worried looking Caroline Gull. Acland seems cool and professionally in control. . . A dependable young chap in an emergency, is Acland. Gull babbles from off panel in the foreground.

GULL (off):
Juh . . . jah . . . bul . . . on . . .

From Hell
Chapter II: A State of Darkness

The account of the stroke suffered in October 1887 is based on the account given in A Biographical Sketch. Reportedly, the stroke had only slight physical repercussions, but severe mental ones, and was marked by an occurence of aphasia---known to cause all manner of strange hallucinations, though the particular hallucinations suffered here are entirely my own invention.

Gull's sinking to one knee during the stroke is as described in his memoir, although I have chosen to interpret this an an act of obeisance, based on its postural resonance with the Freemason initiation ceremony depicted earlier.

GULL (off):
Jahbulon . . .

LADY GULL:
Oh, Dr. Acland, whatever is he SAYING?

LADY GULL:
William? It is Susan. Husband, do you KNOW me?

(PANEL) 6
Still looking through Gull's eye's but now Theodore Acland has moved in front of the distraught Lady Gull and is reaching out towards us to help us to our feet, perhaps taking one of Gull's arms that we see protruding into the panel from off in the foreground here. Caroline and Lady Gull hover in the background, looking very worried. Acland remains cool and professional.

ACLAND:
It appears my Father-in-Law has suffered a stroke to the heart: They sometimes cause Aphasia, with hallucinations and impairment speech.

ACLAND:
Come, Sir William, can you walk? Let us get you to the house . . .

(PANEL) 7
Sir William is now standing, after a fashion, and is being slowly assisted towards the off panel house by his relatives, with Acland and his wife Caroline supporting the old man while Lady Gull hovers nervously behind them. We are

looking down upon the family group from some way above them where as they start up the path towards the off panel house. (Sorry I have no reference for the house. I think it was at a place called Killiecauldie, if that helps.) Since we are above them here and since William Gull's head is hanging down upon his chest as he walks we cannot see his face here, even though we're not yet too far above the party for all their details to be invisible.

    CAROLINE GULL:
Oh, POOR papa. Theodore, will he be all right?

    ACLAND:
I think so, dearest.

    ACLAND:
There, Sir William. Carefully does it now...

(PANEL) 8

We continue to pull up into the sky, so that the party are now considerably smaller and we can see at least some of their holiday cottage as they walk towards it up the path, the rolling grassy hills and the mist widening around them as we pull back.

    WILLIAM GULL:
Jahbulon... juh... juh...

    LADY GULL:
Oh, William, don't try to talk. it frightens me so.

    CAROLINE:
Javelin? Is he trying to say "Javelin"?

The incident depicted here is a necessary elaboration of Knight's hypothesis. According to Knight, Gull was asked to intercede on Victoria's behalf by a Masonic intermediary---none other than then-Prime Minister of England Lord Salisbury.

However, later evidence suggests Salisbury could not possibly have been a Freemason. Thus, in light of Victoria's relatively intimate relationship with her physician, I decided to do without the intermediary and make Victoria herself the source of the request.

From Hell
Chapter II: A State of Darkness

(PANEL) 9
We pull right back up into the grey sky and the rain sodden low clouds. The house is now tiny beneath us; The people walking slowly towards its front door merely a straggling group of tiny black ants. We are so high that a few small and lowly grey clouds are starting to float miserably between us and the bleak landscape below, where the ants stumble along in the wake of their close brush with death. This is what the worlds looks like to God.

GULL (way below):
Jahbulon.

PAGE 28

(PANEL) 1
It is now the early months of 1888, and we are back in the darkness of Victoria's chamber at Buckingham Palace for another static page detailing an audience between Gull and the Queen. Unless you're getting tired of it, I figure we can keep up the tension by making this page almost exactly the same as our last Victoria sequence, even using the same xeroxed picture of her if you think that's a good idea. There are nine panels on this page, and in this first one we have our standard full figure to three quarter figure longshot of Victoria in shadowy profile as seen through Gull's eyes as he approaches her from across her enormous lonely chamber. She doesn't turn to look at him as she speaks, and her face is in a blot of shadow. She doesn't move.

VICTORIA:
Sir William.

VICTORIA:
We trust you are quite recovered from your illness of the heart?

(PANEL) 2
Maybe by enlarging the Xerox™ picture, we close in now so that Victoria is roughly half-figure. She still doesn't move a muscle. Up to you whether we see any trace of Gull in the foreground. . hands or whatever. . just do whatever looks most natural to you.

GULL (off):
Physically never better, Your Majesty. Why, I feel quite another man.

GULL (off):
Your Majesty, Might I ask why I've been summoned?

(PANEL) 3
Now we've completed the close in, coming to rest upon the familiar head and shoulders shadowy profile of the Queen, her face obscured, motionless as she speaks.

VICTORIA:
You may.

VICTORIA:
It concerns our grandson, the Duke of Clarence ... known to his intimates, we believe, as "Prince Eddy".

(PANEL) 4
Same shot as above. Nothing changes. Nothing moves.

VICTORIA:
Recently, his foolish mother took it upon herself to entrust her son's social education to an "artist" of her acquaintance ... a Walter Sickert.

(PANEL) 5
Same again. Nothing moves as Victoria speaks.

VICTORIA:
Under Sickert's "care", our grandson has apparently fathered a bastard child upon some filthy shop-girl.

VICTORIA:
Worse, he has secretly MARRIED her.

GULL (off):
Y-your Majesty ... ? Are you SURE?

(PANEL) 6
Same shot as above. Nothing moves, especially Victoria. She just sits there with the shadows behind her. (Maybe the shadows could move if you need some mobile visual element ... Just differences in the weight of the cross hatching or whatever you think works.

From Hell
Chapter II: A State of Darkness

This meeting between Gull and Netley is entirely my own invention, based upon their alleged subsequent partnership as described in The Final Solution.

VICTORIA:
Our informant, the Duke's coachman, is currently below stairs. You may inspect him as you leave.

VICTORIA:
His name is "Netley"

(PANEL) 7
Same shot again. Victoria doesn't move.

VICTORIA:
Our grandchild and his "wife" have been forcibly separated, and the boy severely chastened.

VICTORIA:
The woman, one "Anne Crook", has been taken to Guy's Hospital to await your attentions.

(PANEL) 8
Finally, Victoria turns her head to look at us full face. Her expression is cold as marble, utterly without human feeling of any kind. She isn't a woman. She isn't even a person: She's a Monarch. An Empress.

VICTORIA:
We have promised our grandson that she shall not be killed . . .

VICTORIA:
. . . but if this scandal is not to rock the throne, she must be silenced.

(PANEL) 9
Victoria turns away again, resuming exactly the same position as the first seven panels on this page. Her face is once moore invisible through the veil of darkness.

VICTORIA:
We leave it in your hands, Sir William.

VICTORIA:
That is all.

PAGE 29

(PANEL) 1
Now we have nine panels detailing the exchange between Dr. Gull and John Netley, who we last saw driving the coach for Sickert and Eddy back at the opening of Chapter One. As we see him here, we are looking at him through the eye of William Gull as he stands by his black coach in a stable yard somewhere out back of Buckingham Palace. Netley is two or three years older than when we first saw him, but has changed very little. He's still a faintly smelly and repugnant looking pit-bull of a man with crafty and ingratiating eyes always looking for the main chance. He stands here with his black coach filling the panel behind him, ready to open the door for Sir William, who cannot see at all here as we look through his eyes. As Netley rests his left hand on the coach door, ready to open it, he extends his somewhat grubby right hand for Sir William to shake, his features split by an unpleasantly broad and pally grin.

NETLEY:
Netley. John Netley. Right glad to meet you, Sir William.

NETLEY:
I trust my efforts have been of service to her Majesty?

(PANEL) 2
Same shot exactly. Netley still stands with hand extended, waiting for Sir William to shake it. The broad smile seems to freeze and die upon Netley's face here as he gradually realises that Sir William has no intention of shaking his hand whatsoever.

GULL (off):
Indeed. You've alerted us too danger which I've been assigned to remedy.

From Hell
Chapter II: A State of Darkness

> GULL (off):
> Please remove your hand, sir. I shall not be requiring it.

(PANEL) 3

Same shot. Deeply embarrassed by his social gaffe, Netley turns his shifty eyes towards the cobbles at his feet, shifting uneasily. He obviously cannot charm Gull in the same way he can other people, and in consequence, Gull makes Netley feel very edgy and ill at ease. The hand with which he'd been going to shake Sir William having nothing else to do, now rises and pretends to scratch at Netley's head just behind hie ear, as if that's what he'd been meaning to do with it all along. With his left hand he starts to pull the carriage door open, so that Sir William can climb in. Chastened, he looks down at the ground as he speaks, unable to look at Sir William.

> NETLEY:
> Oh. Oh, right you are, Sir William.

> NETLEY:
> I, Uh, I hope putting this matter to rights will not prove tiresome to your Lordship.

(PANEL) 4

We are still looking through Gull's eyes as he climbs into the coach, and thus we can't see Netley here, since he's momentarily behind Sir William. Looking through Gull's eyes we see his hands as he pulls himself up into the dark, plush interior of the coach. We shall be seeing the interior of this coach again later in our story, in much grimmer circumstances, so if its possible to give it a certain creepiness here, just subliminally, then please do so. Just make it very shadowy and dark or something, with the odd glint of a brass fitting gleaming from the darkness. Design it with an eye to how it will look when its covered in blood.

> GULL (off):
> Putting matters to my rights is my PROFESSION.

> GULL (off):
> ... and please do not call me "Your Lordship". Sir William will be quite adequate, or simply "Sir".

(PANEL) 5

Gull is now seated, and we are looking through his eyes. Netley, outside the coach, is looking in somewhat apprehensively through the window as he pushes the door closed behind Sir William. He looks as if he's making an attempt to make up for his earlier faus pas, and somehow find a way into Sir William's good books. He looks at us through the coach window with an almost puppy dog expression upon his broad and somewhat ugly features.

NETLEY:
Oh. Right. My apologies, sir.

NETLEY
Please don't mind my rough manner. I hope to prove most useful her Majesty. . and to you, sir.

(PANEL) 6

We are now outside the coach with Netley. We are up in front of the horses here, so that over to the right of the foreground one of the horses is staring at us dully with the black mass of the coach in the middleground to the right, behind it. Netley stands towards the foreground over on the left, perhaps just making some final adjustment to the bridles before swinging himself up onto the box to begin his ride. He could even be in the act of climbing up onto the box here, if that flows more smoothly into our next panel. Sir William's balloons issue from inside the coach, out through a window as he speaks to Netley. We cannot see him.

GULL (from coach):
Useful to ME? Hahaha!

GULL (from coach):
Mr. Netley, were I a student of Physiognomy, I'd undoubtedly find your remarkably shallow brow and closely-spaced eyes indispensable.

(PANEL) 7

Now just a shot of Netley, perhaps a profile, as he climbs up atop his box and takes up the long blackleather whip that lies there. He smiles with a moronic smug pleasure at what he takes to be Sir William's compliment, looking very pleased with himself

From Hell
Chapter II: A State of Darkness

in an almost childish way. Sir William's balloon enters the panel from behind Netley as the Doctor carries on the conversation with his driver from inside the coach.

NETLEY:
Oh. Well, very kind of you to say so, Sir William. I'd be honoured to assist your Lordship in any way.

GULL (off):
Hahaha! Who knows, Netley?

(PANEL) 8

We are now outside the wrought iron gates of the stable yard, which are heavy and black. Footmen to either side of the panel are pulling the heavy gates back over the cobbles of the yard to let out the dark coach, which we can see Netley starting to steer towards us from the background here. Sir William's balloon issues from the coach's window again. We cannot see him here.

GULL (from coach):
The Lord creates us all with good reason.

GULL (from coach):
Though in your own instance his motives would seem impenetrable, perhaps you'll one day discover your Divine purpose...

(PANEL) 9

Now just a closing shot of the horses hooves... or perhaps just the front hooves of one single coach-horse if that looks better, as they clop their way over the slippery and fog-dampened cobbles leading out of the yard and into the street. Gull's balloon enters the panel from off-pic above.

GULL (off, above):
...just as at times I think I hear the footsteps of my own.

GULL (Off, above):
Guy's Hospital, Netley. At the double.

PAGE 30

(PANEL) 1

A seven panel page, set within the confines of Guys Hospital, little changed since the earlier sequence with Hinton some forty-odd years before, except in small details here and there. In fact, on these last three pages we are in almost exactly the same part of the hospital as we saw during the Hinton sequence, so it'll maybe be easier to slightly modernise a few significant details and make the passage of time subtly noticeable to these readers who bother to compare the two pages. In this first panel, we are looking once more through the eyes of Sir William at his son in law, Theodore Dyke-Acland, who is running along the corridor towards Sir William with a look of anxiety as he draws within speaking distance. In the foreground, Sir William lifts one hand towards the younger man, as if to calm his needless anxieties. Beyond them, hospital life goes on.

ACLAND:
Sir William! I raced here to Guy's when I received your message. It is not your heart ?

GULL (off):
No, no, rest easy, young Acland. I am well.

(Panel) 2

The men have turned now, and are looking at a different view of the hospital interior. Gull has one hand upon Acland's shoulder and is gently steering him towards the top of the staircase that we saw him leading Hinton down earlier in this episode. With his free hand, Sir William perhaps gestures towards the stair-top. Turning his head to look at Sir William as he walks along, Dyke-Acland looks somewhat mystified and confused.

GULL (off):
There's an operation to be performed upon one of the madwomen kept for me here. I shall need your assistance.

GULL (off):
It's this way.

From Hell
Chapter II: A State of Darkness

> ACLAND (off):
> But why me?

(Panel) 3

They are starting to descend the shadowy staircase here, with Acland in the lead glancing anxiously back at Sir William as he walks, the shadows of the two men looming ominously upon the stone wall immediately beyond them. It's up to you how you angle this shot, through Gull's eyes or otherwise. So long as we don't see his face for just a couple more pages. Acland still looks a little nervous and uncertain as he gazes back at Sir William, a condition perhaps accentuated by the lamplight and shadows.

> GULL (off):
> The operation involves research of a confidential nature. You are my son-in-law, Theodore, and I know I can trust you to remain silent...

> GULL (off):
> ... even to Caroline

(Panel) 4

Looking through Gull's eyes now as he descends the final few stairs towards the locked door at the bottom, where Acland already stands paused and waiting for us, looking back up the steps towards us as we descend with a look of profound respect and trust that is almost touching. As Gull descends the last few steps, we can see one of his hands holding up the door-key in the foreground.

> ACLAND:
> You have my word, Sir.

> GULL (off):
> Good. The research concerns a cretinoid condition found in adult women. I hope to write a paper some day.

(Panel) 5

We are now at the bottom of the steps, looking through Gull's eyes at his old hands, unlocking the door. If possible the dapper figure of young Acland stands in the shadows to one side, looking at us respectfully as he listens to what Gull is saying with rapt attention.

> GULL (off):
> It is my belief that such women are rendered half-witted by an impairment of the Thyroid gland, which regulates the body's iodine.

> GULL (off):
> Our theatre's just down the passageway, incidentally.

(Panel) 6

Gull is now starting to push open the door, which opens upon the darkness within, too narrow a chink as yet to see much more than murkiness through it. We needn't see Acland here . . . Just Gull's hand swinging the door open, perhaps with the key still dangling in the lock.

> GULL (off):
> Our subject today, whom the orderlies are preparing, is a deranged woman in terrible distress. Be assured that whatever we do to her can only alleviate her condition.

> GULL (off):
> She's through here.

(Panel) 7

Now a big wide panel that fills the entire tier, if that looks good, showing us the miasmic interior of the madwoman's quarters, again, very little changed from the last time we saw them. In the background we see various madwomen sitting around in various madwomens' attitudes. They look so similar to the women we saw here forty years ago, and yet it cannot possibly be them. Towards the foreground, two orderlies stand holding the arms of a wild eyed and terrified-looking woman with unkempt hair. She stands there staring at us with tear-darkened eyes, utterly distraught and confused and with no idea of why she has been brought to this dreadful place.

From Hell
Chapter II: A State of Darkness

[Script page missing]

(Panel) 7

PAGE 31

(Panels) 1 & 2

Alan Moore

(PANEL) 3

We now close in upon Annie, as if with a zoom lens. We see her as the orderlies are just steering her reluctant form through the open door of the small operating theatre. She twists her head round and calls back at us as they drag her in, a wild look in her eyes. There is something madly prophetic about her appearance, and this, coupled with the eerie unconscious coincidence in the words she is saying lend a certain chill breeze of eeriness to this panel.

> ANNIE:
> They dragged me from my lodgings, and I don't know WHY!

> ANNIE:
> I'd just been upstairs, talking to James Hinton, and they dragged me out.

(PANEL) 4

We now stand at the doorway of the operating room, looking in through Gull's eyes. The room is small and sordid looking, with a smell of medicinal evil about it. It looks like a bad place to be dragged in to, especially when you have no friends at all about you. It is dark, lit only by a lamp or two, and the walls look cold and stained and damp. It looks like a little room tucked away in one corner of hell. In the foreground, roughly head and shoulders, Theodore Dyke-Acland turns and looks at us with concern and perhaps puzzlement, trying to reassure

---

Regretfully, the page of Alan's original typescript for the remainder of Page 30, panel 8, and Page 31, panels 1 & 2, are lost.

In fact, Eddie Campbell recalls Alan having to reconstruct the contents of the missing panels over the telephone, indicating the page was lost immediately upon completion.

In their stead, we present the missing panels on the facing page as they appear in the graphic novel itself, reprinted with permission of the creators.

—SRB

From Hell
Chapter II: A State of Darkness

Stephen Knight suggests in Jack the Ripper: The Final Solution that Gull may have operated in some way upon the captive Annie Crook, reducing her ability to function mentally. Given that Gull's memoir reveals one of his last published papers as a dissertation on "A Cretinoid Condition Found In Adult Women," I have decided to marry the two notions so that it is the removal or impairment of Annie's thyroid that has such a disastrous effect on her consciousness.

The notion that Gull's son-in-law Theodore Dyke-Acland assisted with the operation is entirely my own, but does not seem unreasonable in light of what is suspected concerning later complicity between the two.

The oddest coincidence on the page: Annie Crook's reference to a fellow lodger named James Hinton derives from evidence unearthed by Donald Rumbelow for his book The Complete Jack the Ripper (revised edition: W.H. Allen, 1987), in which he tracks down electoral records for No. 6 Cleveland Street, given by Knight as Annie's ad-

us. In the background, the orderlies steer the stumbling Annie Crook towards an operating table with a stained white sheet upon it. Straps hang down from the sides of the table, and in one corner of the room there is contemporary anaesthetic equipment. I think this would have been gas, but I'm not entirely sure. I'll try and find out.

GULL (off):
Hinton? But

GULL (off):
But Hinton's dead.

ACLAND:
Sir William? Calm yourself: The woman obviously lodges with someone sharing your late companion's name. 'Tis a coincidence. Nothing more.

(PANEL) 5
Perhaps in the last panel we could see Gull rest one hand on the doorframe, steadying himself, if that would help convey the shock of hearing James Hinton's name in this stranger's mouth. Here, he still seems a bit unsteady as his balloon issues from off. In the F/G, Acland has turned slightly away from his father-in-law to watch the two orderlies as they gently but firmly help the confused and disoriented Annie up onto the operating table. She shouts at them irritably, but they pay her no attention, their faces as grim and bland as those of statues.

GULL (off):
A coincidence?

GULL (off):
Yes. Yes, of course

ANNIE:
Why am I being put to bed? It's not sleep I need, its my husband!

(PANEL) 6
Annie starts to cry helplessly as the orderlies loop the straps across her body, in preparation to strapping her down to the operating table. She is so intensely miserable and lonely at this moment that she hardly seems to notice what they are doing. With a snotty and imperious gesture, young Dyke-Acland indicates to the stone-faced orderlies that they should strap her down securely. Its up to you whether the orderlies are male or female. Whatever looks most natural and most disturbing.

ANNIE:
Oh God, you're not LISTENING.

ANNIE:
Nobody's LISTENING to me.

ACLAND:
Secure the straps well and then kindly leave us to our labours.

ORDERLY:
Very good, sir.

(PANEL) 7
As the silent orderlies fasten the restraining straps tight across her arms and body, Annie finally seems to un-

dress at the time of her abduction. Although Annie herself is not on the electoral register----unsurprisingly, since women were not allowed the vote at this time----the name James Hinton is clearly listed.

From Hell
Chapter II: A State of Darkness

derstand what they are doing. She starts to shout in a panic as she feels the power of movement taken away from her. She looks very frightened now. In the foreground we see Gull's hands as he raises them placatingly towards her. Up to you whether we see Dyke-Acland looking on here. He isn't essential.

ANNIE:
What? What are you doing?

ANNIE:
You're strapping me DOWN! I WON'T be strapped down!

GULL (off):
There, there, my good woman. All is well...

GULL (off):
All is well.

(PANEL) 8

Gull seems to walk nearer to Annie as he talks to her, so that she gets bigger as we close in, maybe half figure here, strapped upon the operating table beneath us. Gull has now turned his hands so that they are palm uppermost in an empty handed gesture as if to reveal that he conceals nothing and intends her no harm. On the operating table and unable to move, Annie looks less than convinced. She stares at the approaching Willam Gull as if he were a cobra and she a rabbit. Though she is confuesd as to her exact situation, from the look in her eyes she knows that in some sense the man walking towards her signifies her end as a complete human being. She isn't even screaming or shouting any more. She looks at Gull and realises that the situation has gone beyond that. Quietly, she abandons all hope, and it is almost a relief for her to do so.

GULL (off):
Fear not, though thoughts and memories most unendurable beset your mind...

GULL (off):
... for I shall take them all away and quite relieve your suffering.

Alan Moore

(PANEL) 9
We close in now, so that Annie's face, looking up at us, fills the entire panel. Her eyes are wide as she stares up into the eyes of the off-panel Willam Gull, and there is a sort of terrible awe in them, more than merely fear. Annie Crook is about to be destroyed by something much, much bigger than herself; a being with dimensions that she can barely begin to imagine. In these, her final moments as a rational and lucid human being, it looks as if on some level she understands that fact. Her voice small and hushed as she speaks, her throat tightened and constricted

ANNIE:
Oh . . .

ANNIE:
Oh dear God, When I look upon your face I am afraid, and I cannot help it.

ANNIE:
Wh-who are your sir?

PAGE 32

(PANEL) 1
Now a seven panel page, of which the first is the biggest, spanning the whole upper tier. We are looking up through Annie's eyes as she lies there strapped to the bed. Over on the right we can perhaps see a little of Acland, perhaps his arms entering the panel and holding the business end of the anesthetic equipment, the mask or whatever. Otherwise, all our attention is on the figure who stands at the foot of the operating table looking down upon us with the shadowy theatre behind him as a dark and grim frame for his image. He stands with his thumbs hooked in his waistcoat pocket, and his face is exactly the same as the one in the photograph, with that same ambiguous mixture of intelligence, arrogance, power and a certain hidden amusement. He stands there, seventy years old and yet a pillar of physical strength and solidity, gazing down at us. Ladies and Gentleman, I give you the star of our show:

GULL:
I am Sir Willam Withey Gull.

From Hell
Chapter II: A State of Darkness

> GULL:
> Administer the anaesthetic, Acland.

(PANEL) 2

We are still looking up at Gull through Annie's eyes as Acland's hand enters the panel from the right and places the dark shape of the gas mask over the lower reaches of the panel, from whence Annie's muffled speech balloon issues. Looking beyond this, we are still looking at Sir Willam as he starts to take off his jacket to reveal the waistcoat and shirtsleeves beneath. He pays no more attention to Annie at all.

> GULL:
> Now ... what were we discussing ... ?

> ACLAND (off):
> You mentioned the thyroid gland, Sir.

> ANNIE (off):
> MMNF!

(PANEL) 3

Same shot. Gull hangs his coat up, perhaps turning his head into the profile as seen upon the other reference picture I've found of him. He seems briskly professional and quite indifferent to Annie as he goes about his business.

> GULL:
> Ah yes ...

> GULL:
> My theory maintains that if the thyroid is impaired ... or, as in this instance, removed entirely ... then iodine will accumulate within the female body ...

> ANNIE (off):
> Mmnn.

(PANEL) 4

In our last panel, I forgot to mention the most important feature, which was that around the edges and corners of the panel a sort of darkness is just starting to close in, signifying Annie's gradual loss of consciousness under the anaesthetic. Here, the darkness has progressed further, and in the remaining illuminated area at the centre of it we see Willam Gull as he turns to us and starts to roll up his sleeves. Significantly, Gull gazes down at us, without passion.

GULL:
... causing impairment of the brain with consequential loss of faculties.

ANNIE (off):
n.

(PANEL) 5

The darkness has now closed in almost competely, the circle of light at its centre that represents Annie's dimming consciousness is now very small and within another panel it will be gone. Its as if we're being taken away from the world down a long dark canal tunnel, with the light as the mouth of the tunnel receeding in the distance. Into this area of light, Willam Gull leans forward so that his face fills the entire of our rapidly dwindling field of vision. His expression is one of reptillian professional interest as he leans over to check whether consicousness has quite departed from the body yet.

GULL:
Does not the concept spur you to humility?

GULL:
Think of it, Acland ...

(Panel) 6

Total darkness, the lights have gone out. In the blackness hang a pair of tailless balloons. This panel is an exact repeat of Panel Four upon Page One.

TAILLESS BALLOON:
Less than a thimble-full of Iodine divides the intellectual from the imbecile ...

TAILLESS BALLOON:
... of which phenomenon I shall henceforth attempt a demonstration.

(PANEL) 7

Now we close with just a panel of blackness, solid and silent.

From Hell
Chapter II: A State of Darkness

Annie has gone to sleep.

No Dialogue

Chapter III: Blackmail, or Mrs. Barrett

PAGE 1

(PANEL) 1
Hello and welcome to this month's episode of *Eastenders*. It's 1888, and thus 'Lofty' hasn't been born while 'Dirty Den' is just a rumour going round the gene pool. 'Colin' is currently enjoying an incarnation as Sir Alfred Douglas, while Anita 'Angie' Dobson is already a mature and respected actress working the music halls with Marie Lloyd. This first page has seven panels, with the first one being the largest. Along with the space for the titles it takes up the whole top tier. What we see, basically, is Marie Kelly walking towards us with determination down Cleveland Street on a muggy and overcast afternoon in early August, 1888. I want to use this episode to try and convey a little more of the atmosphere, complexity and grandeur of London in all its diversity, so please take the opportunity to work in all your favourite reference shots or whatever, should you wish to. The impressionistic little studies of London that you're been coming up with throughout the strip thus far are a joy, so use this opportunity to take that even further, if you want to. Here, as Marie makes her way down Cleve-

(Alan is referring here to Eastenders, a banal and interminable British TV soap opera about modern life in the East End of London.)
—SRB

The title of this episode, "Blackmail, or Mrs. Barrett" is taken from Walter Sickert's picture of the same name, which will be reproduced in Book Two. (Regrettably, a suitable plate was not available at press time.) According to Knight in The Final Solution, Sickert based the woman in the picture upon Marie Kelly, while deriving the painting's title from Marie Kelly's attempt at blackmail. Knight suggests that the name Barrett is a deliberate encoding of 'Barnett', this being the name of Marie Kelly's common-law husband, or is otherwise a simple mistake upon Sickert's part. The latter option is the one that I have chosen to adopt for From Hell.
The more conventional critical studies of Sick-

From Hell
Chapter III: Blackmail, or Mrs. Barrett

ert's life and work suggest, when it comes to "Blackmail, or Mrs. Barrett", that "Mrs. Barrett" may have been a servant or housekeeper of Sickert's during some later stage of his career. While this is possible, none of the authorities concerned claim to know for certain, and in the end their hypothesis is no better supported than Knight's, while being a great deal less interesting for story purposes. It should also be noted that the Knight hypothesis is accepted and supported by Jean Overton Fuller in Sickert & The Ripper Crimes.

Marie Kelly refers to Prince Eddie as "Prince CollarandCuffs", which was the standard nickname for the Prince during this period on account of his habitual mode of dress. While on the subject of Prince Eddy (or Albert Victor Christian Edward, to give his full name), I should perhaps point out for the benefit of confused American readers that almost every male member of the British Royal family during this period seems to be called 'Albert.' The first was Queen Victoria's beloved consort or husband,

land Street, she is carrying the awkward weight of little Alice Margaret on her hip, more through habit than necessity. She pays no attention to the cabs and carriages and passersby that drift through the background around her, but continues walking towards us, her eyes blazing with suppressed indignation, utterly lost in a world of her own rage. It's worth remarking that throughout 1888, the skies of London were exceptionally dark and it was described as 'A Lightless Year' even before the White Chapel murders happened. It might also be worth remarking that there were an unusual number of green suns, bloodred sunsets and blue moons over London that year. This was blamed upon the explosion of Krakatoa, but since this happened five years previously (almost to the day) one has to wonder ... and if you're one of those skeptics who requires blood before you're convinced about such things, I draw your attention to the rains of blood over the Mediterranean during those months, as mentioned in good old Charlie Fort's *Book Of The Damned*.

TITLES (OUTSIDE PANEL):

Chapter III: Blackmail, or Mrs. Barrett

CAP. (INSIDE PANEL):

Cleveland Street, London. August, 1888

(PANEL) 2

Now we have Marie facing away from us in the foreground, only partly visible with most of her off one side of the panel. We can see her hip and one of her arms, holding the child in place as it sits there, also facing away from us. Looking past Marie we are looking at the open front door of number 15 Cleveland Street. A started and somewhat dismayed looking Walter Sickert is standing holding the door open and gazing at Marie and the child, looking less than delighted to see them. He looks guilty and embarrassed as he gazes uneasily into the off panel eyes of Marie Kelly. He wasn't expecting her.

    SICKERT:
Oh.

    SICKERT:
Marie.

(PANEL) 3

Change angle here so that we're looking over Sickert's shoulder at Marie and the child as they stand facing us on the doorstep, the child in Marie's arms. Marie's eyes have not lost their expression of blazing ferocity as she stands there glaring into the off panel eyes of Sickert. All we can see of him here is his arm and shoulder as he stands just inside the door looking out at Marie and Alice Margaret. His head and shoulder are off panel here. Behind Marie, the relatively respectable and wellheeled streetlife of Cleveland Street winds by. Her eyes are dark and flashing and angry and she is very beautiful. The child clings to her and gazes towards the offpanel Sickert with a neutral and bemused expression upon her chubby features.

Prince Albert. Their son, whom William Gull received a knighthood for nursing back to health, was also called Albert, although the dissipated Prince was more commonly known to his subjects as "Stuttering Bertie". He went on to marry the beautiful Princess Alexandra, known to her intimates as "Alix", and by her produced a son named Albert Victor Christian Edward, better to become the Duke of Clarence and Avondale, referred to by friends as "Prince Eddy". One almost suspects that the bereaved Victoria, who spent the later decades of her reign in mourning for her departed consort, would have changed her own name to Albert and the name of the country to Alberta if she had thought for a moment she could get away with it.

From Hell
Chapter III: Blackmail, or Mrs. Barrett

       MARIE:
    Good day t'ye, Mr. Sickert.
       MARIE:
    Might we come in?

(PANEL) 4
  Now, as I see this panel, we are maybe some way up the flight of stairs that lead down into the hall of fifteen Cleveland Street from the upstairs where Sickert has his studio. As we look down into the hallway we see a very nervous and uncomfortable Walter Sickert as he ushers Marie and the child into the hallway. He stands by the front door, perhaps just pushing it closed in the wake of Marie's entrance, turned to look towards the back of Marie, who has walked past him into the hall and has paused facing us at the bottom of the stairs with Sickert standing behind her. With a grunt of effort, Marie sets the chubby little girl down at the foot of the stairs. As she speaks she does not look round at Sickert, and there is something very frosty and cold in her attitude towards him, both her body language and facial expressions. This is probably why he looks so horribly ill at ease. Here, he is attempting to be cheery in an effort to deflect the bitter recriminations he knows must come for his part in the Annie/Eddy deception and its tragic aftermath. The cheeriness doesn't work, and Sickert comes over as merely shallow and evasive. Marie has a face like a cold marble statue as she sets the child down, the hard and unforgiving line of her back turned to the shuffling and nervous artist behind her as she speaks. Little Alice Margaret alights upon the floor without protest, seemingly resigned to walking upstairs under her own steam.

       SICKERT:
    Uh . . . yes. Yes, of course. Come up to the studio.
    You know, Marie, I haven't seen you since..
       MARIE:
    Since they took poor Annie away.
       MARIE:
    Oof. You'll have to go down, child. You're too
    heavy.

(PANEL) 5
Now a side-on shot of the staircase and its attendant banister-rail as Marie, Sickert and the child mount the rickety staircase to the building's upper floors. The staircase runs diagonally up across the panel here, from lower left to upper right, and Marie and the child are in the lead as they make their way up the stairs ahead of Sickert, with the artist following up behind, wretchedly trying to explain his complicity in affairs to Marie's icy turned back. Marie, a few steps ahead of Sickert, is visible only from the waist down here. In a couple more steps she'll be off the picture all together. Labouring determinedly up the stairs beside and a little behind Marie we can see all of the much shorter Alice Margaret, one of her hands holding the banister and the other clutched tight in Marie's larger hand, a frown of concentration on her face. Sickert, following them up from below, has only the upper part of him visible here, with his imploringly up towards Marie's turned back, his hands spread in supplication as he attempts wretchedly to explain himself. Marie's balloon issues from off the top of the picture here, where her off panel face is. Her reply is brisk and icy and dismissive.

SICKERT:
Um ... listen, Marie, the business with Annie; I've been meaning to explain ...

MARIE:
What wants explainin'? Your royal friend had his fun; a workin' woman SUFFERED...

MARIE:
Why, it's so simple little ALICE here could fathom it!

(PANEL) 6
Now we are upstairs in Sickert's studio, where we saw him sketching Marie back in chapter one. I should point out that since this is early August, both Sickert and Marie needn't be overdressed, although they dress in keeping with how we've previously seen them, with Marie favouring fairly somber and dark colours. Around Sickert's throat he wears the red neckscarf that we last saw him pocking up in Cleveland Street in the wake of Annie's abduction. This is not commented upon by either him or Marie. As we see the

From Hell
Chapter III: Blackmail, or Mrs. Barrett

studio here, up in the foreground we can see the uncompleted pencil sketch of Marie Kelly's face that will evolve, in a few years time, into the picture 'Blackmail, or Mrs. Barrett'. It lies somewhere in the foreground, curling slightly so that we can see clearly the sketchy face of Marie and recognise it as the same sketch we saw in issue two, only a little more worn and dogeared and curled up. From the picture, the roughly sketched eyes of Marie Jeanette Kelly sparkle out at us. Looking beyond this, into the chaotic background of the cluttered studio, we see Sickert showing the real Marie Kelly and her infant charge into the studio. Sickert looks wretched, almost as if he's pleading with Marie doesn't look at Sickert as she replies, her face set into a rigid mask of angry, frosty contempt.

SICKERT:
Marie, please, I swear I didn't know it would go this far . . .

MARIE:
Like you swore Prince CollarandCuffs was your brother?

MARIE:
Oh yes: I tumbled after Annie's capture who your 'Albert' must have been . . .

(PANEL) 7
Same shot, but now the trio have walked right up close towards the foreground. The picture is still clearly visible in the bottom foreground and will remain so throughout the rest of this sequence, with Marie Kelly's pencilled-in face staring out at us. Beyond this, standing to either side of the picture we see Marie and Sickert, with Marie on the left and Sickert on the right. Both of them are so close to us that we cannot see their heads and shoulders, these being invisible beyond the upper panel borders. The only person who we can see the face of (other than the face on Marie's picture) is little Alice Margaret, who stands in the space between the two grownups as they face each other across the panel. Here she stands closest to Marie, but standing so that she faces toward Sickert. Marie's hands rest protectively upon her shoulders, and Alice is craning her neck round to look back up at the offpanel Marie with a speculative expression, perhaps wondering if it will be time to go soon. In the F/G,

the picture smiles out at us from the shadows of its wide brimmed hat.

MARIE (off):
... and pity it is I didn't tumble BEFORE! That poor woman's in Guy's MADHOUSE now!

MARIE (off):
D'ye think after you've PAINTED us ye can throw away the ORIGINAL? God, y'oughter be ashamed.

SICKERT:
Marie ...

PAGE 2

(PANEL) 1
Now another seven panel page, with the first six panels (in the top two tiers) all being from the same basic shot as the last panel on page one, with the picture in the bottom foreground, Sickert and Annie decapitated by the upper frame border to either side of the immediate background and little Alice Margaret standing roughly on our eye level between them. Only the posture of the various people changes over the next six panels. In this first one, Marie shoves her arms (resting upon Alice's shoulders from behind, if you remember) straight out in front of her, so that she propels the child towards the obviously reluctant Sickert across the short gap between them. As he does so, little Alice turns round from looking over her shoulder at the off panel Marie to looking up at the off panel Sickert as

Marie's reference to the fact that Annie Crook's parents resided in Portland Street are based upon the data unearthed by Donald Rumbelow in The Complete Jack the Ripper *(revised edition, W.H. Allen, 1987). Rumbelow states that Annie's parents, William Crook and Sarah Ann Crook, were both living at 18 Portland Street (now renamed D'Arblay Street) in 1902 and had been doing so for forty years. While Knight's* The Final Solution *merely states that Walter Sickert found some third party to bring up little Alice Margaret, Rumbelow's evidence seems to demonstrate fairly conclusively that Alice was very often in the company of her mother, Annie, over the next fifteen or twenty years, according to the workhouse records of the times. She was also occasionally in the company of her grandmother, Sarah. For the purposes of* From Hell, *the best way to reconcile these pieces of information was to make Sarah and William Crook the third parties alluded to by Knight, hence Marie's suggestion here that the child could possibly be raised by its grandparents.*

From Hell
Chapter III: Blackmail, or Mrs. Barrett

she is pushed towards him. She looks surprised as Marie decisively shoves the kiddie towards him, placing it in his care and forgoing all future responsibility for its well being. In the very F/G, the dark, scribbled eyes of 'Mrs Barrett' regard us enigmatically.

> MARIE (off):
> Don't you "Marie" me! It's Mrs. Barnett to you!

> MARIE (off):
> Four months I've dragged this poor mite about; lookin' for someone to keep her; hopin' Annie'd turn up . . .

> MARIE (off):
> Well, no more. Here, Mr. Sickert . . . she's yours!

(PANEL) 2

Same shot, only now little Alice stands over to the right of the picture, where Sickert is. She is standing so as to face Marie, with Walter Sickert standing behind her, head still off panel, his hands resting on her shoulders from behind. Alice cranes her neck round to look up quizzically into Sickert's off panel face as he speaks. Over on the left, Marie makes an angry gesture, or at least strikes an angry looking posture as she replies to Sickert. I realize that they're on the wrong side of the frame, strictly speaking, for the order of their dialogue, but I figure you can put Sickert's balloon towards the top of the panel and Marie's lower down. The main emphasis throughout this sequence is the mute figure of Alice as she is shuttle between the two adults like a tabletennis ball, all the while looking completely bewildered by what is going on above and around her.

> SICKERT (off):
> Look, if it's money you want . . .

> MARIE (off):
> I don't want your bloody money! All I want is that you should be made to mind the consequences of your bit o' sport!

(PANEL) 3

Decisively, Sickert propels Alice back towards Marie, pushing her away from himself by extending his arms, his hands resting on

Alice's shoulders. Mutely, Marie is starting to raise her own little hands as if preparing to yet again reject the custody of the child. Little Alice has turned away from Sickert to look up questioningly at the off panel face of Marie Kelly as she is pushed towards her. In the foreground, the sketch regards us noncommitally.

> SICKERT (off):
> I can't look after a child! My wife would . . .

> SICKERT (off):
> Well, I just CAN'T, that's all. The child needs a MOTHER . . .

(PANEL) 4

With absolute resolution, Marie shoves the infant back towards Sickert. Poor Alice stumbles and looks slightly dizzy with all this pushing around.

> MARIE (off):
> Well, you should have thought about that before they dragged her mother away.

> MARIE (off):
> Annie's family live in Portland Street. Take them the child if you must, but I'll not keep her.

> MARIE (off):
> Good day, Mr. Sickert.

(PANEL) 5

Same shot. But Marie has walked off, out of picture. Sickert stands with one hand resting on the child's shoulder, the other raised in a gesture as he calls out to the departing Marie, off panel. Little Alice, bored with the chatter of the adults, has noticed the drawing in the foreground, frowning slightly with curiosity as she glances at it here.

> SICKERT (off):
> Marie . . . Mrs. Barrett! Wait!

> SICKERT (off):
> I can't just turn up at Annie's parents with a child! What will I SAY?

From Hell
Chapter III: Blackmail, or Mrs. Barrett

(PANEL) 6

Same shot, with Marie still absent, having presumably departed off panel left somewhere. I remember that I said the door was visible in the background in panel six of page one. This seems to rather spoil the effect of Marie's absence in this panel, so maybe you should readjust the panel descriptions on Page One so that the door isn't in the background, but is off left somewhere. See what you think, anyway, and do so accordingly. In this panel, Sickert gradually lets the hand fall that he was gesturing towards Marie's turned back with, presumably realizing that she isn't going to come back. Little Alice reaches out toward the foreground and grabs the sketch of Marie by one corner, crumpling it slightly in the process. As the child starts to drag it towards herself while Sickert's attention is diverted we can see the sketched in features of Marie Kelly staring out at us.

SICKERT (off):
Mrs. Barrett?

(PANEL) 7

Now in this last panel (and in the first few panels on our next page) we have a shot to test your reference sources: In this wide angle panel, spanning the bottom of the page we have the small figure of Marie Kelly walking along the street with the dark Victorian mass of Euston Station behind her. About her, people are getting on with their daily business, but Marie looks somehow detached from them all as she walks along, lost, angry and preoccupied, probably replaying the scene with Sickert over in her head and thinking of lots of cleverer things that she could have said to him. Behind her, the station is a smoke and steam-wreathed edifice, it's roof too grimy to glint in what ever weak sunshine there might be.

No Dialogue

PAGE 3

(PANEL) 1

Now a nine panel page, with the first three panels just documenting various key points in Marie's progress from the area around Cleveland Street towards the east end, where she lives. Throughout, she walks with a preoccupied air, taking very little notice of the city bustle going on about her. I fancy these scenes as having some of the same feel as those Tardi shots of New York in Manhattan (RAW 1), where the protagonist is dominated and indeed almost lost amongst the giant overwhelming buildings of the city about him, a tiny figure moving amongst their dark masses. I want some of the same feel here, so that we get a slight sense of Marie's (and everyone else's) insignificance and transience amongst these impassive and enduring stones. In this first panel, Marie is somewhere up around the King's Cross area, about to head down Pentonville. Dunno if the prison might conceivably being the background (is it even round that area? I dunno) or perhaps some other pertinent landmark. If you can't find reference, then just make it a generalized "Marie walking through London" shot. One thing I do want to get over here is the difference between areas like Cleveland Street and the East End, so I'd like these first few panels to look fairly civilized, with the dirtiness and strangeness increasing the nearer we get to the east end.

Alan's reference in Panel 1 is to Parisian artist Jacques Tardi's story "Manhattan," which was translated and presented to American readers in Art Spiegelman and Francoise Mouly's anthology title RAW Vol. 1, No. 1 (1980).
—SRB

No Dialogue

(PANEL) 2
Now a similar shot, this time show-

From Hell
Chapter III: Blackmail, or Mrs. Barrett

ing the figure of Marie as she makes her way past the angel, Islington, about to head down the city road. Around her, the smokewreathed life of inner London goes on unnoticed.

No Dialogue

(PANEL) 3

In this panel, Marie is around the area of St. Agnes Well, about to head down great Eastern Street and thence down Commercial Street. Her pace seems to have slowed a little, and she is perhaps starting to drag her heels and trudge slightly, looking a little footsore.

No Dialogue

(PANEL) 4

Now we are in Commercial Street, on the corner of Hanbury Street looking up towards shoreditch along Commercial Street. Leaning against the corner in the foreground is a fairly roughlooking man of about fifty, perhaps a costermonger or street seller, with an unlit clay pipe between his teeth. He is glancing idly away from us up Commercial Street to where we see the petite figure of Marie Kelly heading towards us. The area around us is now looking very dirty and strange, with rotten fruit and vegetables and less nameable produce upon the cobbles at our feet. Really lay on the filth and squalor with a trowel ... It's bound to be worse than whatever you imagine. Even in 1988, the place is a shit heap, and I imagine it was much, much worse a century ago.

No Dialogue

(PANEL) 5

Exactly the same shot as Panel Four, only now Marie has walked past the man leaning on the corner of Hanbury Street by a few paces to stop dead in the foreground, facing us roughly head and shoulders as the roughlooking man speaks from behind her. Turning from his corner to address Marie's back, the man removes his clay pipe and smiles through uneven yellow teeth. Marie stops in her tracks as she hears him, but not with apprehension so much as with an ear for business.

MAN:
Art'noon, missis.

(PANEL) 6
Same shot, but here Marie turns to address the man, one eyebrow raised, as he takes a couple of steps towards her and begins to engage her in conversation, smiling at her all the while through his uneven teeth. He tucks his clay pipe away in an inner coat pocket and maybe raises whatever form of headgear he might be wearing as he speaks to Marie, in semimockery of mortal politeness.

MAN:
Sorry t'be botherin' yer, but I was after travellin' to a certain place and wondered as you might advise me.

MARIE:
Well, that depends on where you're wantin' to go, now.

(PANEL) 7
Different shot, maybe so that we're looking away up Hanbury street. I sent you a Polaroid of the place, but I imagine it would have looked different in the 1880s... for one thing there were little courts like Hanbury Place running off of it. Maybe there's some pictures in one of the Ripper books, in which case I'll have a look and see if I can find it. Here, in the foreground, we see Marie and the man in profile as they speak to each other, Marie having to

The phrase "HairyFord-Shire", appearing in the dialogue on the next page, and a rather dim pun upon the pronunciation of "Herefordshire", is one of an extensive array of Victorian slang expressions relating to the female genitalia. The expression, in this instance, was passed on to me by Mr. Neil Gaiman, who has a dirty mouth in at least seven centuries.

Also referenced on the next page: the price for shorttime prostitution in Victorian England was indeed approximately three pence. The exchange would be carried out most often against a wall or fence with both parties in a standing position, and was referred to colloquially as a "Thrupenny upright".

From Hell
Chapter III: Blackmail, or Mrs. Barrett

The yard shown here is a reconstruction of the back-yard of No. 29 Hanbury Street, connected to the street itself by a narrow passage. The yard would, within a few weeks of the events shown here, become as famous as the site of the discovery of Annie Chapman's body. Well before that point however, it was used frequently by the prostitutes of the East End as a place to take their clients, a point mentioned by Colin Wilson & Robin Odell in their book Jack the Ripper: Summing Up and Verdict *(Bantam Press, 1987).*

The central incident on this page, an unpleasant congress against a garden fence, is invented but must undoubtedly have been a commonplace occurrence in Marie Kelly's everyday working life. The trick by which the prostitute would hold the penis between her thighs to simulate intercourse without penetration was, allegedly, a common one during this period. One woman working the area during this period (and unfortunately recorded in a source that I am presently unable to trace) stated that during twenty years of working as a pros-

tilt her head up slightly as she talks to the taller man, with Hanbury Street stretching away behind them. The man stares into Marie's eyes as he answers her, and his lips curl into a suppressed leer. He looks amused.

MAN:
Well, I fancied takin' a trip to HairyFordShire . . .

MAN:
. . . only I don't 'ave above thruppence for me fare.

(PANEL) 8
Same shot as panel seven. Narrowing her eyes slightly, Marie stares into the man's eyes as if weighing him up. The man stares back at her, confidently, still with the same faint smile on his lips.

No Dialogue

(PANEL) 9
Same shot. Marie starts to walk away up Hanbury Street, turning her head to speak back at the man as she does so, telling him to follow her. The man is looking away from us here, towards Marie as she starts to walk away up Hanbury Street in the background. Marie smiles faintly with her lips, more as a professional courtesy than anything else. Her eyes aren't smiling.

MARIE:
I think I know how you might get to that place for thruppence.

MARIE:
Follow me up this way.

PAGE 4

(PANEL) 1

We are now in the back yard behind 29 Hanbury street. The yard is small, dirty and deserted, a wooden fence about five and a half feet tall to the right of the panel here with the passageway that gives entrance to the yard leading away into the background from somewhere in the middle. There are about three steps down from the passageway into the yard here, and Marie is coming down them towards us into the yard, looking around at the yard with evident distaste. Behind her, coming down the passageway that leads from the street, we see the man. He has left the door at the far end of the passageway open, so that we can see him silhouetted against the faint light of the street behind him. The yard is littered with bottles, dried shit of unguessable origin, and bits of rag amongst the weeds and dandelions. It'll do.

No Dialogue

(PANEL) 2

Marie is now standing with her back resting against the wooden fence. In a very business-like manner, she starts to lift up her dress at the front. Beneath the skirt and petticoats she wears black ribbed stockings, but no

titute in the East End of London, she had only been penetrated twice, the rest of the time fobbing off the customers with the trick that Marie seeks to employ upon this page.

The scene implies that Marie, against her wishes, has suffered penetration without adequate precaution. Although no one can state for certain that it was at the hands of a customer, as suggested here, it is clear that Marie did indulge in unprotected sex at some point during this approximate period. When her body was found in the room at Miller's Court in the early November of 1888, a pathologist's report records that she was at the time three months pregnant. Thus, the contraceptive accident must have occurred in early August, the scene included here being our explanation of that event. Most of the books relating to the Whitechapel Murders give adequate reference for the three month foetus that Kelly was carrying at the time of her death, but the one closest to my hand at the moment is Jack the Ripper: One Hundred Years of Mystery by Peter Underwood (Blandford Press, 1987).

From Hell
Chapter III: Blackmail, or Mrs. Barrett

knickers. Holding up her skirts she leans against the fence waiting for her customer to come and get it over with. In the foreground we can see the middle section of the man as he fumbles with his trouser fastenings, trying to fish his penis out. Since his head is off panel, his dialogue balloon issues from off picture here.

MARIE:
Alright, we can do it here . . . but only if you're quick, now.

MAN:
Hold on. I'm just findin' me old man . . .

(PANEL) 3

Change angle . . . or maybe not. Maybe Marie keeps in the same place up against the fence and the man just walks up to her, coming fully into the picture now, and takes his place between her legs, with his back turned towards us. Marie is fishing down with one hand towards the man's crotch, evidently trying to get his cock properly into position inside her. I don't suppose we can see any of his face, but the man looks into Marie's face with a slight frown.

MARIE:
Give it here, I'll put it in meself . . .

MARIE:
There.

MAN:
Is it in?

(PANEL) 4

Change angle now so that we see the pair in profile, about half-figure, as Marie (over on the right here) leans with her back up against the wood of the fence. The man is now looking down towards the intersection where his crotch seems to meet Marie's. It's very difficult for him to see, however, since the bunched up skirts and petticoats that Marie holds in front of her effectively serve to mask what is going on below. The man's frown is deepening now and he is starting to look very suspicious. Marie glares at him angrily as she replies to him, urging him to get on with it.

MARIE:
Of course it is! Now hurry up and be about your business.

MAN:
It's not in. You're holdin' it between the tops of her legs!

(PANEL) 5

Same shot as Panel Four. Resting one arm across Marie's throat, or fore-arm at least, the man pushes her head back against the fence, immobilizing her. With his hand that's free he reaches down towards her crotch, roughly shoving her legs apart, looking down at what he is doing rather than into Marie's face. He looks angry. Marie winces in pain as the man's forearm presses across her neck and bangs her head back against the fence, her face turned briefly towards us here.

MARIE:
Don't be daft, of course I'm not. It's . . . OW!

MAN:
I know cunt when I feels it. Open yer legs, an' I'll see meself as it goes up right.

MAN:
OPEN 'em!

(PANEL) 6

Evidently having located the right spot, the man thrusts his loins forward and pushes his cock up into Marie. We are still looking at them in the same shot as in the previous two panels, by the way. The man grunts in satisfaction, while Marie grunts only in discomfort. Her lip is curled in disgust, and she is maybe biting down upon it here, her face turned away from the man's bad breath and towards us. Her body jerks as the man sinks into her.

MAN:
There . . .

MARIE:
ngh

From Hell
Chapter III: Blackmail, or Mrs. Barrett

(PANEL) 7
Now we are just above Marie and the man as he fucks her against the fence. His back is towards us, but Marie is looking up towards us over his shoulder as he lurches rhythmically against her. Her face is expressionless as she stares up into the sky. It is as if she's detached herself from whatever's going on around her, as we look down upon her here.

MAN:
Umf

MAN:
Umf

MAN:
Ummf

(PANEL) 8
Same shot, but we continue to pull back up so that Marie, her customer and the yard they are in are beneath us. As our vantage widens we can also begin to see some of the surrounding yards as well. Marie and the man are quite small and far beneath us here, still leaning against the fence.

MAN:
Umf

(PANEL) 9
Same shot, but we've now pulled back even further so that we're right up in the air, amongst the smoke and the pigeons, looking down on the maze of yards below. If we can see Marie and her customer beneath us, then they must only be tiny little dots. We can no longer here the sound of the man's passion. It's almost as if we have risen up with Marie's detached thoughts, high above her body and into the London sky above it all.

No Dialogue

PAGE 5

(PANEL) 1
Nine panels on this page. We are now back at ground level in the yard behind 29 Hanbury street, and Marie and her customer have finished. We see his middle section or thereabouts up in the foreground. One of his hands is employed in tucking

his shirt back into his trousers while the other is contemptuously tossing small coins down casually at her feet. Her skirts gathered up in one hand she wipes between her legs with the other, either to relieve soreness or to optimistically wipe away whatever of the man's sperm she can. This action is in vain. In three months' time, Marie will have the man's foetus developing nicely inside her on the night she dies.

No Dialogue

(PANEL) 2

This panel is more or less the same shot as we saw when Marie was just entering the yard on Page Four, with the few steps leading up to the passageway which leads away towards the white rectangle of the open street door at the far end. Marie stands in the foreground facing away from us, with only her feet and lower legs visible here. Around her feet, the coins have fallen in the rough semi-circle. She does not stoop to pick them up. In the background we see the man in silhouette as he walks away from us up the passageway and back towards the street. Perhaps he is resettling his hat upon his head as he does so. Marie stares after him, and does not stoop to pick up the money, lying about her feet in the same way that it will lay about Annie Chapman's feet when she is murdered in this yard in a few weeks time.

No Dialogue

(PANEL) 3

Same shot, only now the man has gone in the background. Marie stoops down, the top of her still off-panel so that we can't see her head and shoulders, and gathers up the fallen coins. Pride is one thing, but this is business.

No Dialogue

(PANEL) 4

We are now in Hanbury street, looking along it towards number 29. The yard door beside the shop is open, and Marie Kelly is peering somewhat cautiously out of it, as if checking to see if there's anyone around before venturing back into the street.

No Dialogue

From Hell
Chapter III: Blackmail, or Mrs. Barrett

The street cries recorded in the background on this page are authentic marketcries of Victorian London, as given in the invaluable collection of temporary portraits and observations, London Labour and the London Poor, *by Henry Mayhew (Penguin Books, 1985). The dialect being spoken offpanel as Marie enters the bar is known as "Backslang", popular amongst the costermongers plying their trade in the East End during that period. Certain words are reversed, so that "Jem! You'll stand a top o' reeb?" translates to "Jem! You'll stand (me) a pot o' beer?" while the reply "On, man. I've been doin' dab," becomes "No, man. I've been doin' bad." The pub that Marie enters, The Britannia, was situated on the corner of Dorset Street and Crispin Street and was definitely used by Marie Kelly and her prostitutes during that period covered in our story. Indeed, after Marie's death, the Britannia was one of the two public houses that contributed wreaths her funeral procession. The other public house was The Ten Bells, which was*

(PANEL) 5
Marie now continues down commercial street towards Spitalfields market, down at the end of Brushfield street nearest to Christchurch. The church itself probably isn't visible here. In the foreground we see the bizarre, dirty, sprawling pocket-world that is the marketplace. Everything conceivable is for sale or display: In the foreground, a man leads a skinny albino male through the street, a rope about the poor creature's neck. The albino's hair is long and straggly, his pale brows turned upwards in abject misery as he's lead through the filthy and clamorous streets. Somewhere nearby, a boy holds up a fistful of yellowing haddock, calling out to the passing crowds. Elsewhere a fat woman with a strawberry mark parades her tray of whelks. From the background, Marie walks nonchalantly towards this press of bodies and vitality, thinking more about the cold sperm trickling down her legs than the various wares upon display.

TAILLESS BALLOON:
Come and look at 'em! Here's toasters!

TAILLESS BALLOON:
SO-OLD AGAIN! SO-OLD AGAIN!

TAILLESS BALLOON:
Now's your time! Beautiful whelks, a penny a lot-ing-uns!

(PANEL) 6
Now Marie pushes through the market crowd, approaching us down

Brushfield street. Behind her, dominating the whole scene like a giant man standing over Whitechapel, we see the ghastly, sepulchral mass of Christchurch; a gothic monstrosity that psychologically overshadows its environment. Around Marie the street vendors are still milling as she walks towards us, ignoring the bustle around her and foolishly turning her back upon Nicholas Hawksmoor's awful, watchful creation, looming there behind her.

    TAILLESS BALLOON:
  SO-OLD AGAIN! SO-OLD AGAIN!

    TAILLESS BALLOON:
  An 'aypenny a skin, blackin'!

    TAILLESS BALLOON:
  Sixteen a penny, fine war-r-nuts! Hurrah for Free Trade!

(PANEL) 7

Having turned left at the bottom of Brushfield street, Marie is now walking along Crispin street towards the Britannia Public House at the corner of Crispin street and Dorset street. We can just see a little of the pub over to the right of the background here as we look across the street at Marie from the mouth of an alleyway. In the alley are a boy of nine and a girl of ten. The boy kneels amongst the filth and rubbish and rotting fruit, his trousers around his knees. The girl, possibly his sister, sits against the opposite wall of the alley with her legs splayed. One of her hands is roofing between her own legs

situated less than two hundred yards from the Britannia, at the corner of Commercial Street and Fournier Street, just across the street from Hawksmoor's Christchurch, Spitalfields. During the 1970s, the Ten Bells attempted to cash in on its historical notoriety by changing its name to The Jack The Ripper. Fortunately, after protests from feminists groups, good taste and historical verisimilitude prevailed and today the pub trades under its original name once more.

The Ten Bells, being situated upon the bustling main road of Commercial street was probably the most popular of the two pubs for working ladies plying their trade. The Britannia, on the other hand, was located nearby and yet still far enough away down the backstreets to miss passing trade. Thus the Britannia was most often used by prostitutes when they were "resting" between clients and wanted a simple drink or a chat without being bothered by prospective customers. In order not to confuse readers at any later stage of our narrative, I should perhaps

From Hell
Chapter III: Blackmail, or Mrs. Barrett

use this opportunity to point out that The Britannia was more widely known locally as The Ringers, after the proprietor, Mr. Walter Ringer, and his wife.

while the other reaches out and takes hold, inexpertly, of the boy's erection. Both children are grinning enthusiastically, and both are very dirty. Neither of them have any pubic hair yet, and their activities have a sort of squalid and yet pure innocence about them that can perhaps only be found amongst those that are born damned. Across the street walking from left to right from the corner of Brushfield street towards the Britannia, Marie glances across the street towards the children in the foreground, her expression one of bland disinterest. The children take no notice of Marie whatsoever.

No Dialogue

(PANEL) 8

We are now inside the run down bar-room of the Brittania, looking out across the bar-top from behind the bar and towards the door. The door is just opening and Marie Kelly is entering, looking around her through the gloom and smoke to see if there's anyone she recognizes. Up in the foreground, a costermonger standing at the bar calls out with a smile to another man who has just entered. The other man shakes his head and waves away his colleague's request for a drink.

1st. COSTERMONGER:
Jem! You'll stand a top o' reeb?

2nd. COSTERMONGER:
On, man. I've been doin' dab.

(PANEL) 9

Now a side-on shot of Marie as she stands at the bar, ordering her drink from the landlady, Mrs. Ringer, for whom I have no visual description as yet. If I find any before I start this episode I'll send it to you. Otherwise, I imagine her as a stout, plain woman in her middle forties, with a hard and shrewd look even though she's not unkindly by nature. The pub her and her husband run, being a little off the beaten track, is more deserted than a lot of the pubs we'll be seeing, and there are more women there than men. The pub is used by prostitutes who are "resting" and trying to avoid trade for a few minutes in order to get a quick drink every now and again. As Marie fishes some coppers out of her purse to pay for her half-pint of beer she smiles up brightly at the landlady, who seems to speak relatively fondly to Marie, also. The balloon belonging to Liz Stride issues into the picture from off panel towards the right of the foreground.

MRS. RINGER:
Oh, hello, Marie. What'll ye have?

MARIE:
I'll have a half-pint of beer, Mrs. Ringer, if you please.

LIZ STRIDE:
Marie! Marie Kelly! Over here!

PAGE 6

(PANEL) 1

Here we have a seven panel page, with three small panels on the top tier, one wide horizontal one taking up the middle tier and then three smaller ones upon the bottom tier.

Alan's acknowledgment of artist Eddie Campbell's superior skills in barroom conversation mechanics is only partially in jest. From Eddie's early photocopy comics through The Days of the Ace Rock-N-Roll Club (collected in 1993 by Fantagraphics Books), the complete Alec stories and novels, Deadface, and his recent collaboration with Dave Sim on the story "The Face on the Bar-Room Floor," Campbell has set countless tales in pubs. He is the undisputed master of barroom staging in comics.

—SRB

From Hell
Chapter III: Blackmail, or Mrs. Barrett

The conversation between Marie Kelly and Elizabeth Stride depicted on these two pages is obviously fictional, as are all conversations detailed in From Hell unless it is clearly indicated to the contrary. Nevertheless, the details referred to in their conversation are as accurate as research allows. According to her autopsy report, Liz Stride was suffering from venereal ulcers at the time of her death, and the fact that she had been treated twice before for venereal disease while in her native parish of Gothenburg in Sweden is recorded in various books, including Jack the Ripper: The Uncensored Facts *by Paul Begg (Robson Books, 1988) and* The Complete Jack the Ripper *by Donald Rumbelow (W.H. Allen, 1987). The above books also confirm most of the facts concerning Liz Stride's history, as given here she was born on a farm called Stora Tumlehed in Torslanda, Sweden, later moving to Gothenberg where she worked as a servant for a man named Lars Oloffson. It would seem that during her four years in Oloffson's employ she be-*

Since I would not presume to instruct you upon how to handle the mechanics of a barroom conversation scene, then the page layouts over the next two pagers are even more tentative than usual. I've made the usual detailed suggestions for how I think it would work, but if you come up with more natural-looking way of telling the story then please be my guest. As I see this first

Liz Stride

panel, we have pulled back from the bar to a table over by the window, so that the table and its attendant seats are up in the foreground and we are looking past them towards the bar, which is some yards away. At the bar, near enough full figure and standing facing away from us but looking back over her shoulder towards us, we see Marie Kelly, who is just being handed her glass of beer by Mrs. Ringer while with her other hand she gives the landlady her coppers. As she does this she glances back over her shoulder towards us in the foreground and smiles in recognition. In the foreground, sitting at the table, we see Liz Stride. We can probably only see her half figure to head and shoulders, and her face is mostly turned away from us here as she calls out towards Marie over in the background, but I'll describe her for your future reference: she is a tall woman, rawboned but of slight build, and though the rigours of the past few years have done their bit in weathering and corroding her once countryfresh prettiness, she might still be described as a striking woman, if one's tastes were sufficiently broad. She has brown hair and blue eyes. Her nose is straight and her face an oval. I see her general manner as somewhat poignant . . . she is a big, goodnatured Swedish farm girl who's a long, long way from home, and while she can usually muster a sort of self-deprecating humour at the absurdly dismal nature of her predica-

came pregnant and was dismissed, although I should point out that there is no direct evidence to prove that Oloffson was the father of the child, as we have Liz claiming here. This is simply my own surmise, resulting no doubt from a jaundiced view of human nature.

Paul Begg's book also confirms that Liz Stride claimed to have lived in Chrisp Street with her husband, John Stride, after arriving in England and marrying. Begg also points out that the only available records that show a John Stride living or working in that area suggest that the address was in fact Upper North Street. Whichever street it was in reality, both touch against or intersect with the Limehouse Cut and are only a short walk from Hawksmoor's church, St. Anne's Limehouse.

From Hell
Chapter III: Blackmail, or Mrs. Barrett

ment, there is an air of bittersweet melancholy about her most of the time. She's not the sort of person who ostentatiously parades her misery, boring and alienating her friends, but rather someone who feels a real hurt and homesickness but keeps it inside as best she can and gets on with her life as cheerfully as possible. Her long face probably adds to this air of melancholy with its basic shape, and her blue, goodnatured eyes are often fixed upon some invisible point in the distance, beyond the kippered walls of London, where she can see a beautiful farm somewhere in the vanished past of rural Sweden; A little girl running barefoot through the wonderful summer. Here, if we can see any of her expression as she calls out to Marie Kelly over at the bar, she has a look of mock-reprimand, her eyebrows raised slightly. From the bar in the background Marie turns and smiles over her shoulder at us and at Liz, smiling despite the scene with Sickert and recent trials in Hanbury Street: She likes Long Liz, and is glade to se a friendly face after such a trying day.

MARIE:
Oh, hello, Liz. Just let me get this, I'll be with ye.

LIZ:
You should be at the Ten Bells. No customers here: Too far from big streets.

(PANEL) 2

Here, we reverse angle as we watch Marie joining Liz at the table. This shot is angled so that Marie is in the foreground facing slightly away from us as she draws back a chair and prepares to sit down, holding her halfpint of beer in one hand while she grips the back of the chair with the other, pulling it back so that she can sit down at the table. Across the table from her and facing towards us we see Liz Stride, looking at Marie over the rim of her own halfpint of beer as she sips from it. Behind Long Liz is the grubby window, maybe lacecurtained, that looks out onto Crispin Street. If we can see any of Marie's face as she draws back the chair and prepares to sit she is still wearing a small smile, and perhaps a mockchiding expression as she tosses Liz's own question back at her.

MARIE:
Me last customer was enough for one afternoon.
I'm resting.

MARIE:
Course, I might ask the same question o' you.

(PANEL) 3
We have closed in upon the table slightly from our last panel, but have maintained the same basic angle. Up in the foreground we can see a little of Marie Kelly (but not her head and shoulders) as she settles herself down in the chair opposite Liz. Looking across the table we see Liz, sitting facing us, just settling her glass down on the table after sipping from it. She glances up at the offpanel face of Marie Kelly and gives a weary, self-deprecating little smile.

LIZ:
Ah, I rest also. My fanny is sore with the, what is it, ulcers?

LIZ:
Since Gothenburg I have them. In Kurhuset, the special hospital, they say I am cured.

LIZ:
Hah.

(PANEL) 4
Now, on this wide central tier we have one wideangle panel that should give you plenty of room to conjure up the atmosphere and detail of the setting. We are probably somewhere over near the bar, maybe even with part of the bar visible up in the lower foreground if you like. There is smoke, and sawdust, and scruffy costermongers exchanging banter or engaging in similar pursuits over near the bar. Perhaps a mongrel dog trots disconsolately around the pub, looking for somewhere to lie down and be safe from people's feet. Any details that you like, basically . . . the whole point of this panel is to give a brief portrait of the location, fixing it in people's minds as a real place which we shall be visiting again. Over towards the background, by the window, we see the table at which Marie Kelly is now sitting, talking across it to Elizabeth Stride. Marie is over on our left here, facing right, with Liz opposite her on the right and facing left. All about them, the bustling and infested life of the gloomy, smokey barroom goes on.

From Hell
Chapter III: Blackmail, or Mrs. Barrett

> MARIE:
> If ulcers is all that last beggar give me I'll think I got off light enough.

> MARIE:
> Shot his load right up, an' me with no sponge.

> LIZ:
> Tch. It is better, I think, to hold, you know, between the legs?

(PANEL) 5

Now we are closer in upon the table, over on Liz Stride's side of it. Maybe we can see part of her up in the foreground, perhaps tilting her glass to her lips and swallowing not looking at Marie here. Looking past Liz we can see Marie sitting opposite, glowering with annoyance into space across the table in our general direction. She looks cross with the world in general and with herself in particular. While she grumbles in the immediate background, Liz quietly sips her drink in the foreground.

> MARIE:
> Well, that's what I WAS doin', but he wouldn't have it.

> MARIE:
> Here's me just this mornin' got rid o' ONE child, and now like as not I'm expectin' ANOTHER.

(PANEL) 6

Change angles so that we're now over on Marie's side of the table, with her sitting maybe halffigure in the foreground, perhaps roughly in profile here and not looking directly away from us across the table towards Liz, who sits on the other side. Here, Marie is not looking at Liz but is looking down at her beer glass as she reaches out and takes hold of it, about to raise it to her lips. The anger has left her face as suddenly as it appeared, replaced by a more neutral expression of resignation. Across the table, Liz sits with her chin resting in one hand, her elbow on the tabletop next to her glass of beer. She is staring dreamily into space with a sort of forlorn and wistful expression . . . or perhaps it would be better if she actually was looking towards Marie here, so that we have her look wistfully into the distance in our next panel. Her expression is still the same look of melancholy in either eventuality, a sort of weariness with life that has gone beyond bitterness. she doesn't have the strength left for bitterness.

> LIZ:
> Children! You don't tell me!
>
> LIZ:
> Expecting baby, I first do THIS for money, to buy clothes. Then, born dead.
>
> LIZ:
> Still I do this. When Gothenburg Police make trouble, I come here.

(PANEL) 7

In this final panel on the page we close in upon Liz, from the same angle. Perhaps in the foreground we can just see a little of Marie Kelly as she raises the glass to her lips and sips at it, but we cannot see her eyes. Looking past what little of Marie we can see we see Liz. She still sits with her chin resting in her palm, but here her gaze has drifted to some imaginary point in the distance off one side of the panel. Her eyes are sort of sad and yearning and melancholy, but her face and mouth are resigned. She doesn't look as if she has any real hope that her situation will ever be better in the future nor does she look as if this fact still bothers her much, beyond the residual sadness it has left behind. Staring off panel, she regards life with a sad acceptance. What else can she do?

> LIZ:
> It is now far away for me, Sweden.
>
> LIZ:
> Very far away.

PAGE 7

(PANEL) 1

This page has nine panels, in three tiers of three, and we continue with our barroom dialogue between the two prostitutes. The first tier on the page, thinking about it, would probably work

From Hell
Chapter III: Blackmail, or Mrs. Barrett

just as well as a wide panel, or perhaps as a continuous background shot that spans the whole width of the tier but which is divided into three smaller panels. Our basic point of view is the reverse of that in the middle tier on page six, in that while we still see Liz and Marie in profile we are now on the other side of the table, standing just inside the window, so that the table is up in the foreground with Liz sitting in profile on the left, Marie in profile on the right and the bar and its denizens visible across the tabletop directly beyond them. If you do decide to do this as a continuous background shot divided into three rather than as one big wide panel, then in this first small panel we see Liz Stride, sitting roughly in profile and facing right, still wearing the same mournful look as in our last panel on Page Six, as she continues to recount the story of her early years. Perhaps she still has her chin resting in her hand. Her glass is half full on the table before her as she gazes dreamily across in Marie's general direction. (Marie is not visible here, being seated over on the far right of this tier, in panel three if you decide to go with the continuousbackground-divided-into-three idea.) Beyond Liz, life in the stygian and smokewreathed barroom goes on as normal.

LIZ:
England . . . so ugly! Once, in Torslanda, I am Elizabeth Gustafsdotter, on my parents beautiful farm, Stora Tumlehe.

LIZ:
Now, in England married, I am Elizabeth Stride.

(PANEL) 2
Panning across we now just have a shot of the table between the two women, with the beer glasses resting upon it. Looking beyond this, we see more of the bar and the shadowy indistinct figures of the costermongers leaning against it, visible through the pall of tobacco smoke. Liz's balloons enter the panel from off pic left here.

LIZ (off):
Arrived, we live by canal, Limehouse Cut. I see the ugly Limehouse church, and I am thinking of Torslanda.

LIZ (off):
It makes me alone, that church.

(PANEL) 3

Continuing to pan across this continuous background we not reach Marie, sitting facing left over on the right hand side of the table opposite Liz. Sympathizing strongly with Liz's obvious disenchantment with England, Marie merely looks gloomily into her beer ... or perhaps, to set up a bit of minor business for next panel, she could be turned away from us and fumbling awkwardly with one of her boots, starting to take it off so that we can maybe see her massaging her foot in the next panel. It's not essential, it's just something natural she'd be doing if she's just spent the last hour or so walking back to the east end from Cleveland street. In either event, if we can see her expression here she looks sort of resignedly gloomy about the condition of England.

MARIE:
Ah, they've some ugly buildings, the English. I'm the same about Ireland ... or even Wales, where we lived after.

MARIE:
Anywhere but bloody London.

(PANEL) 4

Now, if this works out, the first two panels on this tier are another continuous background shot. In it, we have

The fact that Marie Kelly lived in Wales before arriving in London, along with the information that she resided on Ratcliffe Highway, where Hawksmoor's St. George's In The East is situated, is confirmed by Begg's JTR: The Uncensored Facts amongst others. For details concerning the famous Ratcliffe Highway murders that Marie Kelly alludes to here, I refer the reader to The Maul & The Pear Tree *by P.D. James and T.A. Gitchley (Constable & Co., LTD, 1971). The murders took place in 1811 on land that Nicholas Hawksmoor had pleaded with the commissioners to buy up a century before, that he might "properly align" his proposed St. George's In The East by siting it partly upon the ground in question. Theo cmmissioners refused, perhaps unable to see why Hawksmoor's curious obsession with alignments should end up costing them good money.*

From Hell
Chapter III: Blackmail, or Mrs. Barrett

Roughly a hundred years later a young draper named Timothy Marr opened his shop in that location. On the seventh of December, 1811, some person or persons unknown broke in the house, where Marr lived with his wife, their threemonth old son and Marr's young apprentice James Gowen. For no readily discernible motive, the intruder(s) then proceeded to kill everyone within the house, including the baby, by smashing in their skulls with a maul (a kind of mallet, pregnant with symbolic significance to the freemasons) and then slashing their throats from left to right (the same distinctive method as that employed with the victims of the Whitechapel murderer more than seventy years later).

Another family was murdered twelve nights later, increasing the public's sense of helpless panic and outrage. Eventually, a man named John Williams was accused of the crimes, but sadly "hanged himself" before he could be brought to trial. The evidence arrayed by James and Critchley in their book strongly suggests

reversed angles so that we're now on the other side of the table, facing in the direction of the window. We have also dropped down to floor level so that in this panel and the next one (the background of which follows on) we are seeing only the lower halves of the two women as they sit facing each other across the table. In this panel we see the lower half to three-quarters of Marie Kelly as she sits facing roughly towards the right but perhaps turned slightly towards us here. If it works and looks good as a piece of business, we see that Marie has taken off one of her shoes and is rubbing her sore foot through the ribbed black material of her stockings, attempting to soothe the blisters incurred by her walk from Cleveland street. Both her balloon and the balloon of Liz Stride enter into this panel from off pic above . . . from the left and right-hand side respectively.

MARIE (off):
It's like you in Limehouse: I lived near that awful George's church, on Ratcliffe Highway.

LIZ (off):
Bad place. Once they hang pirates there, I'm hearing . . .

(PANEL) 5
Panning across we now see the lower half of Liz Stride, her head and shoulders off panel above as she sits facing towards the off-panel Marie. If we can see her hands she is just raising her glass again here towards her off-

that Williams was not the guilty party, from which it follows that he may have been the scapegoat needed to placate public sensibilities, a fake suicide arranged to spare the authorities the embarrassment of a trial. Whatever the truth of the matter, Williams' dead body was proudly paraded along Ratcliffe Highway where it could be viewed by the massive crowd of spectators that had gathered. Finally, and with some ceremony, a stake was hammered through Williams' lifeless heart and he was buried at a crossroads, as Marie Kelly states here. The James/Critchley book also provides the information that pirates were once hung in chains at the low watermark of the Thames at Ratcliffe Highway, there to drown at the return of the tide.

From Hell
Chapter III: Blackmail, or Mrs. Barrett

panel lips, to sip from it. Beneath the table, lying there with its muzzle resting on its paws, we perhaps see the mongrel dog that I suggested you show trotting round the pub earlier, its belly resting contentedly in the sawdust ... Marie's balloons issue from off panel left here.

MARIE (off):
Hangin' and WORSE! Why, they buried the Ratcliffe Highway murderer at a crossroads, stake through his heart an' all.

MARIE (off):
Why'd ye leave your farm?

(PANEL) 6

Now, up to the right of the foreground, in profile and facing left, we have the face of Liz Stride. She gazes into space with her sad eyes and gives a self-deprecating little smile at the thought of her youthful folly in preferring the bright lights of Gothenburg to the dreariness of rural Torslanda. Looking beyond her and across the table we see Marie Kelly sipping from her half pint of beer, staring keenly at Liz over the rim of the glass as she does so, interested to hear this big Swedish girl's story.

LIZ:
Haha. At seventeen, not thinking so much of farms, I go working as servant in Gothenburg. Lars Olofsson. Man with three children.

(PANEL) 7

Same shot, but in the foreground Liz's expression has lost its little smile, and she just looks sad. This isn't funny. This guy in Gothenburg and his stillborn baby fucked up Liz's entire life, and that's why she's here in London at precisely the wrong time and that's why within a little over a month someone will slice her throat open in Berner street. Her eyes look momentarily deadened with the sadness of her life, and the smile evaporates from her lips as she recounts the story. Across the table, Marie Kelly has lowered the glass from her lips and is looking at Liz with a sort of wince of sympathy, a slight sympathetic grimace contorting one corner of the mouth.

LIZ:
Four years, every night in my bed he wants me not as wife, but as servant. When I expect baby, he say "Go".

LIZ:
Now I am here. Even born dead, baby changes our life, I think.

(PANEL) 8

Change angles. In the foreground, all we can see of Marie Kelly is one of her hands as she raises her half-empty glass aloft into the panel, proposing a solemn toast to the continuing regularity of the menstrual process. Looking beyond the glass and Marie's upraised hand we can see Liz sitting opposite us, once more conjuring her weak little smile as she looks up at what Marie is doing. Her eyes, however, are still filled with sadness and loss. Marie's balloon issues from off panel left.

MARIE:
I've got friends as wouldn't argue. Here's to next month's blood, Long Liz.

MARIE:
Here's to the curse.

(PANEL) 9

In this final panel we cut away to a still shot of Christchurch Spitalfields. It fills the background here, while in the foreground we see an anonymous black man from the West Indies. He wears a long linen smock and has a carefully lettered copperplate sign

I have already explained the reasoning behind my decision to make Annie Crook's parents the third parties, to whom Sickert entrusts Annie's daughter, in my footnotes for Page Two of this chapter. Even so, the scene on these two pages obviously demands a fuller explanation.

In The Complete Jack the Ripper, *Rumbelow casts doubt upon Knight's hypothesis that Prince Eddy fathered a baby by Annie Crook. He does this by pointing out that while little Alice Margaret's birth certificate does indeed leave the father's name and occupation suspiciously blank, when she grew up and married, a father's name was very definitely entered upon the wedding certificate. The name in question was "William Crook".*

William Crook was Annie's father, and thus Alice Margaret's grandfather. But was he her father as well? From the information upon the wedding certificate, barring a ghastly clerical mistake, there would seem to be incest involved. This, in the underclass of Victorian London to which

From Hell
Chapter III: Blackmail, or Mrs. Barrett

Annie and her parents belonged, was a commonplace phenomenon. In one's bleaker moments, it is possible to suspect that incest was not only commonplace, it was almost mandatory. Therefore, Annie Crook may well have slept with her father. The way I have chosen to interpret this scene as presented here is to marry the two notions by suggesting that while Annie may have been sleeping with her father, the baby that she carries is in fact that belonging to Prince Eddy. If, as suggested here, Annie's father allowed his own guilt to let him assume that he was responsible, it would at a stroke explain the discrepancy between the birth and marriage certificates and also go some considerable way towards explaining why Annie Crook's parents never asked any questions about their daughter's impaired mental faculties when they were finally reunited with her.

hung round his neck which declares him to have been bathed in the blood of the lamb. As the negro stands there in the street, a tepid and grimy rain is just starting to fall from the grey blanket of cloud up above. As the rain droplets trickle over his black skin leaving invisible trails of soot he turns his eyes upwards and stares miserably into the overcast London sky. He doesn't know what the fuck he's doing here. He isn't at all important to our story and we never see him again, but I thought it'd be nice to include a shot of him as an example of the unsuspected exoticism of Victorian London. As he stands in the foreground here, Christchurch rears up behind him, its sickly white spire threatening to scar the clouds. The church is a more important image than the black guy here. He's just a bit of foreground business that we have to look beyond to see the pallid, hungry stone monster in the background, waiting in the rain.

No Dialogue

PAGE 8

(PANEL) 1
Now we have a three page scene designed to paper interestingly over one of the rends in Stephen Knight's remarkably stout tissue of lies: Namely, that while on the birth certificate of Alice Crook no father's name is recorded, on her later marriage certificate (which Knight avoids mention of)

the father's name is given as William Crook . . . who was Annie Crook's father and Alice Crook's maternal grandfather, which clearly suggests either incest or a spectacular registration error. Anyway, this first page in sequence has seven panels, with a big wide one at the top, spanning the whole uppermost tier. What we have, basically, is a shot of Oxford street by night . . . I have a beautiful reference painting that should be enclosed somewhere in this package, which shows the murkiness of the night punctuated by the smokey orange glow of carriage lanterns, the warm but crepuscular yellow of gas lamps. If you squint your eyes up a bit it could almost be Oxford Street today, but the painting has a real sense of the Victorian atmosphere in that it shows you how bloody dark a night in Oxford Street was a hundred years ago. These days, one could comfortably read a fairsized novel by the neon glow of the Virgin Megastore, but back in 1888 it was a different story entirely. Anyway, the way I envision this panel is as a sort of adaptation or recreation of the scale and mood of the abovementioned reference shot, only with the figures of Walter Sickert and the Tiny Alice Marie added somewhere up in the foreground, or at least close enough to be recognizable and identifiable, even if they are still small enough to be dwarfed by the bustle of Oxford Street going on all around them. They make an odd pair, physically, as the painter glumly leads the small child by her hand through the nighttime streets of the city. Sickert is a giant by contemporary standards, and next to Little Alice Marie there is something oddly touching or almost comical about their difference in scale. Sickert is leading the uncomplaining infant towards Portland Street, which is just off Berwick Street, which, in turn, is just off Oxford Street. Annie Crook's parents live in Portland Street, and it is to see them that Sickert is taking Little Alice Margaret, which is why he doesn't look very happy, not relishing the awkward encounter. For her part, Alice Margaret just looks stoical as she trots along uncomplainingly beside Sickert, her small sweaty hand clasped in his turps-scented fingers.

No Dialogue

(PANEL) 2

Now we are looking at the corner of Portland Street, where it

From Hell
Chapter III: Blackmail, or Mrs. Barrett

intersects with Berwick Street. (If you look this up on the AZ *of London*, Please not that Portland Street is now called D'Arblay Street.) We thus see the very corner of Portland Street, perhaps with a street sign visible, over to the right of the foreground. To the left, we are looking round that corner and up Berwick Street towards Oxford Street. (I dunno if you remember Berwick Street . . . It's where Bram Stokes used to maintain England's first comic shop, 'Dark They Were and Golden Eyed'. I just mention that in case it helps you get a fix on this scene.) As we look up Berwick street here we can see the shadowy figures of Sickert and Alice Marie walking down it towards us as the head for Portland Street.

No Dialogue

(PANEL) 3

Now we are standing with Sickert and Alice Margaret directly outside number 18 Portland Street. We see Sickert in profile as he stands facing the door, so that the door is over to the right of the panel here, and beyond it we are looking along Portland Street towards the intersection with Berwick Street. I imagine these streets as being very, very narrow . . . from what I remember, they're pretty narrow even today and probably weren't as wide back then. As we see Sickert here he stands full figure, but with his head and shoulders invisible off the top of the panel border, so that we only see him from the shoulders down as he stands there with his hand raised to rap at the front door of number eighteen with his knuckles. Standing slightly nearer to us than Sickert, little Alice Margaret stands beside Sickert but doesn't appear to be even slightly interested in what he is doing. She is looking around, gazing out of the side of the panel with a look of only mild curiosity. I should perhaps point out that little Alice is partially deaf, which perhaps accounts for her slight air of detachment. Having been hauled around town by Marie Kelly for a couple of months she no longer finds it unusual that relative strangers should escort her through the bustling city in the dead of night to unknown and incomprehensible destinations, and thus her overriding expression throughout most of this scene is one of relative indifference.

No Dialogue

(PANEL) 4

Now, although we maybe have a little of Sickert's shoulder or something visible up in the extreme foreground, most of him is offpanel and we are looking from the point just behind him towards the front door of Number Eighteen, which has now been opened. Standing looking out at us with a surly and justifiably suspicious expression we see Mrs. Sarah Crook, Annie's mother. She is woman of fifty years old, but since I don't have any physical description or photographs of her to hand I'm afraid you'll have to construe her features from those of Annie and the adult Alice Margaret. I imagine her as dark haired and bigboned, but with a face that the years have robbed of Annie's vivacity, leaving only a disgruntled stoicism in their place. From her expression, she looks as if she doesn't expect her life to get any better, and sadly she is right. Her life will end after a string of confinements within workhouses and institutions, but for the moment she still looks solid and capable enough as she peers out from the gloomy passageway towards Sickert, squinting as her eyes accustom themselves to the gloom.

SARAH CROOK:
Yes?

(PANEL) 5

Reverse angles so that now we are looking either through Sarah's eyes (so that we can't see her at all) or from just behind her (so that we see a little of her shoulder or something as she stands facing away from us in the extreme foreground.) We are looking towards Sickert and Little Alice Margaret as they stand facing us, Sickert with one hand upon the child's shoulder and an incredibly uneasy and apologetic expression upon his face. Alice, meanwhile is just standing and gazing up at her grandmother (and us) without any look of recognition upon her tiny face, which remains relatively blank and expressionless. Sickert is perhaps taking off his derby hat and holding it to his breast in nervous and uneasy politeness here, as he addresses a lady.

SICKERT:
Mrs. Crook? My name's Sickert. I'm a friend of Annie's.

SICKERT:
This is Alice, your grand-daughter. She...

From Hell
Chapter III: Blackmail, or Mrs. Barrett

                SICKERT:
        She needs somewhere to stay.

(PANEL) 6

    We now pull back from the front door and along the passageway, so that now we are looking towards the front door from somewhere near the living room door, and we can see Sarah Crook maybe half-figure up towards the foreground with Sickert and Alice Margaret visible behind her. Sarah, bidding them enter, is already turning towards us and shouting instructions to her off-panel husband, William, who is in the living room and thus not seen here. Looking flustered by these unexpected guests but none the less efficient, Sarah prepares to bustle about making them welcome even while she's still showing them in through the door. Beyond Sarah we see Sickert hesitantly stepping through the front door and into the passageway. He glances up at the damp and stained walls of the passage as he enters with a look of aesthetic dismay: this place smells of damp and of old people, and if anything it looks worse than it smells. While nowhere near as horrific and unbelievably squalid as the Doss houses of the East End which we shall visit later in the series, the house that Sarah and William Crook share in Portland Street is still pretty filthy and miserable by today's standards. And of course, like everything else in Victorian England, it is oppressively gloomy and dark. I dunno whether Sarah would maybe be carrying an oil lamp or candle to see her way along the passage to the front door... there certainly wouldn't be any light in the hall. See what you think, anyway, and draw what looks most likely and most visually palatable. Alice trots into the hall obediently beside Sickert, but doesn't react to her new surroundings in any noticeable way.

                SARAH:
        Alice...? Gor love us, I've not seen you since you
        was aborn! Come in, come in...

                SARAH:
        BILL? Clear the table off! We've got COMPANY!

(PANEL) 7

    Now we are in the pokey little living room, with a battered old table up in the foreground. Sarah, who has entered the room, if facing us across this as she busily tidies away whatever household debris might have been left cluttering its surface, trying vainly to make things look nice for the visitors. She doesn't look round at either Sickert or her husband as she speaks, but continues to scoop up the items littering the table with complete single-mindedness. Beyond her to one side we see Sickert as he leads little Alice in through the living room door from the passageway, still looking very uneasy and out of place as he does so. (Would he have to stoop slightly to get through the door? How high did they build doors then, anyway?) over to the other side of the background we Annie's father, William Crook, as he rises from his chair with a look of surprise and puzzlement on his broad and not-particularly-bright features, staring at the newcomers in bemusement.

> SARAH:
> Now, what's all this in aid of? Why can't our An-
> nie look after the child herself?

> SARAH:
> William, make yourself useful. Give us hand with
> this . . .

PAGE 9

(PANEL) 1

Now we have a nine panel page, still set in the gloomy interior of the Crook family living room, probably sulphurously lit by an oil lamp, which I hope will add to the disturbing, low-key nightmare quality of this scene. (By nightmarish, I mean emotionally nightmarish rather than scary, you understand.) This first tier of three panels is arranged so that we have a gradual close-in upon a relatively fixed image. What we see in this first panel is a shot angled from just behind Sickert, so that we see him perhaps head and shoulders looking away from us in the foreground, towards Mr. and Mrs. Crook as they hover near the table in the immediate background. The crook couple are arranged here so that Mrs. Crook is closest to us here, with William Crook a pace or two beyond her and thus furthest away. Both Mr. and Mrs. Crook turn to look at Sickert as he speaks from the foreground. Although we can't see much of Sickert's face from the angle at which he is standing, his expression

From Hell
Chapter III: Blackmail, or Mrs. Barrett

is really wretched and sick-looking. He really didn't want to the be one to deliver this news. Beyond him, as Mrs. Crook wheels to face him, her expression is one of startled outrage at the news concerning her daughter. Looking beyond her we see William Crook glance up towards Sickert with a look of worried surprise.

SICKERT:
I . . . I'm afraid she's in a hospital for. . .

SICKERT:
. . . well, for madwomen.

SARAH:
WHAT? What are y'SAYIN'? There's nothin' up with our Annie! What are y'SAYIN', mad?

(PANEL) 2
Keeping the same angle now we start to close in, so that we can no longer see Sickert here and his voice issues from off panel in the foreground. The only figures we can see in this panel are Sarah and William Crook as they stand staring towards us. Slightly closer to us than her husband, we see Sarah's face as her indignant expression crumples to be replaced by one of horror and worry for her daughter. She does not weep, but her eyes are desolate and afraid, unable to understand why this tragedy should have happened. Immediately beyond her, William Crook's face is different. He is just staring at us numbly, his eyes gradually starting to widen as an awful and private realization gradually steals over him. He looks like the news he's just heard has stunned him, but for subtly different reasons to those behind Sarah's obvious maternal grief.

SICKERT (off):
I . . . I don't know what happened. I just know that's where she is . . .

SARAH:
Oh, God. My baby, a madwoman . . .

SARAH:
Whatever has DONE this to her?

(PANEL) 3
Continuing to close in, we now close in past Sarah so that we

can no longer see her either, and so that her speech balloon issues into the panel from off pic in the foreground. What we are looking at here is relatively tight close-up, say head and shoulders, of William Crook. His expression since last panel has changed, if only subtly. He looks sicker, and his eyes have widened still further and are starting to take on a look of tragic horror and understanding. As we stare into the damned eyes of William Crook we understand that he knows the answer to his wife's question.

SARAH (off):
Whatever has UPSET her so?

(PANEL) 4

This next tier also makes use of the close-in effect, but from a reversed angle. In this first panel we are now on the other side of the room, beyond William Crook and looking past him towards Sickert, Alice Margaret and Sarah. Here, as we look on, William Crook raises his hands to his face and slowly crumples to his knees before the expressionless little girl, who simply stares at him uncomprehendingly and with little real interest. Sickert and Sarah are also staring blankly and with evident surprise at William Crook as he breaks down under the sudden weight of his awful, awful guilt. The picture is set up so that William and Alice Margaret are more towards the foreground with Sickert and Sarah looking on from the near background.

WILLIAM CROOK
OHHH GODDDDD...

WILLIAM CROOK
Oh God FORGIVE me. What have I DONE?

WILLIAM CROOK
AHUHUHUHUH

(PANEL) 5

Slowly, we begin to close in, so that right up in the foreground now we have William Crook as he kneels beside the diminutive Alice Margaret with tears running down his weathered cheeks from screwed-shut eyes. He throws his arms around the child and hugs her fiercely to him, protectively and lovingly. Alice looks startled and bewildered but not afraid. William's face is turned towards us

From Hell
Chapter III: Blackmail, or Mrs. Barrett

and he is not looking at anybody as he speaks. Beyond him and Alice we see Sickert and Sarah. Sickert is staring at the kneeling man with a frown of complete incomprehension. What is going on here? What is this surreal episode all about? Sarah Crook, though no less puzzled than Sickert, has a subtly different sort of frown as she looks at her husband. Its puzzled, but it's also shrewd. As she stares at her husband and grandchild we can see that she is trying to puzzle something out, despite her surprise. Her frown is quizzical.

SARAH:
William? What. . .?

WILLIAM:
Oh, I've SINNED . . . me own daughter, me sweet ANNIE, and the shame's made her MAD.

WILLIAM (separate balloon):
B-but don't YOU worry, little Alice. I'm here now, eh?

(PANEL) 6
We have continued to close in slowly, so that if we can see any of William and Alice in the foreground here it is only his old labourer's hands resting protectively upon the little girl's shoulder. Looking beyond this we see Sarah and Sickert staring down at us. Their expressions are near enough identical now: Their eyes widen in sudden understanding as the penny finally drops. A creeping sick horror steals over their features as they realize what William Crook is confessing to.

WILLIAM (off):
Your daddy's here.

(PANEL) 7
Not sure what angle would be best here . . . maybe we could keep to roughly the same angle as on our last tier with William and Alice towards the foreground and Sickert and Sarah immediately beyond them. If this looks okay, then we've pulled back a little here from the close-up of Panel 6, so that we see more or less the whole group. The main action, up towards the foreground, is provided by Sarah as she fiercely grabs the child away from the protective

embrace of her husband. She stares at the old man with her eyes on fire and rage, a fierce protective maternal fury mingled with utter loathing and disgust for what William has done. He doesn't seem to resist much physically as Sarah wrenches the child away from him, but just kneels with his open arms empty and imploring, his face wet with tears and wracked with a look of the purest loss and anguish and wretchedness. Alice, as her grandmother wrenches her from her grandfather's arms, is perhaps starting to look a little scared and uneasy. From the background, Sickert looks on in escalating horror as he slowly starts to understand the complex and hideous nature of the mistake that is being made here. Sarah, for her part, even as she directs her brusque aside to Sickert, does not take her blazing eyes off of her wretched husband for so much as a second. Her glare pins him to the floor like a grub.

          SARAH:
You...?

          SARAH:
You SWINE! You bloody old SWINE! Take your filthy hands off that child!

          SARAH:
Please leave us now, Mr. Sickert. I'LL see the child's alright.

(PANEL) 8

As Sarah starts to hustle Sickert towards the living room door and the passageway beyond she keeps one hand protectively upon Alice's shoulder, leading the child with her as she prepares to escort Sickert to the door rather than leaving her alone in the room with her grandfather. Sarah isn't looking at Sickert as she speaks to him, but continuing to glare down at the off panel point in the foreground where William is presumably kneeling and weeping, looking back over her shoulder at her husband as she ushers Sickert towards the door, Alice in tow. Sickert looks trapped and horrified, suddenly realizing that he has no choice other than to let this man continue to bear the burden of his guilt, even though Sickert knows that the incest was not the cause of either Alice Margaret's birth or Annie's madness. That the incest was nevertheless real only adds to the moral ambiguity of Sickert's position, and from the artist's face it looks like

From Hell
Chapter III: Blackmail, or Mrs. Barrett

>>he's in a hell of guilt all of his own.
>>>SICKERT:
>>B-but...this isn't RIGHT. Annie's madness...
>>surely there's ANOTHER explanation?
>>>SARAH:
>>EXPLANATION? YOU heard what he said! What
>>other explanation COULD there be, answer me
>>THAT, Mr. Sickert...

(PANEL) 9
>Continuing to close in we can perhaps only see Sarah's hand or arm now as she continues to propel Sickert gently backwards and through the living room door out into the passageway. What we mainly see here is Sickert's trapped and horror-stricken face as he stares back into the lamp-lit and sulphurous room where William Crook writhes off panel in his own private purgatory. He cannot say anything. He cannot do anything to ease the burden of this poor couple. He can only feel a great hollow sickness inside, a confusion of thoughts and emotions swirling incoherently around his racing mind.
>>>SARAH (off):
>>What OTHER explanation?

PAGE 10

(PANEL) 1
>There are eight panels on this page, with three on the two upper tiers and two on the bottom tier (the final panel is double-sized). In this first panel we are standing just inside the passageway, with Sarah and Sickert up in the foreground (Alice is there too, but is maybe too small to see here) as Sarah leads Sickert out into the hall despite the artist's feeble protests. Sarah's face, not looking at Sickert as she speaks, has set into a mask of iron, full of a grim and controlled fury. Sickert, not looking at Sarah, is gazing back for a final glimpse into the dimly lit living room, where we see William Crook kneeling on the floor, head hanging, face covered by his hands, weeping to himself. Sickert looks helpless and horrified.
>>>SICKERT:
>>I...I don't know.

SICKERT:
Look, I CAN'T just leave things like this. I'-I'll come back and visit the child, I promise. Take her for outings...

(PANEL) 2
Different angle. We are now in the passageway and Sarah, still holding little Alice protectively by one hand, is steering Sickert towards the front door. Her face is still a grim and determined mask, her anger waiting until Sickert has gone before it explodes. Sickert, for his part, still looks profoundly miserable as the older woman opens the front door for him, not looking at him as she speaks.

SARAH:
That's all well and good, but you must leave us now. I've matters to discuss with my 'usband, the wretched animal...

SARAH:
Good night to you, sir.

(PANEL) 3
Now we are outside in the street with the front door over on the right, looking down Portland Street towards where it joins Berwick Street in the background. Sickert stands full to three-quarter figure facing the door, his hands spread imploringly as he makes his final useless entreaty to the stonefaced Sarah, who we see standing in the doorway here with one hand resting on little Alice's shoulder while with the other she prepares to shut the

Sickert's promise to return occasionally and take little Alice Margaret for outings is based upon similar assertions in Knight's The Final Solution. *Knight suggests that Sickert spent a lot of time in Alice Margaret's company while she was growing up, and that in fact she later became his mistress, bearing a son by him. The son of this alleged union, Joseph Sickert, is the first hand source for much of the material in Stephen Knight's book, and we shall be returning to him and his story in the proposed second appendix to* From Hell, *"The Dance of the Gull Catchers".*

From Hell
Chapter III: Blackmail, or Mrs. Barrett

door in Sickert's face. Alice is simply staring, uncomprehendingly at the two adults. Although her deafness renders her unable to hear the tension in their voices she can feel it in their posture and see it in their faces. Sarah stares coldly at the anguished looking Sickert as she bids him goodnight.

> SICKERT:
> But... but this is HORRIBLE. If only I could TELL you...
>
> SARAH:
> I said GOODNIGHT, Mr. Sickert.
>
> SICKERT:
> But please, I...

(PANEL) 4
   Same shot, but the door has now closed, and Sickert is left standing in the deserted street, staring hopelessly at the closed door, his eyes still sick with horror, his arms drooping slowly and resignedly towards his sides.

> No Dialogue

(PANEL) 5
   Same shot, but Sickert has begun to walk slowly and hesitantly away from the door and along Portland Street towards Berwick Street. Some few yards away here he turns and takes a last anguished look back at the door, as if deliberating as to whether he should go back and knock on it and tell them the whole story. He decides against it.

> No Dialogue

(PANEL) 6
   Same shot. Resolved, Sickert sticks his hands in his pockets and walks away from us down Portland Street and into the night, a small and isolated figure here as he walks away from the door that we still see mutely closed up in the right of the foreground. Although he is very small here, something about Sickert's hunched and oppressed posture as he walks away gives him a profoundly haunted air.

> No Dialogue

Alan Moore

(PANEL) 7

Whoops. I know I said earlier that this was an eight panel page, but it seems that I misread my own notes. It is in fact a seven panel page, and this last panel is a big wide one that takes up the whole of the bottom tier. What we see here is simply another shot of Oxford street by night, different in composition but as evocative and magical as its counterpart at the start of this sequence, in the first panel of page eight. We cannot see Sickert here . . . it's just a shot of Oxford Street by night, a silent beat to close this page and this scene upon before we switch back to Whitechapel and the continuing conversation of Marie Kelly and Liz Stride in the snug of the Britannia . . . or The Ringers, as it was known locally in honour of its landlord and landlady. I may use the two terms interchangeably in future, so don't let me confuse you into thinking they're two different pubs. Anyway, here all we see is nighttime Oxford Street, 1888. The growlers growl along the busy street, dark buildings on either side adorned with signs and noticeboards and old fashioned advertisements. The crowds throng the pavements, all blissfully unaware as yet that 1888 will in any way be remembered as a special year. In another month, most of them will be doublelocking their doors at night and doing their best to sound convincing when they comfort their trembling, night-

All of the literature devoted to the Whitechapel murders agrees that Marie Kelly was living with her commonlaw husband Joe Barnett in a single room at number 13, Miller's Court at the time of her murder (Miller's Court being a small courtyard running off from Dorset Street). The buildings in the court were owned by a Mr. McCarthy, and they were known generally as McCarthy's Rents. Most of them were occupied by prostitutes, and at least one author has suggested that the term "McCarthy's Rents" might have been meant to refer to the girls themselves rather than the squalid singleroom apartments in which they were living.

On the 27th of September, 1888, Liz Stride moved to 32, Flower and Dean Street. This episode being set in early August, she is still residing with waterside labourer Michael Kidney at number 33, Doreset Street. This information is again common to many of the books that make up the burgeoning black library of Whitechapel, but the one that I happen to be look-

From Hell
Chapter III: Blackmail, or Mrs. Barrett

ing at while typing this is Jack The Ripper: The Uncensored *Facts* by Paul Begg (Robson Books Ltd., 1988).

Those familiar with Ripper lore may know that Elizabeth Stride claimed to have lost her husband and family in the infamous Princess Alice Disaster of 1878. The disaster occurred on September 3rd, 1878, when the saloon steamer Princess Alice collided in the Thames with a large screw steamer called The Bywater Castle. Between six and seven hundred people lost their lives.

Why then is Liz Stride sitting in the bar of the Britannia ten years after the disaster and talking of a husband dead only four years? The simple answer is that from all the evidence, it would appear that Liz Stride simply made up the story about losing her family in the Princess Alice tragedy. According to Begg's JTR: The Uncensored Facts, John Thomas Stride died at the Sick Asylum in Bromley on the 24th of October, 1884.

The reference to "The Old Nichol Mob" and a woman called "Emma Smith" made by Polly

mare-ridden children and spouses.

No Dialogue

PAGE 11

(PANEL) 1

Now we have a seven panel page, with a big wide panel taking up the whole of this first tier and then six smaller panels beneath that. In this first shot, we have a view of the exterior of the Britannia, on the corner of Crispin and Dorset Street. As opposed to when we last saw this establishment a few pages back, it is now dark. The surrounding streets have their squalor mercifully cloaked by the gloom of the night, but somehow this doesn't make them any more welcoming. The London fog is not yet evident, this being summer, but even so the darkness has a miasmic quality, where the litter and squalor and junk upon the pavements becomes reduced to ambiguous and unguessable shapes, as do the forms of the occasional passersby that we make up drifting through the background here. The indistinctness of the shadowy forms that make up Crispin and Dorset Street makes for a general air of visual uneasiness... not a horror film dramatic shadow effect, but a sort of dismal murkiness filled with ambiguous solids and lumps. From the window of the Britannia, a dull weak light filters out into the external gloom, but serves more accentuate the darkness than dispel it.

Against this wan glow, perhaps a few vague silhouettes are visible... just one or two... as anonymous pedestrians walk along the dark street from some nameless point of origin to some equally nameless destination. This panel is just to set the following scene, really, and to establish that we are once more back in the distinctive territory of the Spitalfields district. All that's needed is a moody little study of a pub on a dark street corner.

No Dialogue

(PANEL) 2

We are now inside the pub, our eyelevel roughly at the level of the tabletop around which Marie and Liz are drinking. We are looking across the table top from one side, looking towards the window. We can't see anything outside the window expect the simple fact that it is now very dark. On the table top in the foreground are five or six empty half pint beer glasses, each with a delicate lace of foam draped about their inner surfaces. From the lefthand side of the panel we see at least one of the hands of Marie Kelly entering the picture from off, perhaps resting palm down, decorously, over the mouth of her beer glass, as if in resolve not to drink any more even though there's still a good inch of ale left in it. From the right hand side of the picture we see the hands of Liz Stride entering the picture, still cradling her own glass of ale.

Nicholls at the bottom of page 11 are also in need of explanation: The Old Nichol gang was a group of men who extorted money from the prostitutes of Whitechapel, the gang being named after the district around Old Nichol Street which they frequented. This information is according to Paul Begg, but is supported by most of the other Ripper sources listed throughout these footnotes.

Begg is also one amongst many sources to detail the killing of a forty five year old prostitute named Emma Elizabeth Smith on the 3rd of April 1888. Some commentators upon the Whitechapel murders have sought to include Smith as an early victim of Jack The Ripper, but the evidence suggests otherwise. Smith was murdered by a group of men, one of whom had forced a blunt object into her vagina, rupturing the peritoneum and leading to her death from peritonitis four days later. This has no real similarity with the established modus operandi of the Whitechapel killer, and although the culprits were never identified, I have chosen to

From Hell
Chapter III: Blackmail, or Mrs. Barrett

identify the murderers as The Old Nichol mob. This is an invention of my own and has never been verified, although of course the mob was considered as prime suspects for the murder of any East End woman during this period.

The threat made by The Old Nichol mob to Polly Nicholls and her friends in the Britannia is based upon a suggestion made by Knight in The Final Solution to the effect that Marie Kelly had in some way run afoul of the Old Nichol mob, their demands for money prompting her desperate blackmail attempt. It does indeed seems plausible that increased pressure upon certain Whitechapel prostitutes from protection racketeers such as The Old Nichol mob may have presented Marie Kelly and her associates with a sudden and desperate need for money. Given that another prostitute, Martha Tabram, was stabbed to death in a brutal assault on August 6th, 1888 and that the Old Nichol mob were suspected by the police at that time of being responsible, it would seem that there may be justification

The respective balloons of the two women enter from either side of the picture, in the appropriate directions.

MARIE (off, left):
Heavens, look at the time, an' me spent me lodging-money. I'd better earn more before goin' home tonight . . .

LIZ (off, right):
Where living are you now?

(PANEL) 3

We pull back now so that we get a good middledistance shot of the table with Marie sitting on the left and Liz on the right, both of them roughly half to three quarter figure here. Beyond them is only the window, looking out onto the Whitechapel night. Marie looks down into her last inch of beer with a sort of weary resignation at her circumstances, not looking at Liz as she speaks. Liz, for her part, is gazing out of the window into the night with a dreamy and melancholy look, her glass raised towards her lips, about to sip.

MARIE:
In one o'McCarthy's rents at Miller's Court, just up Dorset Street.

MARIE:
My Joe'll be wild if I'm home emptyhanded.

LIZ:
Ah. Once I have husband.

(PANEL) 4

We change angle now so that we are behind Marie Kelly, looking past her across the table to where the melancholy Swedish woman sits facing us, glass in hand, still staring distantly out of the window into the Whitechapel night. More towards the foreground we see Marie suddenly turn her head and look back over her shoulder towards us with a look of surprised curiosity as the balloon of the landlord, Mr. Walter Ringer, issues into the panel from off pic behind Marie, in the foreground. It is towards the source of this loud outcry that Marie is turning her head while Liz continues to talk, gazing out into the darkness.

LIZ:
John Stride. We keep coffeeroom, in Poplar. Dead now, four years.

LIZ:
Now in Dorset Street also, I am with Michael Kidney. Good man, but . . .

WALTER RINGER (off):
Oy!

(PANEL) 5

Now we cut to a shot from just behind the bar, with the landlord facing away from us half figure to head and shoulders up in the foreground. Looking over the bar we are looking towards the front door of the pub, which is being pushed open as two women enter from the dark streets outside. Walter Ringer, up in

for suggesting that protection gangs were leaning heavily upon the tradeswomen of Whitechapel during this period.

Polly Nicholls' reference to her dream is also an invention, although it is true that Polly Nicholls did live on Stamford Street just a short walk over Waterloo Bridge from Cleopatra's Needle, with her husband William before he left her, as she alleged, for another woman. (Or, as he maintained, because of her incessant drinking.) It is also true that Polly's brother had died in a fire two years previously when his paraffin lamp exploded. The dream is invented, but the individual elements from which it is constructed are genuine. The information on Polly Nicholls comes, once again, from Begg's The Uncensored Facts.

The physical appearance of the four women here is drawn from written descriptions, published sketches by police illustrators and, where appropriate, from morgue photographs. These women were neither the sultry, wanton beauties that they are depicted as

From Hell
Chapter III: Blackmail, or Mrs. Barrett

being in the more exploitational Ripper movies, nor the disfigured and toothless hags that some writers have described them as. They were ordinary women, who, despite their deprived and unhealthy situation, were trying to look attractive for the only job that society had seen fit to offer them. Polly Nicholls, for example, despite having front teeth missing, was by all accounts a very youthful looking woman five or ten years younger in appearance than in actuality.

the foreground, is a burly, red faced and blustery man, somewhat older than his wife, who we saw earlier. I'm afraid I don't have any visual reference on him, so you'll just have to make him up as you go along. Here, his expression is cross and suspicious as he calls out his warning to the two women that are entering his pub. He looks apprehensive of trouble and determined to head it off at the pass. Looking beyond him we see the two women. One of them is Annie Chapman and the other is Polly Nicholls. Annie is a fierce looking woman of forty seven years, only five feet tall but solid as a brick shithouse. Her hair is wavy and dark brown, her eyes blue and her nose large and thick. Two teeth are missing from her bottom jaw, although this probably won't be evident here. As she enters the pub she is steering and shepherding the weeping figure of Polly Nicholls along with her. Polly is a couple of inches taller than Annie, but of much slighter build, cutting a less substantial figure. Aged forty two, Polly looks about thirty seven or even younger, taking advantage of this to lie about her age. She has five teeth missing at the front, but when her mouth is shut she looks quite pretty in a weak, frail sort of way. Her dark hair is brown, turning grey, and her facial features are small and delicate in contrast with those of Annie Chapman. Polly has high cheekbones and pretty grey eyes that are flooded with tears in this panel. Trembling and weeping helplessly, she allows Annie to steer her into the pub, dabbing at her eyes with a dirty handkerchief, her eyelids lowered here and not looking at us. Annie, beside her, is staring furiously and defiantly towards Walter Ringer, the barman, up in the foreground, daring him to refuse her entry, her eyes blaze. Annie is a real termagant, and faced with her wrath, all but the brave and reckless will usually back down.

> WALTER RINGER:
> Oy, come on, Dark Annie! Don't go bringin' no trouble in 'ere!

> ANNIE CHAPMAN:
> You shut yer 'ole, Walter Ringer. Can't ye see the girl's 'ad a fright?

(PANEL) 6

Change angle now so that we are back over by the table that Marie and Liz are sharing, by the window. This is up in the foreground here, with perhaps a little of Liz . . . her hand and beer glass or something, entering from the left of the foreground. Across the table and more to the right of our picture here we see Marie, turning round in her seat to call across the bar to Annie and Polly, in the background beyond her. Over in the background we see Annie steering Polly Nicholls through the bar and towards the table where Marie and Liz are waiting up in the foreground. I imagine he'll only be small and sketchy at this distance but we see Walter Ringer behind his bar as he sulkily returns to his work, shooting a resentful but impotent glance at Annie as he does so. Steering Polly across the bar towards Liz and Marie, Annie ignores him. She looks expressionlessly towards Marie and Liz as the former call out to her. Polly, by her side, is still crying too much to really see anything. As I see Polly, she weeps quite easily and is regarded as a bit of a baby by the other women.

> WALTER RINGER:
> Aye . . . well, as long as you keep the noise down . . .

> MARIE KELLY:
> ANNIE! Annie CHAPMAN! Over HERE!

> MARIE (separate balloon):
> Whatever's the matter with Polly?

From Hell
Chapter III: Blackmail, or Mrs. Barrett

(PANEL) 7
Change angle slightly, so that it's almost as if we're seeing this panel through Liz Stride's eyes, although she herself isn't visible here. To the right of the panel we see Marie sitting facing us, turning slightly towards the panel's left in order to pull back an empty chair for Polly to sit down on. She is looking at Polly sympathetically and with genuine concern as she does this. Polly, lowering herself hesitantly into the proffered chair, still has a hand full of handkerchief raised to her face as she speaks, still not looking at us or indeed at anybody. On the left of the panel we Annie Chapman as she helps Polly into her seat. She looks dour and grim as she speaks, looking down at the top of Polly's head as she does so.

Polly Nicholls

> ANNIE CHAPMAN:
> The old Nichol Mob 'ad a word with 'er ...

> POLLY NICHOLLS:
> Th-they said they'd do to me what ...

> POLLY NICHOLLS:
> What they did to Emma Smith. Oh GOD ...

PAGE 12

(PANEL) 1

A nine panel page here. In this first panel we close in upon the image that concluded our last page, so that we only see Polly, now properly seated, and Marie sitting on her left (our right) as she comforts the still-weeping woman. If we can see any of Annie Chapman at all it is only the edge of her coat or something entering the panel at the left, and she needn't be visible at all. Polly, now seated, is still covering most of her face with one hand and weeping copiously. Her eyes are still lowered and not looking at anyone. Marie lays one hand comfortingly upon Polly's shoulder and gives a pained little wince as she tries to quieten the weeping girl.

> POLLY:
> They s-said if I didn't pay more insurance, they'd shove a knife right ...

> POLLY:
> Right up my ...

> MARIE:
> Hush now. We ALL know what happened to Emma.

(PANEL) 2

Now perhaps we pull back to have a shot showing the whole table, so that we can see where everyone is sitting in relation to the others. Moving anticlockwise, we start with Marie Kelly. Polly Nicholls sits on her right, and Annie Chapman is just taking a seat to Polly's right and the left of Liz Stride. We are looking from Liz's end of the table here, so that what we see is Liz over on the right, sitting facing roughly away from us, up in the foreground. To the

From Hell
Chapter III: Blackmail, or Mrs. Barrett

left we see Annie Chapman in profile as she lowers her squat bulk into another vacant chair between Liz Stride and Polly. Polly sits next around the table from Annie, But as we look at her here she is almost facing us. On her left (our right) sits Marie Kelly, also facing us down the length of the table. We cannot properly see Liz Stride's expression here, and Annie Chapman seems to be directing her undivided attention to the task of settling her bulk onto a chair. Polly, however, looks up for the first time and speaks in our general direction as her eyes move round the table, as if speaking to all the women present. Her little face is tearstreaked and her eyes are wild with terror as she croaks out her warning to the women. Marie Kelly, staring at Polly, suddenly has a rather sick expression of anxiety come over her face. Her brow tightens into an anxious frown and she peers at Polly through pained and worriedlooking eyes. Marie has never liked the idea of being cut. The threat of it makes her feel sick.

POLLY:
"Tell yer friends in the Ringer's", they said.

POLLY:
"Either we get bigger cuts, or they do!"

MARIE:
Oh fuck me! Is that right?

(PANEL) 3

Change angle. We are now looking at the end of the table where Annie and Liz are sitting, and cannot see Marie or Polly here. Annie sits with her back towards us, up in the left of the foreground. Her head is turned so that her face is in profile, looking off panel towards the left we see Liz Stride. Liz is staring at Annie in widemouthed astonishment and horror at the mention of this astronomical sum of money. Annie is not looking at her but gazing at the offpanel Marie Kelly with a grim, dour and pessimistic expression upon her thick, coarse features.

ANNIE:
There's worse: They want four pounds, what they reckon we owe 'em.

LIZ:
Four POUNDS? Never I am seeing so much!

(PANEL) 4

Change angle again. Up in the foreground on the right now we can see a little of Polly Nicholl's face entering the picture, right up close to us and in profile facing left. She is staring down at the tabletop in front of her bleakly, seeing nothing but her own fears. Her eyes are still brimming, with saline tracks down her cheeks as she talks. Beyond her slightly and more towards the left of the panel here we have Annie Chapman sitting facing towards us across the table, but turning to speak to Liz Stride, who is unseen off the lefthand side of the panel here. Annie's expression is glum. Polly's is fatalistic and tremulous. We cannot see Marie or Liz. Behind Annie there is a suggestion of the bar room visible, just as in our last panel there should have been a glimpse of the window with the night beyond it immediately beyond Annie and Liz.

ANNIE:
Well, we'll 'ave to find it SOMEWHERE...

POLLY:
We'll NEVER find four pounds. They'll kill us, I know. I've 'ad NIGHTMARES...

(PANEL) 5

Change angle again. We are now positioned behind both Annie and Polly, so that Polly sits facing slightly away from us on our left and Annie sits facing slightly away from us on our right. Beyond these two we can maybe see a little of Marie and Liz, facing us to either side of the background. Polly is looking wide eyed and tearful as she gazes away from us towards Marie and Liz in the B/G, who are listening sympathetically and attentively if we can see them. Annie Chapman, to the right of the foreground, isn't so sympathetic. She curls her lip in contempt, sneering at Polly's dream dismissively.

POLLY:
I dreamed about Stamford Street, where I lived with my Billy before 'e ran off...

ANNIE:
Dreams! It's wakin' life's the trouble!

From Hell
Chapter III: Blackmail, or Mrs. Barrett

It is Knight, in The Final Solution, *who suggests that Marie Kelly and her associates leveled their blackmail attempt against the Royal Family, although Knight never explains precisely how this is carried out. However, since his book clearly depicts Walter Sickert as the only player with Royal contacts who would be personally known to Marie Kelly, it would seem that Sickert himself would be the obvious target for such an attempt, which is the way that I have chosen to depict events here. Since writing this scene, however, Jean Overton Fuller's* Sickert & The Ripper Crimes *has seen the light of day, in which Ms Fuller reiterates much of Knight's theory, apparently from a different source. In her book, she clearly states that Walter Sickert was the man being blackmailed by the prostitutes, thus confirming my intuitions (at least in as much as anything in this morass of halftruth, rumour and downright lie is confirmable).*

(PANEL) 6

The last four panels on this page are all from the same angle and represent a gradual closein upon the face of Polly Nicholls as she recounts her dream. In this current panel we can see Polly sitting in maybe a halffigure, still some feet away from us. To either side of her sit Annie Chapman, on the left, and Marie Kelly, on the right. Annie, her elbows resting on the table, is still scowling with surly, dismissive contempt as Polly recounts her tale. Marie, on the other side, is listening with sympathy and real interest. She likes hearing narratives, whether they be gossip, ghost story or recounting of a dream. She gazes seriously and attentively at Polly as she speaks.

POLLY:
No, no, it was 'orrible . . .

POLLY:
I walked over Waterloo Bridge, down the Embankment, and there were that MONUMENT; that NEEDLE thing.

MARIE:
As, I know it.

(PANEL) 7

We continue to close in. Polly is still halffigure, but now she is closer to us. We can no longer see the faces of Marie or Annie, since they have vanished off the sides of the picture as we close in. All we can see are perhaps their arms or hands entering the picture to either side. Polly is staring out of the panel at us from between them, her eyes wide as she recounts her dream, as if she is watching it being played back before them on some sort of cerebral V.C.R she is just staring into space through her tearmisted eyes. Liz Stride's balloon issues from off panel at the bottom, denoting a voice from the foreground, while Marie Kelly's answering call for silence enters from the right of the panel here, where Marie is sitting just off panel.

POLLY:
Standin' by it was me brother . . . 'e burned to death two year back, when 'is paraffin lamp exploded.

LIZ (off):
Is bad luck, dreaming of dead . . .

MARIE (off):
Shhh!

(PANEL) 8

We continue to close in, so that we really only see Polly roughly head and shoulders here. Nobody else is visible. Lost in the recounting of her nightmare, Polly is just staring into space, looking at some inner scene that only she can see. Her eyes are filling with horror as she recounts the dream, living its terrors over again. Her hands raise up tentatively before her, as if trying to convey the dream more forcibly to her offpanel audience.

POLLY:
I called him, but . . .

POLLY:
. . . but 'e just started BURNIN', like when 'e DIED. I couldn't do anythin' . . .

POLLY:
'E put 'is arms round the needle . . .

(PANEL) 9

We are now right in tight close upon Polly's face, She lifts her hands up into the picture and covers her face, all but obscuring it from our view here. Polly is obviously terribly distraught. Whether from her dream or from her recent death threat is difficult to say.

From Hell
Chapter III: Blackmail, or Mrs. Barrett

> POLLY:
> ... and the NEEDLE burned too! That cold stone, afire ... it looked so QUEER.
>
> POLLY:
> I woke up an' KNEW somethin' bad would 'appen.
>
> POLLY:
> I KNEW it.

Page 13

(PANEL) 1

Seven panels here, with the first panel taking up the whole of the top tier. What we have is a full figure shot showing the whole table and all four of the women seated about it. They are positioned so that over furthest towards the left here we have Polly Nicholls sitting in profile facing towards the right. She seems to have pushed her chair back from the table a little and is sitting with her face sunken into her hands, as she was in the last panel on Page 12. Working across from left to right, we next see Marie Kelly, who is sitting immediately beyond Polly and facing more or less towards us here. She has one hand resting comfortingly upon Polly's shoulder and with the other one she is waving for the attention to the offpanel landlady, Mrs. Ringer, who we presume is somewhere offpanel to the left and towards the foreground, since this is where Marie's gaze is directed as she calls out, ordering a gin for the distraught Polly. Next, from left to right, we see Annie Chapman, who sits on our side of the table with her back towards us but with her head turned to look at Polly and Marie so that her face is partly visible in profile here. She still looks surly and pessimistic. Finally, over on the right we have Liz Stride. Liz is turned in her seat slightly and gazing dreamily and absently in our direction, even though her body is angled to face mostly towards the left. She has a thoughtful frown as she gazes into space, thinking aloud. Her look of concentration has an earnestness to it that is quite endearing.

> MARIE:
> Don't go upsettin' yourself, now.

MARIE:
Mrs. Ringer? Can we have a gin over here for the girl?

ANNIE:
Listen, what WE'VE gotta dream up is some way o' findin' that MONEY . . .

LIZ:
We could sell something, perhaps . . .

(PANEL) 2

The three panels that make up this central tier are all the same shot. Basically it is as if we were crouching somewhere between Annie Chapman and Liz Stride, to our left and right respectively, looking between them towards Marie Kelly, who sits across the table from us and facing us in the immediate background. We can see Annie's hands entering from the left of the panel, gesturing as she talks brusquely to Liz, while we see Liz's calm, long-fingered hands entering the panel from the right, holding her half-empty glass of beer. We can see neither of their faces, and thus all of our attention is upon Marie Kelly as she sits silently facing us from the near background. In this panel, Annie's hands enter from the left with one palm held outwards towards Liz Stride in blunt refutal of Liz's idea. Entering from the other side we see Liz's hand, fingers wrapped around her glass, just starting to raise it from the table here towards her mouth. In the middle, Marie is looking with an

Annie Chapman

From Hell
Chapter III: Blackmail, or Mrs. Barrett

attentive and thoughtful expression towards the off-panel Annie Chapman, listening to what she is saying with a thoughtful little frown. Since Polly had pushed her chair back slightly from the table last panel we do not need to see her here . . . or at least, we don't according to my rough layouts, but you'll have to see how realistically it works for yourself when you come to set it out.

>ANNIE (off):
>Aa, ye great daft Swedish cow! We're already sellin' ourselves at thruppence a ride!

>ANNIE (off):
>What 'ave WE got worth sellin'?

(PANEL) 3

Same shot. Entering from the left, Annie's hands are now spread palm upwards as if displaying the irrefutable truth of her argument for all to see with this little shrug of her hands. The hands are spread as if asking for some answer to her careful listing of their individual poverties, although she isn't really expecting one. Entering from the right, we see Liz's hand raise the beer glass right up to her lips, sipping from it. Sitting between them, Marie Kelly isn't looking at either one, but is staring down at the tabletop before her, her thoughtful frown deepening as she slowly arrives at her fateful decision, urged by neccessity. Annie continues to rant from off-panel left.

>ANNIE (off):
>MY only regular money comes from washin' the PENSIONER, an' I've nothin' o' value bar what I stand up in.

>ANNIE (off):
>Neither 'ave you.

>ANNIE (off):
>Neither 'as Polly . . .

(PANEL) 4

Same shot. From the left, Annie Chapman's hands suddenly grow still, palms flat down upon the tabletop as if stunned into immobility by what Marie has just said. On the right, we see Liz

Stride put her glass back down upon the table top, having sipped from it. Her hands too are still. Facing us in the background, Marie Kelly suddenly speaks, her eyes cold and steely and resolved. She's made up her mind.

MARIE:
I have.

MARIE (separate balloon):
I've got somethin' worth sellin'.

(PANEL) 5

Now, on this bottom tier, we also have three panels from the same angle, but here we reverse the angle of our last tier so that we are looking through the eyes of Marie Kelly at the other three women across the table from her: Liz on the left, Annie in the middle and Polly nearest to us on the right. From the bottom foreground we can see Marie's hands (or hand) entering the panel from off, resting with the fingers wrapped around the base of her glass, there upon the tabletop before her. As we look through her eyes at the three women we see that they are all looking towards her. Liz Stride has a frown of puzzled interest, wondering what Marie might have to sell, while Polly is darting an anxiously questioning look at us over on the right of the panel here. Annie Chapman, between them, sneers in dismissive contempt, perhaps waving away Marie's claim with one hand as she does so. Marie's balloon enters the panel from the bottom here as she speaks from off in the foreground.

ANNIE:
Garn! If it's yer cunny, you'd be lucky to get four pennies, let alone four POUND!

MARIE (off):
No, it's not that. I'm talkin' about secret INFORMATION.

(PANEL) 6

Same shot. On the left of the background, Liz Stride's eyes widen in an expression somewhere between real surprise, mock surprise and disbelief as she stares across the table towards us and the off panel Marie. Next to her, Annie Chapman is now looking angry,

From Hell
Chapter III: Blackmail, or Mrs. Barrett

openly contemptuous of Marie's claims. On the right, Polly is still looking anxiously and seriously towards Marie, as if she wants to believe what she's saying but can't quite bring herself to. In the foreground, looming large, we see at least the upper rim of Marie's beerglass as she raises it to her lip, accentuating her dramatic pause before replying to the women with a sip of her beer. Hope that works okay as a shot, with the curve of the beerglass looming in the bottom foreground.

LIZ:
If worth four pounds, is very BIG secret, I'm thinking.

ANNIE:
She's makin' it UP! What do YOU know about that's worth four pounds, Marie Kelly?

(PANEL) 7
Same shot, only here Marie has lowered the beer glass from the foreground so that it rests on the tabletop before us as it did in panel five. In the near background, the women all appear to be struck momentarily mute by what Marie is saying in the word balloon that issues into the panel from the bottom border from where Marie is offpicture in the foreground. Liz Stride looks bemused and surprised, her puzzled eyes staring at us questioningly. In the centre, Annie's face looks blank and uncomprehending, while on the right Polly's eyes grow as wide as a child's waiting for Christmas. She believes Marie's unlikely story instantly and wholly ... though this is more through gullibility and credulity that through perceptiveness, I should point out. As it happens, Marie is telling the truth, but as a general rule of thumb, Polly will believe almost anything anyone tells her instantly.

MARIE (off):
A royal baby.

Page 14

(PANEL) 1
A nine panel page here, still in the Britannia with the four women as they chew over Marie's revelation. This first tier has

three panels all showing the same shot, which is one of the quartet of women sitting around the table, angled so that we are looking across the table towards the bar ... presumably we're standing just inside the window. Liz and Annie are over to the left, with Polly and Marie over towards the right as we see them here. Approaching the table from the background we can see Mrs. Ringer, carrying a tray upon which rests the glass of gin that Marie ordered for Polly a couple of pages back. Annie Chapman, to the left of the foreground, is glaring at Marie Kelly, almost snarling as she expresses her contemptuous disbelief. Since she has her back to the bar she cannot see Mrs. Ringer approaching. Marie Kelly, over on the right, can see her however, and hisses a sharp warning to Annie, her face wrinkling with urgency and crossness, her eyes measuring the approach of Mrs. Ringer. If we can see Liz and Polly properly, then Liz has also noticed the approach of Mrs. Ringer and is watching her, while Polly is looking with mingled hope and admiration towards Marie Kelly.

ANNIE:
A Royal ... ? Are ye MAD, woman? You can't have ...

MARIE:
Shhh! Shut yer fat Gob, for Christ's sake.

(PANEL) 2

Same shot, only here Mrs. Ringer has walked right up to the table and is just setting the glass of gin down beside Polly Nicholls. Mrs. Ringer wears a fairly neutral expression. The four seated women are all suddenly taking an unnatural interest in their drinks or in the table top, and Marie Kelly doesn't meet Mrs. Ringer's eyes as she speaks to her. Annie Chapman is still scowling, but only at the tabletop. Liz Stride sips her drink, while Polly just sits there not meeting anyone's eyes and looking small and frightened.

MRS. RINGER:
Here y'are, Marie. I've put it on the slate.

MARIE:
S'very good o' ya, Mrs. Ringer.

From Hell
Chapter III: Blackmail, or Mrs. Barrett

(PANEL) 3
Same shot. Mrs. Ringer, visible in the background, has turned away and is walking back towards the bar. All four women watch her depart with their eyes, waiting until she is out of earshot before continuing with their conversation. There is something almost charmingly furtive in the way they all turn their heads, like sea gulls, in the same direction as they follow Mrs. Ringer's departure with their eyes.

No Dialogue

(PANEL) 4
Now a crowded, tighter shot of the four women as they all lean forward furtively over the tabletop, their faces bunching together as they confer in heated whispers. Annie Chapman is angry and disbelieving as she growls at Marie Kelly. She suspects that Marie is just spinning another of her fancy tall stories and that they're having their legs pulled. For her part, Marie's eyes flash with indignation and she stares into Annie Chapman's eyes as she replies, her gaze level and unwavering, her expression suffused with crossness that Annie should cast doubt upon her story. Liz and Polly just look on at this whispered confrontation with interest.

ANNIE:
Now, what's all this Royal baby bull . . .

MARIE:
It's not bull. It was Prince Albert Victor fathered a baby on a poor girl I knew, then had her locked away.

(PANEL) 5
This panel should just be angled so that we can only see the faces of Annie Chapman and Marie Kelly, with Marie towards the right of the foreground facing slightly away from us as she glares at Annie, defiantly, and Annie staring at us from the immediate background, her lips set into a thin hard line as she stares belligerently into Marie's eyes and tries to decide whether the young Irish girl is lying or not. It is a long, hard penetrating look, but Marie does not flinch from it.

No Dialogue

(PANEL) 6
Same shot as panel five exactly, still with Annie staring hard at Marie and Marie staring levelly and defiantly back. The only minor difference here is that both of them have their mouths open just a little as they speak. Otherwise, this panel is identical to Panel Five in every way.

               ANNIE CHAPMAN:
If you're LYIN' about this, Marie Kelly, I'll break your fuckin' neck.

               MARIE:
I'm not lyin'.

(PANEL) 7
This panel is probably more or less through Marie's eyes, so we can just see Annie Chapman and Polly Nicholls, the two sitting nearest to her, as she looks at them. Annie is sitting facing us on the left of the panel here, but is looking away from us and gazing with a deeply thoughtful and troubled expression out of the left hand side of the panel. Polly, more towards the right of the panel here, is looking directly towards us, an anxious and questioning look in her slightly puffy, tearsmudged eyes. Behind them is a backdrop of the bar room, with business going on as normal. (Something I should have stressed earlier when we had the exterior scenes of Whitechapel is just how many obvious Jews there are about, including ones with the full Hassidic beard and what have you. We should remember to make them a permanent and highly visible feature of our Whitechapel background wherever possible. That said, however, I don't suppose there'd be many Orthodox Jews drinking in the Britannia at this time of night. Just look on it as a note for your future reference.)

               ANNIE:
Bloody 'ell.

               ANNIE:
Bloody 'ell, I've gotta think about all this . . .

               POLLY:
This SECRET . . . would people give MONEY for us not to tell?

From Hell
Chapter III: Blackmail, or Mrs. Barrett

(PANEL) 8
Now just a shot of Marie Kelly. Eyelids lowered demurely and smiling a quiet little smile to herself she sits facing us with her almost empty glass held between her hands in front of her. Annie Chapman's balloon issues from offpanel on the left.

ANNIE (off):
Blackmail the Royal family? You're talkin' TREASON, woman!

MARIE:
Oh, we needn't approach THEM. They've got FRIENDS who'll buy our silence.

MARIE:
In fact, I know the very man.

(PANEL) 9
Now just a silent panel to end the page. It is a fairly closeup shot of the bartop of the Ringers. We can see the ale pumps with the towel already draped over them. Entering from one side of the picture, probably the right, we can see the arm of Mr. Ringer as he lives up to his name and rings the bell to call time. This can either be a hand bell that he rings as a town cryer would or perhaps a small bell hanging above the bar which he reaches up and rattles. Up to you. Whatever sort of bell he's ringing, we only see his arm. His face isn't visible here. This panel really just to say "Time has passed. The pub is now closing".

No Dialogue

PAGE 15

(PANEL) 1
Now we have a seven panel page, with panel seven being a big wide one that takes up the whole of the bottom tier. This first panel is a long shot of the front door of the Ringers, a pallid rectangle of light against the dark of the streets outside. Framed in this rectangle we see Mrs. Ringer as she says goodnight to Marie, Annie, Polly and Liz, who she has finally persuaded to leave her pub so can shut it for the night. As we see her here she is just a

stocky silhouette against the light of the bar room behind her. The four prostitutes are just dim and shadowy shapes as they move away into the darkness. The word balloons here are tailless, to give the impression of a general chorus of goodbyes heard over a distance. The first balloon is nearest Mrs. Ringer while the others drift across the panel into the darkness after the four departing women, some of whom are perhaps having goodbye to the Landlady as they walk away.

TAILLESS BALLOON:
Goodnight now, ladies

TAILLESS BALLOON
G'night, Mrs. Ringer.

TAILLESS BALLOON
G'night ...

TAILLESS BALLOON:
Night, Mrs. Ringer.

(PANEL) 2

Now we are in Brushfield Street with the women, looking down it towards the corner of Crispin Street. Up towards the foreground and perhaps closer to the right we have Annie Chapman and Marie Kelly as they walk towards us. Behind and further to the left we see Polly Nicholls in the near background as she bustles round the corner from Crispin Street looking anxious and trying to keep up with the others. Annie Chapman doesn't look at Polly as she speaks to her, but is staring keenly at Marie Kelly. Marie doesn't look at Annie but just looks straight ahead of her, the way she's going. She seems very calm. Up to you whether we can see Liz Stride or not. If we can she is some way behind Annie and Marie but not as far away as Polly, hobbling around the corner behind her. Around the women the night has the darkness of dirty water: A sense of a dark sediment churning.

POLLY:
Wait for ME! I don't like walkin' on me own ...

ANNIE:
Oh, shut up an' don't be so daft.

From Hell
Chapter III: Blackmail, or Mrs. Barrett

ANNIE:
Now, 'ave you got that letter safe, Marie?

(PANEL) 3

Now perhaps a profile shot of as many of the four women as you can fit in comfortably, walking from left to right across the panel. Polly has perhaps caught up here, bustling anxiously into the panel from the left and looking towards Marie as she speaks. Marie is glancing disdainfully towards Annie Chapman as she speaks to her. If we can see her, Long Liz Stride merely looks on and holds her peace. Remember that Liz is considerably taller than the other women, so you should have a good mix of distinctive physical types to arrange your pictures around.

MARIE:
'COURSE, I have. I've not spent all night writin' it to wipe me arse on it now, have I?

POLLY:
Shall ye deliver it tonight?

As mentioned earlier, Hawksmoor's Christchurch Spitalfields is a brief two minute walk up Dorset Street from the front door of the Britannia. It's sepulchral white bulk blocks the mouth of the street where at least three of these women resided near the time of their deaths, part of the ominous furniture of their lives.

(PANEL) 4

We are now probably standing at the bottom of the steps of Christchurch, looking across towards Brushfield Street as the four women come around the corner and start to walk across the dark street towards us. Since Christchurch is directly behind us we can see no trace of it here. We are probably too far away to make out much about the women here, but we can probably tell who they are from their builds and postures: Annie tubby, Liz tall, Polly huddled, Marie defiant. They are about to walk across the tram lines as we see them coming towards us here.

          MARIE:
Aa. I could use a walk

          ANNIE:
Not me. I'm off lookin' for trade to buy me supper.

          ANNIE:
I'm starvin'. Only 'ad broken biscuits all day . . .

(PANEL) 5

Change angle now. The woman have crossed the street and are now walking from left to right across the panel, along the pavement immediately in front Christchurch. As we see them here, the steps of Christchurch and perhaps the lower reaches of the Doric pillars are immediately behind them. The whores do not look at Christchurch as they pass it by but continue to talk amongst themselves. We see Liz Stride wincing expression of pain is quite comical. Marie has an airy expression as she replies to Annie's stated preference for seeking trade rather than enjoying a brisk walk to Cleveland Street. None of the women pay any attention to Hawksmoor's Church, filling the background behind them.

          MARIE:
Sure, an' I'll take sore feet over a sore fanny any time.

Annie Chapman's reference to having eaten nothing but broken biscuits all day gives pretty much a full and comprehensive account of the diet of the East End woman, this being gin and broken biscuits, (Broken biscuits, obviously, may be purchased more cheaply than unbroken ones) This grim snippet of information derives from London Labour and the London Poor by Mayhew (Penguin, 1985). I would recommend Mayhew's book as being the essential reference source for anyone interested in the everyday life of Victorian London. Filled with observations and interviews recorded at the time, it is the best surviving account of how people actually thought, talked and lived, with Mayhew coming across as a kind of nineteenth century Ring Lardner.

From Hell
Chapter III: Blackmail, or Mrs. Barrett

> LIZ:
> Oh, do not speak of it, when I have my ulcers.

(PANEL) 6

Same shot, but here the women are walking off the righthand side of the panel, Marie laughing as she talks to Liz Stride. In the immediate background, unnoticed by the women, the steps of Christchurch rise up and away from us, inviting us up under their inhumanely big portico. Marie Kelly's laughter, bright and infectious though it is, is a small and fragile thing next to the age and power and brutal mass of Christchurch.

> MARIE:
> Ha ha ha ha!

> MARIE:
> Her with her STARVATION, you with yer PLAGUES an' Polly with her DEATHTHREATS...

(PANEL) 7

This final big panel is a shot of Christchurch Spitalfields, standing there, awful and alone against the miasmic night. I figure we are looking at the upper reaches of the church here, with the massive spire rising up above the gigantic portico: One man's strange and twisted ego cast in corpsewhite stone and built to last for all eternity. Marie's little speech balloon issues up from off panel down towards the bottom right corner of the panel here, her words drifting back along the street towards us a she walks on leaving us to gaze up at the pallid hellchurch, looming above us, a tomb of dead gods.

> SICKERT (off):
> We're the four whores of the Apocalypse.

PAGE 16

(PANEL) 1

We return for these last four pages to Cleveland Street and the worsening fortunes of Mr. Walter Sickert. This page has seven panels, with the first one being a wide one that takes up the whole of the top tier. All we see is the distinctive derbyhatted figure of

Alan Moore

Christchurch, Spitalfields - Steeple

From Hell
Chapter III: Blackmail, or Mrs. Barrett

Sickert as he trudges wearily and despondently towards us down the near-deserted expanse of Cleveland Street. You can pick your favourite view of the street, bearing in mind that Sickert will be coming along it from the Oxford Street end towards his studio. From his posture he looks very depressed. Maybe he's even stopped off for a drink on the way home, but its done nothing to lighten his spirits. He trudges towards us, hands in his coat pockets, eyes downcast.

No Dialogue

(PANEL) 2
Now a small panel to kick off this tier, again showing Sickert as he walks towards us down Cleveland Street. (If the shot is a bit monotonous after panel one then maybe in panel one he could be walking from left to right, or even away from us. See what you think.) In the foreground, we are down at roughly pavement level outside Sickert's studio at Number Fifteen. Sickert trudges towards us, looking miserably towards the pavement at his feet rather than ahead of him and thus towards us.

No Dialogue

(PANEL) 3
Same shot as panel two, except that here, right into the foreground, there steps a woman's leg, barefoot, and clad only in a light hospital gown such as the ones we've seen worn by the women kept for William Gull's private asylum at Guy's Hospital. The leg belongs to Annie Crook, as it steps out to block Sickert's path. It is positioned so that Annie is standing facing away from us and down the street, her bare sole resting upon the cold pavement. Sickert, still approaching from the far background, is still a fairly small figure here, and is still gazing miserably towards the ground at his feet as he walks. He has not yet looked up and noticed the woman stepping into his path.

No Dialogue

(PANEL) 4
Same shot, with the leg up in the foreground standing stock still, exactly where it was last panel. The only thing that's changed in this

panel is that Sickert is much closer and larger now as he finally looks up and sees the woman standing outside his studio. His face has a look of surprise as he gazes up, slack jawed and vaguely stupefiedlooking, into the offpanel eyes of Annie Crook. He stops dead in his tracks as he does so, the dark reaches of Cleveland Street stretching away behind him. Annie's balloon issues from off panel above here.

> ANNIE (off):
> Mr. Sickert . . . ?
>
> ANNIE (off):
> Where is she?

(PANEL) 5

Now a shot through Sickert's eyes. We are looking at Annie Crook as she stands there in the nightshrouded street wearing nothing but her hospital gown. Her hair is dirty and tangled, and she has put on weight since the last time we saw her, this being a rapidly noticeable side effect of the king of thyroid operation that Annie has suffered. She isn't obese, but she looks sluggish and heavy. Her face is hard to look at: All the vitality is gone, and the eyes look sad and dead and confused, the muscles around her mouth too slack to conjure the warm, bright smile that we associate with Annie in better times. She stares at us and the offpanel Sickert, who we cannot see here. Her entire body posture is slumped and lethargic and slow as she stands there aimlessly in her bare

Knight states that at some point, according to his sources, Annie Crook returned to Cleveland Street looking for her baby in the wake of her debilitating surgery at the hands of Dr. Gull. The scene on these pages is my interpretation of that event.

From Hell
Chapter III: Blackmail, or Mrs. Barrett

feet outside Sickert's studio, to which place she has somehow found her way through a fog of dim memories and confusion.

      ANNIE:
Where's my baby?

(PANEL) 6
 Now maybe we have Annie facing away from us in the foreground so that we're looking over her shoulder towards Sickert as he stands there facing us and Annie, rooted to the spot with the creeping horror of recognition stealing over his features as he gazes at the wretched creature standing before him. His eyes are wide with a sick and appalled look, and he seems to be having difficulty in getting his jaw to form appropriate words.

      SICKERT:
Oh God . . .

      SICKERT:
A-Annie? Is that . . . ?

      SICKERT:
Oh God.

(PANEL) 7
 Now we have maybe pulled back a little from our last shot, so that we can see both Sickert and Annie as they stand there outside Number Fifteen. Annie is turned slightly so that we can see some of her face as she stands looking dully and expressionlessly up at Sickert. One of her arms is lifted, the fingers playing childishly with the matted coils of Annie's hair. The gesture is unconscious, and Annie doesn't seem aware that she is doing it. In fact, Annie doesn't seem aware of very much at all. Sickert is staring at her in wretched and helpless horror, just stammering and babbling as he tries to think of something to say.

      SICKERT:
Annie, you're . . . you're supposed to be in hospital. You . . .

      ANNIE:
I climbed out of there.

ANNIE:
I want my Alice.

PAGE 17

(PANEL) 1

There are nine panels on this page. I'm open to suggestions regarding the visual storytelling, since the nature of this scene... Sickert and Annie standing motionless and talking in Cleveland Street... makes it relatively flexible. For what it's worth, here's how I think we could do it: Over the first six panels we have a gradual closein upon the pair from some distance away down the street and then reverse angles for a relatively static shot in the last three panels. If that works for you, then here in this first panel we are quite some distance away down Cleveland Street from Sickert and Annie as they stand there outside Number Fifteen, so that they are quite tiny figures here. Their expressions are thus too far away to see, but we can see that Sickert has reached out in an uneasy and impotent gesture of comfort to take Annie by the shoulders as he stands there facing her, looking down anxiously into her slack and vacant face. Annie does not respond to this contact in any way, but simply stands there limply, arms trailing by her sides, staring blankly and unresponsively up into Sickert's face. The street is dark, and their figures are probably indistinct and shadowy, as well as being small.

SICKERT:
A-Alice is FINE, Annie. She's alright. Your parents are looking after her.

SICKERT:
Look, can I fetch you a...?

ANNIE:
Little Alice.

(PANEL) 2

Slowly, we start to close in down Cleveland Street towards the pair. They become closer and slightly larger, but throughout this first tier we don't get any closer than a fullfigure shot, if that gives you any idea of the speed of this closein. It's very slow and creeping.

From Hell
Chapter III: Blackmail, or Mrs. Barrett

Here, we see that of the two figures, Annie is slightly the closer to us, and also that she is standing looking slightly away from us towards Sickert, immediately beyond her and facing both Annie and us as he speaks. From his posture he looks solicitous and worried here. Perhaps he drops one hand from Annie's shoulder but leaves one hand reassuringly in place, stooping down as he peers in to Annie's face anxiously, bending forward with the posture of an adult asking a child why it's crying. Annie is sort of starting to turn slightly away from Sickert here, raising one hand to touch the fingertips to her temple as if to still the buzzing in her head. We cannot see her expression, but it is one of frustrated puzzlement: Just a moment ago she knew exactly why she had come here and what she had to do. It was the single biggest and most important idea inside her head. Now, as she looks around inside her mind for it, it has gone completely, leaving only tantalizing echoes that are too insubstantial to grasp. She frowns and tries to remember, but the effort of trying only seems to push the elusive concept further away.

SICKERT:
Annie? Are you ill? You seem ...

ANNIE:
I ...

ANNIE:
I can't THINK straight. It was somethin' about ALICE ...

(PANEL) 3
We continue to close in. The figures are much nearer and larger now, but still only full figure. Annie, slightly closer to us, is continuing to turn aimlessly towards us, as if dimly checking to see if her missing memories are somewhere behind her. Her hands are back by her sides now, the palms turned outwards as they hang by Annie's waist in a sort of unconscious shrug. All of Annie's movements are very, very slow, as if she is walking underwater. If we can see her expression it is still one of bewilderment ... her eyes squint slightly, as if trying to see more clearly the vague shapes drifting through her murky consciousness, her lips making tentative, abandoned movements as they haltingly shape themselves around words whose meaning she feels slipping away even as she speaks

them. Slightly behind her, Sickert looks on with an expression of increasingly anguished and guiltwracked pity. He did this. He did this to Annie.

> ANNIE:
> We . . . we called her Alice because of that book, what my Albert read me . . .
>
> ANNIE:
> I can't read nor write, so he . . .
>
> ANNIE:
> Lovely. Lovely book.

(PANEL) 4

We continue to close in, so that now Sickert and Annie are maybe threequarter figure as they stand there in the muggy evening darkness of Cleveland Street. Annie is now standing sort of roughly turned towards us, but not looking directly at us so much as gazing aimlessly off to one side of the panel, staring at nothing in particular. As she stands there, more or less motionless, we see that her hands are starting to rise slowly from her sides, still palm upwards, her elbows bending as her hands ascend. She does not seem to be aware of this action, and it happens very, very slowly, taking the whole of this tier to complete their gradual ascent towards Annie's motionless head. This is a visual idea that I got from a documentary film on Allen Ginsberg's lover Peter Orlovsky and his autistic brother Julius. There's a scene with Julius talking to the camera as it gradually starts to rain. His

Annie Crook's assertion that her baby was named after Alice in Wonderland is based upon the fact that it was Lewis Carroll's book, published in 1864, that was responsible for popularizing the name Alice towards the end of the nineteenth century. Since Annie was illiterate, as attested to by the cross that serves for a signature upon her daughter's birth certificate, I have suggested that her beloved "Albert" may have read the book to her at some point.

The film Alan is referring to here is Me and My Brother *(1968), directed by Robert Frank, "one of the f cinema's first serious attempts to deal with mental illness " (according to* The Time Out Film Guide, *Penguin Books, 1991).*

—SRB

From Hell
Chapter III: Blackmail, or Mrs. Barrett

hands rise with eerie slowness, seemingly independent of any consciousness upon his part, and cover his head with their interlaced fingers. This takes about a minute and a half to accomplish and more than anything conveys the distance separating the mentally ill from the rest of the world. That's the effect I'm after over these next three panels. Annie's expression is still a sort of frown of intellectual strain as she gropes around in the darkness of her mind for the scattered fragments of memory that still remain, trying to piece them together into something that resembles a past; a personality. Beyond her, Sickert (who removed his hand from Annie's shoulder in panel three, incidentally, but I forgot to mention it) is standing looking more wretched by the moment. He also looks increasingly horrified as the extent of Annie's mental impairment gradually reveals itself. What the hell has been done to this woman? His hands lift uselessly in an ambiguous and halfcompleted gesture towards Annie, but she is staring into the dark and doesn't seem to register it. Indeed, she almost appears to have forgotten Sickert's presence. Around them, the fashionable and stately buildings of Cleveland Street maintain a reserved silence, aloof in the concealing darkness.

SICKERT:
Annie, listen . . .

ANNIE:
All about a little girl, an' she went down . . .

ANNIE:
Down the hole.

ANNIE:
Rabbit hole.

(PANEL) 5

Continuing to close in upon Annie and Sickert, we now see them half figure, with Annie still the nearer of the two, and still standing with her back roughly towards Sickert and staring confusedly off panel to one side of the foreground. Her hands, continuing their painfully slow upward progress towards her head are now raised a little above her shoulders, as if she were holding an invisible beach ball up in front of her face. Her expression, still groping and confused, now has a more troubled look creeping into it as Annie's mental questing takes her dangerously close to understanding something important about her awful situation. Her frown is still there, but the brows are starting to twist upwards towards the centre in a look of encroaching and barely-comprehended dismay. Immediately behind and beyond her, Sickert falls silent and still, just looking on in sick and impotent horror at this poor destroyed woman.

ANNIE:
A-and there was a QUEEN, a horrible old QUEEN . . .

ANNIE:
And the Queen said . . .

ANNIE:
The Queen said "Off!"

ANNIE:
"Off with her . . ."

(PANEL) 6
We complete the close in just as Annie's hands complete their ascent towards her head. We now see her roughly head and shoulders as she faces obliquely towards us from the foreground. Her hands reach her hair, the fingers digging themselves slowly and almost painfully into Annie's matted hair on either side, as if to stop her skull from bursting with all the fog that's building up inside it. On her face, the faint residual wrinkles of her troubled frown are still there, but in her eyes there is something painfully childlike showing itself. She looks like a child who has finally understood that she really isn't going to the birthday party she'd been looking forward to so much. She doesn't understand exactly why this devastating thing should have happened to her, but she is beginning to understand that it has. In her childlike and puzzled eyes there is a terrible look of disappointment that is almost unbearable to look at. For a second, Annie almost understands the scale of what has been taken away from her; of what she will never, never have again. In her little girl eyes an unendurable selfawareness flickers for an instant and then is gone forever. Her fingers burrow deeper into her filthy hair as Sickert looks on numbly, helplessly, from the background.

From Hell
Chapter III: Blackmail, or Mrs. Barrett

ANNIE:
"off with her head."

(PANEL) 7
We reverse angles here, so that we are just behind Sickert and looking over his shoulder towards Annie as she stands a couple of feet away from him, full figure here, with the darkened reaches of Cleveland Street stretching away beyond her. (I dunno if it's relevant to this panel, but it's just struck me that in the Cleveland Street scenes for this issue we should endeavour to show that there is rebuilding and construction work going on the premises of Annie's flat at Number 6. Just show the place covered in scaffolding and Victorian builder's clutter somewhere in this episode and we should be alright. I just want to get that over to cover the Anti-Knight lobby's quite reasonable claim that 6 Cleveland Street was being converted into flats in 1888.) Anyway, as we see Annie here she is standing facing slightly away from us and Sickert, still with her hands raised to her head, but less frantically now. The expression of realization has faded from her eyes and the fog seems to have rolled back in. She is frowning again now, trying to remember whatever it was that seemed so vaguely upsetting just a moment ago. She frowns and squints her eyes and tries to bring it back into focus, but it's no good: The thought has gone into the cranial dark, perhaps never to return. In the foreground we perhaps just see Sickert's shoulder and maybe a little of the right hand side of his head, viewed

The dispute over Annie's flat and Knight's suppositions relevant to 6 Cleveland Street have been argued by Donald Rumbelow in The Complete Jack the Ripper *among others.*

—SRB

from the back, over towards the left of the foreground as he stands there motionless staring at Annie. We can see more of him if you wish, just so long as our main attention is on the fullfigure shot of Annie, standing there on the chill pavement in her grubby hospital gown, looking utterly bewildered and lost. Nobody says anything in this panel . . . it's just to give a beat after the moment of awareness in Panel Six, during which we can practically hear the vital concept trickling out of Annie's skull and away to some unreachable place in the wells of her unconscious.

No Dialogue

(PANEL) 8

Same shot as in panel seven, only here we see that Annie's expression has changed. She still frowns, but it is now a frown of resolve, as if she has suddenly remembered her real reason for being here, which, while it has nothing to do with whatever she was reaching for a moment ago, now seems every bit as vital and important to her. She turns slightly and begins to crouch even as she starts to gather up her hospital gown around her waist. She wears nothing beneath the robe. In the foreground, Sickert doesn't move, not yet having grasped this latest twist in Annie's internal wanderings for what it is.

ANNIE:
I need a wee.

(PANEL) 9

Same shot, but in the foreground we see Sickert belatedly lift one hand in appalled but useless protest. In the near background, Annie squats on the pavement, her hands closed childishly about her knees, a look of muddy concentration upon her slack face. Her robe is gathered up about her waist, revealing the crack of Annie's buttocks and thighs that have grown fatter and lardier since we last saw them. A thin and twisting ribbon of urine falls from between Annie's legs to spatter against the paving slabs immediately beneath her as she squats. From this spot, it runs across the uneven pavement toward the gutter in bifurcating streamers of wet darkness. Jesus, this looks pitiful and humiliating. From off panel policeman enters the panel from a point somewhere behind Sickert in the shadows of Cleveland Street.

From Hell
Chapter III: Blackmail, or Mrs. Barrett

> SICKERT:
> Oh God, Annie...
>
> POLICEMAN (off):
> OY! Oy, what are you adoin' there?

PAGE 18

(PANEL) 1

Nine panels on this page. In this first one, we are maybe down at roughly Annie's eyelevel as she squats there in the street, her face turned obliquely towards us and gazing off to one side of the foreground with a look of oblivious childish concentration as she takes a piss. She is roughly head and shoulders, up to the right of the foreground here. Looking beyond her and along the darkened length of Cleveland Street we can see Sickert and the police constable who has just wandered up to him. Sickert spread his hands in an unconvincing explanatory gesture as he gapes at the policeman. The policeman, frowning with a businesslike look of professional consternation is staring disapprovingly at Annie as she squats in the foreground. He looks at Annie rather than at Sickert as he speaks to the artist, while Sickert stares somewhat trepidatiously towards him.

> POLICEMAN:
> Come on, what's all this?
>
> SICKERT:
> Constable, this... this woman's ill. She...

(PANEL) 2

Dunno about this, but maybe we could have a pavement level shot here: All we see, in the background of this panel but still quite close to us, are the feet and lower legs of the policeman and Sickert as they stand grouped fairly close together, facing roughly towards us. Across the pavement at their feet and closer towards the foreground we have the dark uncoiling ribbons of Annie's urine on its journey towards the gutter. The policeman is identifiable by his checkered trousers, or whatever he's wearing. The policeman's balloon issues from off panel above, while Annie's balloon enters the panel from the side in the direction which her urine is also entering the panel from. Like I say, I dunno about this. I want Sickert's feet up in the foreground for the next three panels, so perhaps an unrelated footcloseup here would muddy the storytelling. Maybe it'd be better to simply pull back slightly from the shot in panel one to show all three figures, with Annie still squatting and the policeman and Sickert immediately beyond her. If we can see the policeman's expression he seems to have softened somewhat as he realises that the woman fouling the pavement is not in full command of her senses. He looks sympathetic as he speaks to the agitated looking Sickert. Annie ignores them both, concentrating on bodily functions and lost babies. Whichever version suits you best, do accordingly.

POLICEMAN (off?):
Oh ... Oh, it's alright, Sir. I recognize her gown.

POLICEMAN (off):
Gone wandering from Guy's, has she?

ANNIE (off?):
Alice. Little Alice ...

(PANEL) 3

Now we definitely have Sickert's feet and lower legs in the foreground, up to the left of the panel here and standing so that he's facing slightly away from us towards the right of the background. Standing full figure some feet away we see the policeman, who has walked over towards Annie and placed his hand upon her shoulder as he starts to help her gently to her feet. As he does so he doesn't look at Alice (Any more than he would dream of addressing serious comments to a dumb animal) but instead looks up towards the off panel place where Sickert's head must be. As he does so, the policeman has a faint sort of comradely smile of reassurance upon his face. The man means well, obviously, but he has no way of understanding the awfulness of the situation, and his bland and cheerful reassurances seem horribly inappropriate in their true context. Annie, still with a puzzled frown on her face, allows herself to be gently guided to her feet, offering no real physical resistance to the policeman's gentle but insistent pressure.

From Hell
Chapter III: Blackmail, or Mrs. Barrett

> POLICEMAN:
> I'll take her back there. Hope she's not troubled you, sir.

> POLICEMAN:
> They're harmless really.

> ANNIE:
> I want 'er. I want my Alice . . .

(PANEL) 4

Same shot. With a friendly but firm hand upon her shoulder, the policeman starts to lead Annie away, barefoot down Cleveland Street. As he does so he is talking reassuringly and comfortingly to her, exactly as he would do to a lost child. Annie looks up at him with a bewildered expression as she attempts to explain her plight to him without really understanding it herself. In the foreground, Sickert's feet remain stock still as he faces away after them, rooted to the spot.

> POLICEMAN:
> Yes, yes. 'course you do lovey. Come on . . . let's get you home and in bed.

> ANNIE:
> I want my ALICE! I want her, but . . .

> ANNIE:
> But she's gone.

(PANEL) 5

Same shot. Annie and the policeman are now much smaller, much further away as they head away from us into the smothering shadows of Cleveland Street, Annie still hopelessly attempting to explain to the policeman as he guides her along. In the foreground, we see Sickert's feet, still motionless as he stands facing away from us, watching Annie and the policeman as they vanish from view. Dunno if the urine stains on the pavement will be visible from this angle, but they're obviously still there, on the pavement near Sickert's feet. In the background, Annie stumbles away out of our story forever.

> ANNIE:
> She's gone down the rabbithole.

Alan Moore

(PANEL) 6

Reverse angles now for a halffigure shot of Sickert, seen from the front as he gazes out of the panel at us with his haunted, horrorstricken eyes, presumably still gazing into the offpanel darkness after the offpanel figures of Annie and her police escort. As we see him here he is still standing outside the front door of Number Fifteen Cleveland Street. Once hand is in his coat pocket, perhaps numbly fumbling for his front door key. As he stares down the street his expression is sort of dazed. This has been a hellish day for Walter Sickert . . . and its going to get worse before he goes to bed.

No Dialogue

(PANEL) 7

Pull back from the last panel so that now we see Sickert full figure as he stands outside his front door. He has turned his body to face the door and is thus standing sideon to us here, but his face is still turned towards us as he continues to stare uneasily down the length of Cleveland Street in the direction which Annie and the policeman have departed in. His front door key is now in his hand, and he is absentmindedly unlocking his front door as he gazes wearily and hauntedly towards us.

No Dialogue

(PANEL) 8

Now we are inside the darkened hallway of Number Fifteen, looking towards the front door, which now stands open. Framed in the doorway, his face probably mostly in shadow along with the rest of the front of him, we see the figure of Walter Sickert, poised upon the threshold of his studio building. Lying there in the hallway at his feet, on the doormat if there is one, we see a sealed white envelope that has obviously been pushed under Sickert's door sometime during the last hour. Blankly, Sickert stares down at it expressionlessly as he enters his house, the darkness of Cleveland Street behind him, the darkness of the hallway ahead. The envelope just lies there. Sickert looks at it.

No Dialogue

From Hell
Chapter III: Blackmail, or Mrs. Barrett

(PANEL) 9
Now a shot through Sickert's eyes, in which we only see his hand reaching out from the foreground as he reaches down towards the letter, which we see close up here as it lies there on the floor just inside the front door. It's dark and shadowy, but written in neat but underdeveloped handwriting on its front surface we can read the words "To Mr. Walter Siccert". Marie can write and is fairly intelligent and good at spelling, but it seems characteristic to me that she might spell Sickert with two 'c's.

No Dialogue

PAGE 19

(PANEL) 1
Now we have a seven panel page, with the final panel being the biggest and taking up the whole of the bottom tier. In this first small panel we see a full to three quarter figure shot of Sickert as he stands there in his hallway, the door now closed behind him. He stands at the bottom of the stairs, using one hand to shrug his top coat off over one shoulder while in the other he holds the sealed envelope. He peers at it and frowns, perhaps in mild annoyance at the misspelling of his name; more likely in puzzlement as to its sender and contents.

No Dialogue

(PANEL) 2
Now we perhaps see Sickert from the shoulders down, his head invisible off the top of the panel as he mounts the staircase towards his studio. We clearly see him starting to tear open the envelope as he goes, small shred of paper falling from his fingers as he mounts the shadowy staircase.

No Dialogue

(PANEL) 3
Now we see Sickert some feet away from us standing full figure at the top of the stairs, just stepping up onto the landing here. He has extracted the letter from its envelope and is looking down at it and reading it as he walks along. He still wears a slight

frown of puzzlement as he starts to read, wondering who the note can be from. Now, although I don't want to use captions any more than I can help in *From Hell*, it's important that the readers know what the note says, and I don't want to have to angle all the panels so that we're reading it over Sickert's shoulder or ridiculously close in to the surface of the paper. Therefore, I figure that the best thing to do here is to use a sort of paracaption where we just have Marie Kelly's handwriting appearing in sequential fragments above Sickert's head as he walks through the house towards his studio. As I see it, these shouldn't be enclosed in a panel border but should just be floating in the air, written in joinedup writing, above Sickert's head as he walks through the shadowy house. This brings me to my next point: if the house is shadowy, it seems unlikely that you'll have much clear white space at the top of the panels to letter these suspended pseudo/captions in. Therefore, if there is likely to be more shadowy masses of solid black up towards the top of the panel, then I suggest you maybe get the captions reversed out into white-on-black for the best looking effect. Anyway, here we see Sickert as he mounts to the landing, letter in hand, its opening words appearing above his head as he reads them.

>HANDWRITING (no border):
>Dear Mr. Siccert, I know you are an honourable man, and will be concerned for

(PANEL) 4

Now we are inside Sickert's shadowy upstairs studio, looking across the untidy room towards the door, much as we did earlier when Sickert showed Marie and Little Alice up to his studio. Looking across the room we see Sickert entering through the doorway, still reading the letter as he comes. He is full figure and relatively small here, right across the other side of the studio from us.

>HANDWRITING (no border):
>the good name of your "brother". If you do not want the world knowing of his misbehavings as I am sure you

From Hell
Chapter III: Blackmail, or Mrs. Barrett

(PANEL) 5
Same shot, but Sickert has walked further across the room towards us and is thus closer to us and larger here, maybe a half figure shot or something. He is still reading the letter, but his facial expression is changing from one of mere puzzlement to one of mounting alarm as he progresses further in his reading of the missive. The crossing out of the word 'five' in the handwritten text below is intentional by the way, and is meant to appear in the finished copy, crossing out and all. As he walks with increasing slowness through his studio, Sickert's face grows paler and paler as he reads the note through to the bitter end.

> HANDWRITING (no border):
> don't, you must get me and my friends (cross out five) ten pounds (£100/od) at the Britannia as soon as you

(PANEL) 6
Same shot, but now Sickert has walked close enough for what is almost a head and shoulders shot before stopping dead in his tracks. He stares down at the note he is reading with a look of the damned in his widening eyes, all alone there in his shadowy and untidy studio. This is the perfect end to a perfect day for Mr. Walter Sickert.

> HANDWRITING (no border):
> can. Yours faithfully, M. Kelly

(PANEL) 7
Now we have a big, wide panoramic shot of Sickert's studio taking up the whole of the bottom tier. Somewhere fairly central and viewed full figure here we see Sickert. He has sunk into a convenient wooden chair set somewhere in the middle of his cluttered studio, from around the walls of which we see indistinct or halffinished canvasses looming murkily through the gloom. In one hand he still holds the note, crumpled now and just dangling limply, almost forgotten. His other hand, as he sits there with his head sunk forward, is covering part of his face, the elbow perhaps resting on one of his knees. Alone in his studio, alone in all the world by virtue of the terrible knowledge inside his head, Sickert

finally breaks down and weeps. He weeps for Annie and Alice a little, but mostly he weeps for himself: Out of fear; out of sheer emotional exhaustion. Right up toward the right of the foreground, unnoticed by Sickert as he sits there shuddering and weeping, we see the unfinished sketch of Marie Kelly that he will later dust off and turn into "Blackmail or Mrs. Barrett". Through the pall of grey shadow that fills the room, scribbled graphite eyes twinkle darkly at us. An expressive mouth made of looselyknotted pencil lines lifts at the corners into an unreadable smile. Down at the bottom right hand corner of the page we see the bunch of grapes, our little signingoff motif. A couple of the grapes are missing as the fruit becomes gradually whittled down to a bare stem, perhaps something over eighteen months hence.

No Dialogue

AFTERWORD

A Snowball's Chance in Hell

*V*ermont winter winds were screaming the night Alan Moore called me with his ambitious outline for a sixteen-chapter serialized novel he had conceived specifically for *Taboo*.

It was, I believe, December of 1988. I know that *Taboo 1* had just recently been published. As a result, *Taboo* finally seemed a tangible reality for Alan as well as myself after a prolonged two-year gestation period. That premier issue featured a story by Alan that was essentially an acquisition from another publisher ("Come On Down" in *Taboo* 1, originally completed for Harris Publications' aborted *Creepy* resurrection), and I had just rejected a very funny script Alan had offered as being inappropriate for *Taboo*. There was really no reason to expect Alan would approach me with anything more than another idea for a single story. I'd have been thankful for that alone!

As always, Alan exceeded all expectations.

From Hell
Afterword

What he was describing to me over the phone seemed unbelievable. This . . . *this* was an *epic*. *From Hell* was to be a horrifying meditation on the life and times of Jack the Ripper, and it was pouring into my ear in Alan's distinctive Northampton accent with a cool intensity I found unnerving. Here was all the resonant depth *Swamp Thing* had been too shallow to reach, that *Taboo* had as yet remained too amorphous and unfocused to accomplish.

We were disconnected twice during the conversation, promptly ringing each other back so Alan could continue reading his notes to me. Every chapter title and its intended contents were carefully spelled out in that initial conversation. All that was needed was a vehicle and an artist.

Taboo would be the vehicle. The artist—well, we'd get to that. After discussing a number of illustrious contemporaries, my insistence that Eddie Campbell was the only artist capable of maintaining the humanistic focus absolutely necessary to *From Hell*'s execution began to take root in Alan's mind as well.

EDDIE CAMPBELL (S. R. Bissette)

It was essential that the artist in question not be seduced by the violence inherent in the tale—as I would have, for instance, were I the artist drawing the novel (Eddie and Alan had been friends for years and had talked about working together someday . . . with a little persuasion, *From Hell* indeed proved a suitable vehicle).

By the time Alan had finished describing the epilogue, we were both breathless and excited. The possibilities were too intoxicating to consider the many obstacles ahead. For Alan, it was a refreshing challenge in the wake of his success with *Watchmen* and his subsequent dissatisfaction with mainstream comics as a proper vehicle for his fertile imagination. As the appendix which follows this afterword explains, *From Hell* cemented Alan's dedication to creator-published comics, building upon the bedrock laid by his own self-published one-shot *Aargh!*, and anticipating the graphic novels to come: *Big Numbers* (then called *The Mandelbrot Set*), *A Small Killing*, and *Lost Girls* (which also began life as a serialized novel in *Taboo 5*).

For me, *From Hell* promised that *Taboo* would finally have its black little heart in place.

The icy winds outside had little to do with the chill that danced up and down my spine that night.

The delicious chill I felt as Alan described *From Hell* to me was a familiar one. I'd savored a similar frisson in 1983 when I read the first Alan Moore script I was privileged to draw, "The Anatomy Lesson" (*Saga of the Swamp Thing #21*).

For many of you, the book you hold in your hand is probably your first exposure to an actual comic-book script. With the exception of a few of Alan's script pages excerpted in the collected *Watchmen* graphic novel, one of Neil Gaiman's complete *Sandman* scripts showcased in the *Sandman* collection *Dream Country*, and Joe Lansdale's comic-script

ALAN MOORE

adaptations in the Crossroads Press chapbooks of Andrew Vachss' *Drive-By* and *A Flash of White*, precious few comic-book scripts have been made available in any form to either the comic-book fan or scholar of the medium. Alan's scripts in particular have been very much in demand among collectors. With Alan's blessings, John Totleben and I used to occasionally donate Alan's original scripts to comic-book convention charity auctions, and they usually sold at dear prices after heated bidding.

I dare say this book is an historic occasion, akin to the

earliest published screenplays. The earliest book publication of a screenplay I've ever come across is H.G. Wells' *Man Who Could Work Miracles* (1936), with Donald Ogden Stewart's script for *The Philadelphia Story* (1940) a fair contender for second place. A notable precursor is John Emerson and Anita Loos' *How To Write Photoplays* (1920), an instructional text which contains the complete script for a long-forgotten gem entitled *The Love Expert*. At the time of their publication these were, at best, oddities. Cinema had not, as yet, been accepted as an artform, much as the comics medium today is only beginning to be understood as a valid and unique artform. Screenplays were rarely published until the academic communities embraced cinema as a medium worthy of study, though by the 1970s everything from *The Cabinet of Dr. Caligari* to *Billy Jack* had seen print as fully illustrated screenplays in hardcover and paperback.

Certainly, comics scripts by the likes of Alan Moore and Neil Gaiman are worthy companions to the finished illustrated narratives themselves. Unlike screenplays, in which the author's original has usually been subsumed by all manner of obstacles and collaborative dabblings, almost every comic-book script I've ever read or worked from carries its creator's distinctive voice. Indeed, the best of them are strikingly personal and, most compelling of all, carefully worded to coax from the reader (the artist and usually an editor) a full visualization of a shared imaginative world. As such, well-crafted comics scripts invite the reader's active creative participation in a more intimate fashion than either a play or screenplay.

I had been working as an artist in the industry since 1976, and prior to working with Alan I'd thought I'd seen just about everything. Most comic-book scripts I'd worked from superficially resembled the screenplay format, though the best of them recognized and utilized the elements that make the comics medium unique from either theatre or cinema. I had worked firsthand with a variety of approaches, from my first efforts illustrating my friend Steve Perry's carefully detailed scripts (often with accompanying visual page layout suggestions) to the somewhat lazy "Marvel method" instituted by editor-writer Stan Lee, in which the writer initially crafts a story outline.

The "Marvel method" forces the artist to orchestrate the actual storytelling elements which the writer is traditionally responsible for, in effect *rewriting* the story through the process of turning the often sketchy plot outline (some are quite detailed, while others are embarrassingly formless) into finished penciled pages. These finished pages are subsequently "dialogued" (i.e., captions and word balloons are written for the completed pages) by the original author. In fact, my first Marvel assignment was to adapt Ron Goulart's science fiction short story "Into The Shop" from a photocopy of the published story, sans *any* script or editorial guidance. Some artists thrive on the "method," embracing the control it grants the artist, while others are content to tread water or simply drown; nevertheless, it certainly simplifies the writer's job, allowing a constant flow of assembly-line product to stream from the editor-as-*auteur* based "House of Ideas."

Some comics writers like Mike Baron (co-creator of *Nexus* and many other titles) have streamlined their own idiosyncratic approaches to comic-book scripting. Mike actually draws his own rough'n'ready little comics stories, providing an entertaining blueprint for the artist while satisfactorily working out the action, pacing and text, ultimately enhancing his script with a final polish before the pages are lettered. There are as many valid approaches to the craft as there are writers, and in the case of a truly collaborative synthesis of writer and artist, the process may become almost alchemical in nature. In such cases, the script generated in the creation of the finished comics work may not provide a coherent reading experience to anyone other than the creators. Neil Gaiman describes his collaboration with artist Dave McKean on the recent graphic novel *Signal to Noise* as being "written in some strange bastard form that only myself

From Hell
Afterword

and McKean could understand a word of. The script would be completely meaningless to anyone else, because they would ignore the fact that we'd been talking on the phone about this for a month and a half, and are, in a way, telepathic" (quoted from Gaiman's interview in *Comic Book Rebels*, published by Donald I. Fine, 1993, pg. 192).

The most satisfying scripts I had worked from prior to that fateful issue of *Swamp Thing* #21 were the visceral stories crafted by Archie Goodwin and particularly Robert Kanigher for *Sgt. Rock* comics. Kanigher's scripts were terse, taut, stripped to the bone; Alan's script, on the other hand, seemed lavishly introspective and disarmingly conversational.

It was, in fact, a long letter to me, describing an as yet undrawn comic book with the layered density and gripping immediacy of a lucidly recreated dream that plunged, in its final pages, into full-blown nightmare. The hairs literally went up on the back of my neck as I read Alan's blueprint to the greatest horror movie never made ... a secret movie I was to illuminate. It was my task to bring the story to life with my pencils, a task I loved all the more because of the intimacy Alan extended to me through his writing. He has since likened the process to "a kind of cultural sex," if you will, and indeed it is. "The aspect that I most enjoy working in comics is the meeting of minds and the meeting of sensibilities," Alan says, "to grasp what someone else is feeling is thrilling in an intellectual and creative way. This cross-fertilization between different imaginations!" (*Comic Book Rebels*, pg. 165). Let me tell you, it was *great* sex, the best!

Though at the time our editor didn't see the reason for it, obviously John Totleben (fellow *Swamp Thing* artist inaccurately labeled as mere "inker" by our publisher) *had* to read the script himself; John had actually already worked as "inker" (though he had pretty much redrawn the entire issue) on Alan's first *Swamp Thing* script for #20. From then on, John and I shared every single subsequent script, letter, phone call, concept and conversation. We were quickly creating characters and proposing concepts, co-plotting complete storylines with Alan, galvanizing the most volatile creative chemistry between artistic collaborators I have ever enjoyed.

It was later my pleasure to enjoy a very different chemistry with Alan as the editor of *Taboo* and, by proxy, the editor of *From Hell* and *Lost Girls*.

And it is now my pleasure to extend the pleasure of enjoying Alan's scripts to you, dear reader.

I only hope Eddie Campbell will forgive such a public forum for his and Alan's, uh, "cultural sex."

Alan Moore (S. R. Bissette)

When Alan called me that winter evening of late '88 (regretfully, I never kept a note of the actual date), *Taboo* had a bright future ahead of it.

As I write this afterword on the final day of 1993, *Taboo* seems to have reached its last act, while *From Hell* continues to blossom.

I record this with no bitterness or remorse. Indeed, *Taboo* was intended as a launching point for many things, and *From Hell* is arguably the most substantial of its many "children."

Like all children, *From Hell* quickly outgrew its parent and struck out on its own, as did Tim Lucas' *Throat Sprockets* (completed as a novel forthcoming from Dell) and Jeff Nicholson's *Through the Habitrails* (which Jeff self-published earlier this year). I'm sure Alan and Melinda Gebbie's *Lost Girls* will soon find a home, too, and affectionately recall the role *Taboo* played as vehicle for the one-shot stories that spawned Rolf Stark's *Rain* (Tundra Publishing) and Wendy Snow Lang's *Night's Children* (Fantaco Publishing), among other projects.

Any sense of propriety I may feel for *From Hell* and its siblings seems forever inappropriate. I was, at best, a midwife. That is, after all, the most an editor can hope to be. As such, I

From Hell
Afterword

remember every moment of the birth as I experienced it, and I worked hard to nurture and publish *From Hell's* formative chapters.

Though it had never really been orphaned, Tundra aggressively asserted itself as *From Hell's* first foster home, damning *Taboo* even as it gave wings to *From Hell*. Such is life. The little demon has since sidestepped into the shelter of the Kitchen Sink, which, Ganesa willing, shall shepherd the novel to its closing epilogue.

As a reader, I look forward to that final penstroke with the same anticipation I awaited the first.

—*Stephen R. Bissette, New Year's Eve '93-'94*
 The Mountains of Madness
 Vermont

APPENDIX

The annotations written for this publication were originally written for publication in Taboo 5. Those plans were abandoned once Tundra announced its first collected edition of From Hell, and the footnotes were appropriately incorporated into that format. They are included here by arrangement with the creators.

Some of Eddie Campbell's illustrations were originally drawn for the planned publication of the footnotes in Taboo 5. One of these appeared as a frontispiece illustration in the first printing of From Hell, Vol. 1, and was inexplicably removed from subsequent printings.

The rest have been drawn expressly for this publication.

The following article was written by Alan Moore early in 1989 to publicize the publication of From Hell's "Prologue" and "Chapter I" in Taboo 2. It saw publication only once, in a 1989 catalogue from Fantaco Enterprises Inc.

We include it here as an historical artifact in which the author stated his intent for the project, his proposed method, and the particulars of its creation. Though there may be a couple of things in here which make Alan and I wince today at the idealistic fellows that we were back then, it is presented here complete and uncut. (S. R. Bissette)

It's my belief that if you cut into a thing deeply enough; if your incisions are precise and persistent and conducted methodically, then you may reveal not only that thing's inner workings, but also the *meaning* behind those workings. This conviction was shared by the historical personage whose life is central to *From Hell*, although perhaps his beliefs were expressed in a somewhat broader sense than my own. For my part, the thing that I am concerned with cutting into and examining is the stillwarm corpse of history itself. In my chilliest moments, I sometimes suspect that this was *his* foremost preoccupation also, albeit in pursuit of different ends.

From Hell is the post-mortem of an historical occurrence, using fiction as a scalpel. The numerous characters who populate the story all existed once. The motivations I have attributed to

From Hell
Appendix

them and the words that I have placed in their mouths are based, wherever possible, upon exacting historical research. Beyond that point I have relied upon guesswork and conjecture, which, while it cannot hope to be accurate, is at least, I hope, informed. In so far as I know, none of the facts stated within the story contradict those previously reported, and no pertinent fact has been ignored. Theoretically, the events detailed in *From Hell could* have unfolded in just the way we describe them . . . .

But it isn't history. It's fiction. Though it concerns itself with a notable and historic mystery, it does not attempt to be a 'Whodunnit?' so much as a "Wha'happen?" Though in the course of the story we name one relatively obscure historical figure as suspect (One whom other writers have previously pointed the finger at), this is simply a convenience of fiction, and in one sense we are not at all concerned with whether he "Dunnit" or not. What we are more interested in is the attempt to examine in detail the anatomy of a phenomenal human event.

This phenomenon; this apocalypse in miniature touched the lives of characters as disparate as Buffalo Bill Cody and Mr. John Merrick, popularly known as the Elephant Man. It took place in what might arguably be described as the most ominous decade suffered during man's brief history thus far, and it seems to me that such legendary times and mythic players should not and cannot be contained comfortably within the meticulous textbook confines of dusty historic fact. They need an element of the melodramatic and the mythological. An element of fiction.

Indeed, perhaps it's worth remembering that *all* history is to some degree a fiction; that truth can no longer properly be spoken of once the bodies have grown cold. The side that wins the battle decides who were the heroes and who the villains, and history is always written by those who have survived it, their biases often surviving along with them.

This is not to diminish the importance of traditional history: It is vital to the continued wellbeing of both ourselves and our culture that we understand the events that have shaped the world that in turn shapes us. Unfortunately, history is popularly regarded as a dry and dusty province accessible only through equally dusty tomes. The very thought of history can set people to sneezing, and the aversion therapy carried out upon most of us by our school systems has rendered our historical past an object of revulsion to us. Though its currents may alter their lives or indeed wash them away entirely, most people are not interested in history.

Fortunately, *From Hell* is also a horror story, a genre which enjoys somewhat more popularity. It is the horror story of five human beings who were touched by a mythical entity of hideous force and in the process were utterly destroyed. It is a horror story about the fateful patterns that exist in time; in human enterprise; even in the stones of the cities wherein we conduct our lives. It's the horror story buried at the roots of the Twentieth Century, and it just might conceivably be true . . . even if it didn't happen.

The only other thing that need be said about the story is that without the existence of *Taboo* it would not have been written. It is a story that concerns itself with politics, architecture, love, art, history and God. And Sex. And regrettably, with violence of a most extreme nature. The fact that these last two ingredients, though not necessarily the most *important* in the above recipe, could not be approached honestly, other than within the pages of *Taboo*, is one good reason why *From Hell* is appearing there. Another is that I know of no currently available publication other than *Taboo* which can accommodate chapters whose length varies erratically according to their content, a freedom rarely considered by novelists, and yet rarely heard of by comic creators.

It should be said that *Taboo* is also a class act . . . possibly the classiest act of its kind since the heyday of *Creepy* and *Eerie*, if only in the range of the contributors and the editorial commitment to excellence. Unlike *Creepy*, however, *Taboo* owes no especial debt to the foundations established by the legendary

E.C. comics line. Indeed, *Taboo* is one of the first coherent attempts to seriously establish fresh territory for horror fiction beyond the restricting confines of formularized plots that would seem to be all that today's duller talents are capable of gleaning from E.C.'s formidable legacy. *Taboo* copies E.C. only in the sense that like E.C., it copies no one.

Last, but by no means least, it is the way in which *Taboo* is published that has determined where *From Hell* will see print. I firmly believe that creator-publishing must figure prominently in the future of the comic book medium if that future is ever to aspire to the medium's full potential. It's a belief that's prompted the formation, with my partners Debbie Delano and Phyllis Moore, of Mad Love Publishing Ltd., a company originally set up to handle the production of the antihomophobia benefit comic book *Aargh!*, and which will next be used to publish a twelve-issue serialized novel by myself and Mr. Bill Sienkiewicz, entitled *The Mandelbrot Set*.

Phyllis, Debbie and I believe in creator publishing. So do Steve and Nancy at Spiderbaby. As for the illustrious Mr. Eddie Campbell, my artistic partner on *From Hell*, he's *always* believed in creator publishing. Even when it wasn't fashionable. I'm glad to work on *Taboo* for the same reason I was glad to contribute to the self-published *Puma Blues* benefit comic: It's nice to know that there's somebody out there, somebody who sees certain things the same way that you do. Maybe if we all hang together, we can make something of all this. Maybe if we all hang together we won't have to all hang separately.

There is no hanging at the climax of *From Hell*. The verdict remained open, the history books silent, the noose empty. All that we have been able to deduce is recorded in the sixteen installments that comprise the work itself. It is a fiction, but it is also a mosaic of tracings and jottings; an enciphered communication from another age. It is a scarcely legible note of terrible significance.

From Hell.

THE PERPETRATORS

In a little over a decade, ALAN MOORE has earned international prominence as one of the finest writers to ever work in the comics artform. Whether obsessively probing the particulars of England's darkest chapter in *From Hell* or playfully re-inventing the energy and mythos of the "Silver Age" of superhero comic books in *1963*, his style and approach remains rich, engaging and often profound, and his collaborative efforts with a procession of the industry's finest artists has yielded a remarkable body of work. After his debut in his native England in the pages of *2000 A.D.* and *Warrior* (which launched both *Miracleman* and *V For Vendetta*), Moore entered the American comics scene with his innovative work on *Swamp Thing*, *Watchmen*, and *Batman: The Killing Joke*. By 1987, Moore's disgust with the business practices of the mainstream comics industry led to his breakaway efforts with *Brought To Light*, *Aargh!*, *Big Numbers*, and his alignment with the independently published anthology *Taboo* for which he created *From Hell* and *Lost Girls*. His recent work for Image Comics includes the series *1963* and one of the bestselling issues of *Spawn* (yielding a related miniseries). For British publishers, Moore also wrote the graphic novel *A Small Killing* (which was recently published in the U.S.) and is working on his first "non-graphic" novel, *The Voice of Fire*.

*H*ailing from Scotland and currently residing in Australia, EDDIE CAMPBELL has been writing and drawing his own unique comics since the mid-1970s. Emerging from small press and photocopied "stripzines" like *Fast Fiction* and evolving further in the pages of *Escape*, it was Campbell's semi autobiographical *Alec* series which galvanized his skill and imagination. The four *Alec* novels (now available in the U.S. in the single volume *The Complete Alec*) and his recent *Graffiti Kitchen* are potent and deeply personal meditations on life, love, death and sex worthy of Henry Miller. His earlier *In The Days of the Ace Rock'n'Roll Club* has also been recently collected. Contrasting and complementing Campbell's down-to-earth accomplishments are the compelling *Deadface/Bacchus* series, in which the immortal Greek deities continue their eternal feuds and power-plays as paranormal businessmen and superhuman barflies, and his scripts for an upcoming fantasy series for Dark Horse Comics. He is also, of course, cocreator and illustrator of the graphic novel *From Hell*.

*T*aboo co-creator, editor, and publisher STEPHEN R. BISSETTE was a graduate of the Joe Kubert School of Cartoon and Graphic Art. He quickly established himself as an artist in the pages of *Heavy Metal, Bizarre Adventures, Weird Worlds, Sgt. Rock, Epic*, and collaborated with fellow Vermonter Rick Veitch on *1941: The Illustrated Story*. His collaboration with writer Alan Moore and co-artist John Totleben on *The Saga of the Swamp Thing* won numerous industry awards and launched the first mainstream comic industry "Mature Readers" tide. While continuing to work on collaborative efforts like *1963*, Bissette also formed his own publishing company SpiderBaby Grafix to launch *Taboo* and his current self-published title *Tyrant*. A frequent columnist for film magazines such as *Animato, Ecco, Gorezone, ETC* and *The Video Watchdog*, Bissette also coauthored *Comic Book Rebels* and won the Horror Writers Association's Bram Stoker Award for his first novella, "Aliens: Tribes." Bissette is one of the authors featured in Borderlands Press' limited, signed edition of *Cut! Horror Writers on Horror Films*; Borderlands will publish his forthcoming *We Are Going To Eat You! Cannibalism in the Cinema.*